The Greed

The Greed

SCOTT BERGSTROM

FEIWEL AND FRIENDS

NEW YORK

A Feiwel and Friends Book
An imprint of Macmillan Publishing Group, LLC
175 Fifth Avenue, New York, NY 10010

Our books may be purchased in bulk for promotional, educational, or business use. Please contact your local bookseller or the Macmillan Corporate and Premium Sales Department at (800) 221-7945 ext. 5442 or by e-mail at MacmillanSpecialMarkets@macmillan.com.

Library of Congress Control Number: 2017944812

ISBN 978-1-250-10820-3 (hardcover) / ISBN 978-1-250-10819-7 (ebook)

Feiwel and Friends logo designed by Filomena Tuosto

First edition, 2018

1 3 5 7 9 10 8 6 4 2

fiercereads.com

For Sonja and Renata, wise and brave

"It's not the bullet that kills you—it's the hole."

LAURIE ANDERSON

Part One

JUDITA

One

Judita ignores the ghost of her reflection in the window—reflection is, in general, something to be avoided these days. She focuses instead on the figures four floors below her, a pair of lunch-hour lovers strolling along the Playa de los Pocitos, carrying their shoes as they walk barefoot in the sand. They pass an old man standing on the shore, who casts a fishing line through the air that catches the light and makes a silver arc, like a blade made of wire, before disappearing against the backdrop of water that's brown as chocolate milk.

Judita's bare arms, burnt from too much sun, prickle with the cold of air-conditioning set too low. It feels luxurious, and she eyes the white leather couch with the silk pillows and wonders what it would be like to take a nap there. She does not sleep much these days, and when she does, never well. But there's no time for a nap anyway when there's so much work to do.

There's a party about to start. At the dining room table behind her—a heavy slab of dark wood, legs as thick as an elephant's—a dozen china plates are surrounded by eight pieces of silverware each. Chafing dishes cover a sideboard, and the room smells of something foreign and delicious.

"There you are," a woman calls out in English. Her eyes tell Judita she's angry with her for stepping beyond the entryway where she was to wait, but the woman smiles anyway because she's American and smiling is what Americans do, even when they're angry. The work ID from a soft drink–bottling company dangles on a lanyard around the woman's neck as she fishes through her purse. Her hand comes out with a pair of 500-peso notes, not quite enough to cover the bill, much less leave anything for a tip. "Your man shorted me on the salad. Do you understand, dear?"

Judita blinks at her. "Sorry," she says with difficulty. "My English, only little."

"*Te olvidó ensalada,*" the woman says with a grimace, as if the Spanish words hurt her teeth. "I have people here in two hours. So who gets salad and who doesn't? Tell me, please. I'd really like to know."

Judita tries to follow the logic of her statement, then shrugs.

The woman sighs as she hands Judita the money. "I won't pay for something I didn't get. There's enough there to cover everything else." She pinches the bridge of her nose and squeezes her eyes shut, the whole world today a torture.

Judita looks at the money, looks at the woman.

"Next time maybe you'll check the order," she says, and gestures toward the door. "Really, you people."

Judita pedals her bicycle toward the Old Town along the boulevard that skirts the Río de la Plata. She's faster now without the woman's order from the restaurant hanging from the handlebars and striking her knees with every turn of the pedals. If she hurries, she'll be back to the restaurant in thirty minutes. But it's a hot February afternoon, the dead of summer, and the humidity is so thick she can see it. Better to go slow.

The traffic is heavy, but Judita is agile and practiced and weaves between the battered Fiats and new Geelys in bright orange and green that look to her like toy versions of real cars. A truck groans and lurches forward, coating Judita in a cough of black diesel smoke. She grabs hold of a handle on the back and rides for a time, coasting along beside the truck until she breaks free and heads north toward the Plaza Independencia.

It's tourist season, and the Old Town is thick with pink skin and sandals and expensive cameras worn around necks. From the snatches of conversations she overhears as she blurs past them on her bicycle, it's mostly Brits today, a soft, older crowd. They snap pictures of the local kids who mug for the cameras and then hold their hands out. It's quaintness and poverty the tourists are looking for, and what luck finding it amid the charming buildings of the Old Town just a ten-minute walk from the pier. When a good ship is in port, the very boldest children can make maybe a hundred pesos a day.

To avoid the slow throngs ahead of her, Judita takes a left and cuts down a street so narrow she can touch the buildings on both sides if she stretches her arms out. In the heat of the day, the passage smells like piss and roasting meat.

Ahead of her, a woman with frizzy, pinned-up blond hair looks down at a pair of kids, ten or twelve years old. They're hassling her, arguing with her in Spanish, while she replies in English. The knot they form blocks the narrow street, and Judita swings one leg over the back of the bicycle and coasts with the other foot still on the pedal.

The woman is clutching her purse tightly to her chest, but the boys are undeterred and wily. One of them reaches up and touches her earring, and when she swats his hand away, the other yanks the purse free. The pair dash down the alley in Judita's direction as the woman's scream bounces off the stone walls.

Judita steps down off the bicycle and, as the boy holding the purse is about to pass, extends her leg. The boy lands in a sprawl on the cobblestones, sending the purse flying. The other makes a move for it, but Judita's reflexes are faster, and she snatches it up. The boys glare at her, and the one she tripped says something about a skinned knee and how she'd better watch her back. They take off down the alley and disappear around the corner.

The tourist woman is still paralyzed with shock as Judita holds out the purse to her, and it takes her a full ten seconds to understand it's being returned. When she takes her purse back, she does so carefully, as if the thing were now toxic. "Thank you," she says in English. Then, self-consciously, "*Gracias.*" In her expression, Judita can see a reflection of herself: stained T-shirt, skin coated in sweat and diesel grime. The woman opens the purse, takes out a 20-peso note, and hands it to her, taking care that their hands do not touch.

Judita pulls the bicycle through the back door and into the kitchen of the restaurant, leaning it against the wall next to the big refrigerator where the steaks and lamb and vegetables are kept—the very finest in all of Uruguay, or so Judita tells the tourists from the ships that dock just a few blocks away. Emmanuel, at the grill, gives Judita a look. He knows he shorted her on the salad, tomatoes and cucumbers being pricey this year, and he hopes she won't bitch about it. But Judita won't bitch, grateful as she is to have the job. Emmanuel is sleeping with Mariela, the owner, and his opinion of people matters.

Tying an apron around her waist, Judita starts through the kitchen doors to the floor, but Mariela stops her. Mariela is tall and thick and wears too much makeup and the customers find her terribly sexy. She brushes her red hair behind her ear and smiles the way she does. "You're filthy," she says. "Wash up first."

Judita nods and hands Mariela the money from the delivery. Even though it comes up short, Mariela gives her back a handful of pesos anyway. "Americans," she says. "Always teaching the world a lesson."

In the little lavatory where the cooks sometimes go to smoke weed, Judita scrubs at her hands and arms and face with gritty powder soap and avoids looking in the little mirror until she has to. Her face is lean and hard—"unwelcoming" is the way she's heard it put. Her brown eyes are drills that tend to make people look away. She has to practice her smile more, the other servers say, which will lead to better tips. In the absence of a brush, she combs her ink-black hair with her fingers and fastens it with a rubber band into a short ponytail. The ponytail keeps the hair out of her eyes so she can see. And Judita must see everything. Must stay constantly aware.

The restaurant is noisy and crowded with a ravenous, barbarous crowd of British tourists smacking their lips over the slabs of nearly raw beef and lamb and calling out, "Girl! More wine, *por favor.*"

Judita got this job because of her crude, utilitarian English. She keeps it because she's fast and can balance the trays of food on one hand and doesn't ever say no to Mariela or anyone else. She is always willing to swap shifts, or clean the vomit off the bathroom floor, or make the deliveries to the other side of town.

From four in the afternoon until one in the morning, she's on her feet, sweating, moving quickly from the broiling kitchen to the too many tables she covers. There are propositions and ass grabs and spilled wine on her tattered sneakers, but Judita works at her smile and says *no problem* and takes it all until Mariela shoos the last drunken customers out the door and locks it behind them.

Everyone cleans up, swabbing the toilets, putting the chairs up on the tables, then gathers at the bar. A few light cigarettes while Gustavo the bartender pours glasses of leftover wine for everyone. Judita drains her glass quickly, and Gustavo pours her another, which she also drains quickly. In exhausted silence, they count out the night's money, hoping the cash in their pockets works out to a little more than the total of the checks. They pool whatever's left and Gustavo is entrusted to divide it equally among them—servers, busboys, cooks. There's not all that much, usually. Maybe 200 pesos for each of them. Only the Americans ever tip big. It's what they're known for, and the servers fight over who gets their table. All the servers except Judita, who always graciously allows someone else to take the Americans.

After the money is counted, Mariela emerges from the kitchen with parcels of food. Everyone goes home with something, and for most of them, including Judita, it makes up the lion's share of their diet. The orders that were sent back are the best because they're mostly untouched. But no one is very picky. The half-eaten rice from table 10 and the almost-intact lamb chop from table 14 are bundled up in newspaper and carried home to waiting mouths. A woman with five children and a bedridden husband gets all the bones, which she boils for soup stock and sells at the market on Saturday mornings. As for the wine, the kind or vintage doesn't matter. Everything left over goes into the pails kept behind Gustavo's bar. Red mixes with white, Malbec mixes with Pinot. While the rest clean up, Gustavo funnels all the pails into the night's empty bottles. Whole families, whole neighborhoods, get drunk this way.

Judita tucks a parcel of food and a few bottles of wine into her backpack. Her bus doesn't come until 2:17, so she takes her time walking through what there is of nighttime Montevideo. Most of the city shuts down early, but this stretch, near the terminal from where her bus departs, only crawls out of bed at midnight. Bars and nightclubs and brothels are at their fullest and noisiest. The stink of weed hangs like a smelly ghost over the street. Judita doesn't mind, though, so long as the city leaves her alone.

She makes her way down to Piedras and keeps her eyes low, her posture meek, just a girl heading home from work. Which is all Judita is, all she aspires to be. The British ship is evidently lingering in port until morning—a problem with the radio, she heard someone at the restaurant say—giving the more adventurous passengers a chance to experience a night of fun in naughty, libertine Uruguay. A loud argument erupts between groups of men, and Judita knows it will escalate into a fight before long. Someone else trips on the root of a tree jutting through the sidewalk and laughs with blood running down his chin. Judita ignores it all and adjusts her backpack, heavy with the night's haul of food and wine.

"How old are you?" a voice calls out in English. Not drunk, not yet. Just loud.

Judita doesn't reply. Perhaps the question isn't meant for her, but it's best to ignore it even if it is. Then she hears it again: "How old are you?" The man who says it—short-sleeved golf shirt tucked into khaki shorts over a bulging stomach—is too close for his question to be directed at anyone else. He starts walking beside Judita.

He's nearing fifty, heavy through the middle, weirdly narrow in his face. Judita sees he's carrying a camera, a good one. "Again say?" Judita asks in her uncertain English.

"I was asking your age," he says. "Sixteen?"

A flash of something crosses Judita's face for less than a second, as if a foul-smelling memory came to her. She smiles and hurries on. But the man stays at her side all the way to the corner where she has to wait as a bus groans past.

He steps closer. "I guessed it, didn't I?" he says. "Sixteen."

"Yes," she lies. "What you want?"

"We could find a hotel, maybe, but I'm not a snob about it. Anywhere is fine. Two hundred pesos."

She closes her eyes and breathes in deeply, pushing something down inside her. "Two hundred pesos for what?" she asks.

"You know. Keep each other company for a time."

Easy money. Money Judita needs. She asks herself: How hard can it be? "Five hundred pesos," she says.

"Two hundred."

She meets his eyes. "Show me."

He lets out a nervous laugh as he glances around, then moves his hands to the fly of his shorts.

"No. Your money," she says. "Half now."

He pulls the wallet out of his back pocket and hands her a 100-peso note, wrinkled and dirty. But she also sees a fat sheaf of brightly colored British pounds. Crisp, new money. First World money. Pink and green and cream.

Judita tilts her head down the side street. "Come," she says.

He follows her as she looks for someplace private.

"You're pretty," he says.

"Yes?" Judita says shyly. There's a vacant lot between two buildings where piles of rubble from whatever stood here before were in the process of being hauled away. She steps from the sidewalk into dirt rutted with tracks, testing it with the toe of her sneaker to see if it's mud. It's not. "This way."

"I was in Thailand last year," the man says. "But the girls here are prettier, I think. At least you are."

She turns and gives him a smile. A backhoe sits idly near the far side of the lot, like a sleeping monster, and she directs him to the space behind it, where it's darker and out of sight from the street.

"You sure—you sure this is safe?" he asks. All shadow and stone here. Threats could be hiding anywhere.

"Oh, yes," she says, coming up close to him, near enough to smell his nervousness. Blisters of sweat on the side of one soft cheek capture and magnify the ambient light. She removes the camera from around his neck and sets it on the backhoe's track next to her backpack.

He makes a twitchy grin and unfastens his belt.

Judita drives her knee hard into his groin. The man pitches forward where she meets his chin with the butt of her hand and snaps his head back. Breath explodes from his mouth in a gasp as Judita's free fist lands squarely in his kidney and he crumples to the ground.

She gives him a second to recover, expecting him to leap up, take a swing, but there's no fight in this one, and instead he scrambles away from her on all fours in a manic crab walk. Even in the dark, Judita can see his wide, panicked eyes. She steps closer and he starts to say something, a plea, but he can't find his words.

"Stand up," Judita says.

"Take—take my camera," he manages.

"I will," Judita says. "Stand up."

Slowly and with great effort, he does as he's told.

"Fight me," Judita says.

A flash of fresh terror lights up his face, but he takes a sloppy boxer's stance, raising his arms into a defensive position, as if he's remembering what he's seen on TV. He's never done this before, Judita guesses.

She drives a fist straight forward into his nose, the soft cartilage bending and crackling against her middle knuckle. He staggers backward and brings his hands to his face, just as the toe of Judita's right sneaker lands hard on his left ear and sends him toppling onto the ground.

"I have pesos," he shouts. "Pounds. British pounds." He rolls over onto his back and pulls out his wallet. Judita snatches it from his hand. The sheaf of bills inside is pleasingly thick, and she pushes it into the pocket of her jeans. There's more on him, though. She knows tourists never carry all they have in a wallet. There's always a money belt or an emergency hundred in some sweaty crevice.

"The rest," Judita says.

"I don't . . ."

She swings her foot into his side, then reaches down and yanks his shirt up out of his shorts. Just a hairless, milk-colored stomach without a money belt. "The rest," she repeats.

He struggles to reach his left foot and withdraws a folded 50-pound note from his sock. "All I have," he says. "Really. All I have."

The bill is wet but goes into Judita's pocket with the rest anyway. She pins him down with one knee pressed into his bare stomach, then takes his camera from the track of the backhoe. The flash fires as she takes his picture, and on the screen a half second later, she sees the man's face, a shining white moon of terror, creeks of blood running lazily from nose to mouth to chin. Her fingers work their way over the camera body until she finds the hatch for the memory card. "For you," she says, dropping the card on his chest. "To remember your visit."

Judita is gone a moment later, already out of the yard, already pushing the camera into her backpack with the food and the wine. She knows she can fence a nice Canon readily enough. Two thousand pesos, easy. His credit cards and especially his passport would have brought in even more, but that means he misses his boat tomorrow morning and Judita wants to make his exit as easy and free of police as possible. Not that she worries much about that—in the version he told the cops, she would become an entire knife-wielding gang of men. But Montevideo is a small town, and she doesn't want to risk running into him. Running into people is one thing Judita does worry about.

Two

I've gotten good at this, thinking of Judita in the third person, as if she were someone else. Her name isn't my name, I tell myself. Her thoughts—concerned mostly with food and money—aren't my thoughts. She ignores the slights dished out by the customers at the restaurant where she works. She ignores the under-the-breath insults of Americans and Brits as they express shock that the South American waitress and delivery girl doesn't speak English as well as they think she ought to. She ignores all of it until, sometimes, she forgets who she's supposed to be and goes back to her old ways for a little while. But only ever in private. Only ever when no one's around to see.

To live as Judita is like waking up every day in a torturously boring sequel to a torturously boring sequel. Nothing changes. Today's exhaustion is yesterday's exhaustion. Today's endless bus ride is yesterday's endless bus ride. I tell myself to be grateful that I'm alive. I tell myself that I'm extremely lucky to be here in Uruguay instead of dead or in a CIA prison in Turkmenistan. Judita—Judita's life—is a gift.

The Uruguayan passport granted to Judita Leandra Perels lists her place of birth as a small town about two hundred kilometers outside

Caracas, Venezuela. Her surname is not common here in Uruguay. But then, all kinds of people turn up in Uruguay for all kinds of reasons, so nobody ever really asks about it. In the case of Judita Leandra Perels and her father, Dario Javier Perels, they were given citizenship after their names were brought up during negotiations about visa requirements and trade tariffs between Uruguay and Israel. Why Israel should care about two Venezuelans is anybody's guess. But their application was supported by the Consejo Judío Sudamericana, Montevideo branch, with a personal recommendation from the organization's president, Dr. Enrique Goldman, regular tennis partner of Uruguay's attorney general.

That's the official version of Judita's life. And that's the version I'll swear to. I've got enough material to last me two, maybe three, days under serious interrogation.

The bus drops me off a twenty-minute walk from my home. At this time of night, the streets are mostly empty, and all the windows dark. Houses, mostly, and a few three-story stucco apartment buildings. A stray dog prances along beside me, not even bothering to beg, just happy for the company. He was a handsome thing once, a golden retriever maybe, but the mange and grime are so thick, it's hard to tell.

Already, at three in the morning, the scrappers are coming out of their apartments, hooking horses up to empty wagons. The animals are beaten, ancient things, slouching along, heads low as their owners tie them up. In a few hours, the carts they drag behind them will be piled high with salvaged metal and wood, anything that might be of value to someone, somewhere. I always feel bad for the horses, though the guys driving the wagons don't look much happier.

In the Old Town of Montevideo and the barrios near the center, everything looks nice. A city comfortable with its status as a cleanish, safeish capital to a cleanish, safeish country. But the scrap collectors and I know better. We live out here beyond where the tourists and politicians and the middle-class office workers go, on the edge of the city, at the edge of the nineteenth century. My dad and I are lucky to have running water, but most people here fare far worse. I pass them on this street daily on my way to work, kids in bare feet hauling pails of water back to the semilegal shacks made of whatever scrap their fathers can't sell. Life in these quarters makes it hard to give a shit about your horse.

I climb the steps to my apartment building and go inside. The landlady on the ground floor is watching TV, or maybe she fell asleep in front of it. The stairs creak as I climb to the second floor, then the third. I pause at my door, hand resting on the doorknob, brass turned brown with age. It's silent in my apartment, as it always is. I unlock the door and step inside.

"*Soy yo, Papá,*" I say. Just me, Dad.

He looks me over, the light from the table lamp catching his eyes, and the corners of his beard turn up into something like a smile.

"Good day?" he asks quietly.

"Fine."

I slip into my bedroom, take the camera and two of the wine bottles out of my backpack. Then I count out the money. Two hundred and ten British pounds and 300 Uruguayan pesos. Add the camera and it's a banner night. Something to celebrate.

All of it—the money, camera, and wine—go into the space between my bed and the wall. There's a small fortune there now, four cameras, six phones, and, as of tonight, what works out to 1,700 US dollars in cash. What I'm saving up for, I don't know. But I know we'll need it, probably sooner rather than later.

I change into a T-shirt and shorts, wash up, and step into the other room of the apartment, holding the parcel of food and the third bottle of wine like I'd just discovered treasure. "Beef and a little lamb, I think," I say in whispered English. "Also some asparagus."

We own two plates, two cups, and two sets of silverware. I dish the food out and take it to him.

"Any adventures?" he asks quietly, inspecting a piece of lamb on the end of his fork. When we speak in English, it always has to be quiet. Foreign languages arouse suspicion.

"Delivered a big order to an American. She stiffed me on the tip."

"Sorry, kiddo. That sucks," he says. "Still, you get stiffed and bring home the bacon anyway. I'm proud of you."

It's silent as we eat, my dad on the couch, me on someone's dining room chair that ended up at the flea market. After a few bites, my dad places the knife and fork carefully on the edge of the plate and leans back.

"Hot today?" he says.

"Yes," I say.

"Sorry you have to, you know, be out in that. Unpleasant."

"Yes," I say.

"Another month, maybe."

"Another month what?" I say.

"Before it gets cooler," he says.

It kills me. It kills me that he's like this. That he's become this. There was a hero inside him once. But the last time he left the apartment was two weeks ago, and that was because I begged him to. Take a walk, I said. Get some air. He was back in ten minutes, and what I could see of his face behind the gray beard and scraggly hair was white as a sheet from terror.

"You need to eat more," I say.

"Too rich," he says. "I'll eat something later."

I just nod and finish what's on my plate. I'll tuck the rest of his away in the refrigerator. "You didn't touch your wine."

He brushes the knee of his pants. "I'm not thirsty."

"So—what we were talking about yesterday," I say. "The plan."

"The plan," he repeats, as if he's never heard these words before.

I take a long drink of my wine and, when it's gone, reach for his cup. He doesn't like it, how much I drink. He used to tell me that, but in the last few months he hasn't bothered.

"You need to get out," I say. "Into the world. I saw a sign for a chess club at the Jewish Center downtown."

16

"Dangerous," he answers, swatting at a mosquito. "Maybe in a year or so."

"We've *been* here a year," I say through gritted teeth.

"Keep your voice down," he says.

The anger flares inside me, but I look away to keep him from seeing it. "Buenos Aires," I say just above a whisper. "It's close. Three hours by ferry. And much bigger. We wouldn't have to hide all the time. We'd be just part of the crowd. I could, I don't know, go to college."

"Sweetheart . . ."

I know what he's going to say and cut him off. "There's a program at the Instituto Tecnológico, a part-time thing. I could take math, intro courses. I looked it up on a computer at the library. It costs a lot, but if I tutored English . . ."

He reaches across the table, places a hand on my leg. "College can wait."

"For what? Until I'm thirty?"

He squeezes my knee. "Your voice," he whispers, glancing to the wall and the neighbors sleeping on the other side of it.

I pull my leg away.

"We can do it, Dad. We can have"—I gesture around the room to the cracked walls, the bedsheet curtains—"*more.*"

I stand and take our plates into the little kitchen. There's a spider on the wall, a nasty, hairy thing, but it's not bothering me so I won't bother it. I place the dishes in the sink, and when I turn around, my dad's standing there. His hands are folded over the stomach of his yellowed undershirt. He's looking down at the cracked tiles on the floor. *Don't,* I will him. *Don't start now.*

But he doesn't apologize. The last vestige of my old dad is still there somewhere inside him, the CIA operative part, the strong part. "Gwendolyn," he says, using my real name for the first time in months. "It isn't people that are looking for us. It's a thing. With ten thousand heads and a million eyes and a very, very long memory. This—what we're doing, keeping the lowest of low profiles—is a tactical necessity. Do you understand?"

I nod that I do. *Tactical necessity.* Soldier talk. Comrade talk. Not dad talk. "Yes," I say, even though I'm not sure I do. "How long?"

"Until they get distracted by something else. But even then . . ." The thought hangs there, and he shakes his head, not wanting to finish it. "You never see it coming, Gwen. Never. There's not a knock at the door. The floorboards don't creak. You don't see them until after the bullet is in you."

I turn away. "Stop talking like that."

"It's true, Gwen. This isn't the life I had in mind, either. But it's the hand we've been dealt."

"Then change it."

"How?" he says.

"You know how," I say.

I hear him breathe out through his nose, disappointed and a little angry. It's the untouchable topic, the thing-that-must-never-be-discussed.

"Sweetheart," he says. "Money won't fix a goddamn thing."

I turn back to him, eyes on his, willing the message to finally be received. "Let's try it and see," I say.

He may be asleep. Hard to tell. The other room is quiet, but then it's always quiet with my dad, the mouse who thinks every shadow is a cat. I sit on the bed, back against the wall, eyes drifting aimlessly out the window. Sometimes in the morning, if the smog is not too thick, I can see a little slice of the river beyond the shanties. Sometimes, if the river's not too muddy, it actually looks blue, gleaming like a promise. Now, though, the dim yellow lights of Montevideo are all I get, just a scattering of them, as if there were barely a city there at all.

I reach into the space between my bed and the wall and pull out a bottle of tonight's wine, the slurry of remnants left behind by the customers at the restaurant. I have little to compare it with quality-wise, but it's not bad by my low standards, and sometimes it even contains a surprise or two. Tonight's, for example, tastes like rancid blackberries, but in the best possible sense. Complicated and weird. I pour it into a chipped coffee mug and sip it primly, like some exiled, destitute princess.

I don't drink wine because I like it, or to get drunk—both are side effects, distractions from the real reason, which is that wine makes me sleepy. It's a drug, a medicine. When I first started taking it home from the restaurant, a single glass did the trick. But then a single glass turned into two, then became a bottle. Lately, getting sleepy takes a bottle plus one—a full bottle plus a glass from the next. A bad road to start down, but a girl's got to sleep. I can't help it if my mind won't shut off or if my body resists sliding into my personal dreamland hell.

I take out my deck of cards and begin shuffling. It's an old deck, dating at least from my time in New York, maybe before, and I took it with me to Paris and Berlin and Prague. The cards are worn and bent and fraying, and really, I should just break down and spend a few pesos on a new deck. But it's practically the only thing that remains from my other lives and other names, the single thread stretching from Judita to Sofia to Gwendolyn.

As I drink, my hands grow steadier, the shuffles sharper and more precise—another bad sign—but I can't do it properly without the wine anymore. I splay the cards out on the bed in a perfectly spaced, face-down arc, then sweep them over so they flow like a wave and finish faceup. This has, for years, been my therapy, the calm orderly plastic world of chance and statistical probability. Each shuffle is a new universe of winners and losers.

The money. The idea flashes across my mind again, so I take another sip of slurry wine and tell it to go away. But it won't. In the cartoon of the man crawling across the desert, the money is the mirage glass of water on the horizon, the thing keeping him going. But this is no mirage, despite what some people say. The money belonging to the dead crime lord Viktor Zoric, the man my dad helped put in the grave, is now comatose in Switzerland and Liechtenstein, asleep, dormant, waiting to come alive again at true love's kiss.

It's how Zoric paid people off, my dad says. Start a new company, open a new account, and make the payee a co-owner. Bribing an official is as easy as that. I'd had the account numbers. And my dad knew where to find the passcodes and names. This information had nearly killed us both.

I push the cards together and set the deck on the table next to my bed. Then I take the last swallow I'll allow myself—a bottle plus one. I sink back into the bed and close my eyes. What I see projected in my mind are the twenty-odd bodies I stacked up as I gouged my way from Paris to Berlin to Prague. Each face comes back to me. The guy I stabbed on the train, the guy whose brains I blew out in a jail cell, are the most generous, appearing to me only as they appeared at the moment they died—openmouthed, frightened. But I remember the others more clearly. Emil in the blue cast of the dashboard lights of his van, rapping along with American hip-hop. Roman as he bought me a dress, struggling through morphine to count out the money. Bohdan Kladivo as he smiled and lit his cigar and told me that if I wanted to rise in this world, I needed to be crueler than any man.

These faces I see as they were before their deaths. Living faces. The faces of men. My rational, daytime self believes that each and every one deserved it, whether it was the knife or the bullet or the rat poison I dumped in their tequila. But my subhuman, nighttime self is less sure, remembering as it does the blood and toxic vomit and how the idea of justice looks nothing like the reality of justice.

That's why, no matter the volume of wine I drink, my sheets are tangled around me and wet with sweat every morning. But it was all for a good cause, wasn't it? Rescuing one's father. It all worked out in the end, didn't it? Waking to another morning in Montevideo, alive.

Three

See you on the other side.

That's what Yael said, just before I left the German farmhouse a few kilometers from the Czech border. She said it casually, in the middle of a loveless hug concluded with two quick pats on the back. The other side of what? The Atlantic? Death? Good and evil? But instead of asking, I climbed into the trunk of the Mercedes sedan. Someone handed me a bottle of water, a bag to throw up in if I needed it, and two small pills—a sedative and something for nausea meant to be dissolved under the tongue.

I rode in the dark for a very long time—two hours or eight, impossible to tell. My mind went blank in the tight confines, aware only of itself and the discomfort of the body to which it was attached. I rode over rough roads and smooth, through cities and over highways. I puked into the bag once, and nearly again when the smell of it became too much. By the end, I had to pee so badly I thought I'd pass out from the effort of holding it.

When the trunk finally opened, we were in a dingy hangar at a small airport, the air smelling of gasoline and the walls piled high with boxes and spare parts. I climbed into the backseat of a single-engine prop plane, the whole cabin no bigger than that of a small hatchback. A pale guy with terrified eyes and clutching a briefcase to his chest climbed in next to me. "She saw my face," he hissed in French to the man who turned out to be our pilot.

East to another airport, where the signs were in what I took to be Polish. Another plane south, a small jet this time, utilitarian blue vinyl seats with metal rings between them. I stared at these for a while, trying to figure out their purpose, and realized after we'd taken off they would be perfect for anchoring handcuffs. A pretty woman with short black hair smiled at us like a flight attendant, then seized my hand with an immensely powerful grip when I tried to open the window shade.

"Windows are to remain covered," she said.

"Until when?" I asked.

"Until we land," she said.

As she turned away, I saw a pistol holstered in her waistband.

The French guy fell asleep a short time later, his head resting on my shoulder. He snored and murmured something indiscernible as he dreamt. Every once in a while, he shuddered with the briefcase against his chest, as if even now he was fearful of losing it.

With no external reference point, time again slipped away, just as it had in the trunk of the Mercedes. We flew for six hours, or so I guessed, enough for several cycles of terror turning to boredom and back to terror again. Just as my body was telling me it was time to go to sleep, we touched down. The French guy woke in a panic as the wheels bounced and squealed on the tarmac, gasping and sucking drool into his mouth. But this wasn't, it turned out, his stop. Only mine.

When the cabin door opened, I stepped into the queer chill of a desert at night. As I climbed down the staircase to the ground, I saw nothing but a small airstrip with a few hangars and unmarked military trucks, all painted tan. A woman with olive skin pulled tightly over fine features and black hair cut close to the scalp waited for me beside a jeep. She wore a green serge army uniform with no patches or markings, not even a flag.

"Hello," she said in English that had no accent. "We're pleased to have you here, Student 312."

There was no official name for the place, so someone who came before me gave it an informal one: Orphan Camp. We called it that because that's what we were, at least in a way. There was no wall and no guard tower, only a fence, a mere two meters high. This wasn't, the instructors were quick to remind us, a prison; it was the safest place in the world we could possibly be. Besides, who needs a wall and a guard tower when you're surrounded by untold miles of desert?

A few minutes after my arrival, another woman in the same unmarked uniform stood me up before a dozen serious faces and introduced me.

"Welcome, 312," they all said back in frightening unison.

There was a hardness to each student's face, something born of trauma and sadness that had petrified their features into a kind of stony beauty that was nearly angelic. They weren't surprised by anything anymore, nor could they be hurt by anything anymore. The color of the students' skin ran from nearly black to paper white, but there was a commonality of experience that made them appear almost like siblings. We had all, for reasons known only to Tel Aviv, somehow fallen into Israel's orbit. Hence our presence here.

Student 309, a wispy Arab boy who spoke English like a British duke, was assigned to show me around the camp. There wasn't much to it besides a few metal buildings, some farm equipment, and fields beyond the fence where wooden lattices held up plastic plants. Just what kind of plants they were supposed to be—grapes, maybe, but in the desert?—I had no idea. Afterward, 309 helped me collect my bedding, toiletries, and uniform: blue fatigues identical to the instructors' except for the color.

Our final stop was the barracks, where he tapped on a thin mattress on an upper bunk. "Days begin at six," he said. "Except when they don't."

I looked at him with a tired smirk that showed I was too exhausted for riddles.

"Sometimes it's a four-in-the-morning run through the desert," he said. "Other times, it's a tear gas grenade through the door."

"A tear gas grenade?"

"To get the blood flowing," he said. "Orphan Camp coffee."

They allowed me to rest that first day, something 309 told me it was better not to get used to—"As you shan't see much more of it for the next six months." *Shan't.* The first time I'd heard someone use that word in real life.

The heat in the barracks was sweltering, and I knew it would be worse when the others came back, with too many bodies too close together. As I drifted off—too tired to be frightened or even intrigued by what was in store for me next—I heard through the metal walls shouting instructors and, every once in a while, a factory whistle.

I managed to sleep until the students returned in what I took to be the late afternoon. They were beaten and dirty, their uniforms soaked through with sweat. No one had the energy to speak, so they simply stripped naked and either crawled into bed or sat around in exhausted silence. This nakedness, I would come to learn, was no more than a biological fact, signifying nothing other than how hot it was. The temperature was simply too high and our bodies too empty for anything like arousal.

I climbed down off the bunk and saw the person who slept below me was a parchment-skinned woman with red hair, no older than twenty. She went by 303, or, as she pronounced it, "Tree-oh-tree"— hard *t*'s, trilled *r*'s. I recognized her look and her accent.

"*Vuy Russkiy?*" I said. You Russian?

She looked at me coldly. "As I said, I'm 303."

No names here, and no nationalities, either.

Firearms training always came first thing in the morning and was taught by a blond-haired, blue-eyed giant of a man who introduced us to the wonders of the world's most common pistols and assault rifles. Thousands of paper targets later, there were blisters on my trigger finger and on the webbing between my thumb and hand. We repeated exercises on disassembling, cleaning, and reassembling the weapons so many times that by the end the instructor blindfolded us, and we could do it in the dark.

After firearms, it was hand-to-hand fighting, taught by a cheery middle-aged woman who looked like her hobbies included scrapbooking and collecting porcelain cats. She was, however, never to be crossed, and when a boy I thought from his accent might be from West Africa failed to deliver a hard enough blow to her during sparring, she twisted his arm behind his back until he screamed.

This class always ended with the mysterious factory whistle. As soon as it sounded, everyone—students and instructors alike—retreated to the nearest shelter. A tractor dragging an enormous sheet of plywood by a pair of heavy chains went out, driving around the grounds, erasing our tracks. I learned why on my first day. Student 300, an Asian girl in her late teens, pointed to the sky as we waited inside a barn and said, "Satellites."

The schedule of the whistles was fairly regular, but there were enough variations—one day, it sounded a total of thirteen times—that I wondered just how the instructors knew when the satellites were overhead. In any case, the images the satellites sent back to Washington and Moscow and Beijing were of a small farm consisting of a few buildings, some crops, and scattered pieces of equipment. Nothing of interest. And certainly not a summer camp at which "Kumbaya" sing-alongs were substituted for AK-47 training.

Firearms and hand-to-hand combat were only two of the subjects we were taught in what turned out to be a comprehensive education in clandestine life. Other instructors in anonymous green uniforms taught us old-school tradecraft, things like street passes, dead drops, surveillance detection—analog alternatives to the high-tech, and of more use today, they told us, than ever before. They taught us how to hot-wire and drive anything with an engine, from a scooter to an elephantine military truck. We learned how to slam through a roadblock, and how to spin a car 180 degrees with just a flick of the wrist and deft dance on the brake and gas.

There was a special sort of pleasure to the training. The tools of revenge is how I saw it. Especially when I got to the knives. Easy to get, the instructor said, and devastating, even in the hands of an amateur. We started with fancy ones, built for fighting. Then cheap ones, made for cutting tomatoes and available anywhere on the planet. It turns out, knives were what I was good at, and the instructor said she liked my technique. There was, in her words, a certain "elegant aggression" to my style.

That's the thing that happens to anger when you live with it awhile—elegant aggression. The fury doesn't make your hands shake or your skin buzz anymore. It just lives in your veins, like a drug, making you stronger and that much faster. Making your aim at the carotid or femoral or liver or kidney that much sharper. The guns were fine, and the driving fun, but that—the ten centimeters of steel coming to a point like an extension of my very arm—is where I found my real pleasure.

Each night, back in the barracks, there was little talk and almost no camaraderie. It's hard to make friends when you go by a number and aren't allowed to say so much as where you came from. Only 303 became something approaching a friend. It turned out both of us had trouble sleeping, haunted by memories that had followed us all the way here. So after lights-out, we'd sneak into the yard to escape the heat. Hushed conversations were all that followed, and those always in the present and future tenses, never the past.

"We're in Israel, you think?" she said one night.

She'd been better with the *th*'s lately. No more turning them into *t*'s or *d*'s.

I shrugged. "Too obvious."

"North Africa somewhere."

"Maybe."

She leaned back against the barracks wall. "They say someone got a radio once. Climbed up on the roof to listen for a signal, maybe figure out where this place is."

"Did they hear anything?"

"Yes," she said, looking at me through the darkness. "A voice telling them to turn off the radio and get off the roof."

We both laughed into our arms until tears came. It was too absurd not to be true.

People came and went. Student 309 vanished one day, and a week later Student 303 did, too. Where they went, none of us knew. New arrivals showed up at random times. Student 313 turned out to be a kid I thought was Japanese until she opened her mouth and out came pure Chicago; 314 was a Latino boy who became the hand-to-hand teacher's star pupil within a single day.

My time came after I'd been there six months. As the others retreated to the barracks one afternoon, I was summoned to the office of the camp's director, the same woman with olive skin and fine features who'd picked me up from the airfield.

"Your father's doing well, happy to say," she said with no hint of emotion from behind a battered wooden desk. "Question is, how are you doing?"

It was a startling question in an environment where what they teach you is trickery and deception and how to kill. "I'm—doing well also," I said. "Thank you."

"Our goal was to teach you survival skills," she said. "For a new life, in a new world, with a new name. Do you feel we've met that goal successfully?"

I nodded. That had been the line from day one, but it hadn't fooled any of us. Survival skills are how to start a fire or open a bank account. What we'd been taught was more aggressive. We weren't being trained for defense but offense. And it wasn't lost on me that I'd incurred a debt to the state of Israel that they weren't likely to forget.

"Yes," I said. "You did that successfully."

She didn't acknowledge the answer and instead pulled a sheaf of papers from a manila folder. "Your Spanish," she said. "Still fluent?"

"*Tal vez*," I said.

She blinked at me from across the desk.

I tried to smile. "Maybe."

She slid the sheaf of papers toward me. "Montevideo, Uruguay," she said. "Your name is now Judita Leandra Perels."

Four

Dear sir or madam,

Contained in the enclosed documents are details of forty-seven (47) operations undertaken by the Central Intelligence Agency of the United States. All transpired with the knowledge of, support of, and/or participation of members of the Department of Defense, the executive branch, and key members of Congress. The events are described from personal memory, as I was a participant or observer in all the cases described here. Each scream of the tortured, each body disposed of in an anonymous grave or in the sea or left in the sun, is precisely accurate to my memory.

Nothing is conjecture or supposition.

What you are reading is a catalog of crimes. This catalog describes torture and brutality perpetrated against probably innocent individuals, and murder perpetrated against same. This catalog describes the CIA's collusion with dictators and enemies of the United States, as well as collusion with organized crime syndicates, including, but not limited to, the Zoric crime

family based in Belgrade and Sarajevo, the Kladivo crime
family based in Prague, the Solkov syndicate based in Moscow,
the Al-Alwadi smuggling organization based in Damascus, and
several others. This catalog describes the participation of CIA
operatives and agents in arms and narcotics trafficking, and
the trafficking of human beings, often women, often children, for
the purposes of sexual exploitation. This catalog describes the
profiting from these actions by members of the intelligence and
defense establishments, members of the executive branch,
members of Congress, and private interests—all of whom are
herein named.

It is my only hope that my daughter, Gwendolyn Bloom,
likely the deliverer of this document, be protected by whatever
means you have at your disposal. She is innocent in these
affairs, though hardly unstained by them. Gwendolyn's safety
is, as I write this, my foremost concern in this world. Had it
always been my foremost concern—which, as a father, it should
have been—it would not have been necessary to write this
document in the first place.

Yours, in trust,
William Bloom
Montevideo, Uruguay

So begins, in his spidery, formal cursive, the first pages of his confession, what he calls his "doomsday device." It spans some seven children's school notebooks in all—two with blue covers, three with pink, and two Hello Kitty. Each page is filled, front and back, with careful prose in ink, virtually uninterrupted by redactions or corrections, as if he were merely transcribing something that already existed fully formed in his head.

The murder of a French spy by the CIA as a favor to a corrupt colonel in Pakistani intelligence. A meeting in a Saudi hotel suite between American businessmen, a US senator, and a Saudi prince in which advanced weapons technology was traded for cash. CIA officers being treated to a buffet of child prostitutes by Viktor Zoric in the city of Munich.

And so on, page after page, brightly colored children's notebook after brightly colored children's notebook, until he has damned everyone he has ever known, including himself. I read the pages only incidentally, to and from the network of Internet cafés where I scan the notebooks and upload the videos he makes of himself reading the whole confession aloud. There are hours of footage, my dad sitting in dim light, speaking low so as not to be overheard by the neighbors, occasionally fiddling with the camera on the smartphone I'd gotten at his request from a pawnshop.

I don't watch the videos, though, which would make it impossible to pretend the character of "I" in the notebooks refers to someone other than my father. He, William Bloom, the I, comes off better than the others, of course, actively participating in no torture, and only three or four or maybe five murders depending on where one draws the line between participation and observation. At no point does he accept any gift or bribe.

I love him. Still. Despite. Maybe because he's my father and nothing can change that, or maybe because he's the only thing left to love. But it's different now. Since coming here, since reading his doomsday device for myself, the love is different.

Carga Completa, says the screen. Upload Complete.

Counting this, the latest and hopefully final episode of Dad's doomsday device, there are fourteen videos in total—two each for each of the seven notebooks.

My dad put together a list of editors at newspapers, magazines, blogs, and television news networks most likely to be interested in the story. Some were old-school journalists for whom integrity and telling truth to power mattered above all. Others were simply scandalmongers, eager for any kind of scoop. The e-mails to the editors linking to folders in several redundant cloud storage sites around the world are already written and waiting in the drafts folder of several different e-mail accounts. All I have to do in case my dad is captured or killed is log in to just one of them and hit SEND.

I move on to the next cloud storage service and start the process of uploading the video and scanned notebook pages again. Turns out, prepping to bring down the world is tedious business. I have to use the TOR browser for anything I do on the Web. It bounces the traffic through servers all around the world before it finally reaches its destination. It's slow at the best of times, but here in Uruguay, it absolutely crawls.

When watching the progress bar creep along becomes too painful, I turn back to my book. It's hard to concentrate here; the *pew-pew-pew* from games and moaning from porn are relentless. And the book I'm reading, checked out from the library, isn't helping, either. *CIA Involvement in Central and South America, A Critical Analysis.* I keep the book's dust jacket off, so only the plain cover is ever visible to the curious.

The topic is interesting enough, but getting through it is like hacking my way through a jungle. Dense, mosquito-infested text, by an author who has no interest in getting to the point anytime soon.

But at least it's mind work, not physical work, not schlepping steaks to tourists and having my ass grabbed. I delight in sorting it all out, drawing the connections between one thinker and another, of wondering whether the French Revolution of 1789 and the Russian Revolution of 1917 and the state of things today are related, and finding out that they are.

To me these books are more than abstract ideas. They show me my place in the world. There are reasons the world looks the way it looks and behaves the way it behaves. My story—a woman of nineteen caught between borders and ideologies—isn't even original. Everything has happened before. Everything will happen again.

Carga Completa.

I put the book down, go to another cloud service, and start the upload again. It's the last one, thankfully, and moving pretty quickly now by TOR-in-Uruguay standards. I indulge myself and open another tab.

Argentina, this month—just a single border away. Somewhere in the countryside, photos of Argentine cowboys and little villages. The month before it had been China, with wonderful photos of Shanghai and Beijing. Couples on the streets. Children holding balloons. Skateboarders midair.

I'm not an artist, and no photographer, but I know good when I see it, and Terrance's work is good. Forget for a second the colors and the light, and look at how the photos are structured. Their composition. See how that little girl is there, and her grandmother, over there? See how the rake the grandmother is holding cuts at a perfect diagonal that mirrors the shape of the bicycle in the background? It's Terrance's eye that makes him so good. His way of looking at the world.

TerraFirma is what he goes by on Tumblr. That's all that's left of Terrance Mutai IV these days. The wonderful, brilliant, deliriously gorgeous high school kid who always looked like he just stepped out of a Ralph Lauren photo shoot. No more Facebook profile. No Twitter feed. Just a Tumblr full of photos seen by 143 followers.

Harvard, he'd said to me in New York as we sat on that bench in Tompkins Square. Double legacy. A shoo-in. But that was right before the sky opened up and it started to rain and the world—mine, then his—fell apart. It feels wrong, looking at the world through his eyes, seeing the things he thinks are beautiful, with his not knowing that he's sharing them with me.

Carga completa.

Five

A black Lab naps in the sun, tail beating a slow, lazy rhythm on the sidewalk. A street kid of about nine wearing a Red Sox tank top says, "Hey, baby," and asks me for a cigarette. I keep to the shady side of the street and pass a dilapidated old building marked with a sign saying HEILMANN TRADING CO. Through the open windows I hear the sound of typewriters clacking away—actual typewriters. What, exactly, does Heilmann Trading Company trade?

The ship that was in port yesterday is gone, leaving the Old Town mostly quiet. I could find a corner somewhere and get a few hours of rest before Mariela's, but it would just find me there, too, the anxiety. It always comes afterward, when the business of uploading another video is finished and it's just me and the video's meaning. It is a train that hits me in the chest, dull mass, a hundred tons strong. It is a blade that slides upward, past my stomach, the point probing around for my heart, pushed forward by an expert hand.

There is only one way to escape it, so I keep walking, west through the Old Town and through the residential neighborhoods until my little refuge comes into view.

I hear it from the street, rap music and men grunting, and I smell it meters from the door. The cure for anxiety lies within: peace through pain, happiness through suffering.

A fist strikes me on the side of the head—a stupid mistake on my part, letting it happen—but I recover instantly and strike back with an elbow to the neck, followed by a tug of the hair as I pull his head back and drop him with an uppercut to the stomach. This guy's good, though, and bounces back, not flailing and desperate like most of them, but sharp and accurate, swinging a leg around and aiming for my bad left knee. I scoop him up by the ankle and drive a foot into his groin. His eyes pinch shut and he rolls away from me onto the mat. *Sorry*, I almost say.

I reach down to help him to his feet, but the instructor, Zvi, is right there. "No!" he shouts, as he would to a bad dog. *Not done yet*, he means. I know what Zvi expects of me, so I drop myself on top of my enemy, burying my right knee in the center of his back, and circle my right arm around his neck. The man's stubble is wet and scratchy on my skin. I brace my other arm on the back of his neck, then look up at the instructor. *Good*, Zvi nods. That's far enough.

From this position—an arm braced on either side of the neck—you jerk your right arm back and to the side, and if the movement is explosive enough, you break your enemy's neck. But I let the guy go and pull him to his feet. He fistbumps me with shredded knuckles and says nicely done. And that's the point here, the thing, the way you're supposed to do it down at the little Krav Maga studio off Avenida San Martín. It's okay to get beat. Just don't be a child about it.

I make my way to the water fountain, spit out my mouth guard, and drink. The first few swallows have the iron tang of my own blood, but the first few swallows are always like that. I keep drinking until the adrenaline and endorphins beating at the walls of my head recede; then I fall to a wooden bench and stare at the ceiling. It's boiling in here. And what's the point of the feeble little ceiling fan, stirring it all up as if it's making a difference? Christ, that shot to the head hurt.

"He's a cop, you know," the voice next to me says.

"What?"

"The guy whose neck you almost broke. He's a cop. A detective."

"Is he."

It's Marco Levinbach, the owner of the gym. He's twenty-five, with fine black hair cut close to his scalp, the way soldiers wear it. It suits his tight, athlete's face. Even his jaw is muscular. "Rafael has a dentist appointment tomorrow morning," he says. "Can you teach his ten a.m.?"

I shrug. "I'll let you know in the morning."

"How about you tell me tonight," he says. "I miss you."

"I'm working tonight," I say.

"After," he says.

"I'm tired after."

I get up to go and feel Marco watching me. There's not even a locker room for women here, so I change in the women's bathroom. I'm the only one who ever uses it. Testosterone hangs in the air thick as smoke, and the men treat me as something between a novelty and a freak. In Uruguay, nice women aren't supposed to practice a brutal Israeli martial art that's all about fighting dirty and hard. I unwrap the tape from my hands. It's doubled around my knuckles using the webbing technique Marco taught me. "So your hands stay pretty," he said. I don't care, but the customers at the restaurant might if I were serving their food with my knuckles still bleeding.

I move on to the bandage wrapped around my left knee and peel it off. The swelling has gone down, but it's still painful from last week when Zvi nearly broke it to prove a point. About staying aware of your vulnerabilities head to toe, is what he told me. To teach me some humility is what it was really about.

I stuff the bandage and the mouth guard in my backpack, then wash the sweat off my body in the sink, mine and the detective's. I scrub hard—it's important to keep up appearances at Mariela's—and the smell of sweat and the tang of blood would be frowned upon there. I tie my hair into a ponytail and change into work clothes: cheap jeans and a tank top—anonymous Judita. On my way out, Marco tries one more time. His mom's making a roast for Shabbat dinner. He'd love for me to meet his family. Maybe, I tell him, in a way we both understand means no.

But just as I'm about to disappear into the street, I stop. I've got an hour or two now, I say.

Afterward, I close my eyes, content to stay this way for a few minutes or, honestly, forever. The room smells of wet towels and the grimy orange cat that watches Marco and me with detachment as we lie naked on the mattress on the floor of his one-room apartment. Marco drapes an arm around me—a muscular arm, gentle—and pulls me close against his body. He's warm, strong, and, most of all, here. He kisses my neck and it tickles and I smile, even though I'm pretending to be asleep, so he just stays there, holding me, and no one has to talk.

"You can't fool me," he says.

"I'm sleeping," I say.

He pinches my side. "Lazy girl," he says. "It's the middle of the day."

I squirm and push his face away. "Lazy girl has to be at work in an hour."

He drops his head back to the pillow and lets out a mock sigh. "Just use me, then. See if I care."

He's a good guy, Marco. Strong and confident. He was born here in Montevideo, emigrated to Israel to join the army, then came back to open his Krav Maga studio. His family is Orthodox, but he doesn't really keep kosher except for not eating pork and shellfish. I started sleeping with him last July.

He's smart enough for what's asked of him, and he's a decent human being, and a good fighter, and exactly who he appears to be: a business owner who pays his taxes and dreams of a nice house, a nice wife. His world, everyone's world, isn't complicated, doesn't take figuring out. And that's what he sees in me, or rather, in Judita. She's just like he is: a decent human being and a good fighter and exactly who she appears to be.

I comply and play the part. Because for the first time since being on the run, I feel safe. Because for the first time, in Marco's little apartment off a side street off a side street in downtown Montevideo, I feel unfindable. Not a soul besides his knows where I am.

I doze off for a while to the sound of the ticking fan and traffic outside.

"What are you thinking?" he whispers, mouth millimeters from my ear.

One night a few weeks ago, tucked there beneath his arm, his breath warm on my neck, I nearly did it, nearly broke down and told him the truth about everything. My mouth was actually open, about to say the words. And I think he would have accepted it, told me he doesn't care. But there are some secrets no one should be asked to keep. "Nothing," I say.

"Know what I'm thinking?" he says.

"No."

"That I'll make you dinner and you'll skip work tonight."

My eyes snap open. "What time is it?"

"Fourish," he says.

I scramble in a panic from the mattress, pull on my bra and tank top. He watches me, a half-grin on his face. "Come on. Just stay."

"I can't. Pass me my—thing."

"Not unless you say it. Don't be shy around me."

"My—underwear."

"Panties."

"*Panties.*"

He tosses them to me and I slide them on, followed by my jeans.

I hear his words, the words I hate, just as the door to the apartment closes behind me. All of it—the sex, company, warmth, peace—I enjoy. I really do. But every time I leave, I tell myself not to go back to him. I tell myself it's too dangerous. Too easy to slip and tell him everything, especially afterward, as the sweat on our bodies cools and he presses his chest to my back and tells me he loves me.

. . .

Mariela's is ablaze tonight. A new ship just arrived in port and there's an hour wait for a table. I rush in through the back. "You're late," Mariela says, "and do something with your hair." But this is said with a wink, a literal wink, and that smile of hers. I look away, embarrassed, and pull my hair back into a ponytail. Then I grab an apron and head out onto the floor.

A mixed group today, tourists from Russia and Asia mostly, chaotic and drunk and loving the slabs of bloody meat. Mariela calls my name and points to table 14, a guy on his own, and American by the looks of him. He's tall, broad-shouldered, with ramrod-straight posture and short graying hair that makes him look like a military officer in civilian dress—a suit, in this case, with no tie. It's still a pretty formal outfit for this place, but somehow I get the feeling this is the most informal he ever gets.

"I'm slammed," I say.

"Who isn't?" she says, and thrusts a menu into my hand.

I approach the table cautiously. The customer is observing the room, sweeping his eyes slowly from one side to the other, and he sits so that he faces the door, just the way my dad used to. I place the menu on the table and greet him in English. He answers back in perfect Spanish. Not school Spanish, or Spanish Spanish, but Rioplatense Spanish. It's the dialect spoken here and in Buenos Aires, and with its flowing, exaggerated rhythm, it sounds to outsiders like Italian. He orders red wine, whatever I recommend, the beef, and a bean dish on the side that only locals ever ask for.

There's a flirty smile on his face as he speaks. I'm used to getting hit on by the customers, but this isn't that kind of flirting.

"Always this busy here?" he says.

"When a ship's in port," I say.

"Ah," he says. "People from all over the world, I imagine."

I shrug. "Yesterday Brits. Today someone else."

He shakes his head as if marveling at the idea of it. "Seems everyone ends up in Uruguay, eventually."

I walk away in too much of a hurry and feel his eyes on me as I pour wine and serve food at my other tables. When I bring out his order, he simply thanks me and sets to work.

He folds his napkin and sets it on the plate when he's finished, and I bring him the check. "Thank you for a delightful meal," he says as he stands. He counts out the pesos, throwing in a very healthy tip. Then he leans in close and says in perfect American English: "Pleasure to finally meet you, Gwendolyn. Yael says hi."

Six

Yael. The name slides like a needle into my ear and paralyzes me, freezing me exactly as I am. The Mossad operative who trained me in Paris, rescued me in Prague. A friend for life is what I call her, for everything she did for me. But she thinks of the relationship differently. I know this because she told me: *Our interests are aligned at the moment*, she'd said once. *Tomorrow, who knows?*

The man buttons his suit jacket and walks out the door without another word. Only when he's gone can I move, looking down at the money clutched in my hand. Stuck in the middle of it is a business card, one side Spanish, the other Hebrew.

BRENT SIMANSKI
Cultural Attaché — Israeli Embassy
Buenos Aires, Argentina

Scrawled in pen along the margin of the Spanish side is: *Piedras / Bartolomé Mitre—1:30.* It's an intersection not far from the restaurant. I tuck the card into my pocket and go back to work, or try to.

So why does this Brent Simanski want to meet me? And why now? Are we in alignment or have our interests diverged? It's been eight months since anyone from the Israeli government made contact. They'd struck a deal with my dad to get us out of Europe in exchange for his telling everything he knows. How the CIA works. How the decisions are made. How the currents of power flow. Helping an ally is how they put it, but that's because it sounds more appealing than calling it treason.

After they got everything they needed, the Israelis stopped coming around. My dad wasn't sad to see them go. I was there for many of the meetings in our apartment, hovering in the background, serving coffee and sandwiches as they talked. They sent in experts from Tel Aviv for the debriefings, people who made their living getting information out of people. But getting information out of people is what my dad did, too, so a lot of times things devolved into staring contests and uncomfortable silences until I would appear, cheerily asking if anyone wanted a refill.

Of course, all this assumes the man whose business card says Brent Simanski, Cultural Attaché—Israeli Embassy, is really that. Business cards are cheap, and neither his name nor his appearance was anything like those who drank coffee after coffee in the living room of our apartment. Brent. What the hell kind of Israeli name is that? My dad's words from the night before play back in my head: *You never see it coming, Gwen.*

Somehow I finish the shift. Somehow I manage to keep my wits about me. For only a brief moment, I consider abandoning the restaurant and rushing home. But I know that if it's all an American trap, then they're already there, waiting for me to do just that.

At one a.m., I make an excuse to Mariela and follow the last customers out the door. The heat of the day has given way to a warm, humid night, but I find myself shivering nonetheless. I walk along Piedras, each block edging a little farther away from the tourist-friendly barrio near the port. Loud music from the bars here, stray dogs and drunken

42

men and hookers on the street. I reach the corner of Piedras and Bartolomé Mitre early and look around for the man from the restaurant whose card says his name is Brent.

There's a travel agency on the corner, with metal shutters over the doors and windows rolled down for the night, and it's here I decide to wait for him. The nightclub across the street is thrumming with house music, and the windows pulse with pink and yellow light. A dark-haired guy of about forty, in jeans and untucked white shirt, lurches out of a bar. He spots me instantly and staggers across the street. A delivery truck slams on its brakes and honks furiously.

"*Chica,*" he leers, adopting a cocky swagger. "You looking for a date?" His Spanish is lispy, European.

I look at him with narrowed eyes. *Depends on what's in your pockets.* "Already got one tonight," I say.

Brent appears from around the corner, spots the man, and smiles at me. "Darling! There you are."

The man in the white shirt looks Brent over, chest out, another peacock entering his territory.

"Picking up my daughter," Brent says to him. "Thanks for keeping her safe."

Eventually, a slow nod from the man, accepting Brent's line, even if he doesn't believe it. We both watch as he stumbles away, and only when he's gone does Brent speak. "Do you know if there's a good beach nearby?" he says.

I look at him blankly.

Brent sighs. "To which you say, 'There's a good beach down the coast, but you have to take the train.'"

It's called a parol, an agreed-upon way of establishing a stranger's identity. "No one told me," I say. "Sorry."

"You're supposed to check the e-mail account every day," he says. "That's why it's there."

"It's—you're right. Sorry."

He gestures down the street and the two of us walk side by side.

His eyes are always moving, every pedestrian checked out, every shop window glanced at, looking for tails.

"The Americans would have sent a helicopter full of SEALs," he says. "But still. You can't let down your guard. You have no idea who I am."

"I'll check my e-mail. Promise."

We stop next to a little Ford sedan parked at the curb. The alarm chirps as he unlocks it with a remote. "You ride up front," he says. "Where I can see you."

The fear comes and goes in less than a second, the usual warnings about strange cars, strange guys, and dark streets. But this is normal in the world I've lived in for the last few years, so I climb into the passenger seat as Brent settles behind the wheel.

"If that guy in the white shirt got grabby, what was your plan?" he says as he starts the engine.

"Knee strike. I usually start with that," I say.

"Knee strike. Always a good call," he says, putting the car in gear and pulling out into the traffic. "I guess step one is complete. Establish rapport over our shared love of knee strikes."

"Step two," I say. "Telling me what this is about."

"It's just a meeting," he says. "Don't worry, you're not in trouble. Someone just wants to have a chat."

"So they send a cultural attaché?"

He looks at me like I should know better. And I do. The title is practically a cliché in the diplomatic world for an intelligence officer working under official cover.

"Don't knock it. It's fascinating work. Just last week, a puppet theater group from Haifa was stranded in the Buenos Aires airport." He squints at something in the rearview mirror. "Apparently, they had visa 21-A, and what they needed was 22-A. You can't imagine the drama."

I find myself studying his face and accent, or lack of accent, digging for something even remotely Israeli about him.

"Redwing, Minnesota," he says.

"What?"

"The question you want to ask. Where I'm from." He sighs, just a little, like someone tired of having to explain. "When the other kids were playing cops and robbers, I was playing Mossad and Nazis-hiding-in-South-America."

"Many Nazis left these days?"

"Sometimes people call, telling us they saw Mengele getting a haircut."

"And what do you tell them?"

"That Mengele died in 1979, but we'll check it out anyway." Rear-view mirror again, looking for dangers only people like him can see. "Mostly what I do these days is run our local assets."

Assets. Curious word choice. Through the driver's side window, I see the cranes in the shipyard swinging cargo containers through the air, lit from beneath by sodium lamps. "So I'm an asset now?" I say.

"Better an asset than a liability," he says. "What did you think you were doing in the desert for six months?"

"I never agreed to be anyone's anything."

He looks at me from the corners of his eyes. "You're doing a good job. Keeping up with your training. Strong morale."

How would he know? "Glad you approve," I say.

"Most people we relocate, they just have to tell someone about their old life. A friend, a lover. But not you. That shows strength."

Something there in the phrasing—*a lover.* "You've been talking to someone about me," I say.

"We keep track of our friends," he says.

"Who?" I say. "My instructor? Zvi?"

He ignores the question and keeps driving. But the answer is obvious. If they're concerned about me talking, they wouldn't go to Zvi, who's just a teacher, someone I happen to see a few times a week. Which means Brent is referring to someone else, the one person who'd know both about my training and my ability to keep my mouth shut.

An electrical pulse dances across the skin of my neck. Without meaning to, I say his name out loud: "Marco."

"Marco?" Brent says, eyebrow arched, the name new to him. It confirms everything.

I pinch my eyes closed and grip the handle on the door. "Before or after?" I say.

"Before or after what?"

"Before I started sleeping with him or after?"

"After," he says, looking at me with something like remorse on his face. "If it matters, we approached him—not the other way around. And he never accepted any payment."

"Then why?"

"Love of Israel," Brent says with a shrug. "Funny, isn't it? Loving a thing that can't love you back."

I bring my hands to my temples, the rage deafening, not in some metaphorical sense but in an actual roar. Static and rushing water. Furious electrons firing until the lights of the dashboard, of the street-lamps, of the traffic, bend and sway. I did love Marco back, or tried to, or wanted to. Next time I see him, I'll twist his head off in my hands.

"Hey," Brent says. "Hey, listen. It's nothing personal."

"Personal is exactly what it is."

We exit the Rambla and make a sharp left onto an industrial road between the power plant and a row of white fuel-storage containers. There's a car parked alongside the road, headlights off, the silhouettes of two people visible through the rear window.

Brent pulls up behind the other vehicle, shuts off the engine. "In a few minutes," he says, "none of that will seem like such a big deal."

The lights of Montevideo seem faint and distant from across the bay, and the sound of the traffic on the Rambla is only a quiet shush. A man in a leather jacket and dark jeans climbs out of the driver's seat. He's fit and good-looking, and he motions for me to turn around. He does a quick but very thorough frisk, unconcerned about my modesty. When it's done, he taps on the roof of the car, and the passenger door opens.

She is, I guess, in her late forties, pale skin, with silver streaks running through otherwise blond hair. She wears a rumpled business suit, like she'd slept in it on the flight over, and carries a manila envelope in her hand.

"Thanks for coming," she says in English, the Israeli accent present but not thick. "How are you holding up, Judita?"

"Who are you?"

"I'm called Dorit," she says, then motions for me to follow her toward a concrete jogging path that runs along the shore of the bay. "I was at your apartment this afternoon. Had a talk with your father about the situation, yours and his."

"What about it?"

"There's been—I'm sorry, Judita. Things have escalated."

I exhale sharply through my nose. "Just spit it out, whatever it is."

We turn down the path, the waves lapping at the shore only a meter away, leaving behind crescents of dirty foam.

"Your father planning on any trips? Hong Kong, say? Moscow?"

Is he going to be another Snowden, she means. Running to the press, spilling secrets. I think of the doomsday device, loaded and ready to fire, waiting for me to pull the trigger. "He wouldn't do that unless he had no other choice."

"The Americans are convinced it's coming," she says. "They've whipped themselves into a frenzy."

"We've always known that," I say. "That's why we're here."

"Except now they've decided to do something about it." Dorit's hands flutter through the pockets of her suit jacket like she's looking for a pack of cigarettes that isn't there, the habit of someone who quit but just now wishes she hadn't. "There's a list the Americans keep. A 'kill list,' they call it. No trial. No arrest."

"For terrorists," I say.

"Or anyone else they don't want appearing in open court." She breathes in deeply and rubs her hands together. "Last week, they added your father to it."

A wave lands against the rocks and, as it recedes, seems to take all the sound in the world with it. I wander away from Dorit to the edge of the path and sit, my mind struggling to decipher the words she just said. The sounds were clear enough, but the concepts they refer to seem somehow jumbled, mismatched.

The color of the sky is France. Love weighs fourteen inches. Your father is on the kill list.

She's standing behind me, arms crossed over her chest. "It isn't a rumor, it isn't speculation—I want you to know that. We have a copy of the document, with the president's signature."

"The *president*?"

"It's an executive order. The president is the only one with that kind of power."

It's impossible, what she's saying. Has to be. "You're a lying sack of shit."

Dorit sits down beside me. "You're right," she says, and opens the envelope. "Just not tonight."

The paper she hands me is waxy and curls in my hands, but the image on it is sharp enough: a photo of a piece of paper on a desk, the name of William Bloom and the signature of the president clear as can be.

I stare at it a long moment. "How did he react?" I whisper. "When you told him, what did he do?"

Dorit looks out at the water. "He took it well. Well enough. He got up. Pulled the curtain back. Opened the window."

I close my eyes. The man who hasn't had more than ten minutes of sunshine on his skin in the last year is suddenly pulling back curtains and opening windows.

"There's a reason I'm telling you separately," Dorit says. "You need to know that this isn't a death sentence, not necessarily."

"A death sentence is literally what it is," I say, squeezing the paper in my hands until it tears.

She takes it back from me, puts it in the envelope. "We have no reason to suspect the Americans know where you are. And this is about your father. Not you."

I look at her. "I'm just collateral damage."

"That's how they'll see it, yes." The wind picks up, blows her hair across her face. She pulls it back into place. "Question is, what will you do about it?"

"What can I do?" I ask.

Dorit rises to her feet again, crosses her arms over her chest. "I have to go now, Judita," she says.

"Wait," I say. "Tell me what to do."

"Not my job to say. You'll have to ask your handler." She looks at the water again, squints her eyes, as if thinking. "Maybe you—do nothing. Maybe living here as Judita is the safest you'll ever be."

I watch her scramble back over the rocks to her car, leaving me there, alone on the shore. She climbs into the passenger seat, and a moment later, she's gone. Brent—handler Brent—approaches the way Dorit left, stepping carefully over the stones to the path, not in any kind of hurry.

When he reaches me, his hands are in the pockets of his pants, giving him a dopey, aw-shucks quality, completely at odds with what I need him to be. He pulls a flask out of a jacket pocket and hands it to me. "Go ahead," he says. "You could use it."

It's warm from being close to his body, and the liquor inside tastes like scorched wood. I take one long swallow, then a second one. Brent takes it back, saying, "Easy."

I grimace at the taste left in my throat. "So you're my handler," I manage.

He sits beside me, takes a sip from the flask. "Looks that way."

"Now what?" I say, waiting for wisdom as he scratches his chin thoughtfully. "How do we handle this?"

"Option one, ignore it. Live your life here. See what happens." He studies the flask in his hands, then puts it back in his pocket. "The Americans, they get worked up sometimes, but then someone retires, someone gets replaced, priorities shift."

"And option two?"

"Option two is you do what we trained you to do." He swivels his head to look at me. His eyes are cold now, and the flirty smirk is gone. "Viktor Zoric, remember him?"

"Of course."

"The CIA approached his son, Lovrenc. Went to visit him on his yacht when it was docked in Crete. We have photos, no audio." Brent says this without sympathy, just debriefing his asset. "The thinking in Tel Aviv is that the CIA wants to hit the reset button on American-Zoric relations. They started by giving him a job."

"What kind of job?"

"Washington can't very well use a drone in Uruguay, can they?" He rubs harshly on his scalp. "Or rather, they haven't yet."

Assassinate us, he means, or at least my father. The old-fashioned way: a guy in latex gloves carrying a pistol with no serial number. The idea of it is offensive. Better a billion-dollar flying robot than a moron in a leather jacket and track pants whose only value in this world is not asking questions when he's given an order.

"So the CIA kills Viktor Zoric," I say. "Now they're working with his son. How does that make sense?"

Brent gives a resigned scoff. "Welcome to my fucked-up world," he says. "*Our* fucked-up world."

And somehow this is my option two. It's clear enough what he's getting at, but I look at him in disbelief anyway. "So I'm supposed to— do what you trained me to do."

"I hear you're good with a knife." He fiddles with his watch as if he has someplace to be. "This Lovrenc Zoric is a danger to Israeli interests and a danger to you. I'd say the solution is obvious. Only I didn't say that."

"Kill him, you're saying."

A slow, exaggerated shake of his head. "I very much did not say that. Such a request would be illegal."

His not saying it, I realize, is the point. It's why he's here with me, the asset. Things, events, coincidences crystallize suddenly in my mind, the paths between them becoming discernible. The camp in its unknown location, the instructors with their unmarked uniforms and whittled-down accents—all designed for deniability. Even my handler, Brent—the only evidence I have of his existence is a cheap business card.

Brent rises, then tousles my hair like he's my father. "Getting late," he says. "And you've got work to do."

Seven

The living room window is still open when Brent drops me off, and for the first time since we've lived here, the apartment smells of something other than fear. Somewhere, my dad found a clean T-shirt, not too badly wrinkled, and is wearing a different pair of pants, the cuffs fraying where they drag on the floor but otherwise not too bad.

I see the smile beneath the beard. "There you are," he says. "I was getting worried."

"I got a ride. Someone dropped me off," I say.

"I saw through the window," my dad says. "Brent Simanski. Nice guy, I thought."

I realize we're speaking in English at a normal volume. "Nice enough," I say, and set down my backpack. "I didn't bring anything home. Sorry."

"That's all right, kiddo," he says. "I picked up some empanadas and blueberries at the market. There was a cat sleeping next to the cash register, lazy little thing."

He left the apartment. Actually left the apartment. I approach cautiously, this version of him very different from the version I left behind this morning. "What are you doing?" I say quietly.

But he just shrugs and smiles. "Normal stuff," he says. "Buying food. Getting some air. There's a little café down the street with excellent coffee, *excellent* coffee. But you probably knew that."

"Keep your voice low," I hiss. "The neighbors."

"Fuck the neighbors," he says.

"Dad . . ."

"Fuck the neighbors," he repeats, and drops himself to the couch, legs crossed, ankle to knee, arm stretched across the back of the cushion. "Sit," he says.

"In a minute." I step into the little kitchen, pour some of last night's wine into a coffee cup, and drink it. Then I refill the cup and step back out again.

"The order—the kill list—it's real," he says casually. "They showed it to me, Dorit and Brent."

I take the chair opposite him. "How did this happen? Not why, but how—the actual mechanism."

"The Gang of Four decides." He reaches for my mug of wine, takes a sip, and smacks his lips. "It's shit, you know. This wine. Absolute garbage."

"It's whatever's left over," I say. "The Gang of Four, who are they?"

"The committee who decides. Someone from the CIA, Department of Defense, Justice Department, White House. Bureaucrats. Cheap suits, fabulous pensions. They get together every so often to review the candidates." He clasps his hands over his heart, makes a wide-eyed expression of stagey drama. "*It's an honor just to be nominated.*"

He's someone new now, and I am, too. What, exactly, is my job here? Supportive fellow adult or terrified daughter? "They can't just kill an American citizen," I say. "There's this thing called the Constitution."

He gives me a look, head tilted, lips pursed. Dad's disappointment face. "One time in Moscow, you were reading the newspaper. There was an article about someone called Abdullah Sabbagh. Remember?"

I fight through the alcohol—the wine and whatever Brent fed me—and try. When I close my eyes, it comes back to me. Sitting cross-legged on the parquet floor of our apartment, reading the *International Herald*

Tribune by the steel-gray light of a Moscow afternoon sky. My dad was wearing a blue gingham apron as he tried to make cookies, his contribution to someone's retirement party. I alternated between reading and poking fun at him for the apron.

"I remember," I say. "He was—sixteen. Born in Kansas or someplace. Killed by a CIA drone in Yemen."

"He was the son of a terrorist," my dad says. "What else?"

"He was killed two weeks after his father."

"And what did the White House say?"

I shake my head. "I don't know."

"They said he was a twenty-two-year-old Al Qaeda soldier, until a reporter went digging."

I look down, remembering all of it now. It had pissed me off and broken something inside me.

"You asked me," he whispers, like the memory shouldn't be said too loudly, "how the American government could kill a sixteen-year-old kid."

"I said, 'The good guys don't do that kind of thing.'"

He nods. "And what did I say back?"

I lean forward, staring into the wine inside the cracked cup. "You said, 'You're right. Good guys don't.'"

I try eating one of the empanadas, but it's cold and tasteless and I give up after two bites. Maybe it's a bad one, or maybe that's how everything will taste from now on.

For only a moment do I consider telling him the other half of the conversation I'd had with Brent. My dad was furious about the training in Orphan Camp; he called it exploitation and all the other things it was. To tell him I was now being manipulated into assassinating the man trying to assassinate him would be met with fury. He'd head to the American embassy and surrender himself rather than let me fall into the bottomless clandestine void. The bottomless clandestine void that we both just learned has a bottom after all.

I run my finger over the cracked plywood of the coffee table. "That woman, Dorit. She said this might be the safest place we can be."

54

"That's true," my dad says. "It'll take them a long time to find us here."

"How long is a long time?"

He extends his hands, palms up. "Months."

Months. So, not *never*. Not even *years*. The reason for my father's fatalism—and that's what this is, the open window, his good cheer and sudden appetite—is clear to me. All those things you hear about the stages of grief—denial, anger, bargaining, depression—he seems to have flown through them in hours and arrived blissfully at the last, final, terminal stage, acceptance.

The words come stumbling out: "She said, she said also—that this, this isn't . . ." I pause, catch my breath. "It isn't necessarily a death sentence."

His knees crack as he rises slowly and goes again to the window. "What else would you expect her to say?"

"And you're okay with it?"

But it's like he doesn't hear me at first. He's fixated on something in the street. "So many stray dogs here," he says.

"You're okay with it?" I ask again. "Just accepting this?"

"Don't really have much say in the matter, do we?" He sits on the sill, leans his head out. "Look," he says. "A Dalmatian. When you were a kid, you wanted a Dalmatian."

I slam my hand on the table and stand. "Goddammit, Dad!"

He turns, startled. "You did," he says. "You called them 'fire truck dogs.' You kept asking for one, birthdays, Hanukkah."

"We don't have to *die*," I hiss, conscious now of the volume of my voice, conscious now of being overheard by the neighbors. "We have options."

He closes his eyes as if the sun were shining and warming his skin. "*You* have options."

"I refuse to"—the thought freezes in my mind and won't come out, so I correct it—"I don't want to leave you here."

"Of course you don't," he says. "But it's been a long time since either of us could do what we wanted."

. . .

I don't remember how old I was when we attended the Eid feast at the end of Ramadan. It feels like Dubai, maybe, but it could have been earlier. Cairo, maybe. I remember only that I was small and that we flew there special on a State Department jet to the airfield of some dignitary, some sheikh. His villa was deep in the desert, a grand place, with multiple swimming pools, cyan rectangles against endless beige. He and my father called each other "brother" as they embraced, which confused me until my father explained that they were just really good friends. The thing I remember most clearly, though, is that they had a lamb there at the feast, a cute little thing. The other kids—there were a million other kids—played with it awhile. I remember thinking how odd it was, a lamb at a party, like a one-trick petting zoo.

At some point, the sheikh gathered all the guests into a circle, straddled the lamb, and gave it a playful, reassuring rub between the ears. Then he cut its throat with a knife.

As the blood poured out of the lamb and everybody clapped, I buried my head in my dad's stomach. That's why I remember how tall I was. A few hours later, though, I ate it just the same. By the next day, it had already stopped bothering me. Even then, I knew that was how the world worked. Lambs and men. Trust met with a knife.

I don't know why I should think of this now. I'm not nostalgic for the time. I'm not hungry for lamb. Maybe it's because of how I buried my face in my dad's stomach, like he could protect me from the world.

I love him. I do. But no one will cut my throat. I will survive with him and struggle with him, but I won't die with him. Part of me wants to scream about how unfair it all is. But the rest of me knows the world doesn't give a shit about fair. The world is only as it ever was, subject to the desires of strong and cunning carnivores. One does not live by being meek. One does not live by remaining Judita the lamb.

The air is still and humid in the bedroom. I dig out a shoe box from under my bed. In it is a filleting knife in a sheath I bought when I first arrived in Montevideo. For my first six months here, I wore it strapped to the underside of my left forearm every day. Now I'll start wearing it again.

With the knife beside me on the bed, I pour myself another glass of garbage wine and drink. I drink too much for anything like planning, or any clear thought whatsoever. The only thing remaining in my vision as I fall into unconsciousness is that I will not die here. I will not die here.

I find sanity again with the insanity of Mariela's. I relish its immediacy and chaos, how everything happens in the moment and results in money on the table. It's not complicated, not shot through with lies and intrigue. I wonder every time the door opens if it'll be Brent again, but of course it isn't. It's just another clot of hungry tourists, eyebrows raised uncertainly as they ask, "*¿Habla Inglés?*" Mariela clasps her hands together at the joy of seeing them, old friends she's just now meeting for the first time, and says, "Better than your English teacher!" She will be what they remember most.

I'm sad to see the last ones stumble out, buzzed, belts a little too tight. I'm sad when the toilets are clean and Gustavo is finished pouring out the wine. The walk to the bus terminal is torture, knowing that on the other end of the ride is my ebullient, fatalistic father, practically picking out the color of the robe he'll wear in the heaven in which he does not believe. I wish it were possible to go without sleep so I could wander the city until tomorrow's shift. Wish I didn't have to choke down the wine in my backpack so I can get something like rest.

I drink some on the way, right from the bottle, for a head start. I take out my phone, pinch the bottle between forearm and side as I walk, and somehow manage to put a new SIM card in.

An elegant man, in late middle age but attractive enough, is sitting in a café, lonely and sad as he drinks beer from a tall glass. Behind him, in the background, is a woman in early middle age, also lonely and sad, also drinking a beer from a tall glass. Oh, Terrance, the way you see the world.

I scroll through his other photos. Here an old lady laying flowers on someone's grave. Here two women leaning confidentially close as they share secrets on a park bench.

The paranoia of this morning has given way to my exhaustion for this life of mine. So please let there be no danger in a Tumblr user in Uruguay with no profile picture, no posts, no followers, checking out the account of one TerraFirma, who wants nothing more than to share beautiful things with those of us who have none.

No one's around at the bus stop, and there's still twenty minutes to kill. I sit and drink more wine—it is particularly awful tonight, or maybe my dad is right and it always is. In any case, what I think about is Buenos Aires and what it would be like to be there with Terrance. I don't have the eye he does. I don't notice the little dramas, life's walk-on characters, all the world's interesting bits. Maybe you could show me, Terrance.

The Buquebus ferry terminal isn't far. I could walk it, be there by the time the first one leaves, and be in BA three hours after that. But it's a silly thought and would only drag Terrance down further than I've already dragged him.

I take another drink and feel like I'm going to throw up. Fast-acting medicine tonight, and too much of it. My thumb hovers over the photo of the lonely man and lonely woman in the café—too dangerous, I tell myself, don't—and I press down. Behold, NSA, how a photo posted by user TerraFirma was, at 2:09 a.m., liked by user RedShoesForSale.

From somewhere, he's dug out a pair of reading glasses and looks over them at me as I come in. The stack of children's notebooks sits on the table before him in a tidy pile.

I breathe in slowly. "You're doing that again?"

"Just—something I forgot to include," he says. "Some details."

I collapse into the chair across from him. "Tomorrow," I say. "I'll upload it tomorrow."

"Sure," he says. "If you want. It's about the Swiss accounts." He pulls open a notebook with a Hello Kitty cover, flips to the last page, and hands it to me.

Walter Kahn, Pension Alexandra, Hareth bei Bärenbad, Austria. It's a name and a place I've never heard of before. I look up at him.

"If there's a way to get Zoric's money, it will come from the information Walter Kahn has." His voice is so quiet and strained, it's as if the words themselves are sapping the life from him. "I don't know if it'll work, but maybe."

I study the name. Something menacing about it. "Is he a banker?"

"Walter Kahn is an innkeeper. The owner of the Pension Alexandra."

He takes back the notebook, squares the stack. "A kind man. Not—an enemy."

I flash him a smile as I remember something and pull my backpack onto my lap. "I brought a good pork cutlet home. Mostly intact."

His face brightens. "Yes? Good. Maybe later. Did you bring wine?"

"You want some?" I say.

He shakes his head. "But go ahead, if you want to. Then—let's talk a bit."

I get up and step into the little kitchen for my cup. All the cameras and phones I'd collected are arranged in tidy rows on the counter. A pang of pleasant, old-fashioned teenage fear—caught shoplifting, grounded for a month—flares inside me, then dies just as quickly. I take down my cup, fill it.

"You found them," I say, stepping into the other room.

"We do what we must," he says.

I sit in the chair across from him.

"No, kiddo," he says, and pats the place on the couch next to him. "Here."

I slide in beside him, and he drapes his arm around my shoulder.

"I found the money you put away, too," he says.

"Are you mad?"

He's quiet a minute, then says, "The cameras and phones should be worth a few thousand American."

"You think so?"

"Maybe more," he says. "Outside Uruguay."

He lets the words hang there, letting their meaning bloom in my mind. His arm tightens around me, and I slip my head into the crease beside his chest.

"You remember *The Wizard of Oz*?" he says. "It was a thing with us. A tradition. Every year on Thanksgiving."

Suddenly he's in the mood for nostalgia. I indulge him. "Yeah," I say. "Hot chocolate. We always made it. Even in Dubai."

"The scene when the tornado comes," he says. "What's the last thing Dorothy's uncle the farmhands do before going into the cellar?"

"I don't remember."

"Sure you do. Come on."

I close my eyes, picture the scene, black-and-white chaos, wind howling, nature itself in a panic. "They let the horses loose from the barn."

"Every single year you'd ask me why they were doing that." His fingers push through my hair, stroke back and forth along my scalp. "You asked why they would just let them loose when the tornado was coming."

My lower lip trembles and I feel myself start to shake. He holds me tighter, not shaking at all.

I swallow the sob down. "You said—because the horses would have a better chance on their own," I say. "If they were free to run away, they might survive. But in the barn . . ."

The sob comes anyway, silently. He presses his mouth to my head. I make a point to remember the rhythm of his heart, how it feels to have his breath on my scalp.

He lets out a little sound that means contentment and regret all at once. "Better that way, don't you think? For the uncle and aunt? Knowing the horses are alive somewhere?"

"But the horses would come back," I say. "That's what you said."

"Of course they would," he says. "Absolutely."

. . .

I leave the next morning at dawn, when he's finally fallen asleep on the couch and I've finally sobered up. I put what I need into my backpack: a change of clothes, and all the cameras and phones I've stolen. I take the paper cash, the SD cards of his doomsday device, and the original notebooks, two with blue covers, three with pink, two with Hello Kitty.

The horses are being hitched to their scrap wagons and neither they nor their owners spare me a second glance as I make my way through the streets, past the barking dogs, past the tin shacks, to the bus stop where I can catch a ride to the city center.

There could be no good-byes, because things would be said that would prevent it from taking place. *We don't have to do this. We'll find a way.* Emotions would overcome reason, and the parting would never happen.

And how does one do such a thing? Leave one's father, one's only family, the only person to be trusted?

One step at a time. One foot in front of the other. And hanging there, on the horizon, the idea of returning. We'll check in with each other the sterile way, with encrypted e-mail accounts, the way we'd been trained. A secret e-mail account that only we two know about, at an encrypted service in Norway, complete with a duress code, an innocuous statement that meant one of us had been captured. The protocol had seemed ghoulish, and I didn't want to believe it was necessary. But here we are. The kill list. Another Zoric.

I focus on the single fact that survival requires action. With effort and luck, whatever I do next will save us both. But I must be content with the idea that it will not, that I will be the only survivor, and there is no easy way to do this other than to ignore the emotions that press against my chest and urge me to go back to the apartment. The biological commandment to live at all cost shoves me forward. One step at a time. One foot in front of the other.

Through the window of the bus, the first rays of sunshine warm the skin on my arms, melting the edges of my resolve. My eyes swell, but I pinch them shut. My breath catches, but I swallow hard.

When I reach the Buquebus ferry terminal, I linger beneath the white archways, blending into the crowd of smokers sucking down their last cigarettes before they board. Everyone who goes in or out of the terminal gets an appraisal from me, as I search for anybody out of the ordinary. But all is as it always is, a few cops, knots of businessmen and tourists. No military police. No American-looking guys in cheap suits and sunglasses.

I'm only a few blocks from Mariela's and it would have been nice to say good-bye, but with what excuse? Only Marco lingers in my deep pool of regrets with something like pain, but that's his doing—betraying me the way he did—and that makes what pain there is easier to bear.

I buy my ticket and board with the last of the passengers. Inside, it looks like rows and rows of airplane seats, fifteen, maybe twenty, across, but I move past them to the back deck. The rotors of the ferry churn the brown water of the river impatiently, whipping it into an angry cappuccino of whites and tans. A few crew members untether the moorings, and the ferry begins to move. There is no one on the pier waving good-bye.

Montevideo creeps away, receding into memory as the ferry picks up speed. I stand there on the deck a few minutes, then slip inside. Families are breaking out the picnic lunches they brought with them, and businessmen are opening their laptops. The alcohol is starting to wear off, so I'll have to make do without the strength that comes from numbness. I push past the crowd to the outside deck and the boat's very tip. The wind is sharp and the water parts before us. I lean on the railing with my forearms and breathe in the river air.

Eight

It arrives in my encrypted inbox as a message from MackintyreMack 69@yahoo.com. *Thought of you when I saw this*, reads the subject line. The message itself is just a link to an article in a British tabloid, "10 Hottest Real-Life Gangsters." What follows are plenty of photos and breathless descriptions of the sexy exploits, debauchery, and estimated net worth of young and handsome rising stars in the world of organized crime. Sexy arms trafficking. Sexy smuggling. Sexy murder. Three Russians make the list, two Chinese, three Americans, one Colombian, and one Serbian—Lovrenc Zoric.

The photos are paparazzi-surveillance style, candids taken at a distance, a guy coming out of a nightclub with his entourage, a guy climbing out of a limo with his two girlfriends, a guy lounging shirtless beside a luxurious pool, phone pressed to his ear. Lovrenc's, though, is of him standing on the prow of a large yacht, squinting handsomely as his black hair tumbles in the wind. He's thirty-four, according to the article (and single!), with an estimated net worth of 900 million British pounds.

The next e-mail is from JulieKurland2000@hotmail.com. Subject:

Ugh, so want to go here . . . There's a real message this time: *I've never been to Valencia. What do you think? Spring break? We could rent a boat, do a little cruise.* The link is for the Valencia marina. A lovely place, judging by the pictures, and helpful sections about sailboats available for rent, the on-site restaurant and bar, and the newly expanded piers for docking your megayacht.

It takes me a minute to figure the riddle out. I toggle back to the article in the tabloid, and study Lovrenc's picture again. Just beneath him is a sliver of the yacht itself, and on it, the name *Erebus*. So back to the Valencia marina's site I go, where I dig around and find a schedule of upcoming arrivals and departures. The *Erebus* has reserved a slip twelve days from now, headed from Marseilles.

So twelve days from now, that's where I'm expected to be.

Well, Brent, aren't you just the cleverest thing, communicating my orders this way. The arrogance of it makes me angry—just get the job done; how you do it and how you pay for it is none of my concern. But deniability is a two-way street, Brent. Can I be blamed for not carrying out an order that was never really given in the first place?

I've been in Buenos Aires three days, three weightless days free of chains binding me to any responsibility. I'd been right about the city, the idea of it I'd had in my head: It's enormous and disorganized and easy to get lost in. There's a transit workers' strike going on, so taxis are the only alternative to buses and the subway. But the streets aren't moving anyway because demonstrations block the boulevards. Anarchists with red bandannas over their faces have taken up the workers' cause and battle with police every few blocks, throwing tear gas grenades back at them and setting cars and dumpsters on fire.

I'm in love with the place.

Maybe I'll stick around for a while. A week, or a decade.

For the first time in my life, I am where I choose to be.

I start a new session on the computer, reconnect through TOR, and check out Terrance's new photos. He's in Mendoza, Argentina, now. An old man with stained hands making a wine barrel. A woman sampling a glass of what must be delicious Malbec, because she's closing her eyes as she sips, as one does when receiving a kiss. The user RedShoesForSale clicks the heart icon on each of TerraFirma's images, writes a comment on the photo of the barrel maker: "love this so much."

Then RedShoesForSale makes a few posts of her own. The first, a photo grabbed from the Internet of the interior of a record shop, the customers browsing through bins clearly labeled JAZZ. The second, another stolen photo of some random girl alone on a park bench, the skyline of Manhattan clearly visible behind her. I caption the image, "missing new york."

Since I am where I choose to be, I might as well also choose who I'm here with.

I found a cheap hotel in the barrio called Retiro by the main bus station, where it's me and a few dozen prostitutes. Over the past three days, the magenta walls and green tile floor have grown on me, even if the constant noise from the traffic outside and the enthusiastic work ethic of my fellow guests have not.

From my fake balcony—just a wrought-iron railing a few centimeters from a tall window—I can hear the sirens and chants and pop of police grenade launchers. I wonder if the tear gas will drift up here to the third floor of the hotel, but the only thing I smell is burning trash.

Despite my general spirit of weightlessness—this freedom like a new pair of shoes, beautiful but not yet broken in—I continue wearing the knife and sheath strapped to the underside of my forearm. It's my one concession to reality, my one acknowledgment that though I've run away from Judita, she can't be too far behind. Plus, I have business to attend to, specifically, getting rid of the last few cameras and phones I brought from Uruguay.

Just past lunchtime, I leave again, my backpack heavy on my shoulders. One of the women from the hotel who's always out front smoking told me about a strip of pawnshops in the Congreso neighborhood an hour's walk away. I head there for the third day in a row.

By now, I know to avoid the main streets, and every time I hear chanting or sirens, I turn away from them. The last thing I need, the very last thing, is an ID check, or any sort of attention at all, not with a backpack full of stolen goods. When I arrive in the neighborhood, I pick up where I left off, halfway down the west side of the street.

I browse the shop for a few minutes, peering through smudged glass at gold watches and sets of silverware arranged haphazardly in the display cases. A man with an enormous belly and a black mustache stands in the back of the shop, hands on hips, relating a story to a rapt audience of two young men, both in muscle shirts. The punch line—*so I made her eat it, every last bit*—brings on roars of laughter.

Idly, I strum the strings on an electric guitar hanging by its throat along the wall. Then the air over my shoulder becomes warmer, and I hear breathing. "The next Jimi Hendrix," says a man's voice.

The top of my head comes up just to the man's mustache. He's bigger than he looked standing at the back of the shop. Not fatter, bigger. "I'm selling," I say, touching the strap on my backpack. "A camera and phone. You interested?"

"Didn't I see you on the street yesterday?" he says.

"You must be thinking of someone else," I say.

"You're trying to unload merch, you come straight to me next time, okay?" He holds out a puffy hand. "Guillermo."

I shake it. "Good to meet you."

The man gestures to the back of the shop. "Gotta be careful with the serial numbers. They're checked against a database."

"I'm not sure I know what you mean."

"If it comes back stolen, the police take it. No compensation." He opens the door to a back office and nods for me to go inside. "Which is why I never check serial numbers."

He meets my eyes and gives a little smile of mutual understanding.

The fluorescent lights of his office buzz and wash everything in the room with green sickness. A foggy mirror in a gold curlicue frame

66

hangs at an angle above filing cabinets piled high with papers and a single tabby cat, which looks up as we enter, then goes back to sleep. Guillermo sinks into his desk chair and holds out his hands, palms up, *well?*

I set a Canon on the desk and he picks it up, squinching his face as he appraises it.

"Okay," he says.

"Okay what?"

"Okay, what else you got? I invited you back here to do some real business."

One of the two men in muscle shirts leans against the doorframe, arms folded across his chest.

No point in playing him along. There's less money selling the rest of the equipment in bulk, but it's safer than spreading it out between different stores, especially if Guillermo is right about the serial numbers. I lift my backpack onto my lap and unload everything.

Guillermo and the guy in the muscle shirt examine each piece, whispering in some sort of code to each other, then frowning dramatically at the sight of the tiniest scuff.

Five minutes later, Guillermo leans back in his chair and glowers. "I'll be honest, for a thief, you don't have a very good eye. This is consumer-grade crap. Obsolete."

The other guy resumes his position at the doorframe and gives a little grunt of agreement.

"I like you, though," Guillermo continues. "I want to do you a favor, and maybe we can do more business in the future." He pulls a fat wad of cash from his pocket, peels off a few bills, and pushes them across the desk.

I run the math in my head—just less than six hundred US dollars. It's a colossal screw. He'll get ten or fifteen times that when he sells them.

"No thanks," I say, and reach for the cameras.

Guillermo's hand flashes forward, catching my wrist, the handle of the knife just a few centimeters up my sleeve from his fingertips.

In less than a second, I've calculated my response—jerk him forward, fist to ear, foot into the balls of the man behind me.

"How much are they going to be worth to you in jail, sweetheart?" Guillermo smiles.

The man at the doorframe pulls a phone from his pocket. "Detective Moreno?" he says. "We haven't given him a bust in a while."

My eyes dart from Guillermo to his partner. I could take them both, but there's a third man out in the shop, and there's no such thing as a pawnshop without a gun stashed in easy reach. Too many variables, too many things to go wrong.

I reach forward, place a hand on the cash. "Deal," I say.

The day is not a total loss, however. Far from it. Despite the mega-screw at the pawnshop, there is good news: Tumblr user known as RedShoesForSale gets her first like.

It turns out TerraFirma clicked the little heart below her photo of the girl on the park bench in Tompkins Square captioned "missing new york." He even left a little comment: "me too."

My heart pings. Just once, and just a little. But has Terrance connected the two dots I'd left for him, the two photos? So I leave him the third, and most important. User RedShoesForSale posts a photo she took yesterday afternoon, of a jazz club in the ritzy barrio of Recoleta. Look carefully at the photo, and there's a schedule for this weekend's performances, a three-night engagement of an avant-garde trio from Japan.

It's the last attempt I will allow myself. If it works, it works, and if not—no doubt it's for the best. Trying to contact him is against all principles of security, against all the ideas I've been taught about the unbridgeable gulf between new life and old. But Judita Perels has run away from Judita Perels.

I have two days to go until Thursday, the first night shown on the jazz club schedule. And like the path of the *Erebus*, I've plotted Terrance's route through the cities he's visited. If he gets the message, if he makes the connection, if he doesn't hate me, then he'll be there. So it's with that delicious question that I wander the city of Buenos Aires for two more days as myself, neither Judita nor Gwendolyn, but both, the me that's too complicated for names.

Nine

On Saturday, the final night, Terrance shows.

He appears just as the last of the audience trickles into the club for the late performance. Well-dressed, monied *porteños*: blonds in their fifties in short cocktail dresses, guys the same age in fitted suits with heads of immaculately groomed graying hair. Very few young people. Only one, in fact.

Terrance stands out with his youth and dark skin, but that's not what I recognize first. He's in a pair of dark blue slacks and a pressed white shirt and is, at least from behind, at least in his gait, exactly as I remember him. Slim and aristocratic.

My stomach turns like a schoolgirl's at the sight of him, and the sensation of it reminds me of the simplicity of our lives when we'd first met on St. Mark's Place in the East Village in that used-record store, where everything smelled of dust and ozone and old vinyl. Nothing to worry about in the world other than tests and homework. It's all I can do to stop myself from calling out to him. But I have to be careful. Now more than ever.

I watch up and down the street from my sidewalk table at a nearby café, searching for tails. This would be a professional-grade operation, and thus, his followers would blend in. Everyone is a suspect. The bearded bum begging for change. The teenage couple making out on a bench. I watch them all closely, watch whether they move as Terrance goes past, watch what they do next. But he's clean. At least as far as I can see, he's clean. Not that I can ever know for sure.

I order another maté as Terrance disappears into the club. There can be no question of my approaching him at the bar during the show. I don't know what he'll do, how he'll react. So, instead, I resolve to wait as long as necessary for him to come out.

"You all by yourself?" the waiter asks as he brings me the gourd holding the maté.

I take a drink through the steel straw and shrug. "Waiting on my boyfriend," I say wistfully.

He arches his eyebrows and checks his watch. "If he doesn't show," he says, "I get out of here at two."

I smile at the waiter and tell him I'll keep it in mind. Christ, I want a drink, just a little of the Malbec that's cheaper than bottled water here. But I don't dare risk it. I need the focus and paranoia that come from sobriety.

I throw a few bills on the table at midnight, when the ten p.m. show ends. A few of the *porteños* trickle out, then some more, then Terrance. His hands are in his pockets, and his face is sullen. All the Tumblr clues had just been a miscommunication. He starts down the street in the direction from which he'd come, and I hang back, watching again to see if he's followed.

Half a block behind him seems like the right distance. I blend in with the pedestrian traffic, just another girl headed to another bar. Midnight is early here in BA, practically dinnertime, and the streets are so full it's hard to keep track of Terrance through the crowd. He makes a left, so I make a left. He turns right, so I turn right. No sign of anything suspicious, so I pick up the pace.

Ahead, a little square surrounded by noisy bars. The streets are thick with loud, drunk kids our age. I move up to his left elbow, and when he's not looking, say in English, just loud enough for him to hear: "Don't turn around."

He doesn't. In fact, he doesn't even flinch. "Is it you?" he answers back.

"It is," I say.

No reply for a dozen paces, then: "Is anyone following?"

"I don't think so," I say. "Which hotel are you at?"

"Paradiso," he says.

One of the big, run-down hotels with its best years behind it. It's maybe two kilometers away from where we are now. "Room number?"

"Five-oh-two."

"I'll meet you there in an hour."

No turn of the head, no nod, no acknowledgment whatsoever that he's heard me. Instead, he accelerates while I slow down, putting distance between us. He gets it, the need for discretion, for secrecy. And this makes me sad. I expected, maybe wanted, the same boy I'd known in New York. But he isn't that Terrance anymore.

I fall back, watching the people around him, scanning the couples leaning in close to one another, the beat cops waiting for a bust, the lost tourists squinting at street signs. The path Terrance takes is indirect and odd, just as I would have taken. If he were being followed, the pursuers would stand out. But all I see are civilians. Even when we reach the Paradiso, it's an innocent scene: shabby bellmen in shabby uniforms, shoving people into cabs; tourists snapping iPhone pictures.

Terrance disappears into the hotel and I disappear into the crowd on the other side of the street. Eventually, I make my way across and into the lobby. The ceiling is vaulted five stories above us, robin's egg blue, complete with peeling paint and water stains and a massive gold chandelier that looks like it's listing to one side. Aging waiters who've worked here their whole lives serve wine and beer to clots of tourists littered around the beat-up leather couches and threadbare armchairs.

Someone's playing an unseen piano, and the notes echo around the room, like lost ghosts.

I glance around for anything suspicious before walking over to a grand staircase. My ascent is slow, deliberate, running a hand along the wrought-iron railing as I casually survey the guests in the lobby. At the fifth floor I leave the stairs and travel down a hallway, room 508, 506, 504. At room 502 I pause, head canted, listening. I hear a television down the hall, but otherwise it's silent. I raise my hand, hesitate, then give a single, quiet knock.

From inside the room comes a sharp breath and the sound of fabric rubbing against fabric—someone pulling themselves up from a chair. I stand back a little so he can see me through the peephole. The door opens a crack, then opens all the way.

I register the sight of him—handsome, clean, upright—all the things I missed. But that has to wait. I push him aside with my arm and rush into the room, looking for whoever else may be inside. The room is large and shabby, with scuffed parquet floors and walls painted yellow thirty years ago. Tall ceilings with ornate moldings and gold, limp curtains beside tall windows.

"Gwen, what are you . . . ?"

"Change rooms," I say. "Call down to the front desk and tell them you want to change rooms."

He stiffens. "Why?"

"Do it."

He hesitates a moment, then picks up the phone receiver. His eyes never leave mine as he speaks to whoever's on the other end, and mine never leave his. I'm gawking, I realize. At the shock of seeing him, at the joy of it. But his eyes regard me differently, like a stranger he doesn't trust.

He hangs up. "Five minutes."

"Thank you," I say. "It's just—I'm paranoid."

"The room's not bugged, if that's what you're worried about," he says.

I lean forward a little, and he does, too. Then he's holding me, with my cheek against his chest, his arms around my shoulders. I breathe him in, the expensive soap, the nervous sweat, all of it so very real and right here.

"I brought it with me," he says.

"Brought what?" I say.

"The book. The one you gave me."

From a battered canvas knapsack, he fishes out the copy of *1984* I'd given him, along with a folded sheet of paper. I take the book into my hands greedily, then check the paper to make sure it's the same one I'd found in the storage locker in Queens. Zoric's account numbers.

"I scanned the book and the paper, just in case," Terrance says. "It's uploaded to an encrypted FTP site if you lose these."

"Thank you," I say.

"It traveled with me everywhere, you know. In case."

"In case what?"

"In case this. Running into each other."

I embrace him tightly. "This means—everything," I say.

"Did you ever read it?" he says.

"Not the whole thing," I say. "I know there's a sad ending. I don't like books with sad endings."

"Winston betrays Julia," Terrance says, still in my embrace. "He betrays her and then it ends."

The staff at the Paradiso scramble over themselves to switch Terrance to another room. Polite inquiries are made. *Was* señor, *perhaps, displeased by the view from the windows?* In any case, they make it up to the *señor* with a room that's larger and shabbier yet, with a curved bay window overlooking a square and a church. As the bellman finishes showing us around, a manager comes bearing an ice bucket from which juts a bottle of champagne, the French stuff, the good stuff, and on the house. All this is accepted with only a polite *gracias* from Terrance; the world has always fallen over itself this way to please him.

I realize, instantly, my own error in having him switch rooms.

Terrance is now known to them. Someone at the front desk no doubt Googled his name and now he—and therefore I—is on their radar. *The son of a hedge fund billionaire is with us; call the manager at home.* I commit to changing hotels, immediately, tonight. Then I hear the pop of the champagne bottle and forget what I was thinking.

"You want?" he says, pouring so that the bubbles rise exactly to the tops of the glasses and no farther.

I take the glass from his hand greedily and am about to drink when Terrance clinks the rim of his glass against mine.

"To—you," he says. "And whatever this is we're doing."

It isn't easy, like I thought it would be. He doesn't reach for me, as he did in my imagination. Instead, for too long, we simply stand there and drink the champagne. Maybe nothing needs saying. No, everything needs saying. From me: apologies and explanations. From him: forgiveness granted or declined.

Except I don't feel like words right now, so I—all bravery, no skill—do the reaching. I raise my hand and cup the side of his face, then lean in to kiss him. He grabs my wrist instead.

"What is this?" he says, holding my arm with one hand, and with the other, unfastening the cuff of my shirt. The knife in its homemade sheath, strapped to my forearm with tape. I'd forgotten it was there, as if it had grown into me.

"For protection," I say.

"From what?" he says. "Me?"

"No. Not you," I say. "Everything but you."

He shakes his head. Sadness and pity. Disgust. "Who *are* you?"

"I'm—I'm the same," I say, the absurdity of it plain as the knife itself. "Look. I'm taking it off."

I claw at the tape holding the sheath, then when fingernails aren't enough, bite the edge with my teeth. Eventually I tear an end loose and rip the tape off my skin. It leaves fiery red stripes on my forearm, sticky and black along the sides where the adhesive glued my skin to the grime of the city.

But Terrance has pulled away and stands against the water-stained wall, eyes turned to something else, as if he's embarrassed for me.

I move to the couch, humiliated at having intruded in his world. "I appreciate it," I say finally, my voice stiff, official. "You took a big risk, seeing me. And I appreciate it."

"Not much left to risk," he says. "Whoever it is you pissed off. They took it out on my dad and me."

"Took it out how?"

"You think they didn't know about us? You called me, sent texts, from Prague, remember?"

"It was a fresh SIM, I didn't . . ."

"Fresh SIM? So what? Me, who never got a call from Prague in my life, suddenly gets one. That's all they needed." He closes his eyes, breathes in and out slowly.

"It's—that's not proof. It's just circumstantial."

His face tightens, lips stretched, anger being tamped down. "It was enough," he says sharply. "For them, it was enough. They came three months after—whatever you did over there. Is it true, by the way? What they said?"

I shrug. "I don't know. Maybe they exaggerated. Terrance, what did they do to you?"

"They accused my dad of laundering money for terrorists in Syria and Sudan." He drains his glass, then sets it down and takes a drink straight from the bottle.

"I'm sorry, Terrance."

"The whole thing was very—obtuse. Some court no one had ever heard of. Evidence he wasn't even allowed to see. In the end, they dropped the most serious charges, so only five years in a cushy prison in Nevada. Lost his license, though. And between the lawyers and the fines for the lesser charges, there's not much left."

I can't help but look around the room, however worn down it is, and think of all his traveling. For him, *not much left* still leaves him with far more than my dad and I have ever seen. A flash of anger goes off inside me, but I decide to take his point. It sucks to be a millionaire when you used to be a billionaire. I can see that. I guess.

"But you never gave it to them," I say. "The book. The codes."

He looks at me, shrugs. "Of course not."

"You did that—for me."

"I did it on general principle. Fuck them. Fuck their fake court."

I blink, look down. "Thank you. Terrance, thank you."

"Yeah, well. You're welcome." A little laugh sneaks out, then he lifts the bottle to his mouth again. "Harvard double legacy, endowments. So you'd think I'd be a shoo-in, right?"

"I suppose."

"Denied. No reason given." Terrance waves his glass in the air dismissively. "Princeton, same thing. Yale. University of fucking Minnesota."

"What do you do instead? Do you have a job?"

"Freelance, sometimes. Here and there. Network security. But legit companies won't touch me. Maybe they get a phone call from Washington. Who knows." He wanders to the window and pushes the curtain aside with a finger. "Mostly I travel. I was in Australia for a few months. China."

"I know. I saw your pictures." I swallow, look down. "You're really good."

"Thanks." A smile flickers on his face. "Those are just—what I take with my phone. I bought an old film camera for the important stuff. I think it's what I want to do."

"Be a photographer?"

"Kind of," he says. "Printmaker."

Nice to have options.

"Printmaker," I say. "That sounds—kind of cool."

He hears me, the thing underlying my words. Something in his face melts away and he comes around to the couch, hovering next to me. Then he touches my shoulder. "Sorry. It must seem like, just whining. I know it's been worse for you. You've been through—I can't even imagine it."

"No, I—I'm just sorry. About what I did to you."

He sinks into the cushion next to me. "Will you tell me about it?"

"About what?"

"Prague. What you did."

I finish off the champagne in my glass; he pours me more. "Such bad things, Terrance."

Ten

Tell him nothing or tell him everything. That's the decision I have to make, and, without thinking too long about it, I decide on everything. The confession of all of it, the deceit, the murders—the words feel every bit as dangerous as the deeds themselves. Let the rich kid shoulder it for a little while, I think. He won't rat me out. And if he does, all the easier for me. It's a game of hide-and-seek that's gone on too long. I've hidden myself too well, so it's time to dangle a foot out from under the bed, *find me already.*

He takes it better than I would have thought, keeping whatever private judgment he renders about me to himself, behind a face of calm and cool. Another bottle—red wine this time—is ordered from room service, along with two BLTs and a chocolate mousse to share. I eat all the mousse, and Terrance doesn't mind.

It must be noted that Terrance says almost nothing throughout my confession, absorbing the facts as a journalist might. Dispassionately and quietly, except for small, barely audible acknowledgments that he's heard me. When I'm done, when I've told him everything, we're sitting together in silence, Terrance sideways on the couch, me nestled against him, my back resting on his chest, my arm lying on his leg. He takes my hand, intertwines his fingers with mine, and finally speaks:

"How did it make you feel?"

"How did what make me feel?"

"The things you did," he answers.

"Things?" I say.

"You know."

"You want to know about the killing," I say.

"Yes," he says.

I shrug, but then think that's the coward's way out, to suggest that I don't know. Because I know exactly how it made me feel. Since I've put Terrance in danger by bringing him here, and will put him in more danger in the weeks to come, I owe him the truth.

"The first one—it was a guy on a train," I say. "I didn't mean to do it. I felt guilty. I guess. For a while."

"How about the second?"

"The second one was some random bigot. A bully. He didn't really do anything to me directly," I say. "That one—the second one—surprised me."

"How so?"

"How easy it was."

Silence from both of us, in honor of what it means for killing to become easier the second time. He pulls his arms tight around me and the embrace feels like nothing so much as the safety bars on a roller coaster. I let my head tilt back against his shoulder and then fall asleep.

I don't know how long he lets me stay this way, but at some point we move to the bed and retake our positions. I fall asleep once more with him holding me, pressed up to me from behind, his lovely body warm as a beach. Even through his clothes and mine, I feel his heartbeat tapping against my back, steady, untroubled.

And there I sleep for half a day, or maybe just less than that.

When I wake, it's bright in the room, daytime, and Terrance, dressed and shaved, is sitting in a chair he's pulled to the bedside as if this were a hospital and I were a patient.

"Need anything?" he asks. "Water? Tylenol?"

I shake my head, then notice something in his hands—an old-school mechanical camera, slim and black. "What are you doing?"

He shrugs. "Looking at you," he says.

"No, with that," I say. "Did you take my picture?"

"Yeah. You looked so—beautiful." He raises the camera to his right eye, adjusts something on the lens.

"Stop," I say, turning away, knowing my hair is a mess, wondering if there's drool caked on my cheek.

His hand turns my chin back so that I'm looking directly at him. "You are. You're beautiful," he says.

But I'm not. I can't be. A killer isn't beautiful. An alcoholic fugitive isn't beautiful. Everybody knows this. "Liar," I say.

"Gwendolyn, you're beautiful," he repeats.

"Stop calling me that," I say, pulling the pillow over my head so he can't look at me. "And I'm not."

The pillow rips away from my face and he tosses it off the bed. He's standing beside the bed, then he swings a leg over my waist so he's kneeling over me. "It's your name," he says, raising the camera. "And you are."

Before I can protest, I hear the click of the shutter and the polite ratchet of the film advancing with a motion of his thumb. I swat his stomach, too hard for it to be playful, but he laughs and fires the camera again.

"Look that way," he says. "Toward the light from the window."

"My hair looks like shit," I say.

"I'm not taking pictures of your hair. I'm taking pictures of you. Now turn."

I scowl at him but do it anyway. Another click, and I wonder what it was he saw in that millisecond that he liked. Is it possible he's being sincere? Is it possible that after everything I've told him, he still thinks I'm beautiful? Worthy of him, worth remembering forever?

At that moment, some bureaucrat inside me fires off a panicked message to my more rational self: *He's taking pictures of you!* But this is film, and the images are trapped inside the camera, at least for now. And if these photos become the last record of my existence here, let the record show that for at least a little while, I was happy. Because the truth is, in this second, I am. That I'm here with Terrance is a victory. That I'm happy is a victory. Let the record show that for a little while, I won.

"If you're caught with those," I say, "it's proof we were together."

"I'm not ashamed."

"It's not about shame. It's about consequences," I say.

"Some people are worth it," Terrance says.

I turn my head to the side, the way models do in magazines, and look at him from the corners of my eyes. "Like this?"

"Yes," Terrance says. "But stop smiling."

"I can't help it." I curl an arm over my head, doing my best to look languorous and bored like a bedded aristocrat. "This?"

"Good." Another click.

I push back the sheets and lower the shoulders of my tank top. "This?"

Another click.

I lower the tank top farther. "This?"

It is not as it was with Marco. It is not fun, or rather, it is not that kind of fun. The notion that fun can be divorced from pleasure—and in making love to Terrance, there is much pleasure—comes as a surprise to me. This is pleasure as serious business. Pleasure as completing a task too long postponed. And, if I am to be truthful, it didn't work the first time.

It's only later, the second time, after yet more confessions and talk, after—imagine this, a little laughter—that it actually happens. It isn't the playful advancing and retreating, the strumming of fingers over

82

skin, the *that* now *this*, skillful Marco employed. Rather it is a little rough, a little dry, and at one point I bite his lip too hard and he yelps. Afterward, I pull the condom off him and put it on the nightstand.

We are—or at least I am—glad when it's over; the tension of something inevitable having come to pass. Now we can see that the pieces do, in fact, fit; that we are both still human beings that way.

He lifts my hand from where it lies on his stomach and seems to study it, peering at the dents and small scars I've picked up from broken glass and hot pans and sharp knives.

"A tacky question," he says.

"Anything," I say.

"Did you have a boyfriend, where you came from?"

"I did."

"Not anymore."

"He—cheated on me. In a way."

He nods, then laces his fingers through mine. "Asshole."

For only a second I consider asking him about girlfriends, but I really don't care about the answer. Whether I'm one of a thousand others, there's no room in my head for little jealousies. My eyes fall to the nightstand, where his camera sits next to the condom. I pull my hand free from his and reach across him to pick it up. It's heavier than it looks, and its black metal body is rubbed to a well-used, brassy finish at the edges. It's a weighty, important-feeling device and reminds me of the first time someone handed me a pistol. Leica, it says inside the little red dot on the front.

"Thank you," I say. "For taking my picture."

He rolls over on his side, facing me, and spirals a lock of my hair around a finger. "You didn't mind?"

"I felt for once like—like I wasn't hiding." I roll the camera over. "So this is your thing now? Taking pictures?"

He watches me, follows my movements with his eyes. "The taking is just part of it. I want to put them on paper. Something beautiful. That can be touched."

"Something beautiful you can touch. I like that idea."

"There's this guy, Miksa Jò. He's a printmaker." He presses his lips to my shoulder. "My dream is to study with him. Be an apprentice, then start my own shop."

"Miksa. What is that, Japanese?"

"Hungarian. He's in Budapest."

On the bottom of the camera is a recessed turnkey. I flip it out. "What does this do?"

"It opens it up. If you turn it, you'll expose the film and destroy the pictures."

I look at him, his eyes only a few centimeters from mine. "I really should, shouldn't I?"

He closes his eyes, then nods. "You have to," he says.

I twist the key, then twist it back. "Fuck it. Keep them."

"Bad idea," Terrance says.

"I'm full of bad ideas." I set the camera back on the nightstand, then turn to him and cup the side of his face. The words come out spontaneously: "I love—I love that you're here."

Caught myself just in time.

He runs his thumb over my hand. "And why am I here?" he whispers. "To deliver your book?"

I kiss him to shut him up. Let the question be asked in another hour or another day.

He pushes me away gently. "Why am I here, Gwen?"

I swing my legs over the edge of the bed. I'm sore from making love and use the corner of the sheet to clean myself. His eyes are on me; I feel them on my back, my ass, my neck. "Are you angry, Terrance?"

"With you? No. Not anymore."

"No, with them."

"Them?"

I turn to him. He's lying on the bed, head propped in one hand. "The people who did this to me. And to you and your dad."

Terrance closes his eyes. "Sure. But so what?"

"Because it matters," I say. "It matters that someone pays."

He rolls over onto his back. "No one ever pays. Or, the wrong people pay. That's the world."

I take his hand and kiss each slender finger one by one. "And that's okay with you?" I say between kisses. "Isn't there something we can do?"

He scrunches up his face and does his best white-guy voice. "Maybe write a strongly worded letter to the editor."

I smile. Pretend to smile. "No, really, what's your plan? Think they'll ever let you get a real job? Think they'll ever let you, I don't know, live normally?"

Quiet except for the rustling of sheets as he turns and looks at me. Something there, in that look. "Yes. I thought about it. A lot. And I have a plan."

"Which is?"

"There's a trust fund—*irrevocable*. It's in Switzerland; the government can't touch it. I get it when I'm twenty-five. My plan is to start an online publication."

"A blog?"

"No. A real publication. Something big. To fight injustice, government abuses."

"So, a blog."

"*No.* With reporters. On the ground. Making people aware." He squeezes my hand. "I have a business plan. The whole thing is entirely self-supporting, no advertising. I've been working on it for a year."

I close my eyes and nod along. "And in the meantime?"

"Living well is the best revenge. Isn't that what they say?"

"Living well," I repeat. I stand and move away from him, to the curtains covering the window, and push them open. Below me, the streets of BA are thick with midday traffic, cabs and honking horns. I lean forward for a better view, the window glass cold against my breasts. "I thought you wanted to start your shop, making prints?"

"A dream, I said. What I want to do. This, the publication, it's what I have to do."

I reach over to the cart room service left behind and tilt the wine bottle, hoping there's something left, but it's empty. "How does money work, Terrance?"

"What?"

"Tell me how money works. I want you to teach me."

I hear him crawl across the bed and I look at him. He's sitting on the edge, covering his waist with the sheet as if a gust of modesty had suddenly blown into the room.

"I have no idea," he says.

"Yes," I say. "You do. You're smart that way. About rich-people things. Your dad's a billionaire. Or was."

"Then what do you want to know?"

"Swiss bank accounts."

Terrance's shoulders slump and he closes his eyes. He knows what I'm talking about without my having to say it. I'd gone to him for help when I'd first discovered the account numbers hidden in a mini-storage unit in Queens. He'd decoded them, and together he and I learned—learned the hardest way possible—that the hunger for other people's money is what moves the world.

"The Zoric accounts," he says.

"Yes."

"It's not like in the old days," he says. "Thirty years ago, twenty, you were just a number. Total secrecy. But now it's different."

"Different how?"

"Laws. I don't know. The Americans, they call the shots now. No more secrets for anybody. All I know is you don't just walk in with a password and walk out with the money."

"There's a way. Theoretically. My dad thinks so."

"And then what? Let's say you get the money. How do you move it, how do you spend it without paying taxes?"

"I'll pay taxes. I don't care about that."

Terrance snatches his boxers from the floor and puts them on. "It's not about paying. They want to know where it came from. How you got it."

"But people—rich people—they get away with it all the time, right? Moving money. Spending it."

I hear him moving behind me, coming up close. Then his hands are around my waist and he presses his chest to my back.

He kisses my neck. "Want to know the secret?"

"Yes."

"Attorneys. Good ones. Naz Sadik, in Zurich. Whatever you can imagine, she can find a way to do it."

"Who's Naz Sadik?"

"The attorney my dad uses. And all his friends." He squeezes me tightly.

"How much?"

"Expensive," he says. "Thousands an hour."

"Thousands, plural?" I say. "Jesus."

"You want to turn water into wine, that's what it costs."

I reach behind me, touch his head, running my fingers over his scalp. "Come with me," I say. "To Zurich. We'll split the money."

I hear the uncertainty in his breathing. "I don't want the money," he whispers. "In fact, you can have some of mine. More when I get the trust fund. Whatever you need."

He means to be generous, and even though I know this intellectually, the idea makes me angry. "This money isn't just money. It's—justice."

"Revenge," he says.

"Justice," I say again. "You coming with me or not?"

He turns me around so we're pressed chest to chest, hips to hips. He takes my face between the palms of his hands and kisses me. "Yeah," he says. "I'm going with you."

Eleven

Wanting is love. Or maybe wanting is simply *like* love. Or maybe I don't know what love is. But I do know what wanting is. And it's this. The opposite of fear.

When you're afraid, you work like hell to avoid the thing you're afraid of. But when you want, you work like hell to steer toward the thing you want. Thus, there will be no more cowering for me. No more hiding. I will go about the business of obtaining what I want brazenly. I will be fearless. I will be merciless. And I will take the money.

I peel my skin away from Terrance's body, and the air is cold there in the places we were pressed together. We make love again, this time on the floor. In the process, we knock over a stand with a vase of flowers on top and the water is pooling on the ratty old rug. As Terrance stirs, I slip on my shirt and climb into my jeans. From here, I can see the clock on the bedside table: 10:17 p.m. I push aside the curtains and look down on nighttime BA below us, full and buzzing.

Terrance approaches and stands beside me at the window. I see our silhouettes, feel the warmth of his naked chest floating just a centimeter away from my naked arm. "Let's go out," he says. "Get drunk. Dance."

"For tomorrow we die."

"No. We celebrate. The end of being afraid."

"Dangerous for you to be seen with me," I say.

He touches my shoulder. "It's nighttime, Gwen. No one sees anything."

The line along the San Telmo street stretches down the block and around the corner. Beautiful, sexy *porteños* laugh and smoke and eye one another. The crowds I've seen here are not generally given to orderly queuing, but tonight they are on their best behavior for the one-night-only engagement at a rave in a disused warehouse space. Even though he's in a city he doesn't know, the date and time and location of the rave are, of course, known to Terrance. Maybe there's an app just for international rich kids.

The scent of good weed crisscrosses with the scent of good perfume as Terrance pulls me by the hand past the line and all the way to the steel doors at the front, where a pair of oak-tree bouncers stand guard. By the standards of the expensively dressed women in line, my clothing—jeans, tank top, sneakers—is pathetic. The smaller of the two oak doormen glances at us once, then waves us away. But Terrance sidles up next to him, puts on that killer smile. I spot a folded green square in Terrance's palm that's not there a second later. The denomination is apparently large enough for the doorman to actually give a little bow as he opens the door and waves us in.

The bass hammers at my chest and eardrums, and strobes freeze ecstatic faces in the crowd. On a stage in the center of the dance floor, the DJ stands behind a control panel of turntables and laptops. With the music's every shift, every build, every drop, the crowd roars its approval, and the DJ, a glorious blond boy with a mouth full of LED teeth, grins back.

We are sucked into the crowd, pressed into the spaces among them, and suddenly moving with them. Our hands reach up as if trying to snatch one of the lasers cutting across the sea of bodies. It's been years since I've been at a club purely for the pleasure of it. Since my dad was stationed in Moscow, where the drinking age is four and the only thing they check at the door is to make sure your skirt is short enough. Dancing in a club felt illicit and thrilling then; now it's luxurious release. To be among others, feeling what they feel, moving as they move, the music pulling at my stomach as if I'm cresting the hill on a roller coaster.

Terrance takes my hand and leads me to the bar. A moment later, he's handing me a shot glass, something green and sugary-smelling, a mad scientist's magic formula. "I clink the rim of my glass to his, and then we both drink. It's sweet and marvelous. I slam the glass onto the bar. "Another," I say.

He looks at me from the corners of his eyes, then signals the bartender. Too much, too quick, I warn myself. Tactical awareness. Always. At every moment. And this green poison will give me anything but.

But.

But screw it. Let me be the me without a name tonight. Let me live in a different world tonight. I drink, then take Terrance by the hand and lead him into the center of the dance floor. Even as the song drifts into another, morphing into a happy, blipping, bouncing children's version of bass-heavy dance music, we don't stop moving. This is one of this DJ's big hits, apparently, because everyone roars even louder. I have spent so much energy on fear, so much of myself on fear, that it is bliss to spend it on something else. Terrance's body presses into me; I press into the woman next to me; she presses into someone else. So it goes, so it spreads, until all of us are fused in this way.

The sweat on my arms shines in the strobes and the lasers like I'm made of silver. Then Terrance's arm is around my waist and he's leading me off the floor. Another transaction takes place at the foot of a staircase, then another at the top that sees us escorted to a white leather couch all to ourselves.

Bottle service only here, so it's a bottle we'll have to get. Through me as his interpreter, Terrance orders vodka and soda water to mix it with, both twenty times the price they'd sell for on the street.

A trio of women approach. Gorgeous and nervous. Cocktail dresses and artfully piled black hair and sequined clutches. They say something to Terrance in Spanish, and when he can't hear, they say it again, louder. Laughter bursts from my mouth just as I take a sip of the vodka. I cough and cough and spit the vodka into my hand.

"What's so funny?" Terrance asks.

"They're asking if you're a rapper."

"A what?"

"A rapper."

Now Terrance bursts out laughing.

I run through a list of rappers in my head but can't think of anyone he looks like. "Ladies, may I present to you T-Maxus," I say in Spanish, cringing at the name even as it comes out.

They consult, and each in turn shakes her head. One of them hands me her iPhone. "Spell it," she says.

"His debut album is coming out next month," I say. "He's not famous yet, but in a year, bigger than Kanye."

They swoon anyway—a word I've never really appreciated until I see them do it—simultaneously moaning and clutching their stomachs as if they're about to vomit. The three pile in close to Terrance and pull their iPhones out to take selfies with him, but I step in.

"No photos," I say, taking the phone away from one of the girls.

"And who are you, bitch?" one of them says.

"His bodyguard," I say.

I'm about to shoo them away, then don't. Instead, I invite them to sit, and Terrance asks a passing server for more glasses. Here we all are, new friends, living life as friends do. The glasses come and Terrance pours vodka for everyone. It goes down hard and is cold as ice cream and sends a web of tingles outward from my stomach to my head and fingers and toes.

Life feels good as someone else.

They are named Delfina, Marti, and Sol, I find out. Native *porteños* who know one another from nursing school. I learn all this from the first minute or so as I interpret for Terrance. In the second minute I learn that two are Catholic, while the third—the one who called me a bitch—"identifies as Buddhist." They are, all of them, charming and cute, and the girl called Sol has an untranslatable wit that's hilarious in Spanish but doesn't work in English. Terrance and I make up stories of what it's like as a soon-to-be hip-hop star, the grueling tour schedule as an opening act for someone famous, the throngs of fans waiting for him at the Tokyo airport. All of it so much more appealing than reality.

One of them—Delfina?—spills vodka on herself, and Terrance helps her wipe it up. A gentlemanly gesture; he's careful to avoid touching her too much. I use the opportunity to take another drink from the vodka, then another. My eyes close and I see fiery swirls thrumming and breathing in time to the music. This is it, the feeling I was after. Alcohol makes you sentimental. It makes you fall in love. It makes you cry because you've never seen a boy so beautiful.

I stand, or rather, find myself standing. I find myself descending the staircase to the dance floor, too. I find myself slipping into the crowd, arms up, body pressed against other bodies. The music lifts me, carries me. I spin, or rather, am spun. The tempo changes, builds. Soft blips turn to scratches and the sound of tearing fabric. A violent wardrum bass line starts up and I see the heads of other dancers tilted to the ceiling, mouths open, as if struggling for air, their arms reaching up as if trying to climb to the surface. In the crisscrossing lasers above us, our breath coils into plumes of dragon fire. I'm drowning.

A ring of booths lines the perimeter of the dance floor and I fight my way toward them. I find an empty table with unattended drinks waiting for their owners to return and empty one of the glasses in three swallows. It's a room-temperature something that tastes of maraschino cherries and gasoline.

I should leave. I should leave and disappear. It was wrong of me to drag Terrance into this. Selfish of me. Greedy. He is not mine to do with as I please. He doesn't need the money I'll steal. Which I won't get anyway. Because I'll die before I even come close. And so will he.

. . .

An arm is around my waist. A mouth is kissing my neck.

"I thought I'd lost you," Terrance says.

We stumble into the night, me nearly tripping over curbs and obstacles that aren't there, him catching me.

Terrance is angry with me. I drank too much, and now he's angry with me for being sloppy and stupid. As he pulls me upright, I grab handfuls of fabric from his shirt and pull him close.

"You're an idiot," I say.

He tries to pull my hands away, straighten me up, but I hold tight.

"You're an idiot," I repeat. "I'm using you, Terrance. Don't you see that?"

"Everyone uses everyone." He finally gets my hands away and turns me around. "It's just a question of what for."

With one arm around my waist, he extends the other into the street, imperially slim fingers raised at an imperially casual angle, commanding a taxi to materialize. And so one does.

"Look at you, all magic," I say.

"What?" he says.

"Nothing."

Terrance pulls me next to him in the backseat of the old Fiat as we head to the hotel. We bounce along, and somehow I see inside the Fiat's buzzy little engine, at the cyclone of bees powering it. As other cars pass us, their headlights throw beams of fire and glass—searing and cold, respectively, and smooth to the touch. But these are just drunken hallucinations, or shards of hallucinations, unreal properties of things that are real. I squeeze my eyes shut and press my forehead into Terrance's shoulder.

"If they catch you with me, they'll hurt you, Terrance."

"I imagine they'll try."

But he can't imagine, because he's a good person and the imagination of a good person can't see the things I've seen, the things I've read about in my father's doomsday device.

"Tajikistan," I say.

"What's in Tajikistan?" Terrance says.

"It's where they'll send you. If they catch us."

He smiles, patronizing the drunk girl, and curls a finger through my hair. "I hear it's nice there," he says.

I rip myself up from his shoulder and lean forward, about to order the driver to pull over, about to jump out the door and slip into the dark and be gone from Terrance's life.

But we're already in front of the hotel. And Terrance is pulling money from his pocket. And the doorman in a threadbare vest and rumpled white shirt is opening the back door of the cab and grinning.

"Welcome back," the doorman says.

One more night. Then I'll go.

This is my shitty world, not his. How dare I drag him into it. Thank the booze-gods I caught my mistake in time to make my exit.

Terrance pulls the keycard out of the lock and swings the door open.

"I'm going to throw up now," I say.

He follows me into the bathroom, crouches next to me as I kneel and bend my head over the toilet, holds my hair behind my ear with slender fingers as I puke the night out, liquor and pink bile. He touches my mouth with a washcloth white as an angel's robe. He tilts a glass of water to my lips. "Baby sips," he says.

"I'm seeing things, Terrance. Hallucinating."

"How much did you drink?"

"Enough." I wave him away. "Go. I need to wash."

I sit on the floor of the tub, rinse my mouth, spit, rinse again. I rub viciously with the washcloth at the black glue on my arm where the knife and cardboard sheath were held in place with duct tape. The green stuff and vodka has peaked and I'm now stumbling back toward the ground. The shy better angel inside me tells me to hold on to the lessons learned: *Keep your word, Gwen, and leave tomorrow.*

From somewhere outside the bathroom I hear Terrance bump into something. Maybe he's ordered room service and the cart hit the wall. Some dry toast would be nice. That's just the sort of thing he would think of: dry toast for the puking girl.

I turn off the water and wrap myself in a scratchy robe. "Terrance?" I call, rubbing a spot clear on the foggy mirror and combing my hair. No answer.

"Terrance?" I repeat.

Still nothing.

I cinch the belt of the robe tight around my waist and step out of the bathroom. Terrance is sitting on the foot of the bed, arms politely in his lap, wrists bound with white plastic riot cuffs. Two meters away, a man stands with a pistol held loose at his side.

Twelve

The man leans a weary shoulder against the wall and doesn't even raise the gun as I enter. He's in his mid-twenties, pudgy and big, and has done this enough to be casual about it. "Gwendolyn Bloom," he says in English. "Show to me your hands." An accent, Slavic, but not Russian.

Insulted vanity. That's what it is, the thing inside me that in that moment is louder than the panic. Lovrenc Zoric's gift for me is just as I thought: an idiot wearing latex gloves and carrying a pistol. I'd imagined a leather jacket and track pants, but this one is in jeans and sneakers and a track jacket, which is close enough to still be right.

I raise my hands to shoulder level and dart a glance toward Terrance. His eyes are wide and panicked. He has, it occurs to me, never had a gun held on him.

"I have money," Terrance says firmly, keeping his eyes straight ahead. "A lot more than whatever they're paying you."

"Yes?" the man says. "Here? With you?"

"No. In a bank."

"Ah," the man says, raising the gun toward Terrance's head. "Too bad we're in a hotel."

I lift my hands higher, just enough to pull the belt on the robe loose, just enough to let the robe fall open in the front. It is, emphatically, not an invitation. Not a come-on. It is an accident. An accident that I made happen.

The man's eyes turn, and I feel them crawl over me. This thug is of a kind, a sort, a species that I know. In the pocket of his track jacket I will find a pack of Marlboros and keys to a BMW. On his phone I will find American hip-hop and racist German rap and pictures of nude blond women with giant tits.

I lower my hands just a little. Let the robe creep down my shoulders just a little. His eyes catch mine, and I turn my eyes away shyly.

He hesitates, the gun still on Terrance, but looking at me. He has orders, a paycheck waiting at the end. He's been told about me, warned. But he's already picturing himself fucking me. He's picturing himself afterward, telling his friends about it in a bar back home, the gestures he'll use. How raptly his friends will sit. How wide their eyes will be.

He takes a tentative step forward, then a more assured one. I keep my eyes lowered and submissive. Then his fingers touch my breast, clammy because of the latex gloves. He squeezes my breast gently at first, then harder. I feel his breath on my forehead. Cigarettes and gum.

With the tip of the silencer, he brushes my hair back behind my ear and prods the robe the rest of the way off my shoulders. It falls to the floor, and only the end of the belt stays in my hand.

This is far too much for Terrance. He bursts forward from the couch with a furious shout. The man's gun swivels in Terrance's direction, but I catch it with my left hand and twist. There's a snap and a yelp as the man's index finger breaks against the trigger guard. Terrance slams into him, knocking the rest of the breath out of his lungs and twisting the man around. The gun spins from my hand and skitters across the parquet.

I yank the belt free from my robe, loop it once around the man's neck, and pull him close. He arches his back as he tries to get his fingers under the belt, but I pull hard, leaning into him with my shoulder. My fingers turn purple with the effort and the fabric of the belt burns my skin like fire. Rude, that's what it is. Intruding into this little corner of the world Terrance and I had carved out for ourselves. Planning to kill us. Fucking rude.

He's almost a full head taller than me and has at least a twenty-kilo advantage, so I have to get him to the floor where I can control him better. I lower him slowly, steering him to the ground so he can't jerk free. We're lying together on our sides now, and I picture my instructor Zvi back in Montevideo shaking his head in disappointment. Strangling is too sloppy. Too slow. Better to break his neck and be done. But reality is like that sometimes, sloppy and slow. The trick is to not let up, not for a second, not ever, until he's dead. I press a knee against the man's spine, the strength of every muscle in my body dedicated to pulling the belt around his neck tighter, tighter.

He is someone's son, this man. Someone's father maybe. What is left of the alcohol in me entreats mercy and human love, *misericordia*, *compasión*. But I pull tighter, tighter. You get no love without giving it.

Terrance scrambles for the gun and points it uncertainly at the man's chest. He's obviously never held a pistol before and he studies the thing in his hands: Is there a safety? Do I pull back the hammer? What does this button do? Christ, Terrance will kill me, too. Through gritted teeth I seethe at him to put it down, but he can't, or won't.

Fucker just won't die. His face is purple and swollen and his eyes are round and white like golf balls, but still he fights. Strangling someone isn't like it is in the movies. It's not over in ten seconds. It's not even over in a minute. The body of any animal fights for life, savagely, with everything it has. So you need to have leverage, endurance, a good grip on the rope or the belt or the necktie, whatever you're using.

He goes, by my rough estimate, somewhere around two and a half minutes later. That's when his body stops jerking, when his grip relaxes, when his hollow choking stops. There is an eggplant-colored ring around his neck when I loosen the belt, which at points is abraded and seeping blood. I place two fingers where his jaw and neck meet, feeling for a pulse, but there's nothing.

I stand, my own breath raw with effort, looking at my hands, which are bleeding and so cramped I can barely open them. The sensation begins like an electric tension in my guts—wires charging, pulling taut—then climbs to my throat, coming out in a sound like a laugh or a gasp.

I sicken myself.

I am proud of myself.

Terrance is still holding the gun, so I tell him to put it down, and when he doesn't, I tell him again. I make sure I'm well away from the muzzle, then gently, with a mother's touch, unfold his fingers from the grip, take the pistol, and set it on the floor.

"You okay?" I ask. "Need to throw up? It's okay to throw up."

His eyes and mouth are wide open as he struggles for air just like the dead man did. I hear him gasp, then he shakes his head. There's fear in his face, fear and incredulity, like the world has just flipped inside out and he doesn't believe any of what he's just seen. His eyes dart from the body to me, back to the body, back to me.

"You killed him." It comes out of him flatly, no judgment, just a fact.

"This is what it looks like, Terrance." I touch his shoulders. He flinches. "And before we get the money, there might be others. I hope there won't be, but it's a safe bet."

He nods once, then his jaw muscles tighten and he nods again. "I understand."

I sit down next to him on the bed, lean my head against his shoulder. Terrance puts his arm around my waist and pulls me close. I'm not sure who's comforting whom. He takes my hand in his and inspects it, the abrasions like bad rug burns, the dots of blood drying into dark specks.

"We—we can't call the police," Terrance says.

Good. Thinking like a grown-up. "No," I say.

"So what now?"

"Go through his pockets," I say. "Get his wallet, his phone. His passport if he's carrying one. We can find out who he is."

"And the body?" he asks.

The body. There's no realistic way we can move it. And putting the Do Not Disturb sign on the door and running to the airport will only make Terrance a fugitive wanted for murder.

"I can call someone," I say. "A friend. A kind of friend."

I search through my backpack until I find the business card and call the number from a new SIM in my phone. A sleepy male's voice answers.

"This is Judita Perels," I say. "I need to talk to Brent Simanski."

I was right: Marlboros, BMW keys, phone, wallet, passport. The items are spread out on the desk and his phone is hooked up to Terrance's laptop. It was locked, he tells me, but because of a security flaw in the outdated version of Android something-something-something. I don't get it, but he does, and that's what matters.

"Boleslaw Koziol," Terrance says. "He has a Serbian passport but born in Poland. Age twenty-seven. According to public records, he owns a general contracting company in Belgrade, where he also has an apartment. That's his official life."

I watch over Terrance's shoulder as he toggles to another tab on the browser.

He points to the screen and a mug shot of the man currently dead on the floor. "I looked him up in the Interpol records, on the notices they send out to the FBI and whatever," Terrance continues. "According to the Munich police department there is no Boleslaw Koziol, at least not anymore. It's a cover ID for a Bulgarian named Nikko Kucheto, but that might be an alias, too, it says."

"So Nikko Kucheto, who does he work for?"

Terrance scrolls down the screen and points to a line: *Associate of Viktor Zoric.*

Viktor Zoric. Reaching out from beyond the grave to protect his money. I lean onto the table, press my fingers to my temples. "How did he find me?"

"He didn't," Terrance says. "He found me."

Terrance switches screens, pulls up an e-mail. "My travel for the past few weeks, sent to Nikko two days ago. Flight numbers. Hotel rooms. Credit card charges. Then, three hours ago, another e-mail. Giving him my new room number after you had me switch. Gwen, someone put this Nikko onto me. Because it would lead to you."

Something cold inches up my spine. "The e-mail. Who sent it?"

"An anonymous address from a server in Crete, but that means nothing. It's a black box, a TOR relay, just a place where the e-mail took a left turn. It could have come from anyone."

But it didn't come from anyone. It came from someone specific, with instant, real-time access to travel itineraries, bank records, hotel room numbers. Someone who knew about Terrance. Someone who knew I'd reach out to him.

He is being so brave. But the threat that was, just an hour ago, theoretical, is now real. And now his theoretical bravery must be real, too. I pull a chair beside Terrance and sit, then take his trembling hand in mine. Or maybe it's me who's trembling.

Thirteen

Brent Simanski arrives a half hour later, sleepy, unshaven, a suit thrown over yesterday's rumpled shirt. He doesn't come alone. A young woman with hipster cat-eye glasses and a young man wearing a cabbie hat and jaunty little scarf trail behind him, both wheeling suitcases like a pair of cool tourists. They look at me as they enter, sizing me up, but don't say a word.

"You must be Terrance," Brent says, shaking Terrance's hand with the bright enthusiasm of a salesman. I hadn't mentioned Terrance on the phone call with Brent, so how Brent knows who he is, I have no idea. As Brent pulls on a pair of blue translucent gloves, he crouches beside the body along with his two colleagues. The woman traces the ligature marks on the neck with her finger and whispers something to her partner in Hebrew.

"My friend asks if you were trying to pull his head clean off." Brent smiles. "For future reference, you don't have to use so much force. But that's what I like about you, Judita. Everything done with such gusto."

One of the colleagues takes a photo of the dead man's ear with a cell phone while the other takes prints from the fingers. "We'll send these in and get confirmation of his identity in a few minutes," Brent says.

Terrance holds up the passport. "Boleslaw Koziol," he says. "An alias for someone called Nikko Kucheto."

"Know what it means, Nikko Kucheto? It's a nickname. Nikko the dog." Brent rises and examines the other items on the desk. "He arrived yesterday on a Lufthansa flight from Frankfurt, seat 24-D. He was following you, Terrance."

"We know," I say. "We saw the e-mail on his phone."

Brent slides Nikko's passport into his pocket. "He was Viktor Zoric's interrogator. A specialist in getting information. The murders are only incidental. Keep going in the Interpol file and you'll see what he did to a narcotics officer in Romania. Use the search terms 'curling iron' and 'rectum.'"

Brent's colleagues unzip their suitcases. The man removes a folded plastic sheet, like a shower curtain. The woman removes a pair of battery packs, the kind used for power tools, along with an electric saw.

"You have a bathtub, yes?" Brent says.

Terrance pinches the bridge of his nose, nods toward the bathroom.

"We'll let them do their job," Brent says. "Judita, you and I can go for a walk, get some air. What do you say?"

"Anything you can say to me, you can say to Terrance," I say.

"We have business, Judita," Brent says. "Terrance, grab a seat and watch some television. And turn it up. Loud."

In the park a block away from the hotel, there's a late-night crowd not quite ready to head home. A knot of *porteños* sit cross-legged and drink wine beneath a gnarled tree that looks like it's a thousand years old. A juggler performs in the cone of light from a streetlamp to an audience of a handful of tourists. A teenager and his girlfriend sit on a bench. He's playing the guitar and singing to her.

We walk along the concrete pathway. I shove my trembling hands into my pockets. "Thank you," I say. "For—taking care of this."

Brent's eyes catch the light as he turns them to me. "Do you have any idea what you've done?" His voice is so low I have to walk very close to him just to hear. "First, you pull that disappearing act in Montevideo. Then you break cover, contacting Terrance. Tel Aviv is livid with you. *Livid.*"

I gesture with my head back toward the hotel. "I can handle myself. As you see."

"That mess? No, Judita," he says. "That, back there, is a fuck-up. Your fuck-up. You knew the protocol: There's your old life and your new life, and they can never overlap. Never even touch."

A middle-aged couple walks by and Brent smiles sheepishly at them as if he's just a father caught in an embarrassing argument with his wayward daughter. When they pass, he leans in close. "This Terrance. What is he to you? Love him? Just a friend?"

"Why?"

"Tel Aviv is curious."

"What business is it of theirs?"

"Because at this moment, there's a group of old men who've never met you sitting around an office, smoking too much and scratching their asses. Know what you are to them?"

"I don't care."

"A line in a budget. And right now, they're wondering if it's worth it, relocating you and your dad again. New IDs, new cover stories. Or whether to go with option two."

I'm about to ask. Then it hits me violently, Brent's words no different than a physical blow. Option two is to eliminate the one outsider who knows my new name, my new location. Kill Terrance. Kill him and cut him up like Nikko. Easy-peasy, problem solved. I ball my fists, nails pressing into my palms like blades. All my instincts, all my muscle memory, command me to respond in kind, violence for violence. But I choke it down.

"Look, it's this simple," I hiss. "Touch him and I kill you."

"Sorry about the world, Judita. The way it works," he says. "But the one person keeping the lid off your coffin is me. So watch your fucking mouth."

Silently, we reach a truce and start walking again, slower than before, stopping as we near the group of tourists watching the juggler. He's moved from rubber balls to bowling pins, starting with three, then adding a fourth and a fifth.

I look up to Brent as he watches, transfixed. "Terrance isn't like me," I whisper. "He's better. He has a life. A future. This world I dragged him into, it isn't his."

"It is now," Brent says. "Thanks to you."

"You have to convince them, Brent. He needs to stay alive."

"It gets exponentially harder with each one," Brent says.

I blink at him in confusion. "What does?"

He nods to the juggler. "Adding a fourth is twice as hard as three. And adding a fifth is twice as hard as four."

I watch the juggler, too. The bowling pins spinning through the air. His little grunts as he catches and tosses, catches and tosses. I watch him until he fails, the bowling pins crashing to the lawn one by one. The crowd begins clapping anyway: a glorious failure, and so entertaining to watch.

I lean in close to Brent, my words masked by the applause. "You gave me a mission."

Brent grins and claps along with everyone else. "Yes, and when you didn't reply, I assumed you walked away."

"I was wrong to do that. I'm sorry."

"Zoric isn't just our enemy, he's yours." He touches my upper arm and guides me away from the crowd. "Too bad it took a visit from Nikko to make you see that."

"I see it now."

A phone buzzes from inside Brent's suit jacket and he answers it. I can hear the voice on the other end, speaking in Spanish. Dry cleaning is done and ready for pickup. Then there's a question, something I can't quite make out.

"No," Brent says into the phone, his eyes locked on mine. "The young man stays."

Gleaming porcelain, smelling of bleach. I sit on the edge of the tub, run my hand along the side. Cleaner than it's ever been in its life.

Terrance hovers in the doorway. "They took him out in the suitcases," he says. "By the end, they were using these fluorescent lights, looking for drops of blood. When they found one, they cleaned it with a Q-tip."

"I'm sorry," I say. "No one should have to see that."

"Mainly I didn't see it." He sits next to me on the edge of the tub. "They didn't let me in until the end, after it was mostly over. Mainly I heard it. The saw."

I place a hand on his knee and sink to the floor. I scan the room again. Nikko is more than simply gone. He's been erased. Terrance has no idea how close he was to joining him. "I'm sorry, Terrance. I'm so, so sorry."

He pushes the hair away from my eyes, cups the side of my face. "It was the Americans, wasn't it? My credit cards, the room change. They're the only ones with real-time information like that."

I bite my lip and nod.

He looks down, stunned, about to be sick. "So now—I'm being hunted, too."

"They're getting a new passport for you," I whisper. "They'll call me tomorrow. Drop it off wherever we are."

"What do you mean, a new passport?"

"I talked them into it. Brent was going to—anyway, it's the best plan." I lean forward, rub my hands up and down his arms. "A new name, Terrance. So we can run."

A sob comes out of his mouth, then I realize a second later it's laughter. "Who am I going to be?"

I shake my head, try to sound hopeful. "They choose it for you. You don't get to decide."

Fourteen

He is in shock, perhaps as deep in shock as he's ever been. But there is a rationality to him, an understanding of next steps, and he stays in the moment with me. There is, for example, the matter of logistics: finding a new place to stay until we can figure out how to transfer two fugitives to Europe, and, as always, the matter of money. I have close to 1,500 US dollars in cash and he has about the same. Credit cards—so easy to track—are off the table, so he decides that a visit to the bank and a one-time withdrawal from whatever's left of his father's fortune is worth the risk. Just under ten grand each is our plan. Enough for two last-minute plane tickets and enough to live off for a while, but not enough to get in trouble with EU customs officers if we're searched.

I wait at the busy corner of two busy streets amid the anonymous throngs of people while Terrance climbs the grand staircase of a bank that looks like a Roman temple. His image is now being recorded by at least a dozen cameras, and I have no doubt the transaction will trigger a series of events that leads to the footage being beamed by satellite or undersea cable to Washington, where every frame will be pored over and analyzed. Someone will pull someone aside in a hallway: *Why is he still alive? And where's the girl?*

Arms folded across my chest, hovering in the entrance of a deli, I watch the bank's doors like a sniper, waiting for him to reappear. When he does, he's walking casually, smiling at passersby, casual as can be. But when his feet touch the sidewalk at the bottom of the staircase, his expression changes and his gait picks up speed. He barely slows down as he passes me, and I fall into step beside him.

"*Una irregularidad menor*, is what she called it."

"Who?" I say.

"The teller." Terrance wipes his mouth with his wrist. "She got the manager. He said the transfer couldn't go through, but he didn't see a reason. He offered to call New York to clear it up."

"Did you let him?"

"Of course not," Terrance says. "I left. Tried to be casual about it, but I'm sure, *I'm sure*, he's on the phone right now."

I put a hand on his forearm. "We'll be fine."

"Fine how? Without money, we're trapped here."

"Good. Let them think that," I say. "We have alternatives."

We find a little *telos*, rooms rented five hours at a time, in Villa Crespa. We pay for a full day, sliding the cash through a slot in the bulletproof glass of an attendant's window, where a fat man with an artificial arm takes it and passes back a key. It's a small hotel, four stories, at the tip of a triangular block. We get the room on the third floor at the very point. A little balcony opens onto a street buzzing with scooters and facing a little park filled with gnarled old trees and the sound of someone playing a violin.

Terrance's face curls in disgust as he peels the lavender blanket from the bed with his fingertips. "There are cigarette burns on the sheets," he says.

I pick up a little cardboard sign from a table. "But free Wi-Fi."

Above us, the brass-on-wood scrape of a bed being moved across the floor in tiny, rhythmic increments. Then the scraping stops and a man howls like a wolf while a woman laughs.

Terrance sits on the bed, staring straight ahead.

"What's wrong?"

He looks up, face slack. "Just thinking."

From the window, the violin again, notes bending in and out of focus on the wind, while from the room above, the padding of bare feet on the bare floor. The man's footfalls are heavy and sure, clomping toward the bathroom. But hers are soft, tentative. She's at the window now, listening to the music. I can smell the cigarette she's smoking.

"Paganini," Terrance says.

"What?"

"The music. The composer is Paganini." Terrance pulls his legs up in front of him. "My dad listened to it all the time."

The toilet above us flushes and ancient pipes groan.

"We need a plan," I say. "In case we get separated, or one of us gets caught."

"How do you communicate? With Brent? With your dad?"

"Encrypted e-mail," I say. "A service called ParallaxMail with my dad. Something else for Brent."

"I use a different service, but yeah, I know it." He snatches up his bag, pulls out a pad of Post-it Notes. "What's your address there?"

I tell him, and he writes it down. Then he writes down his own and hands it to me.

"We memorize them," I say. "Better if we don't leave paper behind."

We study the addresses for a time, then I take an ashtray and book of hotel matches from a table, watching the two little yellow squares curl and burn, black smoke rising to the ceiling.

When the papers are gone, I look up to see Terrance holding his camera. He turns it over in his hands, then licks his thumb and rubs at a spot on its surface. "It's worth a few thousand US. Enough to get you there, at least."

"What camera is worth that much?"

"A Leica. You won't get full value, but don't take less than three grand for the body and lens together." He holds it to his eye and aims it at me. "You mind? One last time?"

"No point in hiding anymore. They know we're together."

"Is that a yes?"

I nod and the shutter clicks. "Can you take selfies with that?" I say. "We should take one. The both of us."

"We can try."

I go to the bed and pull Terrance down next to me. He makes some adjustment on the lens, then holds it at arm's length above us. I lean in close, press my cheek to his. He presses the button. Now this moment is recorded. Now a half-second slice of us, together, will be left to continue on in the world. Now there's something for the file, to balance out the autopsy photos. Here we were once, alive, eyes open.

I hit the shop just after five in the afternoon the next day, just as Guillermo the pawnbroker thief is walking out the alley door, fiddling with a pair of expensive women's handbags, maybe deciding which to give his wife and which to his girlfriend. I call his name from ten paces away and his left hand darts into the right side of his suit jacket. (Note to self: pistol on right, not the left.) But his hand falls back to the handbags when he sees it's me.

"I need to sell something," I say. "Very special."

"Closed," he says, and wheezes past me toward a parked Mercedes coupe.

"Fine. I'll take it somewhere else."

But he pauses, looks down as if he's searching for something he dropped. "You're the thief."

"It's too valuable to show you here. Inside."

A groan, a sigh, some more back-and-forth. I'm about to walk away, then he pulls out his keys. Better be worth it, that particular way of jangling them says. He unlocks the back door and nods to the darkness inside. "Go."

The fluorescent lights of his office buzz as he turns them on. The tabby looks up from the spot where I saw it before, on top of the file cabinets. It leaps to a shelf high on the wall, wanting to be away from whatever happens next.

Guillermo sits at his desk, and I pull the camera from my bag.

"A Leica? You make me reopen for a Leica?"

"You want it or not?"

He picks it up, works the controls, unscrews the lens. "It's a knockoff."

"It is not."

"I know my Leicas, you thieving little sow, and this ain't one."

He offers me what works out to $350, give or take. Another colossal screw.

"I want American dollars," I say. "Five hundred."

"Three hundred or nothing."

I snatch the camera up and stand. But Guillermo lifts a flaccid hand, two fingers extended like he's suddenly Pope Guillermo lazily anointing the deal. Five hundred American for the Leica is the steal of the year and he won't pass it by. Is physically incapable. "Fine," he says. Guillermo the Charitable.

I set the camera back down on the desk and he lifts his bulky mass from the chair. The safe is right behind him, burrowed in a pile of laptops and broken clocks and antique humidors that were once someone's treasures. He makes a circular motion with his finger as he tells me to turn around so as not to see the combination. I do it, and let my ears be my eyes. I hear his body creak as he stoops, the rustle and stretch of his suit jacket pulling taut over his back, and the scritch-scratch of the safe's dial. Then the door swings open—a raspy, happy sound, like an old man's single laugh, *ha*.

I'm over the desk in a half second. Over the desk and seizing Guillermo's mane of hair with my left hand while my right reaches around
his suit jacket and under, grabbing the pistol he carries in his armpit
and pulling it free. I drive his head forward into the lip of the safe,
twice, three times, and a fourth, because fuck Guillermo. Then I pull
him back. There's a shallow indentation on his forehead, red and purple, a perfect trench running from side to side. His eyes are wide but
unseeing. I swing the pistol through the air, catching him in the left
temple with the butt. He collapses against the desk.

Inside the safe, it's just the usual stuff of pawnbroker fascination.
Necklaces and bracelets. Tiny gemstones in tiny envelopes. A pistol for
those who have to do their killing from across a room. But there are
also stacks of currency held together with rubber bands, portraits of
queens and presidents and tyrants of various nations on linen rectangles slick with the grease of fingers, and it's these I'm interested in. I
haven't got time to count it now, but there's a pleasing thickness to the
stacks as I drop them into my bag. It's enough to get us to Europe and,
for a while, put a cheap roof over our heads and cheap calories in our
stomachs.

As for the rest of Guillermo's shit, I consider leaving it alone.
I'm a thief who takes only what she needs. Then, at the last second,
I grab one of the envelopes of gems and shake its contents into my
hand. Five diamonds, not particularly big or special-looking, but
diamonds nonetheless. Easy to smuggle, easy to sell. These go into my
pocket.

The tabby leaps silently to the floor, slinking its way toward me. It
rolls its head against my ankle, then lifts its tail, shows me its asshole,
and disappears through the door.

Terrance is sitting cross-legged on the bed, his face lit orange by the
light of the laptop screen. He looks up as I enter, holds up a passport
with a dark blue cover.

"My new ID," he says quietly. "A lady I'd never seen before bumped into me on the street. I was out getting food, and she just came from nowhere. 'You dropped this,' she said."

He tosses it to me—Belize, well-worn, the real thing. I open to the first page, and there's Terrance's photo, siphoned from some database, I imagine. Dr. Andre Mason, age twenty-seven.

"You're a doctor now," I say.

"What the hell am I supposed to do with that?"

I toss it back to him. "Live. They wouldn't have given it to you if it wasn't good."

"Who's Andre Mason?"

I set my bag down on the floor. "A dead guy, probably. That's how they do it sometimes."

He recoils, finding the idea just as repellent as I did the first time I had to share a name with the dead. I sit cross-legged on the floor and start pulling the money from my bag.

"Holy shit," Terrance says, springing from the bed and picking up a stack of euros with one hand and American dollars with the other. "Holy shit."

Then I pull out his camera and set it gently on the floor next to the money. The muscles in his shoulders go slack, and he looks at me with horror.

"Is he okay?" Terrance says, sitting cross-legged on the floor in front of me.

"I'm fine."

"No, is *he* okay? The person you took the money from?"

"His name is Guillermo. He's a dick." I pick up a stack of 100-peso notes and start counting them. "And I don't know if he's okay. I didn't check."

His hand lashes out, snatches the money from my hands. "What did you do?"

I take the money back from him, calmly, or as calmly as I can. "I solved a problem. He had money. We needed money. Want me to tell you about how bad he deserved it?"

"Did he?"

"I'll say it if it makes you feel better."

For a long moment he stares at me and I stare at him. I know what he's thinking: how abominable I am, how low I am. But there is no life without escape, no escape without money, no money without violence.

His eyes drop down to the money, then he rises.

"Where are you going?"

"For some air."

"Stay."

But the door closes behind him and I hear his footsteps fade as he moves down the hall.

Terrance tries to be quiet when he comes back just after midnight, but the floor is creaky and the bedsprings old. I roll over when he sits down. He's shirtless, the white oxford hanging from a peg on the back of the door. I touch his skin, kiss one of his vertebrae. "You all right?" I ask.

He's silent for a long time. In the dim light, I see the muscles in his back expanding and retreating as he breathes. "Gwen . . ."

"Look, what I said, I was, I don't know. High on adrenaline, I guess. I'm sorry." I kiss his back again, snake an arm around his stomach.

"You're sorry about what you said."

"Mm-hm." Another kiss.

"But not what you actually did."

I pull away from him, open my mouth, but don't know what to say. I'm not sorry. I'm not sorry a shitty man in a shitty world got beaten up and robbed. I'm not sorry his money is now with good people who need it more than he does. How can Terrance not see this?

"Yes," I lie. "I'm sorry about that, too. What I did."

Another silence. "That guy, Nikko. You know, when they cut him up, they used a saw."

"You told me."

114

"Sometimes, it would get stuck. In a bone or whatever. The motor would—whine, high-pitched."

I grimace. "That's terrible."

"Yes," he says. "Terrible."

I try to think of something to say that will console him, a bit of good news. "About seventeen thousand," I say before I can stop myself.

"Seventeen thousand what?"

I shake my head. "Nothing. Tell you in the morning."

"Seventeen thousand what?" he says, sharply this time.

I roll away from him, face the wall. "What the money works out to. In American dollars."

He snatches one of the pillows from the bed, then lies down on the floor on the other side of the room.

Neither of us sleeps, but neither of us speaks, either. Heavy silence is broken by the sound of scooters outside or laughing or fucking in one of the adjacent rooms. A high-low siren passes by, and a few minutes later, another.

Terrance is right, of course. About the violence, about the rancid person I've become, and the rancid person I'm asking him to become. Theft and violence as regular occurrences, like doing the laundry. But to live morally means to be captured, means to die or wish you could. One instance of seeing what it's like on the other side, my side— Nikko Kucheto strangled, cut apart—hadn't, apparently, been enough to convince him. And too many instances of seeing it have made me immune.

I drift off sometime before dawn, just when the sounds of the city are replaced by the first birds starting to chirp. It's an uncomfortable, dreamless sleep, in which I'm not all the way there and still conscious of things. Terrance moving around. Terrance showering. Terrance dressing and zipping up his bag.

He's standing by the window, dressed in a white shirt and jeans, when I roll over and open my eyes. I glance around the room and see all his things are gone.

"Hey," I say sleepily.

He turns his head. Not his body, just his head. "Hey." His voice is crisp, certain.

I'm not stupid. I know exactly what he's certain of. I swing my legs over the edge of the bed, stand, and self-consciously wobble for a second.

"Got your passport, doctor?"

"Doctor?"

"Andre Mason."

A fake smile. "Yeah. I forgot."

"Better not forget. Your cover legend, it's important. . . ."

"I know, Gwen."

I nod, bite my lips between my teeth. There's a sob rolling up from my stomach, so I pinch my eyes shut and swallow it back down. "You're not the only one," I say.

"The only one what?"

"Who hates this," I say. "You think I like it? Being this way?"

His shoulders sag. Not what he wanted to hear. "You're doing—what you have to. I get that."

"You're in just as much danger as I am," I say. "I'm sorry that you are. I'm sorry that it's my fault. But, Terrance . . ."

"Not this way," he says, his voice on the edge of anger. "If I go to jail, so be it. If I—get shot. I'm living my way. Mine. I'm not becoming—something I'm not."

"Not becoming *me*," I say, angry now, too. "What you mean to say is, you're not becoming *me*."

Terrance opens his mouth, about to protest. Then he closes it. "Like I told you, when you get to Zurich, look up Naz Sadik."

I raise my hand to my eyes, look away. I swallow down the sob again. "Where will you go—no, better if you don't tell me. I'll e-mail you. The ParallaxMail account, okay?"

"Naz Sadik," he repeats. "I'll reach out. Tell her to expect you."

My body sways back and forth, and I reach down to find the bed, then sit. "Tell me—you feel this, Terrance," I say. "Tell me it's hard for you, too."

In a second, he's in front of me, hands on my cheeks, tilting my head up. He bends and kisses me with very soft lips and says that it is.

Part Two
LILA

Fifteen

In Valencia, spring rain and empty streets. It's another month before the tourists come, and so it's just locals here and visitors from other parts of Spain. My accent won't be mistaken for native—too *porteño*, too South American, and none of that gorgeous sibilance that turns every *s* into a *th*. But I understand and am understood here, and have no trouble remaining invisible.

For two days, I play the visitor, renting a motor scooter and taking a room in a cheap hotel off the beach with a pool out front still empty for the off-season. I buy some cheap black ballet flats and a black cocktail dress of the kind of stretchy material you can shove in the bottom of a backpack and wash in the sink. I also buy a pair of small binoculars from a flea market that accompany me every day for my afternoons at the marina. There I while away the hours at an outdoor café, watching the yachts going in and out of the harbor.

A Gulf prince with a vast belly stands in a Speedo on the deck of an enormous yacht. He squinches his mouth beneath a ferret-sized mustache, surveying the Valencia shoreline like he's thinking about buying it. On another yacht, some pink-skinned tycoon with wisps of snow-colored hair smokes a cigarette in a long holder as he strolls around the deck nude. His girlfriend in a gold bikini, age approximately my own, rises from a lounge chair and languidly fixes herself a cocktail.

This is voyeurism at its very best, so much more louche and interesting than the middle-class domestic vignettes I'd see from my apartment windows in Montevideo and New York and Moscow. But as interesting as the humans in my marina-zoo can be, it's the names on the sides of the yachts that I check out first. They range from the curious—*Anonym II, Meduse*—to the stupid—*NautiBoy, Sail-a-bration.* But the one name I'm looking for, *Erebus,* pulls into the harbor right on schedule late in the afternoon of my second day.

It's enormous, even by yacht standards, and only the masculinity of the Gulf prince remains unthreatened after its arrival. A crew of seven, all in white uniforms, scramble about on deck among elegant white curves and black-tinted windows. An impossibly complicated array of antennas and satellite dishes sprout from the top like a silly hat. Three figures, two dressed mainly in black, and one in a tan suit and open-collar white shirt, climb down a staircase from the ship's stern to the pier. The figures in black are of the same species as Nikko Kucheto, short-clipped hair and bulky builds. The man in the tan suit, trim and handsome behind expensive-looking sunglasses, has a conversation with some official in a uniform who comes out to meet them. It's concluded swiftly, and in a few minutes the three are headed to the street.

I throw down a 5-euro note for my iced tea and circle around the men in the other direction to get a good look. Lovrenc Zoric is even better-looking than in the photo I saw, taller, and somehow more commanding with the added element of kinetic movement. None of the three so much as glance in my direction. I cross the street, start the motor of my rented scooter, and watch as they climb into an idling Range Rover. I wait until the SUV is a half block ahead before I pull into the street after them.

With the thin off-season traffic, I have to hang back farther than

I'd like. The Range Rover climbs a little hill, and I nearly lose them as they cut in front of a bus before taking a left onto a narrow side street. I turn at the last second, cutting through a knot of pedestrians who shout angrily after me. The path Lovrenc's driver is taking is circuitous and designed to prevent exactly what I'm doing, but my scooter is agile and quick and the big SUV is anything but. Exactly as I was taught in Orphan Camp, I use larger vehicles as camouflage, vary the distances, and try to stay out of their sight lines.

After twenty minutes, the SUV pulls up to a busy open-air restaurant next to the beach—MARISCOS DE STAVROS, says the sign. I park my scooter, duck into a public restroom, and change into my cocktail dress and ballet flats. In lieu of jewelry, I put on the other souvenir from the flea market where I bought the binoculars: a five-inch filleting knife in a metal sheath, slim and frighteningly sharp. This goes on the underside of my left forearm, beneath the sleeve of the dress in a strap I fashioned by separating two layers of a leather cuff bracelet.

I carry my backpack over one shoulder and look around like a wandering tourist searching for a place to grab a bite. Mariscos de Stavros is lively and loud, with a trio of Greek musicians making their way around the floor, the bleating melody rising and falling on the wind. Pausing at the stand out front, I pretend to look over the menu as I scan the tables inside for Lovrenc. All I need is five seconds within arm's reach of him. A trip to the men's room, stepping outside for a cigarette—any opportunity will do.

He's in a back corner of the vast patio, seated with a man in a gray suit who's older than Lovrenc by at least twenty years. Lovrenc's two guards join those of his dinner companion at an adjoining table, drinking coffee and keeping wary eyes on the room. I take an empty stool at the bar, where I can see them.

It's very early for dinner in Spain, but whatever meal this is for Lovrenc and his associate, it drags on and on. Soup followed by lobster followed by an enormous fish served whole on a platter. It's a business meeting, though. That much I can see. An intense negotiation about something, with both parties angry, taking turns being offended by something the other says.

By the time Lovrenc picks up the check, however, the two have kissed and made up. The men embrace warmly, and Lovrenc starts toward the door, his guards only steps behind him like the overbearing parents of a toddler. They make a stop at the restroom, but both guards remain outside the door. I duck out of the restaurant, recalibrating how to get close.

The Range Rover is at the curb, waiting, and it's unlikely I'll get the chance here. I climb onto the scooter, wait for Lovrenc and the guards, and once again start following them. But evening traffic is too thin, and I simply can't risk it. I peel away from them and head back to the marina.

It's livelier there, with people strolling and taking dinner at the cafés. A juggler and an accordion player with a monkey on a leash compete for children's attention. A teenage couple leans against a lamppost, making out. I hang around, waiting for Lovrenc's return and formulating a plan. I don't know where they went after leaving the restaurant, but it wasn't straight back here. They show up two hours later and begin walking toward the marina's entrance.

I stop at an ice-cream seller and buy a teetering cone three scoops high, chocolate, vanilla, and strawberry, and start toward them slowly, just a young woman on a stroll, absentmindedly people-watching. Just as they're about to pass me, I sway a little into their path, colliding with the larger of the two guards, and crushing the ice-cream cone against my chest. The guard looks down with a growl, then gives me a little shove as he pushes past.

"*Gilipollas!*" I call angrily at him. Then I switch to Judita's accented English. "Stupid asshole, you ruined my dress!"

This gets their attention, particularly Lovrenc's. He stops in the center of the sidewalk and looks at me over the rims of his sunglasses, then swats the guard in the chest with the back of his hand. "Obrad, you stupid ox. Look what you've done."

The guard's eyes shift from me to him as if trying to figure out if it's a joke. Then Lovrenc comes toward me, smiling, pulling a handkerchief out of the breast pocket of his suit jacket. He rests a hand on my shoulder, dabs at the ice cream on my chest.

"I apologize," he says. "Let me help you get cleaned up."

I reach toward my left sleeve, touch the handle of the filleting knife, then stop as the two guards appear by Lovrenc's side. They produce handkerchiefs of their own and try to follow the boss's lead, but I bat their hands away. "Hey, stop it!"

Lovrenc gives them a smile. "Really, you two. Manners."

I back away from all three of them, knowing the opportunity is gone. "Never mind," I say to Lovrenc. "I'll clean it at home."

"But my yacht is very close," Lovrenc says softly. "We can have a drink while the crew takes care of your dress."

There's inherent menace in the idea, and it's said with such suave charm that I'm certain he's used the line before. Risky to go with him, but on the yacht he'll be relaxed, off his guard. I flash to Nikko Kucheto in Buenos Aires, the fury I'd felt at his intruding into the one private corner of the world I'd carved out for Terrance and me. Now I can return the favor.

"A yacht?" I say. "I don't know."

"Come on," he says. "I promise I don't bite."

I smile shyly. *But I do.*

He walks slowly beside me down the pier, interested in everything the local girl has to say. The guards linger behind a few paces, too close for me to use my knife.

"So what's your name?" Lovrenc says.

"Judita."

"Judita," he repeats. "In English, that's Judith, yes?"

"Yes."

"Do you ever read the Bible, Judita? The forbidden stories, not in the official version?"

"The Apocrypha," I say. "No, only heard of it."

"There's a story about a woman called Judith. Israel is at war, and she seduces an Assyrian general." He rests a hand on my shoulder and grins. "Then she uses his own sword to cut off his head. Good stuff."

Beads of sweat blister on the back of my neck. "Like I said, I've never read it."

We reach the *Erebus*, and Lovrenc steps over the wide gap between the pier and its stern. Right away, I see my mistake. On the yacht, I'll be frisked and the knife found. There's no possible explanation for it besides the obvious one.

"Obrad," Lovrenc calls to the guard. "Give me her backpack, then help her aboard."

I slip my hand under my sleeve and undo the cuff. Lovrenc is worth the risk, and I can always improvise with a fork, a broken wineglass, my bare hands.

Obrad tosses the backpack to Lovrenc, but it turns in the air, sending my boots tumbling out onto the deck. All three men move quickly to keep them from bouncing overboard, and I make a flash decision, dropping the knife into the water between the boat and the pier.

The open deck at the very tip of the yacht is paneled in honey-colored wood polished to a high shine that gives it the appearance of plastic. Soft white light from the lamps embedded in the overhang make the table and china and wineglasses below it glow. The guards have left, but we're very noticeably not alone, either. A female server in a white shirt and black pants stands against the wall, a pressed white towel over her arm.

"Your dress," Lovrenc says, as the server opens a closet and removes a folded blue robe. "Take it off, please. You can wear that in the meantime."

"Take it off here?"

"Yes. Now."

His tone is very plain, businesslike. Nothing predatory about it. Maybe that's the way he operates, like there's never a need for anything but direct orders, casually given.

I pull the dress off over my head, and stand there a moment in bra and underpants as the server helps me into the robe. It's lovely silk, the real thing, with embroidered birds over the breasts. Lovrenc, for his part, doesn't stare or ogle but just looks on indifferently as if I were no more or less interesting than any other object passing through his field of vision.

Then the boat starts to move.

Lovrenc smiles radiantly. "I thought, why not a little cruise? Valencia by night?"

"Stop the boat, please. I'd prefer to stay here."

"Don't worry. You'll be back in a few hours." Lovrenc gestures to a chair. "Sit. Let's talk awhile."

I look for something I can use as a weapon. There's a plate on the table. Pickles and fish and cheese and bread—finger food, no silverware. But there are wineglasses, useful in a pinch.

The reverse motion of the *Erebus* slows, then the yacht shudders as the powerful engines jerk us forward. The server catches me as I stumble. She's a woman a few years younger than Lovrenc, heavy-breasted, and thick through the body, with her face half covered by black hair that hangs down at the sides.

I glance to the side of the boat, estimate four meters to the railing of the deck. I can sprint and be over the side in a few seconds. But Lovrenc knows what I'm thinking and preempts me by pulling a small pistol from beneath his suit jacket. He holds it loosely against his thigh, as casual as a threat can be.

"Plenty of time until the boat turns back into a pumpkin," he says. "That clever thing you did with the ice cream. That's when I knew it was you."

The other yachts, docked for the night, are slipping past as we head toward the exit of the harbor. In minutes, we'll be in open water.

"Knew it was me?" I say.

"The one following us on the moped, the woman at the restaurant bar." He taps the muzzle of the gun on his chair, as if the pistol were an extension of his hand. "Please, you're making me feel like a bad host."

Slowly, I take my seat, ready to burst forward as soon as the gun is down. "I don't know what you're talking about."

He gives me a tired smile. "Tell me: Why did I have you change into that robe?"

"To clean the dress."

"No. So that I could be sure you didn't have a second knife on you. Like the one you dropped in the water."

The boat picks up speed, and I cross my arms against the cold. "I'm not who you think."

"Don't be ashamed," he says, as if trying to comfort me. "Gwendolyn Bloom should never be ashamed of who she is."

Sixteen

Remember this, always: Your cover legend is the only friend you have. So hold on to it as long as you're physically able. Through interrogation. Through torture. And if necessary, die with it. If you can't save yourself, you can at least save the operation. That's what they taught us in Orphan Camp.

But they also taught us this: Rules, held to regardless of circumstances, will kill you. Improvise. Read your gut. Even if it contradicts your training. To surprise your enemy is to subvert him.

Thus, my dilemma.

"Don't you find it tedious, the little narrative they tried to set up?" Lovrenc says, gesturing expansively with the gun, to the boat, the world beyond it. "Your father kills my father, so now we have to kill each other. Amateurish. Amateur bullshit. Please tell me you see that."

I glance over my shoulder to find the server still standing there, face blank, unbothered by her employer's pulling a gun on his guest. "Like I said, I'm not who you think," I say as calmly as I can.

Lovrenc slams the gun down onto the table, hard enough to rattle the wineglasses and plates. I jump at the sound.

"I'm so—disappointed," he says. "Look at you, acting the coward. A monster, they said. Killed a dozen men in Prague, they said. *Pfft*."

He reclines in his seat, gun hand tiredly rubbing the back of his head, daring me with his eyes to go for the pistol on the table. I reach forward tentatively and take my wineglass.

There is, I see now, no way out, no tidy answer to my dilemma. Admit who I am or not, this yacht is where it ends. The fear melts away and is replaced by a not-unpleasant sort of certainty. Getting shot on a yacht off the coast of Spain. So much more interesting than getting hit by a bus or dying from the flu. And the wine really is excellent.

The lessons from Orphan Camp be damned. Lovrenc knows. And more, he knows I know he knows. The labyrinthine circuit is complete, so there's nothing to be gained from pretending. Besides, I may have more to gain with the truth than by continuing a cover story neither of us believes.

I raise my glass in a toast. "To our heroes," I say. "May we never have the disappointment of meeting them in real life."

A relieved grin breaks out across his face. He toasts me, takes a long drink, then looks past my shoulder to the server behind me. "You can take it from here," he says to her in English.

She approaches the table and extends her hand. Perplexed, I rise and take it.

"My name is Dragoslava Zoric," she says. "Lovrenc's sister. Viktor's daughter."

Dragoslava tucks the pistol from the table into the waistband of her pants and says a few words to her brother in Serbian. Lovrenc replies with something that makes her laugh, then he disappears through a door that opens onto a staircase to the lower decks.

"Poor Lavro," she says. "He likes the clothes and the money and the girls, but he never had the appetite. Not for this."

"And what is this?" I say.

Dragoslava brushes back the hair from the left side of her face and

I see a quilt of scar tissue running from her temple to her jawline, some faded to white, some inflamed pink. "If someone came to kill you, how would you answer them?"

"Same way I answered Nikko Kucheto."

"Ah," she says. "Poor, stupid Nikko."

"Your employee," I say.

"Always the idiot of the group," she says sadly. "Did you do it yourself? Personally?"

"Yes."

Dragoslava sighs. "Well, I'm sorry you had to kill him. Sorry, too, for the path that moron put us on."

"Nikko put us on that path?" I say. "And here I thought it was you."

She takes some bread and cheese from the plate, makes a little sandwich. "The CIA trash who came here—well, they never said they were CIA, but one knows. They painted a little picture for us—your father oversees the killing of our father, so now we should continue the pattern."

"The difference is, my father isn't a monster."

She looks at me without emotion. "You're right," she says finally. "The man the world knew as Viktor Zoric was a monster, even if the Viktor Zoric I knew was not. The world is a better place without him in it."

"So why did you send Nikko Kucheto after me?"

"I didn't. Revenge is a silly business. That's what I told the CIA, right before I kicked them off my boat."

A lie. Obviously. But since it ends for me the same way, why bother? I take my glass, take a long drink of wine. "Wish I could believe you," I say.

"No, I suppose you shouldn't," Dragoslava says. "By the way, who was it that sent you? Israelis, I assume."

"I don't work for the Israelis. I came on my own."

"Right," she says. "Well, if you happen to run into them, maybe you could pass on a message."

—

"Sure," I say, playing along as if there's any way she'll let me off this boat alive. "What is it?"

"That the Zoric family is out of the arms business. We don't sell to Hezbollah. The PA. Al Qaeda. Anyone. Can you do that for me?"

"I'll pass it on."

"You don't believe me," Dragoslava says.

"Does it matter?"

Dragoslava rises to her feet and gestures to the staircase. "Come. Something I'd like you to see."

The thrum of the powerful engines on the inside of the boat is a constant roar but not unpleasant. I walk ahead of Dragoslava a few paces, conscious of the gun in her waistband. Conscious, too, of Obrad following behind her. I'd gotten a good look at him as he shoved me aside. Shaved head, a roll of fat on the back of his neck, but sharp eyes, like the intellect inside him is badly represented by the outside.

Dragoslava directs me down a staircase to the level below and along another hallway toward an open door at the end, where I see the gleaming steel of an industrial kitchen. The men inside are speaking in Serbian and laughing until I appear in the doorway. From their card game at a table littered in beer bottles and ashtrays, they look up and stare. Then Dragoslava appears behind me a second later, and they all rush to their feet.

Dragoslava surveys them, then points to a heavy man with a blond crew cut wearing a leather jacket and track pants. "Sergei," she says. "Let's talk awhile."

The others look away from her as they scramble to leave, even Obrad, who shuts the door behind him, leaving the three of us alone. Sergei stands nervously at attention, shoulders straight, eyes forward.

"We'll speak in English, so she understands," Dragoslava says to Sergei. "Now sit. And for God's sake, relax. You're not in trouble."

Sergei does as he's told, clearing his throat and moving his eyes from me to her. His lower lip is trembling.

"I'm told you're Nikko's best friend. Like brothers, everyone says." Her voice is soothing, like an elementary school teacher gently trying to suss out the truth.

"Yes, Dragoslava."

"So then he must have told you where he went on this vacation of his."

A long pause as Sergei works through the problem. "Back to Bulgaria. His father is sick."

Dragoslava nods slowly, then folds her arms over her chest and stares at him, her eyes unblinking through the long silence that follows. Sergei's anxiety is painful to watch. His eyes shoot between her and me and a pack of cigarettes on the table. With each moment, he becomes twitchier to the point I'm almost rooting for him, hoping he comes up with something clever to defuse the situation.

"Nikko is not with his father," he says finally.

"Ah," Dragoslava says. "But you told me otherwise. So you lied?"

"Yes."

Another long silence, then Dragoslava's face brightens suddenly. "Well, you're just protecting your friend, I suppose." She leans forward, places her hand on his. "But I do need to know where he is, Sergei. It's important."

"He's—he took that job," Sergei says quietly, eyeing the pack of cigarettes again and turning a lighter over and over in his one hand. "The Americans who came. When you said no, they went to him. A lot of money, Nikko said."

His whole body is shaking now, and he can't even look at her. Dragoslava leans back in her chair and smiles at him. "Thank you, Sergei. I know that wasn't easy." She pushes the pack of cigarettes to him. "Go ahead."

Sergei fumbles one from the pack, nearly puts the wrong end in his mouth, then finally lights it. His shoulders relax, and he even manages to give a little smile back at her as smoke curls up from his mouth and nostrils. "I'm sorry, Dragoslava. Look, I was scared."

"Of me?" she says. "You were a loyal man to my father for, how long was it?"

He coughs, ticks off time on his fingers. "Ten years, I think. Eleven."

Dragoslava reaches for the pack of cigarettes, pulls one out for herself. "You never need to be afraid of me, Sergei. Remember that. Lighter?"

He slides it along the table toward her. She picks it up, then clumsily drops it to the floor. Sergei bends from his seat to retrieve it.

The gunshot deafens me, sends me to my feet and staggering backward. Dragoslava rises, the pistol from her waistband held loosely in one hand, blood covering the front of her white shirt. She drops the unlit cigarette in an ashtray and pushes Sergei's body over on its side with her foot. A pool of blood starts forming beneath his head, widening with every second.

The door swings open and Obrad rushes in, followed by the others. Without a word, Dragoslava opens a closet door and pulls out a mop and bucket. The men need no explanation; this is just the way things are sometimes. One of them hoists the bucket into the sink and begins filling it. Two others lift Sergei's body by the armpits and haul him toward the door as if he were merely drunk and needed to be put to bed.

She says something to them in Serbian, the words close enough to Russian that I get the gist: *Waters are strong here, so use a lot of weight.*

With the bucket full, Dragoslava sets to work, soaking up the blood and rinsing the mop in water that turns pink, then red. She says something else, a joke I assume, because the men laugh. One of them offers to take the mop, Dragoslava protests, he offers again, and this time she accepts. Another man hands her a towel when she's done washing her face and hands.

The lights on the shoreline twinkle in the darkness like humble stars. There's just a few of them, a little village, though how far away I can't tell. Hard to measure distance on the water. Dragoslava and I are alone on the deck on the port side as the *Erebus* runs north. She's leaning on the railing three meters down from me, while Obrad is off somewhere getting her a change of clothes for her blood-soaked shirt.

She holds the pistol in one hand, a bottle of vodka in the other. "Always be the first to pick up a mop. Those under you respect that," she says. "It shows them you're not too big to do the work yourself. You cold?"

The air is frigid, but Dragoslava seems unaffected by it. I fold my arms over my chest. "A little."

"Here," she says, holding out the bottle by the neck. "Put on your vodka coat."

I take the bottle but don't drink. Just as with the cold, Dragoslava seems unaffected by what just happened, or by the body now making its way to the bottom of the sea. She had pulled the trigger without a second thought, in the midst of a comforting deception. More or less as she's doing now with me. A drink together, a chat on the deck; it's coming any minute.

"These idiots, always testing you, always wanting to see whose dick is biggest." She pushes back from the railing, turns to me with arms crossed. "Never let them doubt who's in charge. Nikko, Sergei—they never would have pulled this shit when Papa was around. There's a saying about power—walking a tiger or something. How does it go?

I take a step closer to her. "Power is like riding a tiger. Hard to get on, even harder to get off."

"Not when the tiger's dead. Then it's the jackals you have to worry about." She takes the bottle back from me. "Two months after they shot my father, a bomb blew up my driver. I was supposed to be in the car, should have been, but I wasn't."

"The risks of the profession," I say.

"Not mine. I never chose this." She takes a drink of the vodka, grimaces as it goes down. "My father's death was the opportunity of a lifetime. Know who set it up?"

"No."

"Bohdan Kladivo," she says. "He was planning a second try when you killed him in Prague."

"You're welcome."

Her fingers tighten around the pistol. "Tell me something. After you killed Lovrenc, what was your plan? Go home? Or go to Switzerland, try to get your hands on those mythical accounts everyone's talking about?"

Once more, she knows the truth without my even having to say it. A little incredulous laugh sneaks out. "I didn't think I was that obvious."

"It's the desperate move; you're a desperate woman." Dragoslava shrugs. "For the record, my father pulled everything out of Switzerland ages ago. If there are any accounts there, it's because they're waiting for someone."

"Waiting for someone?"

"You don't give money to a prime minister or CIA bureaucrat directly. So you set up a company, make them a partner under some fictional new identity."

Exactly as my father described in his doomsday device. "So they're already accounted for."

"Yes. And as far as I'm concerned, someone else's problem. If only the greedy little jackal had asked nicely." She takes a drink of the vodka and smiles at me. "It's too bad about us. I kind of like you. We could have been friends."

I shrug. "Next life, maybe."

"Sure. We'll get coffee." Dragoslava's eyes catch the moonlight as she says this. They're strong and unwavering and go well with the calm on her face. It isn't so different, what she's been through and what I've been through. If not the same species, then at least the same genus. The things I could learn from her.

"I'm glad it's you," I say.

"What do you mean?"

"Who pulls the trigger."

She looks down at the gun in her hand. "Too dangerous to keep you around. Then again, killing someone who saved my life. Some kind of special bad karma there."

Obrad appears on the deck, holding a folded sweater in both hands. Dragoslava slides the gun into her waistband and unbuttons her blood-covered blouse. Her body is just as I thought, thick, with a layer of muscle just beneath the flesh that moves and shifts in the dim light as she balls the blouse up in her hand and tosses it over the side. Obrad hands her the sweater and she puts it on.

A few words between them, and Obrad disappears again.

The two of us are quiet for a time, Dragoslava looking out at the sea, keeping me just in her peripheral vision. A cluster of lights comes into view on the shore. She nods to it. "That town, I stayed at a little inn there once. Woke up at ten, ate clams and drank sangria. Went for a swim. Best afternoon of my life."

"Sounds—like a wonderful place."

"It was. Still is, I imagine," she says. "Good coffee, too. Maybe that's where we'll go. In the next life."

I watch as we approach the lights. The town is on a little penin-sula jutting from the coast. We're about to pass in front of it, a hun-dred meters, maybe two. From here I can see the silhouettes of piers and bobbing boats, small buildings with yellow windows, strings of lights and moving people.

I smile at her. "Why wait?"

Dragoslava blinks. "Wait for what?"

"The next life." I pull the robe off, let it fall to the deck. "Let's have that coffee now."

And then I'm over the side.

Breath explodes from my lungs in a silent cry of shock as the frigid water grates the skin off my body. My primitive dive breaks apart under the surface and I'm scrambling madly back up for air. Just as my lips open to inhale, a wave crashes over me and I suck salt water into my lungs.

But panic will get me nowhere. I cough the water out, take a deep breath of air, and launch myself away from the looming black silhouette of the *Erebus*. I'm no swimmer, have never been a swimmer, and can brag only that it would take me a long time to drown.

I thrash my legs madly, find some kind of rhythm, and manage a graceless backstroke toward the shore. Waves lap over me like nasty, icy surprises and it's all I can do not to gasp each time one strikes. There's another splash beside the yacht, and I lift my head just far enough to see Dragoslava coming toward me in a powerful crawl.

Searchlights erupt from the boat, strafing the water, then land on us. Two more splashes into the water and shouting from the deck. Dragoslava pulls up beside me.

She's obviously a stronger swimmer than I am and, even without the gun, could easily overpower me. But instead, she's in a backstroke beside me.

"You insane bitch," Dragoslava shouts. "What the hell are you doing?"

"Problem with killing," I shout back just as a wave crests over my face. I choke through it. "It gets so easy after a while."

"Drowning is better?"

"Coffee is better."

Dragoslava lifts her head, looking at some activity on the boat. "They're lowering the motor launch. Obrad will have a rifle."

"So decide," I gasp. "Coffee or that. Your choice."

It takes forever to reach land, the motor launch gurgling along behind us the whole way. The certainty I'd felt that she was going to kill me has turned into certainty she won't, at least not now. The bad karma, and the family resemblance: what certain kinds of trauma have etched into both of us. She'd seen that, too. I stumble out of the sea, exhausted and so cold I'm not even shivering anymore, just numb.

Dragoslava sloshes out at the same time, clasps a cold hand to my shoulder. Like me, she'd stripped out of her clothes before jumping in and wears only her bra and underpants. "That hotel," she says. "The restaurant better be open."

Obrad leaps from the launch, pulls it onto the beach, and two more guards climb out. Dragoslava turns to them, shouts instructions. One rushes to us with a pair of blankets. They're thick, scratchy wool, and just the thing we need. My teeth start chattering.

"This way," Dragoslava says, pointing down the beach to a group of small two-story buildings. I follow her, and Obrad follows behind. The two other guards push the boat out to sea, heading, I assume, back to the yacht.

Only three couples are on the patio when we shuffle in, barefoot and dripping from beneath our blankets. A waiter approaches, perplexed, as if we needed medical help.

"Just went for a swim," I say in Spanish, doing my best to smile at him. "Could we have a table?"

He starts to tell me they were just closing up, then Obrad produces a sheaf of euros and suddenly they're open again. So, a nice table for two next to the outdoor fireplace and a pot of coffee, black and strong. Obrad takes his at the bar.

"Can't very well shoot you here," Dragoslava whispers.

I take a sip from the mug, let it scald my throat all the way down to my stomach. "That's the idea," I say. "Something else then. We can arm wrestle."

Dragoslava leans forward, and I see her shoulders heave as if she's weeping, then I hear her laugh. "So—how does this end? Do we hug? Promise to write?"

My eyes are heavy with exhaustion and terror. I let them close. "I don't want to die. Not for shit our fathers did. I'm tired of it."

A long silence and, when I open my eyes, I find Dragoslava looking at me.

"You love him, your father?"

It's a harder question than I want to admit. "Yes," I say. "Do you?"

She stares down into her mug as if the answer were inside it. "He rescued me. Saved my life. So, yes."

"Rescued you?"

"He was Serbian. But born in Bosnia and loyal to it. He found me in Sarajevo during the siege. I was an orphan. Do they teach about Sarajevo in school? Or is it just another far-off event?"

"They mention it," I say. "The Serbs shelled the city."

"And when there was nothing left, they shelled it again anyway. For four years." She lets out a long, tired sigh. "I was half-starved, bleeding, covered in filth. Yes, Viktor Zoric was a monster. But once, for a single moment, in the winter of 1994, he wasn't."

"And your biological parents, they died in the siege?"

"My mother did. As for my father, who knows. In a ditch somewhere, along with the other Muslim men."

"I'm—very sorry."

She's silent for a long moment, dragging a plum-colored fingernail through a long cigarette burn in the table's surface. "But you know all about that, don't you? The file the CIA showed us said your mother died when you were young."

I look down, then nod. "Algeria. I was seven."

She leans forward, meets my eyes. "We don't need to die for our fathers' sins, do we? Can we agree on that?"

"Yes."

"I meant what I said. The Zoric family business is closed. You are not my enemy. And I'm not yours—and whoever you're working for."

"I'm sorry," I say. "For coming after you."

"If there's anything left in Switzerland, you're welcome to it," Dragoslava says. "Compensation for Nikko. And a show of gratitude for killing Bohdan Kladivo before he killed me."

I look at her. The fearsome scar on her face glistening in the firelight. The fearsome gangster she is, or was, still there in the calm of her expression. But despite her power, despite her ability to have killed me at any moment in the past hours, here I am, still alive. Maybe she pities me, or maybe it's something else, or maybe it doesn't matter.

A pair of newcomers enters the patio, and both Dragoslava and I raise our eyes to them. It's the two other guards from the launch, and they hand Obrad my backpack and a small duffel bag, presumably clothes for Dragoslava. Obrad approaches us and sets both down on our table.

"Time to go," Dragoslava says, rising to her feet. "I have just one request."

"Of course," I say. "Anything."

"That you never come near me again." Dragoslava snatches the duffel bag and starts walking toward the door leading to the restaurant.

I pull my jeans and a sweater from the backpack, then dress right there at the table.

Seventeen

My body is exhausted, drained of everything, but I need to keep moving, to get as far away as possible. Dragoslava letting me go was an act of generosity. Of sisterhood and benevolence. But decided then and there, on an impulse. The kind of decision one soon regrets, maybe within minutes. I put on my socks and boots in a little square a block from the hotel and start down a wide road that I hope leads somewhere I can catch a train.

The town ends abruptly at a highway, and I walk along the shoulder for an hour before I hit the next town. It's not a quaint seaside village like the one I just left, but a collection of prefab concrete shops closed for the night and a gas station where eighteen-wheelers chuff and snort as they pull away from the diesel pumps. So no train for me tonight, but maybe the cab of a truck.

I enter the gas station and find an all-night snack bar with a few tables. I buy a coffee and a sandwich in plastic wrap. Avocado turning brown, yellow cheese, and some kind of meat that might be ham or turkey or a Frankenstein hybrid of both. From my seat, I appraise each person who comes in. I could handle myself with any of them when it comes to my safety, so what I'm looking for is someone who looks like they won't ask too many questions.

I put a new SIM card into my phone and log in to the encrypted e-mail I share with my father. The drafts folder is empty except for the two I'd sent him from Buenos Aires and the one I sent from the café table at the Valencia harbor. No replies from him, which means either there's nothing to say or he's been taken. I shiver, both from the cold and the thought, and leave a quick update: *All OK 4 now.*

Sitting here has its own dangers, too. I'm getting sleepy, and the clerk behind the counter keeps eyeing me, waiting for trouble. A call to the cops, a problem with my passport, then it's all over. I run my fingers through my hair and realize it's dried into a snarly mess from the salt water. So I fish a comb from my backpack and head to the bathroom.

In the mirror, I see any driver I might have approached would have been unlikely to take me anywhere. Besides my hair, the makeup I'd put on before going to the restaurant has run down my face and dried in black-blue streaks. So I bend at the faucet and wash as best I can, using hand soap as shampoo.

Someone comes in when I'm in the middle of rinsing, goes into one of the stalls. I don't see her, but I hear her singing to herself in German. I start pulling the comb through my hair when I hear her call out angrily, *Scheisse.* Shit.

"*Bist du ok?*" I say.

Silence for a moment, then a sigh. "You got a tampon?" she says.

"Pad," I say.

"Would you mind?"

I dig through my backpack, find one, then gently tap on the door. It opens a crack and a ruddy hand with bitten-down nails reaches out and takes it.

I finish up at the sink and wipe up the counter just as she's coming out.

She bends over the sink, the tan jacket she's wearing pulled taut over her wide body. "*Danke,*" she says.

I meet her eyes in the mirror. "*Wohin gehen Sie?*" Where you headed?

North, it turns out, traveling empty through Barcelona to Marseille. There she picks up a load of industrial equipment and passes through Italy and Austria and the Czech Republic before dropping it off in Krakow, Poland. The pad I gave her gets me to France, she says, and after that, meals are on me until I get off at my destination, Vienna.

Cordula is the driver's name, and she's been schlepping across Europe for twenty years, she says. Livestock, car parts, toys, gasoline, frozen vegetables—anything that moves by truck, she's moved. Her cab smells dankly of banana peels and spilled coffee, but the seat is accommodating and the music, Chopin, soft.

"Have kids?" I ask as we pull out from the truck stop.

She raises her finger to her lips and gestures with her head to the sleeping area behind us. "She's napping," Cordula whispers.

"Your daughter?"

"Another stray," she says. "Like you."

The other stray, it turns out, goes by the name Sabiha. Cordula picked her up outside Malaga, at a gas station, just like me. "Refugee girl," Cordula says in a low voice. "Syria. Speaks English. Educated."

We talk in whispers for a while longer, then somewhere outside Barcelona, I fall asleep to the sound of Cordula humming along with a nocturne.

I'm out for a solid six hours. Deep, restful sleep, the kind that's rare these days. I don't wake up until we're halfway between Barcelona and the French border.

"So she's alive," Cordula calls out in English when I open my eyes and stretch. "Sabiha, this is—what's your name?"

My mouth opens, but no sounds come out. Then I remember. "Judita," I say.

"Spanish?" says Cordula.

"From Uruguay," I say. "I'm—a student."

"I as well am a student." This from a soft voice behind me. I turn and see Sabiha, a small woman, thin, about my age. She's sitting with her knees tucked up against her chest on a cot that folds out from the wall. She corrects herself: "I am a student as well."

I extend my hand, and she shakes it weakly. "Good to meet you," I say.

"Yes. For me also."

"What did you study?"

"Art. In Beirut. Painting," she says. "Then, in Aleppo, a year of medical school. When there was still a medical school."

"I'm sorry," I say.

"Why? I hated medical school," she says.

In Marseilles, a bit of rest for Cordula. She's parked on the road outside the port in a line of other trucks, waiting for their loads of whatever they'd come for. Sabiha and I walk for a while, squinting into the warm Mediterranean sun as we look for a place to buy food. Cordula had given us a list: tampons, coffee, bananas, toothpaste, supplies for sandwiches.

"Sun feels good," I say.

"Yes?" Sabiha says. "I'd rather the rain."

I look at her. "Why?"

She ignores the question and breathes in sharply through her nose as if trying to identify a smell she doesn't like. "There. A shop."

The store is well-stocked and clean. We split up to gather what we need, and I find Sabiha lingering in front of a cooler of soda. She grabs a few tall bottles, tries to fit them in her full basket. I take them from her, put them in my own.

"I saw tables out front," she says. "We can sit. If you like."

We leave the store with a pair of bags each, settle at one of the tables beside the parking lot, and open two bottles of orange soda.

Sabiha takes a long sip, closes her eyes with her face to the sun, as if she's been waiting for this for a long time.

"Where are you headed?" I ask.

"Artists go where it pleases them," she says, eyes still closed, then spouts a line as if from memory: "*Borders are arbitrary lines drawn by patriarchal agents wishing to preserve their power.*" She laughs at what might be a joke meant only for herself.

I smile along with her. "Berlin might be a good fit," I say. "Lots of artists. Cheap rent."

"Mm," she says. "Maybe. Where go you?"

"Austria first. To see a family friend. Then Switzerland. Zurich."

"Good art in Zurich. A colony, in the west part. I read about it on-line. Maybe there for me, too."

"Expensive in Zurich."

"Artists care nothing about money."

It isn't hope I pick up in her voice, but something closer to certainty. That it will all work out. That what she'd seen before—war, the brutal trip across the sea, whatever horrors the refugee camps provided—were aberrations in her mind, not the real Europe.

I take another sip of soda. It's cold and sweet and very good.

Fifteen hours to my destination, with Chopin turning to Brahms and then Tchaikovsky for the daytime drive, Cordula humming along, knowing every note. An accident outside Venice and the road work between Villach and Klagenfurt in Austria slow us down, so when she drops me off in a little town just west of Vienna, it's too late to catch a train.

Cordula lets me off in front of a plain little hotel. I climb down, thank her again, say good-bye to Sabiha, and watch as the truck pulls away. It stops again fifty meters down the road. The passenger door opens, and Sabiha clambers out, holding a small duffel bag.

She approaches me, grinning, as Cordula drives off. "I decided," she says. "Zurich. The art colony there."

But the last thing I need is a companion. I tell her I have an errand here in Austria, but she's welcome to stay the night with me.

She agrees, and so we take a hotel room together. Thankfully, the clerk doesn't ask for her papers, only mine. In the room—small, with two twin beds, but very clean and smelling faintly of fresh paint—I shower while she watches television. She's still watching when I come out, fascinated by a game show in German, a localized version of an American show where people guess some name or phrase and buy vowels to help them along.

"Do you know German?" she asks, not looking away.

"Some," I say.

"Can you guess this?"

I look at the screen as I comb my hair: St _ _ t _ _ _ t _ _ c _ t f _ e i, says the game board.

"No idea," I say.

"Come on, guess."

I keep combing and sit on the end of the other bed. A contestant, a heavyset man in a suit who looks like an accountant, guesses *d*. A pretty blond in a sequined dress turns a letter in the first word.

"*Stadtluft Macht Frei*," I say.

Sabiha looks at me with delighted eyes. "Yes?" she says. "What does it mean?"

"It's—I don't know. An expression. 'City air makes you free.'"

"Why does city air—have this property?"

I rack my brain, trying to remember the context, or even where I read it. "In medieval Germany, if a peasant could escape to a big city and live there a year, they'd no longer belong to the landowner. They'd be free."

She smiles at the TV screen. "I like this idea."

"I do too," I say.

She doesn't sleep but pretends to. I lie awake, facing her in the other bed, and watch her back lifting the blanket up and down too quickly.

Traffic rumbles by outside all night in a constant low rumble, but it's the soothing kind of noise, like a waterfall. It explains why I don't hear her crying until a long time after she must have started.

I close my eyes and try to ignore it: her problem, not mine, I tell myself. But I know the nature of this particular way of crying, its qualities and causes. It sounds soft, easily defeated, but it's not. It's the sobbing that comes from hopelessness and exhaustion. I'd done it every night my first six months in Montevideo, until I discovered alcohol.

"You okay?" I whisper.

She freezes under her blanket, holding perfectly still.

"Sabiha, you okay?"

A long silence, then, "Fine."

"Are you sure?"

The pain radiates from her like heat, and I feel it all the way over on my side of the room. "Yes," she says. "Fine."

In the morning, we both have breakfast at the train station, croissants and coffee, all of it pretty good for train station food. She's bright and hopeful again, checking the clock on the wall over and over, waiting for the 9:17. That's the way our kind of sadness is, though. The worst of it always comes at night. Whatever hopefulness you can pull together in daylight is never enough to get you through a full twenty-four hours.

She gives me her mobile number, and I promise to call.

"Zurich." She grins as if the idea were impossible, like Shangri-La. "I'll be with much experience when you come. I can show you about."

"Yes," I say. "You can show me about."

An electronic chime signals the arrival of a train, and I rise, throw my backpack over my shoulder. "See you," I say as I give her a hug.

"Very soon," she says.

Eighteen

The train pulls away and I'm alone on the platform. Not much of a station here, just a ticket booth, a sterile waiting room with benches, and a coffee cart already closed for the day. I take a pamphlet from a dusty display—the chamber of commerce welcomes you to Hareth bei Bärenbad. Hot springs, good for relieving arthritis and gout. Hiking trails, breathe the healthful air. St. Michael's Lutheran church, purify the soul. There's a little map on the back, and I find the road where the Pension Alexandra is located.

Late afternoon light reflects off the street, and a somber sedan passes by, shushing over pavement silver with the rain that only moments ago stopped falling. It's Austria here, but Bavarian in spirit. Steeply gabled buildings with stucco walls and exposed beams, two old men chatting on a corner, both wearing russet-colored lederhosen and green caps with feathers—not a costume, just what they wear. If I have my bearings right, Hareth bei Bärenbad isn't too far from Berchtesgaden, where Hitler took his summers, breathing in the cool air scented with pine, every bit as healthful as the brochure promises.

Only two or three shops are still open—just like Valencia, it'll be another month before the tourists start coming—and what few people there are on the streets look me over as I pass. I'm younger than all of them by at least four decades, and my presence here in the off-season is a mild curiosity. A small market on the corner catches my eye. It has shelves out front, piled high with squash and potatoes and apples. Next to the front door, there's a rust stain on the sidewalk in a perfect circle, as if something had stood in that spot for a long time and now is gone. A signpost? No, says something in my mind. Something else. For just a half second, I hear a sound in my memory, laughter, and a tune played over a loudspeaker. A memory mixed with something imagined.

A woman in a long dress and thick-soled sneakers comes out of the shop, hunched over her cane. There's a loaf of brown bread just visible in the burlap shopping bag she carries. She nods at me; I nod back.

Then the sidewalk ends, as does the town, and I'm walking along the shoulder of a road. The hill climbs and the road winds, disappearing at each curve behind overgrown pine trees heavy with rain. How the hell did my dad ever think to hide something here?

In time, I see a little break in the forest, a gravel path barely wider than a car. A small wooden sign, the words PENSION ALEXANDRA painted in white, is posted next to it. Even on foot, I barely see it. Someone driving would have to know it's there. I turn up the steep path, leaning into the climb, my boots crunching on the wet stone. Then the inn comes into view. Gables with blunted points and walls of weathered wooden shingles rise up grandly from the forest floor. A few of the windows are lit, rectangles of yellow cut into the shape of diamonds. I expect a cuckoo to come bursting through a balcony door on the second level and chirp the time. But, instead, the door opens and a woman in a white bathrobe appears. She lights a cigarette, leans on the balcony railing, and taps her ash into a pot of purple flowers hanging over the edge. I can smell a fire burning, and something layered over it—baking pastries. Only a few cars are parked on the unpaved lot out front: a little red roadster, a black BMW just smaller than a limousine, a boxy SUV in white. People with money escaping for a midweek weekend.

In the lobby, the smell of baking pastries is stronger, and in a little parlor off to the side, a maid—hat, frilly apron, the whole thing—is vacuuming a faded rug. At a reception counter at the end of the room, an old man with a head of silver hair is bent over a ledger, writing figures in a column. He's handsome, north of seventy, trim and elegant in a spotless black suit.

"*Guten Abend*," I say.

"*Abend*," he says coolly without looking up.

"I'm looking for the owner," I say. "Walter Kahn."

The writing in the ledger stops, the nib of the pen forming a broadening black period where it came to rest on the paper. He looks up at me over the top of silver eyeglasses. "Just missed him," he says.

"I can wait," I say.

"He'll be a while," the man says.

"I'm not in a hurry."

He studies me as he screws the cap onto the pen. "Gone for the night. Perhaps I could be of assistance."

"I was told to ask for him specifically."

Something flashes on the man's face. A grimace. Anger. Curiosity. "Then why don't I take you to him," he says. "You may call me Herr Mucha."

The loden-green cape over his shoulders snaps in the wind as he climbs the path through the forest. It's dusk now, the light growing thinner with each passing minute. His walking stick taps twice on a root jutting through the soil, a warning.

We hike for what must be a kilometer along a trail that grows narrower and darker with each step. Thick, ancient forest surrounds us. Fairy-tale forest. Talking-wolf-disguised-as-grandmother forest. The wind whistles and groans through it, swinging branches through the air, and it's only my reflexes that keep the woody fingers from slashing at my skin. *You're not welcome here tonight*, the forest seems to say. From somewhere nearby, I hear something enormous and powerful crashing through the brush, and my body tenses in anticipation of the attack that, in any event, doesn't come. The sound bleeds off into the distance as the fearsome whatever moves away from us.

"Stag," the silhouette of Herr Mucha says. "If Walter were here, we'd eat like kings for a month."

The trail ends at a clearing at the top of the hill. The light is hard blue, and there's enough of it that I can see the clearing ends abruptly at the edge of a cliff. There's a valley below, and more forested hills on the other side. I turn back to Herr Mucha expectantly, but he's standing at the end of the trail, hands resting on his walking stick.

"You wanted me to take you to Walter," he says.

I look around, then see the punch line hiding in the shadows of the pine trees on the far end of the clearing. Two gravestones sit side by side, with precarious piles of small stones atop one of them. I approach, not wanting it to be true, not wanting the gravestone to say what I know it says. I fall to my knees, lean in close, and read the inscription. WALTER KAHN. I pinch my eyes shut.

"Four hundred thirty-three," he says.

"What?"

"How many stones there are." There's an implicit sigh in his voice, mourning with the edge worn down. "I bring one every day."

I've missed him by over a year.

Herr Mucha approaches me from behind. "The other grave is mine. For someday. Soon, maybe. Or not."

"I'm sorry," I say, meaning it.

"Why? Did you love him?" His voice is stern again, coming from very close behind me. "There are those who love us. And there are those who want something from us. You are the second, I think."

I nod, slowly, admitting guilt for whatever sin this is. "I'm looking for—for information. It was given to Herr Kahn. Left with him by someone, a mutual friend."

"Whatever secrets Walter kept, they are with him."

"I understand," I say. "I'm very sorry to have disturbed you."

A firm tap of the walking stick on the ground. "No, they are *with* him. There. Beneath. *Buried.*"

"In the—?"

"Good God, no. Just half a meter down. Papers. Myself, I would have burned them, but the old fool insisted they remain intact. Promises and oaths, he said. Someone would come, he said."

A pang of hope lifts my stomach, and I run my fingers over the soil. Rocky. Packed hard. But only half a meter—I could do it with my hands.

"Who did he say was coming for them?" I say.

Herr Mucha clears his throat, lets out a little chuckle. "The Bloom girl, he said. The one who used to come here."

I blink at him through the darkness.

"And here you are, as predicted," says Herr Mucha. "You look just like your mother, you know."

Herr Mucha sits on his own gravestone, watching as I dig. A very slow, very cold rain patters against the dirt as I scrape my fingers through the soil, my nails catching on rocks and twigs. It occurs to me I'm burrowing like a dog, throwing the dirt behind me, between my legs. Is there a polite way to do this, desecrate a grave?

"A young man came down from Paris. Brought the papers personally." Mucha adjusts his cape, pulls it tight over his body. "I didn't know him, but Walter did. Ahmed Tannous."

Something about the name—not the first name, but the last. I know it from somewhere. *Ahmed Tannous who came down from Paris.* That's it—the last name of the man Yael had tracked down right after my dad was kidnapped, Hamid Tannous. He died in front of my eyes, my hands sliding over his chest from bullet hole to bullet hole as I tried to keep him from bleeding out. In the dark, the blood looked just like black ink.

"Ahmed was here only an hour. Didn't even stay the night. He and Walter, they talked in the sitting room. Your father's name was mentioned, and someone else, someone I took to be Ahmed's brother, could that be right?"

I stop digging. "Yes," I say. "That's right."

"You knew him?"

"The brother. Hamid. We met. Once."

"The two brothers, they were friends of your father's. Or colleagues, of a kind. Hamid died, but he left the papers and instructions for Ahmed to deliver them," Herr Mucha says. "Tragic when the young go. I'm sorry to hear about your mother, by the way."

"Long time ago."

"But still." Herr Mucha coughs, shifts on the gravestone. "Your parents—our favorite guests. Winter. Summer. Didn't matter to them."

I glance up at him but can't see his face through the darkness. "You remember them?"

"Oh, certainly," he says. "As for you—quiet, curious. Liked to explore."

"I came here, too?"

"You were a great friend to Frau Wexler—she was the housekeeper then. Off to the market the two of you would go, for bread and vegetables. *Mein kleiner Helfer*, she called you."

My little helper. I close my eyes, remember the odd nostalgia I'd felt passing through the town in the valley. The sound of laughter and music from a tinny speaker. Then, an image: a pink hippopotamus made of cracked fiberglass. Motion. In a circle. "I remember—a carousel," I say. "Pink. And purple. It was old."

"Ah! Exactly so. In front of the grocery. Cost a pfennig—back when there were pfennigs. You'd beg Frau Wexler for a ride every time. '*Nilpferd reiten! Ich will das Nilpferd reiten!*' Your German isn't much better now, by the way."

Strange to be with a stranger in a strange place and find everything so familiar. I imagine us, me and my parents, walking the path to this clearing. My father and a shadow that is my mom, the space where her face would be a Cubist's mosaic of my memories and the photos I've seen.

I'm standing in a hole that's just past my knees when my fingers slide across the surface of something smooth. I probe through the dirt to find the edges, then pry it free. Herr Mucha's flashlight switches on as I hold the object up and squint at it. Black plastic sheeting bound tightly with electrical tape. It's a package the size of a ream of paper. I glance over to him.

"There it is, what you came for," he says. "Now fill it back in, if you please."

I set the package aside and start pushing the dirt back into place, feeling Mucha's eyes on me as I work. Fifteen minutes later, I rake my fingers over dirt that's quickly turning to mud in the rain, blending it in with the soil around it as best I can. I keep doing this until Herr Mucha rises and says, "Enough." Then we begin back down the path, he in front with the flashlight, me in the rear, the dirt-caked package held tightly in my hands.

"You will stay the night, of course," he says over his shoulder. "I'll have it made up for you—room thirty-three—your parents' favorite."

"They came here a lot?"

"Four, five times a year. All of them did. Like a club." The lights from the inn come into view, warm-looking, welcoming. "For some reason, our place was popular among their type."

"Their type?"

"*Der Geheimdienst*," he says.

Spies.

The door of the room clicks shut behind me, and I set the key with its flat diamond-shaped fob—*Zimmer 33*—on top of a dresser. Moonlight streams through the window, catching the gauzy curtain and making shapes on the white eiderdown folded across the bed. Once again, I picture my parents. They're lying on the bed while I play on the floor. Or maybe my mother's over there, in that worn-out armchair, the brass lamp next to it switched on as she reads a book. Or maybe I've gone to the market with Frau Wexler, and they're giggling and cuddling and trying to keep quiet.

I look away, squeeze the package in my hands. Whatever's inside is why I'm here, I remind myself. It's the only why that matters. I scratch at my left cheek, where something is tickling me, and discover my skin is wet.

In the bathroom, I turn on the lights and start the shower, passing the head over the package, letting the water drill away at the caked soil. When it's clean, I tear at the plastic sheeting and tape with my fingernails.

Herr Mucha had packaged whatever is inside with great care, wrapping it so well that it might have lasted decades, if not centuries, there in the ground above Walter Kahn's coffin. When I finally get the plastic off, I'm holding a rectangular metal ammunition box, dark green and dented, a discarded bit of trash from someone's army. I undo the latches cautiously and lift the top, as if there might be a monster inside waiting to be set free. But it's just a fat envelope made of cardboard with accordion sides, held shut with red string around a little tab. The envelope has the formal, old-fashioned feel of something a lawyer might use to protect important documents—the deed to the house, someone's last will and testament. I undo the string and slide a thick packet of papers into my hand, and a little surprise, just for me.

The passport was issued in Budapest by the government of Hungary, to one Lila Kereti, aged twenty-four. She bears a striking resemblance to me. In fact, she is me. I recognize the picture as identical to the one on Gwendolyn Bloom's old US passport. Its presence here, however, doesn't surprise me. As soon as the burgundy passport slipped from the envelope, I knew I'd find my own photo inside. That's the way it is here; this is what gifts look like.

It's my father who sent me here, so I can only assume this is his doing. But why this—I flip back to the identity—Lila? Why Hungary? I don't speak the language and haven't even been there. As far as cover identities go, it's paper thin, certainly nothing to build a life on.

I set it carefully on the floor and turn to the papers. It's at least one hundred pages total—no, more than that, twice that. Some of the documents are in densely typed German legalese. Those that aren't, mostly have officially stamped translations in English or French attached. How to begin? Where? This piece of paper, for example, looks very important, with embossed seals and indecipherable signatures printed on a single sheet of creamy linen paper. *Freistellungsbescheinigung,* it says at the top. Exemption Certificate. But what is it exempting, and from whom? The rest of the document would require someone with far more fluency than me. I flip to another document and drag my finger over a random sentence, translating as I go: "... shall be deemed to be in compliance with the *Bundesdatenschutzgesetzes.*" Federal data-something-something. Oh, sweet German, how you just roll off the tongue.

I switch on the bedside lamp and it forms a gold semicircle of light on the parquet floor. As if beginning an enormous jigsaw puzzle, I spread out the papers, looking for the squared-off corners, the continuations of lines and colors between pieces. The documents are, to a one, dull and lifeless, meant for a lawyer's eyes, not mine. Then I see it, the thing bringing them all together. I spot it first on a list of shareholders for a company called Webb-Rosenthal AG. No one named Webb or Rosenthal is mentioned, but three Russians are, along with three Chinese, an Arab, and one Hungarian. The Hungarian's name is Lila Kereti.

In the next stack, a certificate of incorporation for a company called España Shipping AD. Despite its name, the certificate was issued by the government of Macedonia. The company owns three ships flying Liberian flags, and leases two more, flagged in Panama. Again, a list of shareholders, German, Italian, and Spanish names mostly, except for the single Hungarian, Lila Kereti.

I thumb through a set of excruciatingly detailed documents spelling out the terms of sale for a company called Fomax Optical Instruments, based in Zagreb. It was sold to a group of investors in Paris five years ago for 75 million euros. Once again, Lila Kereti's signature appears on the final page as the seller. Same with the lease for something called a strong room at someplace called Ports Francs et Entrêpots de Genève SA. The lease is for twenty years, and Lila Kereti paid it all in advance, in cash.

In total, there are documents for five corporations and two non-profit foundations. Construction. Manufacturing. Shipping. Medical research. Each organization has a different purpose. Each was formed in a different European country. In fact, there is only one point of overlap, a single shared node of DNA: the signature of Lila Kereti.

I rise from where I'd been crouching and feel a rush of blood as my vision tunnels into blackness. I stagger, feel for the bed, and sit. The passport isn't a cover ID at all. It's an escape hatch from whatever destruction the doomsday device will unleash. Just as my father and Terrance described, the key isn't account numbers and passcodes, but documents, paper, lawyers' handiwork. It doesn't lead me to the money, so much as lead the money to me.

My fingers roll the passport over and over in my hands, and I touch each page looking for a sign of cheapness, a sign that it's just a counterfeit. But it looks and feels as real as a passport gets. It, *she*, is a gift to me, a gesture from father to daughter, an act of protection. He's a brave man, my father, and, I believed—and perhaps still do—a good man. But this, all this, shows a cunning I hadn't thought him capable of. A fluency in the ways of high-functioning thuggery that means he was more than an observer to bribes and swindles but was maybe even their organizer. It's obvious why he pointed me in its direction only at the last moment; it shows he's guilty of more than he let on, and this was the only way he could find to save the horses.

There's a polite knock at the room's door. I scramble to pick up the papers and answer it. But it's just the maid, sent to tell me dinner will be served in the dining room in five minutes.

I change into the black pants and sweater I'd brought, both horribly wrinkled from being rolled up in the bottom of my backpack. Then I wash up at the bathroom sink in the light of two flickering yellow bulbs. I catch my face in the mirror, and for just a fraction of a second, a photograph of my mother lingers in my sight instead. She would have looked in this mirror, just as I am now. She would have scrubbed soap in circles over her cheeks, just as I am now. Combed her black hair. Gathered it into a ponytail with a rubber band.

A weekday evening in the off-season. Only four couples—hushed conversation, the quiet clinking of silverware against porcelain—share the dining room with us. Herr Mucha's table sits apart from the others, in the far corner, pinched between an enormous stone fireplace and a window with lace curtains. Leek soup is followed by duck breast. A sweating bottle of Riesling rests on a coaster.

"Walter's cancer—it took its time. When it ended, part of me was glad. For his sake."

I try to think of something to say other than a feeble apology, but I can't.

"We were so fond of them, your parents." Herr Mucha looks at me, smiles. "They would put you to bed, and Walter and I would drink brandy with them in the parlor. Your mother's German was perfect, like an aristocrat's. Not a preposition out of place. Your father's was—barbaric. Like yours."

"You said before, 'their type.' Security services. Was she—also part of that?"

Herr Mucha blinks, understanding the question. "Certainly it was never said, not directly. But I have no doubt. Your mother, she was respected by the others—*deferred* to."

So another lie of omission from my dad. I try not to be angry, or at least put the anger on hold for when I see him again. I would have been happy to keep her the way she is in my head, all love and good-ness, the soft things. But of course she wasn't just that—it's not how the world works.

"And what were they like? Personally. With each other."

"That disgusting kind of newlywed love. Hands always touching. Kissing between dinner courses. I didn't approve, of course. 'So Ameri-can,' I'd say. But Walter—he'd say, 'They're the reason we do this.'"

I look down, trying to feel them here. Touching hands, kissing, maybe at this very table. The soft yellow light, the white of the table-cloth. *Gemütlich* is the adjective for it in German: homey, cozy—but deeper than that, almost untranslatable. It's how you talk about the place you always want to be, the place you wish you were whenever you're not. This inn, this dining room, it would have all been just the same as it is now. Places like this don't change. Men like Herr Mucha don't change. It's what makes the Pension Alexandra *gemütlich*.

"Now, here you are. Carrying on the family business," Herr Mucha says with a little smile.

"No," I say. "I'm not like them."

"You didn't *choose* to be like them, you mean," he says. "But the world doesn't care much for what we choose. How is it, by the way?"

I swallow a sip of Riesling. "The dinner? Very good."

"No. Walter's package. Did it solve all the world's mysteries?"

I watch him carefully, eyes sharp for his reaction. "It's just—legal papers. Contracts. Certificates. I don't know what they're for."

"That's Walter." Herr Mucha gives a shrug and a sad smile. "How better to answer a riddle than with another riddle."

I lean forward. "Do you know the name Lila Kereti?" I say quietly.

He stabs a piece of asparagus with his fork but otherwise shows no sign of recognition. "Hungarian, by the sound of it."

"Yes. Or so I would assume."

"Can't recall anyone by that name," he says. "Perhaps no one can. Perhaps she's just paper."

"Just paper?"

He looks away, eyes lingering with an innkeeper's indifference on a couple at another table, a middle-aged man and a woman of maybe twenty-five. "Those two," he says to me very quietly. "Checked in yesterday. 'Herr Schmidt,' he says. Then he gives me a passport with his picture and the name Herr Schmidt."

I study the couple for a second, then shake my head. "I don't understand."

"He is Herr Schmidt," Herr Mucha says. "Because his passport says he's Herr Schmidt."

Just then, a waiter arrives with dessert, Sacher torte, of course. They like their cakes dry here and it crumbles beneath my fork.

I take a bite and study Herr Mucha. My parents trusted him, and I find myself trusting him, too. "I need a favor," I say. "If you can."

He looks up from his dessert.

"The identity papers I'm using. I'm worried."

A sip of wine and a nod of his head. "Getting a little worn out, is she?"

"You were involved in that world."

"On the margins only."

"But still. Do you know someone who—can help with that?"

He thinks for a moment. "Where are you headed?"

"Zurich," I say quietly.

"You go east, Poland, Romania, I know a few. Best forgers in the world, those old communists. But in Zurich—" He looks down, dragging up something from deep in his memory. "Vidor. He was called Vidor. Ran a store. Antiques."

"And he's good?"

"Never had a call for such things myself, but his reputation was quite good." He reaches for the bottle of Riesling, refills both our glasses. "Vidor Sonnenfeld, that's it. At least what he went by."

"Thank you," I say. "For that—and everything else."

Herr Mucha wipes his mouth with a cloth napkin. "It's nothing. We all need friends," he says. "In desperate times, most of all."

. . .

In room 33, I spread the papers out again, searching for some link besides Lila Kereti, but I can find nothing. The businesses and charities are nonsensically diverse, as if Lila had purposely chosen them so no link could be drawn, one to the other. And who was this Lila before she was me? A paper person, as Herr Mucha had said, a fictional notion someone, perhaps my own father, crafted? Or had she been real, or still is real, before I stole her name?

Eventually I fall asleep on the floor surrounded by the contents of the package. At some point in the middle of the night, I wake up and climb into the bed, where I shiver beneath the eiderdown. Sleep comes and goes in nervous fits, the storm of paper and big German words and a faceless woman in my mind never quite leaving me alone.

In the morning, Herr Mucha waves his hand dismissively when I ask him what I owe. I thank him again, and he inclines his head gravely, once more the formal innkeeper.

I hitch a ride with the handyman who's heading to the hardware store in town for a new showerhead. He drops me at the train station and I buy a ticket to Zurich from a sleepy clerk reading a fashion magazine. One-way or return, she asks. One-way, I tell her.

Nineteen

Sublime chaos in the Zurich train station, masses of people moving in perfect coordination, no one tussling, no one breaking the rhythm. I slide out onto the street and find myself in what a map on the train station wall says is the Altstadt, Old Town. Fussy, well-kept architecture. Neckties worn tight. Jackets buttoned. Shoes gleaming. There are no bums, no drunks, no litter. A particular German idiom pops into my mind: *Alles ist in Ordnung.* Not merely all is in order, but all is as it should be—an aesthetic commandment, but also a moral one.

I buy a prepaid long-distance card with cash and find a phone booth. On the train, I'd checked the encrypted e-mail again and found nothing since the message I'd left in Spain. Thus, drastic action, breaking cover, if only for a moment. I thumb through the scraps of paper in my backpack until I find the number I'm looking for, then dial it. It gives a scratchy ring, and I picture the phone on Señora Lopez's kitchen wall, mustard yellow, forty years of accumulated cooking grease.

An old woman's voice answers, and I hear a soap opera in the background.

I deepen my voice, try to sound bureaucratic, official. "Señora Lopez?"

"Sí?"

"I'm looking for a tenant of yours. Perels. Do you know how I can reach him?"

There's a long pause, as if the old lady had turned back to her television and forgotten about me. "Perels," she repeats. "He's gone. They're gone."

I freeze, have to move my mouth away from the receiver so she doesn't hear my shaking breath. I clear my throat. "Gone. Very interesting. Did he—move out?"

"Last week. I saw him leave with one bag. He owes me rent."

"Did he leave alone?"

"No, with his entourage of a thousand friends. Of course alone. Perels is always alone. Who is this?"

"I'm—collecting a debt."

"Try that daughter of his, Judita, she works at . . ."

I hang up the receiver, press my head to the phone-booth glass. Alone. On the run, alone. Better than the alternative. Something spooked him, sent the mouse scurrying. I have no choice but to calm myself, rely on faith that he'll be in touch soon.

For a time, I walk down a cobblestone street of elegant little boutiques, cocktail dresses and shoes and handbags displayed in windows with the style and reverence of treasure in a museum. A blond woman, some Scandinavian-looking goddess, departs through the door of a shop, carrying her customer's bags to a waiting dark-windowed Range Rover, speaking to her in chummy Mandarin. Even on the cobblestone street, she never falters in her heels, never even looks down.

I stop at another kiosk and buy a SIM card and three-day transit pass, then call the number Sabiha had given me. It goes to voice mail, so I text her: *in zurich you free?* An answer comes a few minutes later: *address hard to find meet you aarhauerstrasse tram stop 45 min ok?*

The passengers file onto the number 4 tram in an orderly fashion, no shoving, no rudeness. A schoolboy of seven or eight, riding unaccompanied, gets up from his seat immediately as an elderly woman steps in. Only a whispered exchange of *thank you; of course* takes place; this is what schoolboys do here, and not doing it would be unthinkable.

It's a quick ride to Sabiha's place northwest of the Altstadt, the old part of the city giving way to arching concrete railroad bridges and gleaming glass-and-steel cubes, like an architect's dreamscape of utopia's gritty side. We pass by a design museum, an ad agency, a public library that looks sleek and clean like a science lab, funky restaurants and clothing boutiques—hipsterland with Bauhaus discipline.

The tram's robot-voice announcer calls out the Aarhauerstrasse stop and I climb off with two or three others. A woman in a canvas jacket and baggy, paint-spattered jeans rolled up at the ankles leans against a light pole. Her hair is tucked under a baseball cap, also spattered in paint. "Judita!" she calls out.

Sabiha is transformed, her face bright and every movement electric with excitement. A long hug, with her rocking me back and forth as if I were a returning sister. She pulls back, eyes shining from within thick circles of black liner. "You made it, Judita!" she says, beaming.

Sabiha leads me down a street of industrial sheds and fenced-off empty lots. "You'll stay with me, of course. With us. It's not much, but there's a place on the floor for you, if you want it."

"Us?" I say. "You're staying with—a friend, relative?"

"No, I have a job. Artist's assistant. His name is Peggo. He's a painter. Also, mixed media. You've heard of him?"

I shake my head. "I don't think so. You're roommates, or—something else?"

"He lets me stay in his studio." Sabiha squeezes my shoulder. "Others, too. It's an artists' collective."

We come upon a yard stacked with steel shipping containers a few hundred meters later. As Sabiha leads me into a courtyard between them, I see the containers have all been converted into houses and studios and shops, some welded together horizontally, others stacked on top of one another. The battered steel walls are fading yellows and reds and blues and still bear the names and logos of the companies they belonged to.

"This is where you live?" I say.

"I call it Lego Village," she says, opening her arms expansively in a Y. "And we're all just tiny villagers living tiny lives."

A few of the other Lego Villagers mill around, arguing about art, smoking, sorting through piles of scrap metal. They pay no attention to us.

Sabiha leads me into a complex of five shipping containers at the end of the row that appear from the outside to be arranged and stacked randomly at odd angles. Inside, however, they've all been welded together to form a contiguous space. Wooden shelves are stacked neatly with rolls of paper and canvas, and tables are arranged with careful rows of brushes and tubes of oil paint. Five or six others, men and women, are gathered here and there, working or in earnest discussion. The man Sabiha identifies as Peggo looks up at us from his position in the center of a large canvas spread across the floor. He wears a paint-splashed set of white coveralls that looks like a hazmat suit, and he has a long reddish-brown beard with hair clipped so close I can see his scalp. He steps carefully over the canvas and removes a pair of white shoe covers.

"Viewing hours aren't until tomorrow," he says tiredly. "Sabiha, you know better..."

"She's not here to buy, Peggo. This is my friend," Sabiha says. "I told you, remember?"

"Ah, the Argentine," he says. "Judas?"

"Judita," I say. "Good to meet you."

"Sorry, *Judita*. Welcome to our home." He gestures around the studio. "Take what you need. Here, all belongs to all."

Part of Sabiha's role as assistant is making Peggo's dinner. So I give her a hand preparing the kale-and-tomato salad and buckwheat porridge that are, Sabiha tells me, his dinner seven days a week. Afterward,

Peggo climbs a ladder to a shelf two shipping containers up and is asleep by nine. Getting up every day before dawn, Sabiha tells me, is another part of his routine. She and I depart to another shipping container down the path, an improvised bar where the other Lego Villagers gather around a fire pit just outside for beer and whatever food the owner feels like making. We eat grilled sausages and some kind of dense, chewy oat bread, and wash it down with bottles of pilsner. In the firelight, Sabiha's face is orange and happy.

"He's kind, Peggo. Teaches me in exchange for cleaning his brushes and making his meals." She finishes the last of her beer. "Another?"

"That's all he has you do?"

Her eyes narrow as she looks at me, hearing an implication I may or may not have intended. "Poor little refugee girl," she says in a high voice. "Careful the big city doesn't take advantage!"

"That's not what I meant. . . ."

"It is exactly what you meant," she says. "Now, do you want another beer or what?"

Sabiha heads to the bar for another round, and I watch her, giddiness expressed in every step, hope in the tone of her voice—*Stadtluft macht frei*. Maybe I was patronizing her. Maybe I'm a cynical bitch who just needs to be somebody's big sister. Or maybe I'm right. Maybe even in Lego Village there are monsters.

She returns, bearing another bottle for each of us.

"How long will you stay?" she says.

"I'm not sure," I say.

She takes a long drink, then stiffens. "You miss it, where you're from? Where was it again?"

"Uruguay." I shake my head. "It's just a place."

"But you must miss, I don't know, your people."

I close my eyes, the beer and exhaustion hitting me at once. "I don't really—have a people."

Sabiha rolls her eyes. "Everybody does."

I shake my head. "Then I haven't found mine yet."

The mattress is old and stained, the horse blanket smelly and scratchy. All night, artists snore, water drips from a thousand sources, eighteen-wheelers wheeze by on the road just outside. And whenever I close my eyes, there he is, my father on the run.

He's good at running. Must be, with his experience. He knows where to go. Whom to trust. How many times when I was growing up had I seen him work a salesman in a bazaar, a traffic cop, a dignitary with medals on his chest? He was a master of the well-placed idiom in the local dialect, the sly joke, just barely off-color, that made a co-conspirator of whoever heard it. He almost always got what he wanted, a better price, a torn-up ticket, maybe a secret or two.

But all that was before Montevideo. Before Prague and Paris. Before the world had broken him and pushed both of us to the very edge of what two people could endure, then a little beyond. So which version is on the run, old Dad or new?

In the morning there's the chaos of breakfast and too many people around and not enough privacy. Washing turns out to be low on Peggo's list of architectural priorities. So when it's my turn, I bathe in a garden behind his studio surrounded by corrugated steel, using a hose and standing in a child's inflatable swimming pool. I'm frozen, nearly hypothermic by the end.

On the train from Austria, I'd noticed a tickle in my mind, something just there beneath the surface of consciousness, like an idea that didn't know it wanted to be an idea. Now, as I dress and slide my stocking feet into my boots, I find something digging into my right sole. I reach in and discover the small envelope with the diamonds I'd taken with me from Buenos Aires. It had slipped from between the layers in the insert where I'd stashed it. And that's when the idea breaks free.

The 4 tram drops me off across the river past the Altstadt, and I peek through the windows of the jewelry stores, looking for one that's well-off, but not too fancy. I find it a few blocks in from the river, dingy carpet and flickering fluorescent lights, but well-stocked glass cases.

The man behind the desk wears a jeweler's loupe over one eye and doesn't look up from his work when I enter. Egyptian pop music plays softly from the radio next to him. "What can I help you find?" he calls in German.

"I'm selling," I say in the same.

"What a coincidence, so am I," he says, still not looking up. "You'd have better luck elsewhere. Take the train up to Antwerp for the day."

I switch to Arabic. "They belonged to my grandmother. I just want to get rid of them."

The loupe goes up, and he squints at me from across the room. "All right," he says after a moment. "I'll take a look, but I can't promise anything."

I give him four of the five diamonds, keeping the largest in my pocket, and watch as he sets the stones out on a velvet cloth and inspects them. He's a careful appraiser, holding each one in tweezers and squinting through the loupe. When he's done, he turns to an old Rolodex and starts flipping through the cards. "Mendy, in Antwerp. A friend of mine. I'll give you his number. . . ."

"What will he give me for them?"

"Five or so thousand for this one, and the others—three to four each."

"Fifteen all together?"

"If you find Mendy on a good day."

"Antwerp, though. So far." I look at him from across the desk. "How about you give me ten?"

The man sighs, inspects them again. "Let me call my wife," he says.

So it's back on the 4 tram, north to the sleek public library I'd seen from the window when I'd first arrived. There's no temple-like quality to the place as there is in the best libraries elsewhere, no soaring ceilings or well-loved wooden furniture. My initial impression had been right— this library is like a science laboratory: clean white surfaces, humming computer stations, immaculately even rows of books, all in pristine condition. I find an empty computer and start working.

Publicly available news sites first, then legal databases. When I turn up nothing, nothing at all, the lack of results delights me. So on to the second step, the search string, *Vidor Sonnenfeld antiques Zurich*. Sketchy information here, irrelevant or old. The Facebook page of a music producer in San Francisco with the same name, who worked on an album called *Zurich* and collects antiques as a hobby. A mention in a travel forum from 2007 about places to find rare books in Switzerland. A community directory of businesses in the neighborhood east of the Altstadt. I jot down the address.

I take two different tram lines to a sober neighborhood of older apartment buildings. MANUSCRIPTS RARE AND UNUSUAL, it says on a hand-lettered sign in the shop window. A bell tinkles as I open the door and step inside. Dust motes dance in the light like far-off galaxies and the air smells of aging paper and an old woman's perfume, the strong stuff, unsubtle, meant to be noticed. Shelves filled with old books line the walls, and documents in cheap wooden frames hang in the spaces between. A signed letter of congratulations from Pope John Paul II to a Spanish soccer star. A note from President Reagan to an Austrian diplomat wishing her a happy birthday. I pick up a book from a table, a German-language copy of *Catcher in the Rye*, and read the handwritten English inscription inside the front cover: *Best Wishes! Your friend, J.D. Salinger.*

From the back of the shop, a tiny silhouette appears, filling one corner of a doorway. "We are closed. Come back Tuesday," the silhouette says, voice feminine but gravelly with age. "Or maybe Wednesday, I don't know yet."

The silhouette steps into the light. Her gray hair is pulled back into a bun, and she's wearing a man's baggy black suit pants, old-fashioned suspenders, and a white dress shirt rolled at the sleeves.

"I heard J.D. Salinger never gave autographs," I say.

"He didn't," the woman says. "For you, twenty percent off." She smiles, as if reading my mind, then takes the book from my hand and sets it back on the table. Her nails are painted fire-engine red.

"Novelty collectibles," she says. "If other people claim they're authentic, that is their concern."

"A friend told me about your shop. I'm looking for Vidor Sonnenfeld."

"*Vidor.* Vidor's retired. Alzheimer's." She hooks her thumbs behind her suspenders. "Anyway, as I said, we're closed."

She turns and starts back toward the stockroom in the back.

"Herr Mucha sent me," I say suddenly. "From the Pension Alexandra. Said I could—said Vidor would help me. Please."

The woman stops and turns slowly, eyeing me carefully. "How is the old man?"

"He's well," I say. "His partner, Walter . . ."

"Died. I know." She sighs like I've interrupted the rhythm of her day with something unpleasant. "Mucha called me a day or two ago. Said to expect someone."

I hold up the J.D. Salinger book. "I'm looking for a novelty collectible," I say. "Custom made."

She purses her lips and nods, then moves to the door and locks it. "My name is Miriam. It would be better if you didn't tell me yours. Come."

I follow her to the back of the shop through a cluttered room stacked high with books and papers. She produces a key and unlocks a narrow wooden door that opens onto a descending staircase. "Mind the third step," she says.

Miriam leads the way, climbing gingerly over yet more stacks of books and papers, skipping the third step, which is only half there. In the basement, most of the plaster has been stripped away from the walls, leaving bare brick.

"Vidor's studio, now mine," the woman says, switching on a lamp on the corner of a desk. "So, a collectible you're after. A passport, I suppose?"

"A passport I have. What I need is everything else."

"And the purpose? Your goal? You want to get through more than a casual police inspection, I imagine."

"Much more," I say.

She leans forward. "How much more?"

I feel my shoulders stiffen. "I need to—prove who I am. Legally."

"Pinocchio wants to become a real girl." The ends of Miriam's mouth curl into a faint smile. "Very well, then. A full suite of supporting documents. Birth certificate. Driver's license. Apartment lease. A nice, rounded-out picture."

I place the Lila Kereti passport on the desk in front of her. "Everything needs to match this."

"Hungarian, current issue, Series C," Miriam says, squinting at it with an appraiser's eye. "*Örvendek*," she says.

I blink at her. "Sorry?"

"It means 'nice to meet you' in Hungarian." She laces her fingers in front of her and leans back in her chair. "Really, you couldn't pretend to be someone whose language you actually speak?"

"No," I say. "It has to be her."

She sighs and picks up the passport, inspects the pages inside. "All right, then. You moved as a child. Speak French? Spanish? Your German is . . ."

"I know. Spanish, then. I'm fluent."

"So a nice address in Barcelona for"—she flips to the identification page—"Miss Lila Kereti."

"How is it? The passport?" I say. "Does it look—real?"

Miriam inhales sharply. "No, I'm sorry to say."

"What's wrong with it?"

Miriam slides the passport toward me, taps a red nail in the center of the page. "Look closely," she says. "You see the tiny musical notes? It's an anti-counterfeiting device introduced in 2009, almost impossible to reproduce." She turns to another page where a holographic seal twists and undulates in the light of the desk lamp. "Same again here, found only on the Series B and C, changed to something else for the Series D."

I shrug. "I don't understand."

Miriam closes the passport and gives it a little pat. "This is either an authentic issue, or the best forgery money can buy."

"So, where's the problem?"

"What's missing, darling, is you," Miriam says. "This passport is too perfect. It needs to be lived in. A work of art like this, it *deserves* to be lived in." She opens a desk drawer and slides the passport into it. "Leave it with me. Miriam will take care of it."

Twenty

A new life for 7,000 francs—half now, half on delivery. Miriam bitches mightily that the specifics are too specific, that the new biometrics are going to take more time than I'm giving her, that 7,000 isn't nearly enough, not for quality work like this. But Miriam is also an artist, and complaining about restrictions and deadlines and costs is what artists do. So come back in four days, Miriam tells me, and don't bother showing up unless you have the second half of the money.

So for four days I linger around the studio, helping Sabiha and Peggo and the artists who are a breed apart from Miriam. Their work is creating truth from the tools of imagination: paint, scrap metal, expression. Whereas Miriam creates lies from the tools of literalism: official stamps and fingerprint scans and the fetish objects of bureaucracy.

My tasks—cleaning brushes, preparing canvases, tearing out the springs from old mattress frames—are pleasant, requiring just enough attention that I can lose myself in them for hours at a time. I even learn to handle an acetylene torch and how to talk about art: negative space, simulacra, juxtaposition, form, and material. With a little practice, and without my actually making anything, the artists accept me as one of their own.

Late in the afternoon on the third day, I sit in paint-spattered cover-alls with Sabiha and the others in the yard outside the Lego Village bar, drinking coffee. Sabiha is arguing about how the disparate shards that make up postmodernist art can't really find an audience until they define themselves the way modernism did. The others take issue, arguing that postmodernism is defined precisely by its rejection of definitions.

Peggo wanders into the firelight and takes the seat next to me, sipping a cup of tea and smoking a joint. "Have some, Judas."

I pinch the joint between my thumb and forefinger, take a puff for form's sake. It was never my thing, but I tell him it's good and pass it back.

"So, does Judas have a manifesto?" he says, taking another drag, talking through a clenched throat.

I look at him.

"What is your philosophy? What guides your work?"

"I'm not really political."

"No? Good for you. Myself, I used to be a Marxist-Leninist, until I discovered Anarcho-Syndicalism."

I nod, wondering how long before I can shake him. "I see."

"These days, though, I'm an Anarcho-Primitivist." He coughs into the crook of his arm. "But I'm asking about your art. What's your artistic manifesto?"

I try to think of something to say. "Realism, I guess."

"*Realism.* We have a radical among us. And what's your medium? You're not a painter, that much is obvious. Not a sculptor, either." He tries to pass me the joint again, but I wave it away.

"I'm—a performance artist."

An arched eyebrow from Peggo. "Yes? Have I seen your work?"

You're seeing it now. "I'm still learning," I say.

Peggo eyes me. "My advice: don't trust in abstract theory," he says. "Go with what your bowels command."

When I go back to her basement studio four days later, Miriam's art—in the medium of paper and stamps and ink—is perfection. Lila Kereti's

Hungarian passport is now storied with visits to Seychelles and Panama and Macedonia exactly corresponding to the dates on the certificates I'd shown her. A Spanish driver's license and Hungarian birth certificate and Barcelona library card and a beautifully creased and folded apartment lease in a nice, but not too nice, Barcelona neighborhood, all of it meticulously worn and scuffed and frayed, as if they'd lived in my possession for years.

She's reluctant at first, then succumbs to artist's vanity and shows me her tricks. A little vinegar to damage the official ink—*really, you wouldn't believe what I have to do to get this*—followed by fine-grit sandpaper rubbed over the documents just so. It precisely mimics the effect of being carried in the front pocket of a pair of jeans, she says.

I pay her, gladly, the remainder of the 7,000 francs. She licks her finger and counts the money I lay out on the desk before her. When the transaction is done, she shakes my hand, wishes me luck, and tells me it would be best if I never mentioned her to anyone, lest her sons— big boys, all four of them—come looking for me. I don't know whether it's an idle threat or a very real one, but I agree and leave her shop a different person than when I came in.

The offices of Frau Doktor Sadik are across the river from the Altstadt, in a hilly neighborhood of winding, narrow streets where the buildings are worn with age and all the more elegant for it. Smart shops and little restaurants punctuate uptight offices of accountants and bankers and lawyers. I find her address in a building nearly identical to the others, but with gaudy curlicue brass railings on the stairs out front and tall windows divided up with complicated, swirly patterns.

I approach the receptionist in the lobby with a smile, but it isn't returned. "I'd like to see Frau Doktor Sadik, please. My last name is Perels, first name Judita. I don't have an appointment."

It's the name Terrance would have used to introduce me to her. However, just as I knew it would be, all is, in the favorite phrase of the Swiss, *nicht in Ordnung.* "Frau Sadik has no appointment today for anyone named Perels." There's no hostility from the chinless reception, just the tyranny of rules and schedules above all else.

"I know, sir. As I said, I don't have an appointment, but if I could make one . . ."

"Frau Doktor Sadik is not taking new clients at this time." He turns back to his computer as if I'd vanished.

"Look, I'm sorry. I'm a friend of Terrance Mutai. She's been his attorney since . . ."

Then, a cheery voice from behind me: "A friend of Terrance? Of course, dear. I was expecting you."

I turn to see a petite woman in a canary yellow trench coat and a bright blue headscarf peering at me from above overlarge Audrey Hepburn sunglasses. She carries a bright red briefcase and red umbrella, rounding out the trio of primary colors.

She removes her glasses and smiles. "Our friend mentioned you'd be ringing me up. How *are* you, by the way?" Her voice is like a perfectly tuned bell, with expensive, British-university English. There's a professional warmth in her tone, the kind that's paid to be there.

I shake her outstretched hand. "Pleased to meet you, Frau Doktor Sadik."

"So formal," she says through a smile. "You may call me Naz."

Coffee is served in nearly translucent china cups, poured from a silver pot by a man in a suit wearing white gloves. Naz, in a cream-colored suit, sits on the opposite end of a leather couch from me and pushes a strand of auburn hair back under her headscarf. The attendant sets down the coffee service and brings Naz a crystal carafe of liquor.

"Like whiskey with your coffee?" she asks.

"Whiskey?" I say. "No. Thank you."

Naz catches me watching her as she pours some of the liquor into her own cup. "An observant Muslim drinking during the day," she says, smiling as she reads my mind. "Do I have it right?"

"Sorry," I say. "I didn't mean to stare."

"You weren't. You were observing. So tell me, what conclusions can you draw?"

"I'm not drawing any conclusions, Frau Doktor—"

"*Naz.* Please. No need to be so Swiss about it." She sets the carafe down and takes a delicate sip, pinky out for show. "So—observant Muslim who drinks. Is she an alcoholic? Is she even a Muslim? Maybe she just likes headscarves?"

It's a test of some kind. Gauging me. Measuring me. I straighten my shoulders.

"My assumptions are wrong," I say. "Your actions don't match your appearance, and now I have to reconsider. It leaves ... whoever's on the other side off balance. Wondering who you are."

A smile and a nod. "Correct." She pulls out a notepad and a slender pen. "Now, how do you know Terrance?"

"We're—friends. Since school," I say.

She gives a conspiratorial look. "Quite a young man now, isn't he? I watched him grow from the time he was a baby. And all the troubles his father has been through lately, he showed himself to be quite strong."

"Yes. I'm very fond of him."

"In the e-mail, he said you were looking for very specialized services. Services that only I could provide. 'Please treat Señora Perels as you would me or my father,' is how he put it—tell me, am I pronouncing your name correctly?"

This part is said differently, a cloying interrogation, delivered so sweetly I'm not even sure it's really there.

"I—I need to ask you something," I say. "I've never used ... an attorney before."

"No? Fortunate life." She smiles.

"I need to know—what I tell you, it's all confidential, right? One hundred percent. Completely."

She gives me a very slight bow and the smile disappears. "Of course."

"Then let's just—start with this," I say, sliding the packet of documents down the table, along with the list of account numbers. Naz doesn't touch them.

"These accounts, they're at a bank here in Zurich," I say. "I want what's in them."

"And are they your accounts?"

I lean back, bite the inside of my lower lip. There can be no lying with her, not if she's to do her job. "They're—owed to me," I say. "What's in them is a debt owed to me."

Naz's head tilts ever so slightly to the side, then picks up the packet of documents and pages through them. "The account numbers are associated with the, let's see, seven entities?"

"I was told they are," I say. "Or—that's what I assume."

Naz sets one document aside, then another, and another, studying them for a painfully long few moments. "It looks like someone named Lila Kereti has full fiscal authority over—all of them." She looks up. "If you believe she owes you something, we should get in touch with her. I can help with that."

I take the passport from my pocket, slide that down the table, too.

Naz opens the cover, then slowly, almost without my noticing it, her lips pull back into a smile. "I see," she says. "And did Terrance know this is what you were asking me to do?"

"No," I say. "He knew it had to do with the money, but not this."

Naz looks at me gravely, folds her hands together. This is the part where she rises, tells me to get out before she calls the police.

"Do you know what I do?" she says. "What my profession is?"

"You're an attorney."

"I'm a magician, actually. The best magician. That's why your friend, why his father and his father's colleagues, rely on me. Do you know what's required for magic to work?"

I shake my head.

"Complete trust," she says. "*Total* trust. And an hourly rate. Tell me, Ms. Perels, do you know what I charge?"

"I know it's a lot."

Naz writes a figure on a piece of paper and slides it toward me. I don't look at it. Instead, I fish the last diamond from my pocket and set it on the table.

"Is that enough?" I say.

Naz picks it up, holds it to the light. "Enough to get started, at least."

For another hour, the story unfolds. It feels like therapy, more than anything, or confession. And only a few thousand dollars an hour. The difference is, though, I only have to give her the relevant bits. No backstory necessary. No feelings. She never even asks why I want the money. It is, for her, a matter of paperwork, not morality, not even reasons. As I speak, however, I find the weight lifting from me, and the heat dissipating. I watch her every expression, every movement of her hand as she writes down something I've said, searching for a sign that what I'm asking her to do is impossible. But I never see it.

"Dormant accounts. Abandoned. That's what we're talking about," she says when I've told her all the parts she needs. "*If* they're actually abandoned. *If* they contain anything at all."

I look at her. "So—now what?"

"First step, we see who Lila Kereti is." She clicks the pen closed, rises to her feet. "Second step, we visit the bank."

All of this is thrown out there with a note of hope, but not fear. All of this is routine, doable—nothing to worry about. It's clear she's finished with me for today, but I remain seated.

"Does—does any of this . . . ?"

"Bother me," Naz says, finishing my thought.

"Yes," I say.

She takes a seat by my side, so close I can smell the soap she used this morning and the scotch she had an hour ago. "Strange thing, money. People start wars for it. People fall in love for it."

"I know. But how can—how is this permitted?"

Naz sighs deeply, pats my thigh. "Say it. Go ahead."

"Say what?"

"The system is corrupt. It's what you're thinking, isn't it?"

I nod.

"What you see as a corrupt system, I see as a system functioning exactly as intended. It isn't broken; it was made this way." She stands, rolls her shoulders like a boxer, and gathers up the documents. "It was made this way so that people like you, and people like me, can do things like this."

"I see. Thank you." I rise and shake her hand stiffly.

"Stealing and taking what you're owed. The difference is all in having a good lawyer." Naz gives me a wink. "Make an appointment with my secretary for tomorrow. I'll look these papers over tonight."

We say our good-byes, and I head toward the door. Only when my hand is on the knob does she say from across the room:

"And pick up a suit, will you? This is Zurich, not a farm."

Mostly, among Peggo and the others, I stay quiet and listen. But to the artists' credit, they don't ask many questions. People come and go from here all the time, I've learned. Lego Village is simply a stopping-off point for a night or a week or a year. No one ever presents anything new, and when there's nothing new, there's nothing worth asking about. So when we gather around and drink in the evening, the talk is about art—one's *work*—or about things outside the self. Personal background, stories from growing up, all of it is banal bullshit. If it's because they're haunted by violent fathers and memories of not enough to eat, it doesn't matter. The net effect is that Lego Village is an excellent place to hide.

I ask them where I might buy a suit without spending too much money. This is met with much laughter, the idea of a suit being inherently funny. After a time, one of them gives me the name of a mall—a "bourgeois playground," is the term he uses—a long tram ride away.

I go there the next morning, and the sales clerk shows me a pantsuit in the same dark gray everyone but Naz seems to wear. It's conservative and dull, and I give it a little scowl. So she shows me something else, something, she says, that will appeal to a younger woman with a wild streak. It's the same suit in a slightly lighter shade of gray.

I choose the first one—best to look as conservative as possible—and pair it with the least expensive blouse and pair of shoes I can find. Still, when she rings it all up, I realize that in Zurich, dull is expensive. It's a little loose and a little long, but I wear it out anyway and take the train to Naz's office.

She looks up from beneath a lime-green headscarf as I enter and smiles because that's what she's paid to do. "Mm," she says. "Well—I did say a suit. And that's what you got."

I hold out my arms, give her a twirl. "Like it?"

"Very—summer intern," she says. "Remind me to give you the name of my tailor. Now sit."

She nods to a chair in front of her desk, a silk-upholstered monstrosity. The seat is overstuffed, nearly rigid, and the arms are carved with sharp little curlicues that dig right through the fabric into my skin.

Naz remains seated behind her desk and holds up a thin packet of paper in a file folder. "She was, as far as we can tell, never real."

"She?"

"Lila Kereti. A birth certificate and passport, which you have copies of. But there are no school transcripts, no arrests, no electric bill, no credit rating."

I squirm in my chair, trying to find a comfortable position. "So—a ghost?"

Naz looks out the window, where the rain is coming down softly. "A bureaucratic glitch. Set up by someone like me. A paper person to hide the real people behind the transactions."

In other words, don't feel guilty.

"That's good," I say.

"It's *ideal*," she says. "As for the accounts, they're held by Hindemith & Cie. Small, private bank, family-run since sixteen-whenever. Their client list, it looks like an index from a history textbook."

"So what do we do next?"

"Hindemith & Cie is popular because they provide—certain things. One of them is poor record keeping, when it's convenient for the client."

"Poor record keeping?"

"According to the paperwork you gave me, Lila Kereti is what's called the 'beneficial owner' of the accounts. Meaning, she has control over the money. In theory, all banks in Switzerland are supposed to keep copies of the beneficial owner's passport."

"In theory," I say.

"But in practice, clients sometimes prefer to have the account under an alias. It's illegal, and the bank can be fined, but to Hindemith & Cie, it's just a cost of doing business." She leans back, bites the end of her pen. "So what do you say, Frau Kereti of Budapest? Time to pay them a visit?"

Twenty-One

Hindemith & Cie occupies a sand-colored mess of a building just off the Paradeplatz, a fifteen-minute walk from Naz's office. Columns, capstones, corniches, friezes, ivy, cherubs, gryphons, all packed together like a three-dimensional glossary of architectural bullshit. Inside, we're greeted by a trim man with pursed lips in a suit that is precisely the same shade of gray as mine. He exchanges a few words with Naz, then—and this, I may have imagined—he clicks the heels of his polished black shoes together as he turns to fetch someone.

He returns with a banker in tow, who shows us to an office off the lobby. Formalities are exchanged; Lila Kereti's passport is produced and quickly examined.

"We would like you to check some balances," Naz says.

The banker nods as if this were a sacred honor, and Naz feeds him the first account number. He enters it into the computer, says *ah* and *hm*, then frowns gravely. "The account was closed, I'm afraid, since three years."

Naz feeds him the second account, and gets the same answer.

On the third, however, the banker gives a hopeful sigh, then smiles and takes up a pen. "Here we are then, like so."

Naz takes the paper from him, looks at it, passes it to me. Just over 10,000 francs.

Fomax Optical, the next account, is a bust, already drained. As is Education des Artes, Ltd. And Caldex Imports. España Shipping, on the other hand, yields 75,000 francs. My heart ticks at the sight of the number. It's more than I've ever seen all together at once, and back in Montevideo, I could live on it for a decade. But it's not enough, not nearly, not for all this, and not for what's been done to me. Naz relaxes a little, though; at least now I can pay her bill.

"Now, Rosenthal-Webb," Naz says, and gives the account number.

The banker types it in, then straightens his already straight back. He looks at me with different eyes now. "Ah, well. Good news."

Naz smiles as she looks at the number, slides the paper to me.

A gasp sneaks out, and my hand flies to my mouth to suppress it. I look to the banker, then to Naz, then to the number again. It's a little more than 1.3 million Swiss francs—about the same in American dollars. My hands tremble, so I shove them under my thighs.

I'm all set to leave, and leave happy. I even rise a little in my seat, but Naz interrupts me.

"There's—just one more account," she says. "Genza Securities."

The banker enters the number as Naz feeds it to him. "Genza Securities," he mutters to himself, and clicks through to another screen. "Based in Seychelles, yes. Account managed by . . ."

Then he pauses and looks down at my passport. He studies it for a long time before going back to his computer screen.

"*Alles gut?*" I ask.

He doesn't answer, and instead lifts the receiver of his phone, presses an extension. "Unusual, yes . . . perhaps if you could . . . yes, herr doktor . . . as I said, this is . . . no, herr doktor . . . no, herr doktor . . . very good, I shall tell them." He hangs up the phone.

"What is it?" I ask, voice urgent.

Naz holds up her hand, then leans forward. "Who were you speaking with?"

"The bank manager, Frau Doktor. He will—I'm very sorry. It will be but a moment."

Naz looks at me reassuringly, but there's tension in her jaw and neck.

A polite tap at the office door brings the banker and Naz to their feet. I do the same, standing primly with hands folded in front of me. A gnome of eighty or ninety enters, gray peak-lapelled suit, the knot of his tie so tight it juts straight out from his collar. He bows, showing us the liver-spotted top of a bald head, as the banker introduces him with a preposterously long title. Herr Doktor Kolb is the gist of it, though, and he shakes our hands with shocking strength.

The banker and Kolb study the computer screen for a moment, the elder man saying, *ja, ja, klar,* as the younger walks him through his work. Finally Kolb looks up. "Frau Kereti and Frau Doktor Sadik, would you please join me in my office?"

Suddenly, another level of formality, and another attendant in white gloves, just like at Naz's office, who pours coffee from an elaborate silver service. It's clearly part of a ritual here, like a sacrament taken whenever business is discussed. Herr Doktor Kolb brings in two attorneys to join us, the original banker apparently too lowly to participate . The two newcomers know Naz by name, familiar with either her or her work.

We're all seated around a conference table, deep brown, nearly black, with centuries of use. Heavy velvet curtains, rich maroon, hang sullenly along the sides of windows that face out on a gray Zurich sky.

"A pleasure to finally meet you, Frau Kereti," says Kolb. "Hard to believe, after so much business together, this is your first visit in person."

All of this is said with a friendly enough tone, but Naz stiffens, preparing her counterpunch. "Herr Doktor Kolb, if we might see the balance of the account."

"It was not shared with you downstairs?" he says.

"It was not."

Herr Kolb takes up a pen, writes something on a piece of paper, and passes the folded sheet to Naz, who reads it like a poker player, utterly without reaction. I expect her to show me, but she doesn't, so, instead, I move my eyes from face to face, looking for clues, and wondering why people in this town have such an aversion to saying numbers out loud.

"As you can understand, Frau Doktor, a sum like this—precautions must be taken. Identities verified, and so forth." Kolb intertwines his fingers in front of him as if praying.

"You yourself have copies of the articles of incorporation for Genza Securities that give Frau Kereti fiscal authority, yes?" Naz says.

A nod from Kolb.

"And the documents I've shown you today—passport, driver's license, even a library card—they correspond exactly with your own records, yes?"

A pause as Kolb exchanges glances with his attorneys. "It appears, our own records are, in that regard . . . inadequate."

The attorney immediately to Kolb's left, a pretty young man, trim and pink-cheeked, clears his throat. "Frau Doktor, records are occasionally misplaced, and we have only the names of the beneficial owners. Frau Kereti's name is among them, but . . ."

Naz sees her shot, and cuts him off. "So your own records are not in compliance with Swiss banking law. Herr Doktor, I am aghast."

The attorney wrinkles his lips at the distasteful drama. "Since Genza Securities is not based in Switzerland, banking disputes, must, by law, revert to the law of the country in which the company is registered— Seychelles, in this case."

Naz looks at him, just a hint of a smile on her lips. "Oh, you're saying this is a banking *dispute* now?"

"Of course not," the young man says. "Only a question of— authenticity."

"And poor record keeping," Naz says sharply. "Article one, Section nineteen of the commercial code. When there is no financial dispute, only a claim, Swiss law applies."

Kolb's posture stiffens. "Frau Doktor, you can't expect us to hand over control of a sum like this based simply on what you've shown us today."

"I do, Herr Kolb," Naz says. "Article forty-two, Section three of the Civil Code of 1907, under which you have more than enough proof to verify my client's identity. Now, if you're going to continue obstructing my client's right to her own property, we can have the courts settle it."

I sink lower in my chair and give Naz a look. She ignores me.

Kolb and the attorneys whisper among themselves, then Kolb turns to us and gives us a thin smile. "Frau Doktor, since it is our own records that are, apparently, not in optimal compliance, we would prefer to handle things privately."

The lawyer on Kolb's other side, a heavy woman of around forty, raises a finger. "A declaration confirming Frau Kereti's identity from the Office of the Registrar will be sufficient for us."

Naz smiles, looks at me. "I think we can agree. Wouldn't you say, Frau Kereti?"

I flash her a worried expression: *Do we?* But I can tell it's the answer she's looking for. "Certainly," I say.

Details are hashed out between them, then we all shake hands, without my being certain what just happened. It's only on the staircase to the ground level that Naz squeezes my forearm and gives me a wicked smile.

She doesn't speak until we're on the street in front of Hindemith & Cie. Then she turns around suddenly, her face beaming. "It's a simple hearing," she says. "Have your papers looked at and verified."

"And—will they be?"

Naz tilts her head, that strand of auburn hair breaking loose again. "It's a formality, really. To cover their asses. If your papers are as good as they look, then—I'd say better than fifty-fifty."

I swallow. "And the amount. You never showed me the amount."

She closes her eyes, inhales deeply. "A drink," she says. "Let's have one. I know a place..."

Then she's leading me by the hand like we're two old friends down the block and around the corner into a narrow alley that ends at the river. Naz opens a wooden door with no sign and nods for me to enter. Soft piano and dim light and a curving wooden bar, still empty at this time of day. We slide into an empty booth.

Naz removes the folded piece of paper Kolb had given her and hands it to me.

My body is numb, from my face to my fingers, and the numbness makes them clumsy. The paper slips to the floor and I pick it up.

The thing about numbers is that they're written differently in different countries. Sometimes sevens have a slash through them, nines look like lowercase *g*'s, and ones look like little tents. Sometimes the decimal place is marked with a period or apostrophe or even just a space instead of a comma. Thus my brain stalls out at the numbers on the paper: *17'394'117*, which look like coordinates instead of an amount. I look up at Naz, mouth the words, *seventeen million, three hundred—*

She nods violently—emphatically, gleefully. Then she's hugging me, which seems like an inappropriate thing for a lawyer to do until I realize she's actually keeping me upright.

I brace my hands on the table. "Altogether, the amount." My voice cracks. "The math, it's kind of hard right now."

Naz calculates the total from all the accounts in her head. "Just under—nineteen million francs."

I nearly cry and have to look away.

Just then a waiter appears and Naz orders champagne.

We're buzzed by the time we leave, and I find myself stumbling back over our conversation as I take the tram back to Lego Village. There will be a hearing in a day or two, where someone called a registrar will examine my papers and hand down an edict that answers the question, am I really Lila Kereti? Or, as Naz is quick to emphasize, *legally* Lila Kereti. My odds are better than fifty-fifty, she'd said. A cautious estimate on her part, or an optimistic one? We'll find out soon enough.

As the tram rumbles along, I consider how to tell my father, and decide to wait until the situation resolves itself, one way or the other. So much wisdom out there about announcing things prematurely. Counting chickens before they hatch. The hallmark arrogance of the fool. Still, though. Nineteen million francs. *Neunzehn millionen.* So much fun to say. Sorry, German, I take back all the nasty things I ever said about you.

That night I lie on my makeshift mattress at the side of the studio wrapped in a scratchy wool horse blanket. In another corner of the structure, two artists are giggling quietly and passing a weed pipe between themselves as they discuss work.

It's the artist's identity, his identity, that money destroys, says one.

Bullshit, says the other, *we do it to ourselves—art is masturbation, has been since cave paintings—so take the money and stop bitching.*

What about what Mao said? says the first. *Art as the purest form of revolution.*

Fucking Mao is dead, says the second. *Anyway, he never even said that.*

From somewhere else in the structure, there's a loud *shhh*, and the two fall silent. They sit for a time, smoking and saying nothing, then drift off to sleep.

But there's no silence in the structure and there never is. Outside, trucks hurtle past on the road, and the vibrations shake the metal walls. I hear dripping water, too, from a few different places, none of the drips timed to bring anything like a steady rhythm that one could fall asleep to.

The goal of the money—at least the goal I'd told myself—was a better life for me and my dad. Not safety; there can never be that. But school. A good shrink. A life a rung or two higher than submerged.

However, the estimate I'd imagined—one, two million tops—had been far, far off the mark. Now my greed has multiplied with it and I must adjust my expectations accordingly. What life can't you lead with 19 million francs? It's not private-jet level, but it's never-having-to-worry-again level. It's good-doctors-and-a-comfortable-ass-in-a-safeish-country level. A lusty thought: some dilapidated old villa on the beach somewhere, Dad on a chair in the sun, me—should I take up painting?—sure, painting, my easel set up by the water. White cotton dress, long hair. Hire a local kid to bring the groceries. Never bother the outside world with my presence again.

The hearing takes place beneath gold ceilings eight meters above us, my body dwarfed by the vast courtroom. A woman in a robe and powdered wig, glowering from high up behind a mahogany judge's bench, listens to Naz's argument carefully before heading back to her study, where she consults an enormous book filled with a thousand years of Swiss law.

That's how I picture it, anyway, and it's why I'm both relieved and a little disappointed when Naz and I find ourselves waiting on a bench in a hallway with worn-out vinyl floors in front of a clerk's office.

Promptly on the hour of two p.m. the door to the clerk's office opens and we're led to a woman in a white blouse in a tiny office barely big enough for the three of us. There's a clear plastic container with the remnants of a salad in the garbage can next to her desk. I can smell the vinaigrette from my chair. The registrar is a round, lovely woman, a grandmother maybe a dozen times over, with a cheerful ruddiness to her skin and a friendly, singsongy voice. I understand almost none of the Swiss-German legalese that comes out of her mouth, but I could fall asleep listening to her; I bet she's good at telling bedtime stories.

Naz makes some obscure but emphatic point, points to a spot on some document, references Article Something, Section Something, of the Swiss Civil Code—that's all I'm able to make out. The registrar frowns, and I have to look away or I might throw up—it all rides on her. There's a framed picture on a bookshelf, three of her dozen grand-children, as ruddy-faced as she is, cavorting in some meadow with the Alps in the background. I think of *The Sound of Music* and name her grandchildren accordingly, Gretl, Friedrich, and pretty Liesl, the old-est, the cause of so much trouble, dating that bike messenger and aspiring fascist, Rolf.

Naz pats my arm and I snap back to the room. The registrar is look-ing at me expectantly, and so is Naz, *answer the question.*

"Excuse me," I say in German. "Please repeat."

The registrar sighs. "Shall we administer the oath?"

I look to Naz, who gives me a single slow nod.

"The oath," I say. "Yes. Of course."

The registrar rises, opens the door, and calls for a clerk. When he arrives, the four of us gather in the hallway, and I'm asked to raise my right hand. I repeat after the registrar:

Do I affirm that I have not given false testimony, under penalty of law?

Yes, I affirm it.

Do I affirm that I have not forged, stolen, or in any way misap-propriated the documents used in today's proceedings, under penalty of law?

Yes, I affirm it.

Do I affirm that my legal name is Lila Kereti, citizen of Hungary, who is the owner of the accounts at the bank known as Hindemith & Cie, currently at issue, under penalty of law?

Yes, I affirm it.

With that, the registrar coughs into the crook of her elbow, places a document against the wall. The clerk signs in the witness box, then the registrar signs it herself.

The visit to Hindemith & Cie is a surprisingly agreeable one. When the certification is presented to Herr Doktor Kolb and his pair of attorneys, Naz tells them I'd prefer to keep the money just where it is for the time being, only under a new account. This delights Kolb, whose cheeks rise in a gnomish smile. With coffee served and Kolb and the attorneys satisfied, the paperwork begins.

From time to time, I'm handed a sheet of paper to sign. Lila Kereti's signature flows naturally from my pen. It's only halfway through the ceremony that I ask for a moment alone with Naz. I expect the two of us to step out into the hallway, but instead, Kolb and the attorneys are the ones who leave. Evidently, this is the kind of courtesy a client like me can expect from now on.

"Could I—I would like some cash." The words come out shyly, almost embarrassed.

"Ah. Of course. Everybody does," Naz says. "How much?"

"I was thinking—half a million."

Her eyes narrow and she purses her lips. "They don't have cash like that in the bank, but I'll see what I can do."

When the others come back, Naz makes the request. Kolb blushes, and the pink-cheeked attorney smirks. But a hushed phone call is made, and just as the visit is about to end, the money arrives. The same white-gloved attendant who'd served the coffee places five packets of notes on the table and presents a withdrawal slip for me to sign.

Five hundred thousand francs in 1,000-franc notes. My head cants to the side as I look at it, and the pink-cheeked attorney makes a comment to the other attorney that causes her to smile. Kolb fires them a look like a father to unruly children in church.

There are handshakes all around, wishes for everyone's mutual success and continued relationships, but I process none of it. Instead, all I feel is the weight of the large zippered envelope of fine, pebbled leather that Herr Doktor Kolb himself had given me. A gift, he said, from Hindemith & Cie. I feel self-conscious about the cash, that maybe I'd come off as childish or provincial by asking for it. But it's my cash, and that goes a long way toward making me feel better again.

On the steps in front of the bank, I ask Naz whether I'm safe carrying this much. She just smiles, reminds me we're in Zurich. Naz squeezes my shoulder, then tells me we should celebrate tomorrow because there's much for her to do. Whole corporations to conjure up for me to be president of, new certificates in a variety of tropical and business-friendly nations to be filed, preparations made for the movement of nearly 19 million lovely, colorful, cream-textured Swiss francs into entities controlled by me.

I watch her tighten her headscarf—pink today, elegant as always—and slip away into the afternoon crowd. The streets are thick with people now, and it's getting dark. Quitting time for the owners of the world. I clutch the leather case to my chest.

People bustle all around me in the little square I've wandered into, and everyone seems to be laughing—groups of friends at café tables and old ladies with little dogs and an ice-cream seller who's doing an excellent business despite the cold. Suddenly, there's a riot of church bells, not just from one church, but from all of them, all over the city, as if a royal wedding were concluding, or a war had ended.

And so it had. Look how easily all this had come to me. Lawyers. Paperwork. A passport. A new identity. A hearing before someone called a registrar. That's all it had taken. No blood. No bodies. No rat poison. Look how civilized I am now. Me, in a suit. With clean hands.

Now I'm on a little bridge, crossing the river, the tolling of the bells still going strong. You won. You won, Gwendolyn Bloom. You brilliant, lucky, brutal bitch, you won.

Twenty-Two

How true my aim had been, how steady my trigger finger. And when the bullet landed precisely in the center of the target, how cleanly it had cut all the way through a thousand years of bureaucratic history designed, or so I thought, to prevent precisely the thing I'd just pulled off. The system is corrupt. The system is functioning as intended.

I am the most sober I've ever been, the most clearheaded, yet I feel delirious. I can't help it if the response in my brain and heart and bowels is chemical in nature. I'm just flesh and squirting adrenal glands and electricity leaping between neurons. The endorphins and adrenaline are very nearly toxic, and they cause me to tremble and veer unsteadily in my steps. This is happiness, as happy as happy gets.

But with happiness comes the fear of it being snatched away. So I am also cautious and once again paranoid. Even though this is Zurich, one does not simply walk around with the 500K nearly undisguised. So I stumble into a shop, buy a big baggy sweater and a cheap tourist's fanny pack to wear under it. As the shop clerk rings me up, I panic that I don't have any small bills. But she doesn't flinch when I hand her a 1,000-franc note.

In a café, I order a cappuccino to go even though the last thing I need is caffeine, then head to the bathroom to change and to enjoy a moment of privacy. God bless Europe for its sense of bathroom architecture, with walls and doors between stalls that go all the way to the top and bottom. I open the leather envelope from Kolb and pull the packets of francs out to inspect them. It's not that I don't trust Hindemith & Cie's ability to count, it's just that I want to have the pleasure, too.

The 1,000-franc notes are maybe seven inches long and three inches wide—elegantly slender, with gradations of purple and blue, stripes of pastel green and yellow, spots of pretty pink and tomato red. *Tausend Franken*, it says, the hard German standing notably apart from the *Milli Francs, Mille Francs, Mille Franchi*, also printed on each bill—these sounding almost like a mantra when you say them together.

Terrance would laugh at me, or, less cruelly, just be disappointed. Fetishizing money this way is a rookie move. But he's not here, so I'll do what I like. My mind flashes to my dad: I need to tell him, share this with him. A kind of joy comes over me, an exponential form of skipping home with a good report card in hand. I fumble with my phone, taking three tries to unlock it, and five to log in to the account I use for communicating with him. Still nothing since the message I'd left him from the truck stop in Spain. My thumbs skitter clumsily as I type the e-mail: *At destnation. Everthing great. Got it!!!!!!!! Contact me asap pls. I DID IT!!*

Such a stupid, childish way to write it. I almost consider deleting the message and starting over, but no—he should see a sliver of it, the immediacy of the joy filling me like a balloon. I save it before I can change my mind.

On the way out, I leave the cappuccino sitting on the counter and race toward the tram, the strap of the fanny pack pulling heavily at my skin under my sweater with every step. When I arrive at Lego Village, Sabiha is out front, smoking a cigarette—something else she's taken up. She crushes it out when she sees me approach, like I'm her mother.

"Judita, you are okay?" she says, worry on her face.

"Yes. Fine."

"You look distressed."

I shake my head, then motion for her to follow me around to the back and into the garden we use for bathing, the only semiprivate place I can think of.

"Judita, you're scaring me," Sabiha says as she wipes a place clean on a rusted metal bench and sits.

I sit beside her. "There's something I want to give you. But first, you must promise me that you'll use it for yourself, only yourself, you understand?"

"I cannot promise anything until I know."

I'd expected her to give in immediately. The last thing I want is for the gift to be squandered by Peggo and the others. But it's her gift, her decision, her life. I pull a bundle of francs from the fanny pack, place it in her hand.

She looks at me, eyes horrified. "Judita . . ."

"It's one hundred thousand francs." My fingers wrap around hers, closing them around the money. "It's not stolen. It's mine. And now it's yours. A gift."

"No." She shakes her head softly, then emphatically. "*No.*"

"You can do whatever you want. Go wherever you want."

"I want to be here."

"Then be here, just do it because you want to."

She shoves the money back at me, and it falls onto the ground, landing in a spotty patch of weeds and mud.

"I'm not your project, Judita."

She jerks away when I grab her by the arm, so I grab her again and hold tight. "Listen to me—this isn't charity." I scoop up the money and press it to her chest. "All the shit the world did to you, you earned this. The world is making a deposit on what it owes."

Sabiha takes a stumbling step backward when I let her go, but holds on to the money. She looks down at it, turns it over and over in her hands. "And before it was yours? Whose was it?"

I shrug. "Someone else's."

"Who?"

"Someone whose fault it is that bad things happen."

"So why give it to me?"

I step closer, wanting to touch her, to connect the circuit between us so that she understands, but she moves back. "Because—I don't want bad things to be my fault."

Someone raps loudly on the corrugated metal fence, shouts that he needs to use the hose. Sabiha tucks the brick of francs under her shirt.

In the studio, I feign interest for a few minutes in a silkscreen project everyone has gathered around, building up to the announcement of my sudden departure. I mutter something about heading up to—I think I say Rotterdam, but it doesn't really matter. They're all cool about the transient nature of things here, accepting that sometimes people do, in fact, go to Rotterdam. I clean up the place where I slept, slip some money, not much, to Peggo for beer or paintbrushes. Everyone gets a little *Tschüss*—bye, casual as it gets—maybe we'll see you around sometime, maybe not.

Sabiha watches me, and when I leave, gives me no more than a *Tschüss* back.

Somehow I always understood what would happen next, somehow this part was a fixture of my fantasy. On the tram, I take my phone and e-mail Terrance. A simple message, thought through verbatim ahead of time, but trying to appear casual and insouciant: *I'm so sorry about BA. But things are different, I'm different. I got what I came for and would love to share it with you.*

The closing is a simple *G*, along with the phone number to my new SIM. I have no idea if he'll call, but I'd meant what I said: The struggle, the fighting, it's over now. I'm different, and the old, violent Gwendolyn is locked in the past. I can finally afford for her to be.

I pull up some hotels on my phone, scrolling around for the most absurdly expensive one. I settle on a spike-helmeted castle on a hillside overlooking the city called the Obelisk Grande. It takes almost an hour to get there on the tram, east past the Altstadt climbing the winding hills in what looks like a rich residential neighborhood.

I hike up the driveway with only my backpack as Mercedes and Bentleys crawl past me, conscious that I'm without not only appropriate luggage, but the matching luxury sedan to go with it. I enter the lobby ahead of a twelve-member Gulf family in flowing robes and chadors, a platoon of bellmen behind them pushing luggage carts loaded down with exquisite suitcases and steamer trunks.

Every one of the people inside is flawlessly dressed and groomed. Moving, talking mannequins, the men wrapped in shimmering wool suits, the women in bare-shouldered cocktail dresses, beads and sequins glinting. As for me—baggy sweater over a blouse, cheap suit jacket in hand—I simply stand out, and for a moment I'm frozen in fear, stupefied by my own non-belonging.

Just own it, says a voice inside me. Tell them what you want. Make them get it for you.

And so I do, addressing the clerk behind the counter with a tone commensurate with my new position. "A room, please," I say. "Four nights."

The woman—blond hair pulled back tightly, fine features, and just a dusting of makeup she doesn't need—regards me with a bland smile. "The name of your reservation?"

"I don't have one."

The smile widens as she delivers an answer she likes. "Unfortunately, there is nothing."

"Nothing at all."

"Suites only. An Executive-Premier." She gives me the price, a nightly rate that's a month's rent on an excellent loft in Manhattan.

"I'll take it," I say.

"Pardon?"

"I'll take it. Four nights."

Her posture stiffens and the ceremony begins. I reach for the Lila

Kereti passport, then think better of it. She's like a special outfit, or set of china—special occasions only. So Ms. Judita Perels of Uruguay produces her passport, slides it across the counter.

"And your credit card?"

I peel off a small fortune in 1,000-franc notes. "I'll be paying cash."

"A credit card is required as a deposit, I'm afraid . . ."

I shrug. "Wouldn't you know it, I lost my purse. How much is the deposit?"

"Ten thousand francs."

I peel off ten more bills and add them to the pile.

A bellman shows me to the suite. In the center is an enormous bed covered in a white duvet that makes it look like a slab of ice cream. Glistening parquet floors and silk carpets in pinks and blues, and bloodred curtains with modest Zurich twinkling in the distance. Instinctively, I resist touching any of the furniture, as if it should be cordoned off with a ribbon like at a museum, lest we peasants touch the Louis-Whatevers. I run my finger over a dresser anyway.

The bellman takes note. "Madame, is the room not to your liking?"

I crinkle my nose. "Just a little dusty."

"I shall call housekeeping . . ."

"Don't bother."

I tip him a hundred for carrying a single backpack to the room and pointing out where the minibar is, then feel like a show-offy ass. But it's going to take some time to get comfortable with this new reality, and one has to start somewhere.

When he's gone, I leap onto the bed and bounce like a child.

Strange, but I don't gorge myself, not in the way I'd imagined in the fantasy, asking the chef to send up a sampler of everything with a special sauce made of gold. Instead, it's a club sandwich and a salad and a slice of carrot cake for dessert. To be clear, it's a very good, very expensive club sandwich, but still. It all feels a little tentative, a little too unreal. Besides, all the guests for my celebration haven't arrived yet.

I check my e-mail again, hoping for a reply from either Terrance or my dad, but my inbox in empty. So I take a bath, wrap myself in a white robe that's thick as a fur coat, and open the minibar, selecting the predictable choice: a bottle of champagne. It's a full-sized one, 750 milliliters of the thing the French do best.

Out on the balcony, the pop of the cork is like a gunshot. My skin puckers in the cold from my feet to my head as I pour myself a glass and sit in the elegant wicker chair. When the glass is empty, I fill it again and drink that, too, wondering if this is what I'd been so greedy for the entire time.

Certainly I couldn't dream up anything better. This is it, the perfection of the human condition, the point beyond which no more progress can be made. Should this night, this moment, happen again tomorrow, and for however many tomorrows I have left, it will not be better, just more.

But who am I kidding. Should this happen again tomorrow, well, that will be nice. But if it happens again the tomorrow after that, that will be a surprise. And so what? I pull on strands of memory from history classes, wondering if there've been kings or queens who only ruled for a single night. Surely there must have been. And what is it mountain climbers do when they reach the peak of Everest? Do they live there? Set up home? No. They take a look around, are proud of themselves, then go back to their lives selling insurance. It's only the Sherpas like Naz who get to experience it again and again.

Anyway, wouldn't it be a pity if all this grew boring?

My phone purrs in the pocket of the robe. It's a number I don't recognize, but the caller ID says *Netherlands*.

I answer tentatively, holding the phone a little away from my ear as if something might reach out and grab me. "*Ja?*" I say. Yes?

A crackling pause, and in the background, the sound of a train station announcement chime. "Is this—hey, it's me," says Terrance.

I slide lower in the chair. "Hey," I say back.

Another pause. "I got your e-mail," he says. "Congratulations."

"Thanks."

"Are you—you're good?"

"Very."

"That's good," he says. "It's good you're good."

I laugh a little, then he joins in.

"You're in—where?" I say.

"Amsterdam. For now." In the background, a conversation and people singing.

"Look, I'm ..." we both say together.

"Go ahead," I say.

"No, you go ahead," he says.

"I'm sorry. That's what I was going to say." I tighten the robe, take a sip of the champagne. "About how I acted. But that's over now. Really."

"You did what you had to."

"But, Terrance, I did it. It's mine. It's—official. My dad and I, we don't have to worry."

"Well," he says. "Then you got what you wanted."

"Not quite."

Another long pause, an announcer calling out the train to Paris. "We shouldn't be talking like this," he says.

"Probably not." I close my eyes. "Can you come?"

"You're in—you met with her, the one I mentioned?"

"Yes. She was amazing."

I hear him breathing into the phone. Then he answers, "I'll be there tomorrow."

I wait for him at a coffee shop across the street from the train station. Despite the clouds hanging over Zurich like skeins of filthy cotton, my body feels like I've spent the day in the sun. *Here,* says his text. Which is all it needs to stay.

When he appears a few minutes later—head low, shoulders tense—I have to stop myself from running out to him.

A cool "hey" from him.

"Hey back," from me.

But I see his face and shoulders relax, can hear something like happiness in his breathing as he slides into the chair next to mine. He takes my hand under the table, and I lean my head on his shoulder. Once again, too much to say, the intervening time a collection of events strange and not quite believable. But he'll believe them. That's the thing about Terrance.

"It's weird, traveling under someone else's name," he says.

"That's right. It's sexy Andre now," I say. "Any trouble?"

"None. It's just, uncomfortable."

"How was Amsterdam? Get stoned?"

"No."

The waiter comes, and Terrance orders two cappuccinos and two croissants. When the waiter goes, I put my head back on his shoulder. He smells like travel, like trains, and the cologne of the man who sat next to him. And now he's here.

I tell him about staying with Sabiha, then remember I never mentioned her, so I tell him about meeting Sabiha. Then I tell him about Peggo and Lego Village, how weird it all was.

"It was like a—dream," I say.

"Is Peggo a nickname?"

"I don't know. It's just Peggo," I say. "And he couldn't remember my name. Kept calling me Judas."

The coffee and breakfast arrive and it's his turn to play back his time in between Buenos Aires and here. Amsterdam. Helsinki before that. Amazing photographs, he says. Can't wait to see them, I say. When we finish with the cappuccinos, I tell him about Naz and Lila Kereti.

"Who's that?" he says.

So I open my new passport.

Terrance looks away, and whatever relief and happiness was there a minute ago vanishes. "You did this? On your own?"

I nod, then shake my head. "Kind of on my own. Partly. Look, I'm done, Terrance. I am. No more shit. Just me. Just trying to be as normal as I can."

"I see that," he says. "I'm glad."

I press my lips to his cheek. "So come to the hotel with me."

Terrance stands at the window, one arm against the glass, weight shifted to one leg. He's the person a room like this was meant to have in it.

"Look," he says. "The city. It's so—I don't know."

"What?"

"Zurich. If money were a country, this would be its capital."

"The capital of capital." I grin.

He groans and smiles back.

"Whatever," I say, squeezing the world's softest duvet between my fingers, plunging my head back into the world's softest pillow. "I can pay someone to come up with something better."

He lowers his nose to his armpit and grimaces. "Can I take a shower?"

"No," I say. "Not until you come here."

"I'll shower, we can have dinner."

I throw a pillow at him. "No, first come here."

He approaches the bed slowly, a half grin lifting one side of his face.

"Wait," I say. "Stop."

Then I point languidly to the minibar. "First, get me one of those million-dollar mineral waters."

Dr. Andre Mason does not have a reservation at the restaurant on the ground level of the Obelisk Grande, but the maître d' shows us to a table anyway. It's an excellent spot, near the windows overlooking the city; some country's prime minister is at the next table over. I try taking apart the transaction that happens between Terrance and the maître d', but I can find no magic in it. It's not a function of clever code words or secret handshakes. Rather, it's just about the way he asks, the tone, so that *do you have a table?* becomes *you do have a table*. That Dr. Mason is the only man not in a suit, and his date is the only woman not in a dress, is of no consequence, either. He only makes the other patrons look foolishly overdressed.

A groveling waiter presents us with menus. When he leaves, I squint at mine in the dim light.

"There are no prices," I whisper.

Terrance does not—emphatically, does not—roll his eyes when I say this. But still, that's what I see anyway.

"That's the women's menu," he says.

I look at him, give a *so what?* shrug.

"Prices are on the men's menu."

Then he laughs at whatever expression pops onto my face—wide-eyed shock, maybe, that such a thing exists in the twenty-first century. "That's sexist," I hiss, quietly as I can.

He stares back blankly, as if contemplating how, after everything, this is what shocks me.

"The tasting menu. Six courses," he says. "How's that sound?"

I'm about to ask how much it is, then don't. Prices are, evidently, not a woman's concern. "And champagne," I say.

Terrance holds out his hands, palms up. "Naturally."

Roasted lobster and artichoke soup with black truffle is followed by seared foie gras, which is followed by quail with winter succotash and asparagus, which is followed by rose sorbet, fucking rose sorbet.

When it's done, paid for by me in cash, we ride the elevator back to the room, fourth floor, fifth.

I press my face to his shoulder. "If the cable were to snap . . ."

Terrance looks at me. "Yes?"

"I'd be okay with that."

He laughs. "You're buzzed."

"Even so."

Back in the room, making love again seems obligatory, so we do, not halfheartedly, just half-bodily, exhaustedly, sleepily. He dozes off somehow a minute later while I'm still peeing in the bathroom, but I don't mind. I don't feel like talking. I don't feel like planning or making sense of things. All I want is what's here. Not just Terrance, but the duvet of white silk he's spread across, the softest pillow in the world scrunched under his head, the Louis-Whatever dresser and the blood-colored curtains. I curl up beside him like a cat and wait for sleep.

Terrance wakes me in the morning with kisses to my arm. I pretend to stay asleep for a long time after he starts, just so that he keeps it up. After a while, though, I can't hide the smile anymore. "Wake up, buttercup," he says into my ear. "Time to go to work."

So just like a pair of normal people, that's what we do. I shower first, he goes second. While I dry my hair, I watch him shave. When he dresses in the same sweater and dark jeans, I tell him he really does need to get something nicer.

"And buy a tie," I add.

"A tie?"

"So in the morning I can straighten it for you."

We leave together, but I take a taxi to Naz's office, and he heads into the Altstadt with his camera.

"So—a company in the Canary Islands," says Naz when I've settled into the couch in her office. "How does that sound?"

I shrug. "Sure. Fine. Can you—tell me what the company does?"

She bites the end of her pen. "Maybe—financial management. Why not?"

"Why not."

"And something else in St. Kitts, I think," she says. "The Caribbean, always a good choice. They have an economic citizenship program. Easy passport if Lila Kereti ever needs it."

"Aren't the Canary Islands in the Caribbean?" I ask.

"Cayman Islands," Naz says. "Canary Islands are off the coast of Africa."

"Oh, that's right," I say. "I just—never mind."

So two entities for me, a company that never has to actually do anything besides exist, and another to own the first. A double-curtain of privacy. It's done in a few hours, and the paperwork, a few hours after that. Phone calls will be made to expedite the process, and the accounts will be funded within a day.

And that's it. That's all it takes to steal almost 19 million Swiss francs.

Twenty-Three

After leaving Naz's office, I go promptly to the address she'd given me, a stately old building off the Paradeplatz just a few doors down from Hindemith & Cie. The plaque on the front of the building says Feldman Capital Services.

Inside, it looks every bit like a bank—and is, in fact, a bank. But a division for, as Naz put it, *specialized services*, is segregated from the rest, and this is why I'm here. The specific specialized service for which Lila Kereti has come is the leasing of a specialized kind of safe-deposit box.

Virtually every question on the application form has next to it the word *optional* in parentheses, even those asking for passport number and name. The only two that do not are the boxes where one checks consent to a retinal scan and the method of payment, which will be taken in advance, five years minimum. This, Naz told me, is the niche FCS has carved out for itself, the class of wealthy clients for whom passport numbers and names might, on occasion, become inconvenient.

A pretty blond woman with clever green eyes shows me into a

mahogany-paneled booth the size of a small bathroom and hefts a narrow steel box about eighteen inches long onto the counter.

"Let me know when you're finished," she says, and closes the door behind her.

I press my fingerprint against a panel on the front of the box and an LED goes from red to green. The inside is lined with a black rubber mat.

One by one, the things I'm leaving behind go into the box. Three hundred thousand in cash. Lila Kereti's passport and identity documents. A small plastic bag with a dozen SD cards containing copies of my father's video testimony. The original hard copies of the doomsday device scrawled on children's notebooks.

The sun is setting, and the air is filled with a magnificent yellow-orange that surrounds everything, casts it in gold, touches everyone's skin and makes it glow. Terrance is waiting in the Paradeplatz, right on time.

"All finished?" he says.

"All finished," I say.

A tram rumbles into the square and sets a flock of pigeons into the air, turning them into dark darts on a hundred bending trajectories. I duck and laugh, then see Terrance has bird shit on his shoulder and laugh again.

"It's good luck," I say, fumbling for a tissue and not finding one. "Really. It's a thing in, like, a dozen cultures."

But he's aghast, scowling at his sweater.

I fish a newspaper from a recycling bin and do the best I can. "You needed a new one anyway," I say, adding spit to the mix in the hope that it will help. "Let's go; I'll get you one, my treat. Look, there's a shop."

Still-laughing me and shit-shouldered he cross the street and enter Lorber's Haberdashery. Nothing new here for the elegantly suited clerks; the pigeons in Paradeplatz have simply claimed another victim. Terrance is given a stack of shirts to sort through, and I entertain myself with a wooden box filled with swatches of elegant wool. This must be the place where those princes hanging out in the lobby of the Obelisk

Grande get their fix: the very deepest blues and the very deepest browns, blacks, checks, pinstripes—everything you can imagine.

A man materializes beside me. "We create for women, as well," he whispers.

He's well beyond sixty, with a thick body wrapped in an electric-blue suit and a fabric tape measure over his shoulders like a priest's vestment. He introduces himself as Marcel, then presses his fingertips together as he takes my measurements in his mind. I catch the glint off the cuff links in his white shirt, which are silver like the wings of hair pressed back to the sides of his head.

"I—don't really need anything."

Marcel looks at me and very nearly winks as he plucks a square of fabric from the box. "A certain prime minister prefers this one. For evenings, of course, when she's feeling daring. The *mystery* of it."

The fabric is black and deep, like oil or ink, then he turns it in the light and for a moment it's unmistakably blue.

"Midnight," he says, answering the question before I can ask. "It exists on the line between one color and another, and it can appear to be both."

I take the swatch and repeat the trick, black to blue, blue to black. The effect is subtle but distinct. By the time I look up, Marcel has a sketchbook of drawings open, his maybe, or Lorber's, but all rendered by hand with notes beside them in elegant script. He runs his finger over a pencil-line woman, her shoulders broad, lines straight, bearing strong and purposeful.

"Madame prime minister—she's a little thicker here and here, of course, and she doesn't have your shoulders, but . . ." His voice trails off as he gives a very salacious smile. "For you, yes. You'll wear it as well as she can. Better."

I twist the swatch in my hand, steal a look at Terrance, busy with a dozen shirts unfolded and spread about him as the clerks around him fuss.

I ask Marcel how much. The number he gives me is painful, and practical reasons for saying no queue up in my mind. But then I'm shaking Marcel's hand and saying yes.

He leads me to an empty spot of floor and begins measuring, calling out the number to an assistant summoned from the back room. Terrance watches me, corners of his mouth curled up. I nod to him, and he nods back.

"Can you be back in Zurich in six weeks?" Marcel asks from his knees as he measures me from crotch to ankle.

"Is that how long it takes?"

"Oh, yes. We can send it by courier, but for final alterations . . ."

"I'll be here."

"Very good. We take half now, half when you're satisfied."

I look down at him, the bald top of his head, the breadth of his shoulders as he measures the circumference of my ankle.

"Better if I pay the whole thing now."

A white shirt. After all that, Terrance went with a white shirt. It does look wonderful on him, though, as does the jacket I bought for him, something soft and black that's a pleasure to touch as I hold his arm walking through the Altstadt. There's a dinner, of course, in some moneyed place the bankers all seem to gather. Steaks and cocktails, the whole thing very American. The meat and wine sit heavy in my stomach, and afterward I can barely move.

"I had too much," I say.

Terrance groans into his napkin. "Me too."

"I think I'm going to be sick."

"Me too."

"God, how we wealthy love to bitch," I say.

There's nothing left to eat or drink in the city of Zurich that we can fit inside ourselves, so it's a cab ride home to the Obelisk Grande. Home, as if we'll stay in the hotel forever, growing old, the two of us. Christmas trees set up by bellmen and Passover seders delivered by room service.

We slink into the room guiltily, as if sneaking away from the sin of having gluttoned down in one sitting the entire caloric intake of a small, poor nation. I collapse to the bed and think about my suit.

Terrance is hanging his shirt on a hanger in the closet, buttoning the top button so it doesn't fall down.

"You should've gotten more," I say.

"I only need one."

"Why, though? I mean, we'll get you a suitcase."

He says nothing. Goes to the bathroom and washes up behind a closed door. When he comes back, I'm nearly asleep but snap back as he sits heavily on the edge of the bed.

"Get in," I say.

"In a minute," he says.

I see his back expanding, the ribs and muscles stretching, relaxing, stretching again.

"Hey," I say, reaching for his shoulder. "Hey, what's wrong?"

"Nothing," he says.

But the inflection's off, like the word isn't what he meant to say. He turns slowly, looking at me with his serious face, then slides onto the duvet next to me. "I was thinking—I was thinking about—since I can't go back. To the States, I mean."

I run my hand down his arm.

"Budapest. That printmaker I told you about, Miksa Jò. I could go there, apprentice maybe. If he'll have me."

I shrug. "Sure. I hear Budapest is great. We couldn't stay forever, though. I mean, I don't know. And I have to contact my dad."

He nods, settles his head into the pillow. "Right," he says. "Your dad."

"Something wrong?"

He closes his eyes, wiggles his head no. "Just tired."

My friends—champagne, the balcony, cold night air—gather with me again just as they had the first night. A low-key celebration this time. A contemplative celebration. If this is a celebration. I'd been wrong about how tired I was. The dinner wore off after a half hour of watching Terrance pretend to sleep. I slipped out of bed only when the real thing came and he started that gentle snoring of his that I love.

Jesus, how could I have been so shortsighted? My plan had only ever led to yesterday. Never further. As to what happens now—it had seemed so unlikely there would even *be* a now—no thought had been given at all. At least by me. But Terrance always had a plan for after, or at least a dream. He'd told me about it. Budapest. Miksa Jò. Is there room for me there? Had he planned on my being part of that?

Those darting pigeons in the square. Together on the ground for a time, but then comes the tram and it's off they go—trajectories this way and that, bending together or not. I am only one force of many, a single influence on Terrance's trajectory. And what have I given him to fall in love with besides greedy, gluttonous Gwen? My worst self—and also the only self I've known for years.

Good thing the money's here to fix things.

I refill the glass again, brain thumping now, held aloft on a cloud of fizz. I turn around and look at his sleeping form on the bed, all long lines and plans for the future. We still have tomorrow, and one last night at the Obelisk Grande to figure it out. Things'll be better in the morning. They always are.

Hangovers for the both of us the next day, and a message from Naz that the transfers to the accounts of my shiny new corporations began this morning. All should be resolved by this afternoon, she says, so early congratulations.

Just some toast and coffee for us. Terrance works out some issue between himself and his camera and says he'd like to try to get some shots in. I smile and tell him it's a great idea, that I can't wait to see them because I'm sure they'll be great. Laying it on a little thick, I think, but just in the performance, not in the sincerity of the thought. When he leaves, he kisses me for a long moment. Then he runs a thumb over my cheek.

I take a bath, lolling around in fat suds until I prune up and force myself to endure the small torture of climbing out. But the robe makes up for it with a mighty hug, and I lie on the couch flipping through the tourist magazines and discovering new things I want to buy.

After an hour of this, I'm disgusted with ads for jewelry and watches—*Schmuck* is the word for that here, bangles, adornments, but all I see is *Schmuck*. All the things one doesn't need but buys anyway. Like a custom suit in a color called midnight. How foolish that had been. I take up my phone and check my mail for a message from my dad, but there's still nothing.

I try not to let it bother me. Try to tell myself it's no different from yesterday's lack of contact, or that of the day before. But at a certain point, the empty inbox has to mean more than he just didn't get around to checking in. I fidget there on the couch for a while, trying to ignore the building anxiety. Then I dress and head out, substituting fresh air and motion for some kind of productive action. A buzzy, anxious tension creeps into me as I walk down the driveway of the hotel toward the tram, every noise too crackly and sharp, the sunshine shifting from blinding to meek every other second as clouds scuttle over the city.

The tram is nearly empty when I get on, and it shushes peacefully along the tracks toward more interesting neighborhoods. Trees and cars slide by, mothers pushing strollers, old men arguing about something.

We slow down to a stop and a single passenger boards. A business-woman, prosperous in a Burberry trench and good suit and good pumps. Her black hair is worn very short, and her skin is dark brown with fine cheekbones and a slender nose. She glances through the car and approaches me, the trench she wears swishing through the air and sending up a faint smell of perfume. Maybe fifty seats are open, but she chooses the one directly across from me. I look away but feel her eyes on me.

Another stop, then another, a few passengers get on and off, but the woman remains just where she sat.

"Excuse me," she says in English. The accent is very slight and from nowhere in particular. "You look familiar."

I glance at her. "I don't think so."

"Yes," she says. "We had a class together, at university. History of the Israeli-Palestinian Conflict, I believe it was."

I try to smile. "No, I've never . . ."

"Professor Brent Simanski."

I glance around, but the few other passengers aren't paying attention. We look at each other for a moment. She's smiling, I'm not. There's something about her I recognize now, not in her physical features but in the way she holds herself—relaxed but ready, certain of her own intentions but not mine.

The tram slows as it enters the first station in the Altstadt. The woman rises, then gestures with her head for me to follow.

On the sidewalk, I fall into step beside her. She walks quickly, like she has someplace important to be.

"I'm called Mazal," she says.

"What is this about?" I say.

But Mazal doesn't answer. We've entered a busy square, crisscrossed by tram tracks running between café tables and street cart vendors, the polite, convivial anarchy of afternoon Zurich.

Mazal takes my arm like an old friend and leans in. "Lovrenc Zoric is alive."

"Lovrenc isn't in charge," I say quietly. "It's his sister. And there's no more arms trafficking. That was their father, not them. The business is shut down."

"Do you have confirmation?"

"They told me," I say. "She did. Dragoslava."

"You had orders, which you ignored." She squeezes my arm. "The baby stroller we just passed. Tell me about the woman pushing it."

"Black yoga pants, blue jacket. Thirtyish."

"Did you see a man eating ice cream while talking on a phone?" Mazal says.

"Pink shirt, gray suit. Tall, athletic. Indian. Or Pakistani. Forty, maybe."

Mazal nods with a sly smile. "Now, who else do you see, up ahead? Who's ours?"

I scan the crowd, looking for clues, the ordinary-out-of-ordinary. "Construction worker," I say. "Beard, yellow vest, and helmet. Smoking a cigarette."

"And?"

"A woman, blond hair in a pageboy. Green jacket. Walking a bike."

"Anyone else?"

I keep scanning, but no one else jumps out. I shake my head.

"Two out of four," Mazal says, giving my arm a squeeze. "Not bad for a rookie. Tell me, how did you know?"

I shake my head. "A feeling."

"Good," she says. "*Good.* Then you're not overthinking it. It's like muscle memory in that way."

Praise, but also something else. She's telling me I'm surrounded.

"Why are they here?" I say.

"We're going to have an unpleasant conversation, Judita," Mazal says brightly. "They're here so you don't get stupid."

"What kind of unpleasant conversation?"

She gives me a quick smile. "I'm going to pull a cigarette out of my pocket and light it. That's the signal that everything's all right between us. I drop the cigarette, they drop you. Clear?"

I nod.

"Good." The cigarette appears between her lips and she strikes a flame on a cheap plastic lighter. She inhales once and coughs. "You failed your first mission. So we gave you a new one, which you completed successfully."

"What are you talking about?"

The pace of her walking slows. "The money you got out of Zoric's accounts. Nineteen million francs. The old-timers in Tel Aviv who were doubting you, they've changed their tune. Calling you a prodigy now."

Something that feels like helium fills my veins, about to lift me into the air. My back straightens, my face goes slack. "First, I don't work for you," I say softly. "Second, that's my money. Mine."

Mazal inhales and lets smoke wander from her nostrils. "This is the part you aren't going to like," she says. "The part where you really need to control yourself. No sudden movements, okay? Let me hear you promise, 'No sudden movements.'"

"Fine," I say with a trembling voice. "No sudden movements."

Mazal holds my arm tightly. "We intercepted the money this morning, as it was being transferred. It's our money now. Sorry about that."

Twenty-Four

It is everything I can do, everything, not to drive the heel of my hand into Mazal's chin, get my arm around her neck, and murder her. But the construction worker is watching me, hand under his yellow vest, and so is the blond with the pageboy, who appears to be digging for something in her messenger bag.

"My lawyer, Naz Sadik—she was working for you," I manage to say.

"Oh, no. We took a peek at her e-mail for the wiring instructions. Spoofed the bank's credentials when the transfer was initiated. She knows now, though. And believe me, she's terrified."

"Terrified of what?"

"Of you," Mazal says. "My advice: Let it pass. It's not your attorney's fault. But take her out if it makes you feel better. Just be discreet about it, please."

The world starts to slip away, the people in the square fading into blackness, the murmur of the city turning into the harmony of a thousand wasps buzzing in concert. Only Mazal remains.

"I need to sit," I whisper.

She guides me by the arm to a bench and takes the seat next to me.

"You had no right," I whisper. "The money was mine. It was mine."

"Your money?" Mazal's voice becomes stern. "Because you deserve it, for what you went through?"

"Yes!"

"Keep your voice down." Mazal looks around, then leans in close. "So all Gwendolyn Bloom's suffering is worth more than the suffering of all the women and children Zoric trafficked, more than the suffering of families destroyed by Zoric's weapons."

"I never said that."

"Who earned the money you call yours? You or the fifteen-year-old girl Zoric sold as a slave? You or the kid with no arms who picked up Zoric's cluster bomb?"

"It was mine because I *took* it."

"And such a good job you did, too." She points with the end of her cigarette toward a jewelry store and a mirrored display case gleaming silver and gold even in the steel-gray light. "What was your plan for all the money, anyway? Look, there you can buy a twenty-five-thousand-dollar watch. Or how about a few Bentleys—maybe one for each day of the week."

My mind clenches, pushing out the profane idea that she's right, that she's right and I'm wrong. "And what is Israel going to do with it?"

"Those passports you burn through, the escape routes, the training. You think those are free?"

"They're not nineteen million francs."

She follows a couple walking past with her eyes, speaking only when they're out of earshot. "When I was four years old, I walked with my mother from Ethiopia to Sudan, smearing shit on our bodies to keep the bandits in the refugee camps away. Know what happened next?"

"No," I whisper.

"An Israeli cargo plane came, landed on a dirt airstrip, the markings painted over. Loud as the devil. I was terrified; I'd never seen a plane before."

Her face is firm, as if ordering me to hear her.

"The woman who came up to us, I'd never seen someone like her. An Arab, we thought, but in army fatigues. She told my mother they'd come to take us home, to Israel, where we wouldn't be slaughtered anymore. Imagine that. Home, to a place you'd never been."

Mazal's eyes linger on me, as if determining whether her words are getting through. "The money pays for that, too."

I can hear the breath whistling fast in and out of my nostrils, the anger inside me not wanting to buy her argument. "Humanitarian work," I say. "That's what Israel's known for, right? Parachuting hugs to the kids of Gaza."

"Sometimes the wrong people get killed." She takes a drag from the cigarette. "Sometimes the right people get helped."

I close my eyes. Goddamn her. Goddamn her for being right. This cash had run in dank streams from all over the world until it collected here in a little pond called Switzerland. Zoric had stolen it from the victims. I'd stolen it from Zoric. Tel Aviv had stolen it from me.

"Be angry, that's okay," Mazal says quietly. "Just don't confuse your anger with righteousness."

Take away the sense that somehow I'd been wronged, and what kind of fury is left? A pure one that burns white and very, very hot. It's not just sudden, unexpected defeat, but victory stolen when the rules changed at the last second. But even this idea, that there ever were rules, seems so pathetically naive that my fury is directed back at me, too.

Mazal shifts, takes another drag on her cigarette. It's burning low, close to the filter. Either the conversation will end soon or I will. "You took, what—five hundred thousand?" she says. "In cash. For yourself."

"Yes."

"You may keep it. A bonus, call it. For your good work."

I glare at her.

"Seven years," Mazal says. "That's how long I have to work before I see that much. Before taxes."

I shove my hands in my pockets, nod. "Then I guess we're done, you and me."

"I guess we are."

"Be seeing you," I say.

"Probably." Mazal stands, starts to walk away, then turns to me. There both is and is not a smile on her mouth as she says, "The State of Israel is grateful for your efforts."

They disappear a moment later, all of them, sliding from view like shadows into sunshine. Even Mazal, who steps across a set of tracks just as a tram arrives, evaporates into the crowd of afternoon commuters. I remain on the bench where she left me for a long time, unable to move.

The white-hot anger burns out quickly, though, when there's no more fuel. Mazal and the others are gone, and as for me, I'm gone, too, an immolated metal husk, a 1/36 fraction of what I was. My ghost rises and feels nothing, passing through matter, unseen by the living. A vague urge to get off the tram as it nears Naz's office. But then we're leaving the stop and the urge is gone. Let her be, I tell myself. It's not her fault.

Then the ghost is back in the room at the Obelisk Grande, opening Terrance's laptop, carefully typing in the log-in for the banks in St. Kitts and the Canary Islands. They are, as Mazal promised, empty. I fumble for my phone, manage to dial Naz's number. I hang up when it goes to voice mail, but she calls back a second later. The word *unprecedented* is used several times, as is *tragic*, and *regrettable*. Promises are made, even an oath. We'll reconvene tomorrow, she tells me at the end, adding that she'll know more then. But her tone is of an attorney far outside her ability to promise anything anymore. Here again Mazal was right: Running through every word Naz utters is fear.

An hour later, I hear fumbling at the door, the aggressive tone of a Swiss lock saying the card key went in the wrong way. It's Terrance, of course, gorgeously oblivious for the three seconds it takes to scan the room for me.

"Why are you sitting on the floor?"

And evidently I am, though why, or when I moved here, I can't remember. The tears come, and I clutch my fingertips over my face as if trying to tear it off. "*It's gone, it's gone. They fucking took it, they fucking took it, Terrance. . . .*"

He's at my side, on his knees, pulling me into him, stroking my hair. "What's gone? Gwen, what happened?"

The story comes out in a greasy mess, sliding too far ahead, and my having to backtrack. Then I fill in some useless detail as if it mattered, the color of the jacket the blond with the bike was wearing, the brand of cigarette Mazal smoked. But by the end, though, he hears everything and understands.

His face is spread wide and open with disbelief, as if trying to take it in with all his senses, as if the story could be seen and tasted and sniffed. He goes calmly to his laptop, asks me for my log-ins and passwords, then nods. "Yeah," he says. "Gone."

"*I'm sorry I'm sorry I'm sorry I'm so fucking stupid. . . .*"

Terrance paces a bit, back and forth across the room, sneakers squeaking on the wood.

"*Jesus fucking Christ I fucked it up. . . .*"

Then he stops, comes over to me again, pulls my hands away from my face so that I can see him. His mouth and jaw are set, eyes narrowed, breathing even and controlled. "You're alive, Gwen. You're going to be fine."

I start up again, but he squeezes my wrists until they hurt, demanding I listen.

"It's money, Gwen. Paper. Not even that, electrons." He forces a smile, leans in close. "And—the safe-deposit box, you said you put three hundred in there."

I suck in air noisily, wrestle back control of my voice. "It's still there. They let me keep it. *Let* me."

"So you have that and whatever you have on you—Gwen, you're fine. I swear it."

"*You're* fine. *You're* fine, Terrance. Your father's money, waiting in

222

the trust fund..." As soon as the words are out, I hate myself for saying them. The shot hits him right in the chest, and he recoils a little. A muscle twitches in his jaw.

"I'm sorry," I say. "That was shitty of me."

"It's all right," Terrance says. "It's all right."

He sits in front of me, cross-legged.

"When the feds took my father's money, I thought I'd die. My father said there are worse things, but I didn't believe him." He scoots closer to me, moving his head with mine so that I can't help keeping his gaze. "Then they sent him to prison. And it turns out, he was right."

I nod slowly. "I understand."

"Do you? Because you're alive, and you have lots of cash in a metal box. The rest of the world would kill to be in your shoes, Gwen."

I turn and lower my head onto his thigh, and he strokes my hair.

We'll check out in the morning, and after that, go east. That's as specific as either of us feels like getting. I try to stay calm about Mazal and the money, and with Terrance's help, it mostly works. But I might be mistaking calm—manifested in the deep desire to not move from where I sit, ever—for shock and despair.

Through it all, I repeat what Terrance said, that faultless logic about three hundred thousand hidden away and whatever I have on me being an excellent start. Obscene to think it isn't. But when you're on the run, where working legitimately or even enrolling in a school means papers and living in the open, exposed—well, it's an expensive way to live, and Terrance doesn't know as much about that as I do.

A last hurrah, a last blowout: döner kebabs brought in from a street vendor. Terrance licks sauce from his fingers, and I have a strand of cabbage or onion dangling from my mouth like a shoelace. He smiles at me, points to my chin.

"You feel better? Even a little?" he asks.

"I think I can be happy as long as there are döner kebabs," I say, mostly to please him.

"Not cheap here. Almost fifteen dollars."

"They're three in Berlin," I say. "We should go."

"The CIA will look for us there," he says.

"They'll look for us everywhere," I say.

When we finish, he collapses onto the bed, and I do too, landing in the nook between his arm and chest. A flare of anger again, but I ignore it, breathe, ignore it, breathe. He used the word *us*, that's something.

"Fun while it lasted, though," he says, nearly reading my mind. "I'll miss this place."

"I don't want to waste it by sleeping."

"Me neither."

So we just lie there, looking at the excellent ceiling.

Twenty minutes of this in a nearly trancelike state, then the phone next to the bed lets out a shrill ring. Both of us jump at the sound and look over at its source. A red light on top flashes urgently as the warbling continues. It stops after four rings, though, and we go back to the way we were.

Then it rings again.

"I'm not going to get it," Terrance says. "It's a wrong number. Nobody knows we're here."

Unless they do.

The thought occurs to both of us at once. Terrance picks up the receiver. "Yes?"

I hear the voice shouting into Terrance's ear, "*Get out, get out, get out, get out . . .*"

We're on our feet in less than a second. Terrance scoops his laptop and phone into his backpack. I throw what I see lying around into mine. Terrance is at the door first, ear pressed against it, then mouths the word *empty*.

On some instinct, I reach for the desk, where our döner kebab wrappers are still balled up, and snatch the lovely gold-plated letter opener with OBELISK GRANDE written in script down the handle.

He opens the door, and we slip into the hallway. Empty, as Terrance had said, and nearly silent. We move toward the elevator, hear it chime as the door opens, and backtrack, dashing in the other direction. Over my shoulder I hear heavy footfalls in a dead run coming up behind us. At least two men, breathing hard as they sprint. I hit the door to the staircase first and burst through it, Terrance right behind. Three steps at a time, then four. The men from the elevator are only a flight behind us.

More footfalls on the concrete stairs below us, too, coming up quickly. Terrance and I are pinned in between those following and those up ahead, so I grip the letter opener just as the men coming up the stairs appear on the landing. The blunted tip of the blade lands hard in the first one's neck, pushing deep inside his throat just below his Adam's apple. With everything I have, I shove him backward into the second man and snatch up his pistol as it skitters across the concrete floor.

Both Terrance and I glance back over our shoulders to see the traffic jam on the landing, the two coming down colliding with the others, one of them gasping loudly. A shouted command to move, move, keep going—all delivered in English that is unmistakably American.

We explode into the lobby, tearing past elegant couples who shriek and leap for cover, creating a useful melee behind us that slows the men down. I shoulder through the revolving door, and Terrance follows. The carport is brilliantly lit as couples arrive in taxis. Two Chevy SUVs hulk at the curb, distinctly out of place. For a moment, Terrance and I both freeze—the driveway is very long, but it's the only way to the street. If we run, they'll be back in their SUVs and on top of us before we're even halfway down.

Then a Mercedes sedan pulls up and a valet approaches. I push him aside just as the driver's door opens and level the pistol at the driver. He raises his hands, and his face goes as white as his tuxedo shirt.

"*Raus! Raus!*" I shout. Get out! He scrambles from the car as the woman in the passenger seat does the same. I climb behind the wheel and launch the sedan forward as soon as Terrance clears the door. More shrieking as bodies dive out of the way. I floor the gas through the turn and race down the hill.

Classical music is playing, a tinkly, pretty piece, Mozart maybe. Terrance fumbles with the controls, trying to turn it off. It blares loudly for a second, then disappears.

At the end of the driveway, left takes us farther into the Zurich residential neighborhoods, and right takes us to the city itself. Or maybe it's the other way around. I jerk the wheel to the right.

The sedan is powerful and fast, but it's also very large. It charges down precariously winding streets that have a habit of becoming suddenly narrow without warning. Headlights are following us a block or so behind. I can hear the SUVs crashing over speed bumps, their engines deep and throaty.

"Where are we going?" Terrance shouts.

"I don't know," I shout back. "Away."

"They're Americans—those guys are Americans. Did you hear them?"

I take a hard left through a red light, kicking the tail end of the Mercedes out behind us before it finds its footing and roars forward. A car coming up behind me swerves and nearly crashes into a truck going the other direction.

"They want me, not you," I yell. "I'll get to the city, we split up, got it?"

"No. Never. Not a chance. I'm not leaving you alone with them."

"Goddammit, Terrance, listen to me." I see the SUVs rounding the corner we'd just taken and coming up hard on the little sedan. "They'll be searching the Zurich stations. So take a taxi east, don't use the trains until you get to a small town. Then keep going."

Up ahead, an intersection with a wide multilane boulevard. We have the green light now, but when it turns red, we'll be trapped. I stomp down on the gas pedal and the burst of speed presses us back in the seat. The SUVs behind us see it, too, and do the same.

Yellow.

Brake lights pop up on the cars in front of us. I swerve into the lane for traffic going the opposite way. Cars panic and veer to the side; some collide with the dead crunch of steel on steel.

Red.

I press the gas all the way and rocket forward. Traffic is starting to creep into the intersection. I flash my headlights, hammer the horn.

Then we're spinning, the world silent, and a mass of white clouds explodes in my face. Spinning three times, four, five. Something hits us from the opposite direction and we spin the other way. Terrance's body is on mine, or mine is on his. This is, of course, the end, as I knew it would be. But better than whatever the boys in SUVs had in mind.

I'm proud of that. Choosing this way. Not their way.

Then motion stops, and the world becomes loud again.

A horn sounding. No, several of them. Stuck that way, a maddening dissonant orchestra of cars braying as they die. The air bags are deflated now, a chalky mass of thin white plastic that I have to fight through to get out the window that's no longer there.

I land hard on the pavement, the side of my head striking the ground, but I drag myself to my feet and see Terrance on his feet, too, studying the blood pouring from his mouth, his eyes glinting in the glare of headlights.

"*Go!*" I gasp at him. "*Go!*"

So he goes, and I do too, shocked our legs work, shocked any part of us does.

Traffic is piling up around us, cars edging forward, curious, then stopping, putting on their hazard lights. People are getting out, shouting at us, asking whether we're okay. I shove past them, then hear screams behind me. I glance over my shoulder and see the men from the hotel in full sprint, pistols out.

Terrance is ahead of me by three or four cars, his backpack flapping like an animal stuck to him, trying to break free. He dodges right, up another lane, then dodges right again and disappears along the side of a bus as it comes to a stop.

I keep going forward, then a door opens in front of me and I launch myself onto the hood of a car, dash over the roof, and leap onto the hood of the station wagon behind.

Two of the men do the same, their footfalls landing heavy on the steel and denting it as if they were giants wearing shoes of stone. I leap again, and this time my foot catches the hood wrong, and I'm tipping to the side. My face hits the windshield, cold glass through which I see a woman's terrified face as she starts to scream.

Part Three

GWENDOLYN

Twenty-Five

My father and I sit together in the last row of the Air France flight from Algiers to Paris.

A fat man sits next to us, fat fingers working fat wooden prayer beads over and over in an eternal loop. He smiles at me, black-and-gray mustache rising up at the corners like a bad guy's eyebrows. In French, he tells me I look like his granddaughter.

We had three seats when we came here.

We'll send her home in a few days, when the military police release the body. This from my dad's boss, the woman I was told to call Ambassador Cassie. My arms were around my dad's waist, head pressed to his hip, as the adults worked out the details.

I look at the fat man and wonder how it'll happen. Will they belt my mother's body into a seat? Who'll sit next to her?

A scratchy announcement over the PA, first in French, then in Arabic, then in English. A collective groan from the passengers. *Air France values your safety and appreciates your patience.* It's hot on the tarmac and hotter inside the plane. I smell everyone, onions and smoky clothes. The fat man smells of cologne and fruit.

My father's head is against the plastic window, face slack and un-shaven and pocked with sweat. He looks at me from the corners of his eyes. What does it mean to look at someone this way? At age seven, I didn't know.

But now I do:

I want to shoot myself—

That look, finally decoded:

And now I can't.

Does one feel actual pain in a dream? Maybe one only feels the *idea* of pain. Maybe one only feels the *fear* of pain. So the actual pain, the specificity of the pain in my wrists and ankles, is maybe a clue that it's not a dream at all.

With no distinction between sleep and consciousness, the real and unreal, it's important I keep doing this, formulating sentences. Sentences with words that mean things, with words that refer to concepts, concepts that refer to the reality of the world I know exists, or existed, before this.

It's starting again.

A vanishingly small musical note—violin? no, electronic, computer-made—lasting no more than a half second. It's in my left ear. A single note, a high-pitched *fa*. Normal. As far as these things go.

A few seconds later, another note. *Fa*-sharp, also in my left ear.

Sweat rolls down my skin. I clench everything that can be clenched. My body shivers. The teeth on my limbs gnaw.

Start counting, I tell myself.

When I make it to three, there's a *re* in my left ear. I start over, and this time make it to seven before I hear *ti*-flat. At thirteen, another *ti*-flat.

It helps if I count off the time between tones. Even if there's no order to them, at least I can measure it, or come close. It works for a while.

Until it starts in the other ear.

A louder *mi* comes from the right, overlapping a *do* from the left. I try to maintain a separate count for each ear but have to give up right away. It's too hard.

In moments, the notes are all over the place. High and low. Long and short. Quiet and loud. Well-spaced and right up against one another. The randomness is what makes it impossible to keep count or even hold on to a thought. It is designed—I am certain of this—to make analysis impossible, to render the mind unusable.

Hours of this. Or so it seems. But I need to be clear: The duration isn't the important thing. The tortures—nightmare, hallucination, madnesses, of which the sound-chaos is the mildest—start and stop randomly. It's that randomness that's the important thing. The thing that really gets you.

In between the tortures, there are pauses, intermissions. Darktime, I call it, a period of absolute lightlessness, absolute *un*light. It's a featureless nonexistence, but at least there's space for me to build thoughts again. With time—if that's how darktime is measured, and not in centimeters or grams or some other dimension—I learn a trick.

Memory. It exists still.

It may, in fact, be the only real thing left.

My mom and dad, snoring in the bed of Pension Alexandra's room 33, beneath the eiderdown, a cold morning in fall, or maybe winter. I bound up onto the bed.

Dad groans, rolls away.

Too early, says Mom.

So I climb under the eiderdown between them, warmth radiating from both sides, a pocket for tiny me.

Light comes through the window, gray turning white. Snow today? Sunshine? It doesn't matter here beneath the eiderdown.

A fart—no sound, just smell. Last night's dinner. I make a gagging noise.

Goddammit, Will! My mom swings her arm over me, crashing her fist into my dad's shoulder.

His body shudders and he lets out a pained *Ow!* He turns over, and the two of them face each other, big Mount Rushmore faces looming on either side of me. *Wasn't me*, he protests.

So I giggle, pull my nightgown up over my mouth.

I keep it together, just enough to say, *Mine.*

Tickling.

Then the darktime ends with the wailing of a baby.

It is wailing of a particular quality: pissed, frantic, in pain. It hits me in the lizard brain lurking at the center of my mind—*save it, save it before it dies*—a biological imperative, a human must. And this would be bad enough if the wailing were just as described. But it is not just as described, not quite.

Because the wailing is backward. It begins at demonic peak-wail and gets sucked in reverse into the baby's mouth, as in a vortex, a black hole of suffering. And there's so much of it, the sound going on and on, all the pain in the world, whistling through a tiny hole.

Somebody help her.

The sweat pours now, along with a sensation like the crawling of a billion insect feet over my skin. I twist and writhe, trying to avoid what happens next, the thing that always happens next.

Images fill my vision, so bright that even when I close my eyes, they're still somehow there. It's an illusion, must be.

A knife pressing into a man's throat.

Time lapse of a human corpse decaying to bone.

A child on a swing, slow motion, face ecstatic.

Knife again, a close-up, hitting the carotid.

A woman's mouth, open in orgasm.

Sewage flowing down a hill.

A human tongue being pierced by the stinger of a wasp.

Time lapse again, sunflower blooming.

Sewage flowing.

Knife.

Mold.

Child.

Knife.

And through it all, the backward baby.

Rain, so much of it. Right there—two, three feet away. Splattering against my red Doc Martens and the legs of my jeans. It's chilly here in the entryway of the East Village tenement. It forms a nook, an eddy, for the wind, and a flyer for a DJ's performance swirls around us. I should be cold, shivering, but I'm not. Someone is holding me.

His name has a number in it. Terrance Mutai the Fourth. Spelled, no doubt, capital-I capital-V. Roman numerals, to make them fancier. *What are you, royalty?* I ask.

I'm the same as you, he answers. *We're both royalty.*

Of what? I say.

King and queen of this, he says.

The tenement entryway, he means. Or maybe all of New York. Or maybe just of our lives. Which are ours. Which are ours alone. To do with as we please.

A cab comes—how unlikely that is in New York, in the rain—and we climb into the backseat of our royal carriage, yellow as the sun. Up the boulevard we travel, past diners and bodegas and mattress stores. I dread the climbing of the street numbers, Forty-Fifth Street turning to Forty-Sixth turning to Forty-Seventh, which means we're getting closer to my apartment.

Terrance the Fourth rubs my hands, red from the cold, while his are always just brown and beige-peach and warm and so much bigger than mine, with long, aristocratic fingers. We're strangers to each other, but we already know everything that's important.

The cab pulls to the curb.

He kisses me.

We'll be together, he whispers, *until the day we die.*

. . .

Maybe I need to rethink my original premise. Maybe the dream-or-real binary is the wrong binary. Maybe the binary I should be looking at is alive-or-dead.

If that's the case, then the answer is obvious:

I'm dead.

And this is hell.

I've done enough to deserve it. There's no question. A stack of bodies that would make a psychopath pucker and look away. The corollary to this conclusion is that it's not a human hand orchestrating my current state but a divine hand. And the corollary to *that* corollary is that I'd miscalculated, badly, since the age of seven, and there is a god after all.

I don't know if it's some human-shaped infinity with a beard, some Yahweh or another, or some Baal or Athena or Gaia. All I know is that it's someone whose job it is to weigh souls and punish those found wanting.

And, lord, have I been found wanting.

Lusting, actually. Greeding. Greed for money that wasn't mine. Greed for a life that apparently wasn't mine, either. Win at any cost, I'd said. Well. I'd won. And here's the cost.

The tortures, the sound-chaos and the images and the wailing babies, they're part of what makes this hell hell. But only a part. The memories aren't there as darktime respites from the bad stuff. The memories have a didactic purpose and torture of their own: Look what you had; look what you wasted. Nineteen years of stuff, from the nasty to the neutral to the sublime, cast into the incinerator, and for what?

I imagine that at some point I'll run out of memories, and every one of them will become an old and stale rerun. After ten years of this, cycling through them will be exhausting. After a million, it'll be unbearable.

The problem with infinity is that getting through it takes forever.

He's dancing, whirling madly. Like an idiot, my dad. Our apartment in—where was it now?—Cairo. I'm a child, tenish, *sad*. To cheer me up, he plugs his phone into the stereo and cranks it all the way.

> *They say love awaits us all, high up in the sky*
> *Where heaven's open to all God's children if we try*

He spins, arms extended, face grinning fiendishly, a pirouette, an attempt at a pirouette. The song, the sappiest of sappy 1970s folk-kitsch, a multicultural chorus of gleaming smiles.

> *Wouldn't it be nice, if we all could learn to fly*
> *Wouldn't it be sweet, if we could sail up in the sky*

The rug in our living room—the red and orange and blue Kilim he bought from the Souk al-Gomaa—binds up around one stocking foot. His arms wave frantically and he falls, *kwa-lumph*, on the parquet floor. I laugh. Hard. Harder than I ever laughed before. He lifts his head and I see a little creek of blood at his hairline.

> *We'd fly together to heaven's gate, you and I*
> *Chasing peace, love, and happiness through the sky*

He's hurt; I'm panicked. Then he laughs, too. My dad wipes away the blood—*just keeping it interesting*, he says, *nothing to worry about*—and gathers me up, pressing his face to my tummy and blowing *bluuuuuuuumph* through my cotton T-shirt. I laugh again; it's been years since the last *bluuuuuuuumph*, and laugh and laugh until it hurts and he holds me. I had to throw the T-shirt out, though, because of the blood on it.

> *A groovy flying pair of fools gettin' high*
> *As we soar high, so high . . .*

For the sake of human scale—measured in rotations of the Earth around the sun, then in rotations of the Earth on its axis (365 units and 24 units, respectively)—I was dead for seventeen days, thirteen hours. That's a made-up number. It might have been four days and eighteen hours, or thirty years and one hour, or just one hour. But for the sake of making it specific—long enough to be long, short enough to not be forever—I'll call it seventeen days, thirteen hours.

It happens painfully, and all at once, my head bursting into the sterile and very white light of a hospital room. It smells of disinfectant here, in this world.

But the obvious metaphor of birth is just an obvious metaphor and, as such, unhelpful. Because that's where the similarities end.

A woman, early forties, dark hair pulled back into a ponytail, stands next to my bed. In her hands is a helmet. It is large and full, to cover the ears, and there's an opaque visor that covers the eyes. Even now, so immediately after my second birth, or my un-death, whatever, I know that this helmet had been the universe I'd lived in, the source of maddening tones and ghastly sights and that fucking reverse baby.

There is a generic quality to the woman, a plainness in her blandly pretty features and neutral makeup and navy blue suit. Her gold earrings are shaped like seashells, a touch of suburban whimsy. She is the mathematical average.

And it's this that confuses me at first. There is something in her I recognize, a specificity, as if she were the most average of average, and that's what makes her unique. Where? A stock photo in the lobby of a bank? *Meet your friendly loan officer.* A commercial for a tasty yogurt? *Even busy moms find time to indulge.* No. Nothing so bland as any of that. There is, emanating from her like a perfume, a kind of menace.

"My apologies, Gwendolyn," she says. "It's Gwendolyn, right? Not Gwen?"

Her voice. I knew that's what it would sound like. Chirpy and calm.

I open my mouth to speak, but there's no sound. Just a gummy dryness and saliva thick as school paste.

"Oh, I'm sorry—water!" she says brightly, fetching a foam cup with a bending straw from a stainless steel tray. "Ice chips," she says, pressing a button on the bed that raises my back. "Baby sips, now—can't have too much too soon."

Instinctively, I move my hands to take the cup, but a biting pain stops me. A pair of wide leather cuffs hold my wrists to the hospital bed. I can see the skin below and above them, red and raw, covered in tiny scabs. Another pair of cuffs are fastened to my ankles, and the skin around them is in the same condition.

"Use the straw," the woman says. "Some of it must have melted by now."

My lips close around the end, but even such a simple thing is suddenly difficult. My lips hurt, and they tremble, and the first of the water I suck through the straw runs down my chin. On the second attempt, I manage to swallow a few drops. It burns its way down my throat like vodka.

The woman presses a towel to my chin, then wipes my mouth. "We've met before. Do you remember?"

I nod, though I'm still not sure where.

"Prague," she says.

Another dream now, vivid as reality, or at least this reality, if this is reality.

A hotel suite, a comfy couch, a comfy bathrobe. And a needle.

A psychiatrist, I was told. Sent to help me get through the debrief.

I'd led her through it all, how I'd rescued my father, how he'd been shot in the process. How I'd sent him away with someone named Sam. How I'd capped off the night by murdering a dozen men with rat poison.

But this was of no interest to her. Was never of interest to her. What she was after were the bank accounts my father had discovered, the accounts I'd tracked down, the accounts I'd just emptied and, in turn, saw emptied by someone else.

She had given me something, injected it into my arm. *Something to help you relax*, she said. *To relax and remember.*

Her name is Dr. Simon.

I pull uselessly at the restraints, shake my head violently until I feel the blood slosh around and my brain bounce off the insides of my skull. *Wake the fuck up now.* But when I open my eyes again, I'm still here in the hospital room smelling of disinfectant, and she's still here, the average of all averages, smelling of menace. In fact, she's stroking my head now, shushing me, telling me it's all right. Everything's all right. A beeping sound in the background begins to slow, and I realize I'm attached to a heart monitor. "Shhh," she says, eyes on the readout. "Shhh."

The cup again, and a few more sucks of water through the straw. Easier this time.

"The anxiety you feel is normal," she says, hand still stroking my hair, not moving from my side. "I've been tapering you off the sedatives since I got here. When I found out what they were doing—Gwendolyn, I want to tell you how sorry I am."

She holds both sides of my head in her hands and stares into my eyes, sincere as anyone's ever been to me. "Barbarism," she says. "There's no other word for it."

The chirping of the heart monitor is more even now. I see the readout over her shoulder. *102, 102, 101, 99.*

She sighs, shakes her head. "You have no reason to trust me, I know that. But even so—what they did, it's over now. Okay? Over. Nod if you understand."

I nod.

She's waiting for me in a chair when I wake up again, laptop braced on her knees. It's a thick, black laptop. Rubberized. Ruggedized. Made for environments more demanding than a hospital room in—

"Where am I?" I say, my voice gravelly and small.

Dr. Simon looks up, gives a quick smile, and closes her laptop. Her nails, medium pink—the average of all pinks—drum on the plastic lid. "Sleep well?" she asks.

I nod, try to raise myself, but the leather cuffs hold me in place. Dr. Simon slips the laptop into a tasteful briefcase, brown pebbled leather—you can find it in the local mall if you want one. In a moment she's at my side, pressing the button that raises my back. There's melted ice again through the straw, and it's like a blade down the center of my body.

"Where am I?" I say again.

She arches her eyebrows. "A research facility. Like a hospital."

"So, not a prison."

"Oh, no," she says. "Not a prison at all."

"So I can go? If I want?"

Pursed lips, *you know better than that.* "We're under contract from the American government. To keep you safe, Gwendolyn." Dr. Simon retakes her seat and crosses her legs primly. "How did you like South America?"

I don't answer.

"Did it agree with you? The climate, the people?"

I turn away. "Where is he?"

"Who, your father?" she says. "Or Terrance?"

"Either. Both."

"We found the apartment in Montevideo," she says.

Despite my attempt to hold it back, there's a little tick in the corner of my mouth. She sees it. I'm sure she does.

She continues. "But he had already, you know, *poof.* Disappeared. Vanished."

I look back at her. "Good."

"Your landlord, she identified the both of you. Gone *dos semanas,* she said."

Two weeks. They missed him by two weeks.

"I don't know where he went," I say.

"No," she says. "Of course you don't. And that's okay. We can talk about that later."

"What about Terrance?" I ask. "Where is he? Do you have him?"

"We did, but not anymore. Terrance is back in the States. We're helping him find a college. We're very grateful to him, actually."

No emotion on her face, not even a little smirk of victory.

"Grateful for what?" I say, already knowing the answer.

"For giving us you," she says, the answer I already knew.

Twenty-Six

There can be no conversation after that. We both know it. So, instead, she turns to a glass dome in the corner of the room and says to it, "Go ahead, cue up the tape." There's a moment's pause, a moment in which everything on me from my eyes to my teeth to my asshole clench shut, before the recording begins with a digital hiss, of ones and zeros coming together into a string of human words in the shape of a bit-crushed voice that belongs to Terrance Mutai the Fourth.

He's whispering, less to be quiet than because the words hurt him to say.

Terrance: She saved me, okay? She saved me. The guy she strangled, he was there to kill us.

    Male voice: Gwendolyn's going to be fine. We have no interest in punishing her.

Terrance: Then why did you send, whoever he was . . .

    Male voice: We didn't, we didn't, Terrance . . .

Terrance: Bullshit.

    Male voice: Not our style, Terrance.

The recording scrubs forward, the voices of Terrance and the other man melting into racing tones, a dense burst of dissonant *mi so la's, do fa mi's*. Then it slows, the tones sucking back into a pair of human voices.

Male voice: Terrance, listen to me, Terrance, this is important.
Terrance: I'm listening. Goddammit, I'm listening.
Male voice: We want to protect her, we want her to be safe. . . .
Terrance: Cut the shit. She's already safe with me.
Male voice: Terrance, if you love her like you say you do . . .
Terrance: Fuck you, using that like it's some bargaining . . .
Male voice: If you love her, you'll tell us where she is.
(Pause, crackling sound in background, Terrance's breathing.)
Terrance: She's here. In the shower.
Male voice: At the hotel? The Obelisk Grande?
Terrance: If you fucking hurt her . . .

The recording ends with a gasp from me, the taste of blood in my mouth from where I've bitten into my lower lip. Dr. Simon stands, makes a slashing motion at her throat.

Through the tears, I see her approach, compassion, or something resembling it, in her slow, deliberate movements. She presses a tissue to my right eye, then my left. Uses another to wipe my cheeks. Uses another to dab my eyes again.

"What is it you're feeling?" she says. "Right now. First word."

"Betrayal."

"Yes." She nods. "Yes."

"I hate him," I seethe. "I hate you more."

"And you're not wrong to feel that way. But what I'd like to show you, Gwendolyn, what I'd like to demonstrate"—she crouches next to me, her voice just a whisper—"is that it just might be exactly as Terrance says. That he did what he did out of love."

I shake my head violently, wrenching at the restraints—I can feel them breaking through the skin again—and let out a sound that might be a scream, except I can't hear it.

"This hurts," Dr. Simon says, still gentle, still quiet. "I know it does. Getting well always hurts. Seeing reality, especially—you've been unwell for so long."

She touches my cheek, I recoil. She touches my other cheek, I recoil the other way.

The following day, the restraints come off and I'm brought to an office and seated in an armchair, comfortable by clinical standards, with tan vinyl upholstery and real wood armrests. Dr. Simon sits in an identical chair across from me, like a peer, an equal. It's still a hospital room, but only in the sense of still being a room in a hospital. The fluorescent lights hanging from the concrete ceiling are dark, so we can see each other by the light of two floor lamps. There's even a rug, a carpet rectangle the same color as the vinyl on the chair. From my seat, I can't even see the guard standing behind me.

"Would you like some coffee or tea? I think your body is ready for some, if you want it."

I nod. "Coffee."

"Milk or sugar?"

"Both."

Dr. Simon rises and gets it for me herself from a stainless steel tray on a cart against the far wall. "Usually, at this stage, I'd caution against stimulants," she says, turning to me as she stirs a foam cup, "but it's just a little caffeine, right?"

She hands it to me and I hold it with both hands. My wrists are a disaster, bright red, scabby. My ankles are, too, but I can't see them beneath the pants of the pink hospital scrubs and paper slippers. "Thanks for the coffee," I say.

She settles into her chair and waits until I take a sip. There's no laptop or even a paper notepad on her knees. *Just two people talking* seems to be the theme she's going for.

"It's a failure on our part," Dr. Simon says. "Everything. We accept full responsibility. This should have never happened."

Through concentration and will, I'm able to keep my breathing slow, my voice calm. "What does 'everything' mean?"

She holds out her hands, palms up. "All of it. That you felt you needed to run, that you felt in danger. This—machine. The state. *Our* government. It's a blunt instrument, Gwendolyn." She crosses her legs, shakes her head. If this sadness I'm seeing in her, this contrition, isn't real, it's a very good performance. "The state, when you're outside of it, it can crush you, crush anyone. That's why it's important you're on the inside again. Where it's safe."

"I'm inside it now," I say. "And, funny thing. I don't feel safe at all."

A polite smile and nod. "That's what I'm talking about. Men with guns, that psychological monstrosity they put you through. But I came as soon as I heard, Gwendolyn. You don't have to worry about all that anymore. We'll focus on getting you well. And getting you home."

I look down, study the swirl of curdled creamer in the coffee, the shelf-stable chemical dispensed from a plastic thimble meant to be milk.

There's no way I can manage anymore. The tension inside me, it's a steel coil, winding up, pulling me in on myself, squeezing everything else out. The sob comes out as a gasp, then a sad little girl's moan.

I take a handful of tissues from the box on the table and press them to my face. Dr. Simon sits patiently, no attempt to quiet me. I take another handful and blow my nose, filling it with snot and spit and tears. When I'm done, the tissues are balled up on my lap. I inhale sharply, sucking air through my nostrils to clear them. "How did you do it?" I manage to say. "Get Terrance to—do what he did."

"After the thing, the incident in Buenos Aires. That—hit man, who-ever he was. Terrance was scared."

"Of course he was scared. He almost got killed."

"No, Gwendolyn," says Dr. Simon. "He was scared of you."

I look up at her.

"Scared of you. And *for* you. What we did, forcing you to go on the run, it changed you, mentally. He recognized that. Reached out. Said you were—headed to Zurich. To get the money, he said."

"It's gone, by the way. The money. I had it for all of about five minutes."

Dr. Simon nods. "The money doesn't matter, Gwendolyn."

Bullshit. It's all that matters. Money is all that ever matters. I see it now, Dr. Simon's game. Win my confidence. Wait for my sin to become too heavy to bear alone.

"I mean it, it's gone. Really."

"Let's promise each other something," she says. "I won't ask about the money. Ever. And you won't bring it up. Ever."

"So what do you want with me?"

"Once you're better, you'll go back to the States. You can have a new name, if you like. A new legal name. Social security number. Even a credit score, a good one." She smiles warmly, leans forward, elbows on knees. "You're young still. Colleges to consider. We can help you with that, just like we are with Terrance."

I take my coffee again, swallow some.

That creamer, it's a lot like real milk.

Two guards—a man Dr. Simon referred to as Mr. LaBelle and a woman she called Ms. Rossi—follow me down the corridor. Both wear cargo pants, polo shirts, and boots—not combat boots exactly, but they wouldn't be out of place. They're of a kind, these two, the strutters I'd see in embassy hallways with my dad, athletic even under a layer of mid-thirties padding, intelligent faces, seen-everything-before eyes. There are no handcuffs on my wrists, but the pair walk a few steps behind me, their confident footfalls echoing off the concrete floors of the tunnel to the concrete walls and concrete ceiling.

The doorways are very few, and each is like the one to my room, with no window and a slot along the bottom for the passing of trays. Next to each is a stenciled letter and number combination in no particular order: A-14, A-15, C-12. Conduits for the fluorescent lights run down the center of the ceiling like a gray stripe.

I look over my shoulder to Ms. Rossi. She's the one who stood behind my chair in the session with Dr. Simon. Her expression is blank, and it's the blankness that infuriates me. That amoral American professionalism: *I'm not evil; it's just my job.*

"What do the letters mean?" I say. "Next to the doors?"

"Eyes forward," she says.

"Are there even any windows in this place?"

"Eyes forward, please," she says.

"Eat my ass."

It's a child's bravado, though, an attempt by the powerless to claim some. Rossi knows this better than I do, and my eyes are forward before she has a chance to repeat herself a third time.

We stop before a door marked C-19, a different room from the one I'd been in last night, C-7. It's a straight shot to the room where Dr. Simon and I met, B-3, as if this entire facility were a single long corridor.

In this new room, the hospital bed is gone, replaced by a cot. There's a pillow on it, and sheets, and a blanket. All of it is institutional in kind but not punitive in quality. Comfortable enough, as far as government bedding goes. They've also given me a clone of the same tan vinyl armchair. And next to it, a small stack of books. A history of NASA. A collection of American poetry. The autobiography of a heroin addict who finds Jesus.

In the corner, I even discover a little luxury: a handheld showerhead mounted to the wall, a drain on the floor, and a thin plastic curtain that goes around it in a quarter-circle, creating a space barely big enough for me to stand.

There's a towel, a fresh set of scrubs, and a pair of white rubber-soled shoes without laces waiting for me on the chair beside it. There are also toiletries, little bottles of shampoo and toothpaste, a flimsy plastic comb, a toothbrush with a flat round tab as big as my thumbprint for a handle. So I can't make a knife out of it, I suppose.

My body shivers under the brassy water and I shower as quickly as I can, not really rinsing the shampoo properly and wondering if it would have killed them to give me a little conditioner. When I finish, I reach from behind the curtain, grab the towel and scrubs.

As I work the comb through hair matted as a stray cat's, I see something has been slipped through the slot in the bottom of the door. It's a cardboard tray, and on top of it, a bowl of soup, beige and hot; and white toast; and a foam cup of orange liquid. I lower my nose to the bowl and breathe in the smell of chicken broth, salty and metallic. I lift a spoon of it to my mouth and burn my tongue. So I take a sip of the orange liquid. It's a sugary something that tastes like a chemist's idea of orange juice, re-created from memory as best he could. I scoop the toast through the broth, then let each bite collapse under its own weight on my tongue.

When I finish, I look up at the camera. It's high in the corner of the room and hidden behind dark glass. Who's on the other end? I wonder. Dr. Simon? No, she couldn't always be there, could she? So a guard, with the unhappy task of recording my sleep, my meals, my bowel movements, my showers.

I give the camera a little wave. "No fair," I say. "You can see me, but I can't see you."

If I sleep, I don't remember falling asleep, which is why it feels so strange when I wake up.

I lift my head and look—yes, I was right. The slot in the door is open. That's what woke me. Instead of the usual tray of hospital food, I see a wooden chessboard, and on top, the pieces all set up and ready to play. A dream, I tell myself, some bizarreness in some cortex or another, a blip or short-circuit.

But no.

I can tell by the feel of my body as I swing my legs to the floor that it's real. I can tell by the coldness of the concrete and the whisper my feet make as they walk to the door. I crouch, listen at the open slot, then drop to my knees to try to see through it. Someone's there, looming just out of sight, their shadow cast on the corridor floor.

So I move a piece, a white knight, two ahead and one to the side, everybody's opening move. Then I slide the chessboard back.

A hand descends, male by the looks of it, peach skin that hasn't seen sunlight in a while, and stubby, strong fingers. He moves a center pawn two spaces forward.

I move my own pawn, mirroring his.

He moves a bishop to center court.

I move my other knight.

He takes my pawn.

I lower my face to the slot. "Who are you?"

"Your move." The voice is deep and hushed.

I move the knight again, to a square precariously close to enemy lines. "Who are you?"

"Max," he says, and takes my knight.

I sneak another pawn one square forward, positioning it diagonal to his bishop. "You a—guard?"

The pawn disappears and his second bishop replaces it. "Do you actually know how to play?"

"I know how the pieces move," I say. My bishop launches an attack and takes one of his pawns in retaliation. My first kill.

He lets out a little snicker—not cruel, just amused—then takes the bishop with his queen. "Bad at chess, good at life. Isn't that what they say?"

"Isn't that what who says?"

"I don't know. People."

I deploy my own queen, moving it diagonally to the right side of the board, hoping he won't notice. "What about the camera in the corner?" I say. "Won't you get in trouble?"

"That's me. I'm the one who monitors it." His bishop again, repositioning for a kill. "You really do suck at this."

"Then I must be good at life," I say.

We continue for a short time longer, with my losing almost everything, even my queen. I manage to take only one more of his pawns.

"If you want to surrender," Max says, "you do it by tipping your king over."

"I know," I say, and move my king forward.

"Check," Max says. "Give up?" —

"No." I move my king back.

In the morning, Dr. Simon is waiting for me outside her office. "I'd like to show you something, Gwendolyn," she says. "Might give you some—insight. Into what we might achieve together."

We walk deeper into the tunnel, Dr. Simon beside me, Rossi and LaBelle five or so paces behind. The farther we go, the shabbier the place becomes. At some point, someone stopped bothering with the paint on the walls and it becomes bare concrete, deep gray and brown, wet, crumbling. I can actually hear water trickling. The doors here are older, too—battered steel, with old-fashioned keyholes, and lightbulbs in wire cages hanging above them. I fold my arms over my chest against the damp cold.

"On our files, what does it say next to your name?" Dr. Simon asks.

"How would I know?"

"It says, *enemy combatant*. No rights, that means. No lawyer, no anything," she says. "So ask yourself why you're not dead, Gwendolyn. Ask yourself why you're here."

"Because you want something."

The clicking of her heels on the concrete slows—plain black leather pumps, not expensive but well-kept. "Yes," she says. "I want to help you. In a way only I can."

I feel icy water sloshing over my laceless institutional sneakers and look down to see I'm standing in a puddle a centimeter deep. It runs in a stream down the slope of the corridor in the direction we're heading.

"Sorry," Dr. Simon says. "The water, it wants its tunnel back."

"Tunnel?"

"Over a hundred meters deep where we are."

"What is this place?"

"It's a dream, Gwendolyn."

I look at her.

"For me, at least. A research facility all to myself. Off the radar. Quiet."

"You built this?"

"Oh, no," she says. "Nazis built it, during the war. Or rather, Jews and Gypsies and whoever else built it, but, you know . . ."

The damp chill of the concrete suddenly seems more than skin deep, and I find myself squinting at every bolt, every crack in the concrete, as if these inanimate objects could be infused with evil. My body shudders.

"It's just a place, Gwendolyn. One has to do something with it, after all. The Poles have a seismic observatory in one of theirs. Looking for earthquakes. This one, the Nazis used it for developing nuclear weapons, but the Russians got here first." She stops before a metal chain-link fence and a padlocked gate. "It was abandoned for a time, but the East German government, they set up a lab of a different kind. For some of psychiatry's most gifted minds."

"Could we go back to your office, please?"

"I'm sorry, I thought you'd be interested. This is a special place. No one, I mean no one, really gets this kind of access." She motions to LaBelle, who goes over to a gray electrical panel on the wall and flips a series of switches. Down the tunnel beyond the gate, lights come to life, illuminating a patchwork of broken concrete, wooden crates dark with age, old desks, and rolling office chairs littered about. Rossi unlocks the gate.

Dr. Simon and I walk together deeper into the tunnel, leaving the guards behind. The place feels less like a laboratory than the gut of a snake, mouth leading to ass, one way in, one way out.

The desks are wood laminate, and the chairs plastic with moldy orange and mustard-yellow upholstery. They look like something from a German office circa 1975.

"The psychiatric work the East Germans were doing was secret and unorthodox by our narrow Western standards. Thus their charming offices." Dr. Simon opens a desk drawer, where I can see a few paper clips and a pen and someone's pocket change. She roots around for a second, then pulls out an ID badge, the photo of a balding man with horn-rimmed glasses still visible. A pink nail taps on the words beneath the picture. "*Streng Geh-guh—*"

"*Streng Geheim,*" I say. "Top secret. Who is that?"

"The good doctor Stanislaw Richter. You've never heard of him." She tosses the ID back into the drawer and closes it. "He was a pioneer of what was called 'political psychiatry.' East Germany's best. People were so jealous of his work that they discredited the whole field, called it monstrous. But Dr. Richter, he found it. Yes, he sure did."

I take a step back. "Found what?"

"Love. He found love."

"Love?"

"Or rather, beauty. Maybe truth." Dr. Simon smiles, looks down at her pumps. "A medicine, anyway. To cure citizens of what makes them sick. It was all very philosophical. Took me two years just to get my head around it."

I feel the edges of my mouth trembling as if I'm about to break out into a smile. Her words are madness. This place, madness. My eyes dart away from her, first back the way we came. The guards are standing there in silhouette, watching us. Then I look the other way, deeper into the tunnel. The lights end a hundred or so meters farther, but the tunnel keeps going after that, into darkness. Again, the sound of running water.

"Gwendolyn. Tell me, Gwendolyn, what do you want? More than anything?"

"To go home," I say.

"Home," she says. "Curious word choice for someone without one."

"To be out of here, then."

"No," Dr. Simon says. "That's not what you want."

This time my smile actually happens and comes with a raspy laugh. "Yes, it is," I say. "I want to get out of here."

"What you want is deeper than that," Dr. Simon says, leaning forward, smiling along with me, as if we're sharing a joke. "'Out of here' is just a negative. Like 'freedom.' But these words don't really mean anything, do they? They're just the absence of something." Hands on my shoulders, a friendly squeeze. "What you want, Gwendolyn, is safety. You want peace. You want to be loved."

Twenty-Seven

Lunch on a cardboard tray. A white bun in a perfect circle, a square of meat, and a square of cheese. There's potato salad, safety yellow, blended to the consistency of toothpaste, and a cookie in a plastic envelope. I balance the tray on my knees but barely touch any of it. Dr. Simon serves coffee. After inquiries about my feelings, my progress, my bowel movements, Dr. Simon reclines slightly in her chair, so her face is in shadow, out of the floor lamp's reach. I decide not to tell her about chess with Max.

"In the end, it's not so different, what you want and what we want," Dr. Simon says.

"Peace," I say, repeating back her words from the tunnel. "And safety."

"Was I right about that, Gwendolyn? That that's what you really want?"

I have to think for a minute. "Yes," I say.

"Us too," she says. "Us, meaning your government. The state. When it comes down to it, peace and safety are universal needs." She gets up and stands beside me, looking down at me. "So you think we can make a trade—what you want, for what we want?"

It's obvious what she's after: my father, delivered up like lunch on a cardboard tray.

"I don't know where he is," I say.

"I know. Funny that's where your mind went first, though. You really care about your father. That's clear." She takes her seat across from me, folds her hands in her lap. "I mean, you're a . . . I don't know. Warrior. Ninja. That's for sure. But there's a soft, chewy center to you, isn't there? The daughter part. That's interesting to me."

"Like I said, I don't know where he is."

"How was he, while you were together? What was his behavior like?"

I look down, study the texture of the potato salad, too yellow and smooth. "He was—probably how you think he was."

Dr. Simon nods. "Depression, anxiety."

I look up, shooting my eyes into hers. "Lot of that going around these days."

She leans forward with that gentle earnestness she's so good at. "Revenge. You want it, which is perfectly reasonable. But did he?"

I shrug.

"Someone in your father's situation, they might try to create a bargaining chip for themselves. Release information, say."

She's talking about his doomsday device. The fourteen videos and their handwritten transcripts I'd uploaded, the links ready and waiting to go out. Dr. Simon alluded to it so casually, so undramatically, that I almost missed it. But the doomsday device is, in fact, the point. Of this conversation and all our conversations. Maybe even the point of my being here in the first place, and not dead. The thing they wanted all along.

"I don't know anything about that," I say flatly.

Dr. Simon clears her throat politely. "I have something for you. A little gift. To celebrate the progress we've made."

I set the tray on the table next to me and look up.

"It's news. About Terrance."

"News?"

"Yes. He was accepted into Tulane University. And his father is being released early. He's moving to New Orleans to be with his son."

I close my eyes, try to picture it. But it sounds like just so much bullshit, a fantasy that couldn't possibly be true.

Then, as if reading my mind, she holds up a postcard. "Here," she says. "He wanted you to have something. A snapshot he took. A photo."

She holds the postcard forward, a small black-and-white print: a street scene, a black man in an open-collar shirt and ratty old fedora laughing as he walks down the street, pointing his finger at a shop window. Whatever he's laughing at is out of the frame, but his expression is joyous, the light undulating over the lines of his face, his delight in this moment, this thin slice of a second, complete and total. New Orleans? Maybe. Must be. That's why Terrance sent it. Look, he's telling me, look at the kind of happiness that's possible here.

I imagine him lifting the old Leica to his eye, seeing the shot before it happens, knowing this is the one, the four-by-six-inch rectangle of light and shadow that will be my window into the real world.

And on the back, a note:

G,

I don't know how to write this, but I know why I need to. I'm sorry. But it was the only way I could save your life. It was the hardest thing I ever had to do. The only thing that would make it worth it is knowing that you're alive and healthy again. That's all that matters to me.

Love always,
T

Dr. Simon allows me to take it back to my room, where I lie on the cot and hold it up to the light, wondering what I'll find—a secret message, something erased and written over? But there are no secrets in the words themselves. I don't think I've ever seen him actually write anything, but the letters feel like the letters he'd form with those slender, aristocratic fingers. I don't know his handwriting, but I know those fingers' touch, and this is it.

But the proof of the thing isn't in the note at all. It's in the photo on the other side. This is *his* photo, the evidence of *his* eye. Taken from up close, an intimate moment, as if he were speaking to the photo's subject, sharing a joke. He wanted me to see this, the subject's smile, a code that means it's all going to be all right. If I cooperate. As he did.

I press the photo to my face. Chemicals, that's what love smells like.

The slot in the door shuttles open, and the chessboard slides in. I expected this somehow, as if something so weird simply had to be repeated. So I slide down the wall next to the board and move my white knight in an L.

Today, Max is in fine form and it's a slaughter for the white forces due to their inept leadership. But at least I'm trying.

"You like being CIA, or are you a contractor, too?" I move a rook, and as soon as my fingers leave the piece, I see how he's going to kill it.

"Just play," Max says with a flat voice. He can't talk about it, his tone means. My rook is replaced with his bishop.

"Either way, it must get tiring, keeping all these secrets." One of my knights makes a mad, suicidal charge and takes one of his knights.

Max kills the knight with a pawn. "Yes. Very tiring."

I oblige him with a neutral, pointless move of a bishop. "I guess if you don't like it, you can always quit."

Max laughs. "You don't quit this. You know that." He advances a knight. "A helicopter ride over the ocean. That's what happens. For real, they do that."

"So run away," I say.

"What?"

"Run away," I repeat.

"Because it worked out so well for you," Max says. "Move already."

I tip my king over. "Oops," I say. "You win." I hear his body slide over the concrete floor.

"What's wrong?"

"I don't like games." I lean down to the slot, peering through it to the wall on the opposite side of the corridor. "Let me see your face."

"It's not allowed," he says.

"But playing chess is?"

A pause as he considers, then his chin appears, then pale lips and his left cheek. Finally, his left eye, greenish-brown, speckled. We stare at each other for a moment across a distance of only six inches, but at least two of them are steel. From what little of him I can see, I guess his age to be about twenty-five.

"Hi," I say.

"Hi," Max says.

My hand is in his hand, and the snow is falling. It's not cold, though, or I'm not cold, even though December in Moscow is always cold.

Pavlik spins me, and I hit a patch of ice under the snow and nearly fall.

But he catches me because he's good at catching girls after he spins them, which he does a lot.

Which is why my dad hates Pavlik. *Arrogant Little Shit* is my dad's nickname for him, as in: *Did you see the Arrogant Little Shit at school today? Who walked you home, that Arrogant Little Shit?*

And Pavlik is arrogant and shitty, to other people. But not to me. A dozen flowers today, produced with a flourish and a bow of his head as we walked out of school. They're white as the snow that's falling, even the stems, because they're made of tissue. It took him, he said, all of last night.

You were up all night? I ask.

How could I not be? he says. *I was thinking about you.*

An eye roll at nineteen, but at just-turned-fifteen, a wave of delight that's indistinguishable from nausea.

So—

Sure, I'll come back to your apartment.

Snow falls on my face like I'm in a movie about love. I gather up a snowball and throw it at him. He throws one back. It misses me and hits something else instead.

A pedestal, almost two meters high, with no statue on top.

That's what they did after the Soviet Union died, tore down the statues of their heroes, left the pedestals for whatever heroes came next.

I squint in the light at the plaque. Faded. Hard to read. *Hey*, I say, *hey—he has your name. Pavel. Pavlik.*

Morozov, he says.

Pavel Morozov, 1918–1932, I say, reading the rest: *Child hero. Example to all.*

Pavlik's arms are around my waist and he pulls me in. I feel his open mouth on my neck, and his saliva is cold when he moves on.

What'd he do? I ask.

Who?

Pavel Morozov.

He pulls back, strokes the side of my head with his thumb. *Pavlik's father hoarded grain to feed his family*, he says. *So the secret police shot him.*

They shot Pavlik?

He smiles at me in the way Russians often smile at Americans.

No, dummy. Pavlik turned his father in.

Give-and-take is how the world works, and even the kind Dr. Simon is determined to remind me of it. Quid pro quo. Tit for tat. Daughter for Father.

That's why the guards have brought me to someplace new, a kind of bunker within the bunker, instead of the usual stage set of a shrink's office with soft lamplight and comfy armchairs. The new room has unpainted concrete walls, damp with decades of neglect, that are cast in sickly green fluorescent light. There are two long folding tables, each

lined with monitors and hooked up to a pair of laptops, the same rubberized, ruggedized kind Dr. Simon uses. On each monitor is a different room. I recognize mine, and Dr. Simon's office, and the room with
the hospital bed. But there are others, too: live motion video of corri-
dors and stairwells, all empty of people, and an enormous steel door,
big enough for a truck to pass through.

Dr. Simon pushes back from one of the tables, the wheels of her
old office chair squeaking. She tells me to sit and kicks another rolling
chair toward me. "I won't ask you to trust me, Gwendolyn," Dr. Simon
says. "Trust is earned, and I haven't done that yet."

I sit, then look over my shoulder at Rossi.

"What do we do when we want someone to believe us but haven't
yet earned their trust?"

"Offer proof."

"Exactly," she says, and lifts something from the table beside her.
It's an old telephone, red plastic, the dial removed and replaced by a
metal plate. "So here's proof. Of my intentions."

She places the phone on the floor in front of me, tugging out a little
slack in the cord that connects it to an outlet in the wall. "Sorry it's a
bit grungy, but it's what we have. Problem with being off the grid is,
well, getting on it again is such a pain in the ass."

I look at the phone. "Who do you want me to call?"

"There's someone already waiting on the other end," she says. "All
you have to do is pick it up."

My hand reaches for the phone, but just as I'm about to touch it, I
stop. "And in return?"

"If, after your phone call, you believe me, that everything I've told
you is true"—she slides forward, gives that earnest look again—"then
you tell us one thing. That's all. One thing."

"Which is?"

Hands out, palms up. "Where it is. The information your father
plans to release."

I look away, first at the monitors on the tables, then at the phone

261

cord, tracing it from the wall to the handset in front of me, red plastic, no more dial, a single path forward, one way out. I study the cracked floor, the wetness seeping across it. How had Dr. Simon put it? *The water wants its tunnel back.* I turn my head to the coffeemaker in the corner, tan plastic, the glass pot hissing. I do all this so that I give Dr. Simon and the guard the impression of being lost in thought. Of thinking the unthinkable, which is to say, betraying the unbetrayable. But the truth is, I've already made up my mind.

Child hero. Example to all.

So I reach for the phone.

And I pull it into my lap.

The red plastic is just a shell, but I can tell from the weight the inside is all metal. I lift the handset and press it to my ear.

"Hello?" I say.

The static of old wires—hissing and crackling, the occasional pop—is all I hear for a few seconds, my voice maybe connecting to a cell phone tower on the surface above us, or maybe continuing by cable and wire all the way to the other end, over mountains and under oceans.

Then, a breath and another voice. "Hello?" it says. "Hello? Hello?"

"Hello, hi," I say.

"Hello, hi. Gwen?"

"Hi, it's Gwen—hello."

"My God..."

Far away, the voice, but even through the static I hear Terrance's sincerity. I gasp.

"I can hear you," he says. "I can hear you, don't worry."

Dr. Simon rises and shoos the guard out. The door closes behind me.

"Terrance?"

"Yeah, yes—Gwen, it's me..."

"Terrance."

"Yes. Gwen, I'm—Jesus, Gwen, how are you? I'm sorry, Gwen. I'm sorry. How *are* you?"

My hands are shaking, and it takes both of them to keep the handset stable against my ear. "I'm, I don't know. I'm shitty, Terrance. But better. You know? It's . . . God, Terrance, it was awful, but . . ."

"Where are you?" he says.

"Where are *you*?" I say.

"New Orleans. I got a place here. It's little, but—Gwen, I'm so sorry. I'm sorry about what I—did to you. It's okay if you hate me, please know that. If you hate me—I just was, I did it to *help* you."

I think I can hear the ocean as it courses over the ancient, fraying cable. It could be I hear whale songs, or maybe it's birds resting on the line as it rises out of the water and travels over land, strung pole to pole to pole to pole across farm fields all the way to a damp old building on a humid night in New Orleans.

"Let me hear it, Terrance," I say. "Let me hear the city."

"What?"

"Let me hear the city. Go to the window."

"Okay. In a sec. I've gotta—Gwen, where are you? Are you coming back?"

"Let me hear the city, Terrance."

"The window, the latch is—okay, it's open."

Filtered through thousands of miles, I hear car horns, a crowd passing by. Drunk people laughing, high-pitched and loud. And even—is that music?—yes, music. The strum of an electric guitar, a snare and cymbal, a band setting up.

"Gwen, can you hear it?"

My fingertips touch my mouth, and my breath pulses hot against the skin.

"Gwen?"

"Yes. Yes, I hear it."

Wood grating against wood, the window shutting.

"How fucked-up is this, Gwen? They called me like twenty minutes ago. Asked if I wanted to talk to you."

"And you're safe, Terrance? You're—they didn't hurt you?"

More static. "No. No, in fact—did they tell you about Tulane? I got in, Gwen. I got in."

I wander in the direction of the coffeemaker, just three steps, then the cord catches on the wheel of the chair. "That's amazing, Terrance. College."

"I'm sorry, Gwen. For what I did."

"I'm sorry too," I say. "For what I did."

"What did you do?"

"I—I fucked up your life, Terrance. I did. I'm sorry about, you know, dragging you into this."

Dr. Simon snaps her finger and I look at her. *One minute*, she mouths.

"It's okay, Gwen. Really. Look, it was an adventure, right? A fucked-up adventure."

"I'm sorry about—the mess we made in the hotel room. You know?"

"Yeah. That was—intense. But it's okay. It's okay now."

"And when I got drunk at that club. You were so good to me."

"It was nothing, Gwen," he says, and I hear him breathe, in and out, his voice catching like mine did. "Gwen? I want you to know something. I love you. I do. I love you."

"I love you back, Terrance. Really. As much as ever," I say. Then I laugh, just a little. "And your camera. Your poor Leica. I'm sorry about that, too."

"Forget it. Really. I mean, it's just a camera."

I look at the coffeemaker, where the pot meets the burner, the glass sizzling with anger. "I'm sorry I sold it. At the pawnshop. We needed the money, though."

"Oh, Gwen. It's—you know. Material things. They're not important."

"No," I say. "They're not important at all."

"What's important, Gwen. What's important is that you get better."

I pinch my eyes shut, curl the phone cord in my hand. "Yeah. I know."

. . .

With the receiver back in its cradle, I weigh the phone in my hands, a solid object, a forever object. You could pound nails with it if you had to.

The guard reenters the room and stands with her arms folded as Dr. Simon arches her eyebrows, *well?*

I nod, telling her I'm satisfied. That the phone call has met the requirements of our deal.

"Emotions. They can be confusing," Dr. Simon says. "It's okay if they don't make sense right away. Takes a while to sort things out."

"Sometimes not, though," I say. "Sometimes, they make sense right away."

I close my eyes and inhale as deeply as the breath will go, filling my belly with it. Then I swing the phone—red plastic over metal, heavy as a stone—into the side of her head.

Twenty-Eight

But it doesn't work.

The swing at Dr. Simon, it doesn't land clean. I hadn't accounted for her reflexes—which are good, it turns out—and my weakened ones, so atrophied after however long my imprisonment has been. In the end, the phone hits her shoulder and just glances off her ear. Rossi has an arm around my neck within a second. Within two, I'm on the ground with her knee in my back. She cranks my wrists behind me, nearly pulling my shoulders out of their sockets in the process.

Darkness after that. Whether it's the guard choking me out or Dr. Simon with a syringe full of horse tranquilizer, I don't know, because I never see it. That's what I get for acting in haste.

I wake up back where I started, in a hospital bed and strapped down with leather restraints. There are sensors taped to my chest and temples again, and a machine off to one side bleating out my vitals to Dr. Simon, who sits in the chair eating a sandwich wrapped in wax paper.

There's a bandage on her left ear. That's all. Just a bandage. Not even a black eye. A coin-sized drop of mayonnaise lands on her knee and she says *shit, shit* as she attacks it with a napkin and water.

She catches my eye as she wipes and actually gives me a thin smile, almost apologetic.

"Where is Terrance?" I say.

She goes back to her sandwich, chews thoughtfully. "Whatever I say you won't believe," she says, covering her mouth to be polite. "So what's the difference, really?"

The pain in my shoulders and neck is incredible, and I feel a throbbing on my forehead, just at the hairline, where I must have hit the floor. "I give up," I say, voice slow and flat. "Tell me the truth about where Terrance is, I'll give you whatever you want."

Dr. Simon nods, sucks grease from the sandwich off her middle finger. "Yes, you will," she says. "Give me whatever I want."

This said flatly, too, but with a difference. Games are over, it means. No more bullshit. She folds the wax paper and slides it carefully into the outside pocket of her briefcase.

"Want to know how to contact my father?" I say.

"Sure. But we'll get there soon enough in the next part," she says.

"The next part," I say. "Torture."

Dr. Simon cants her head to the side, and a smile ticks across her mouth. "The American government doesn't torture people, Gwendolyn. You know that."

"But you're not the government," I say. "You're a contractor."

"Well, that's true. A small distinction, but an important one." She scratches a pink fingernail at the dark spot on the knee of her pants. "Tell me, when you say 'torture,' do you mean pain?"

I manage a small shrug, *what else?*

"There are some people who get off on pain, you know—resisting it," she says. "Athletes, for example. A pride thing for them. Ego. But there are more extreme cases. You, I think. You like to defy pain. Say 'fuck you' to pain."

My eyes squeeze shut. "Just tell me. What comes next?"

I hear the feet of Dr. Simon's chair squeak against the concrete as she rises. I hear the soft click of her shoes as she approaches slowly.

"What comes next," Dr. Simon says, "is the fun part."

The terror, starting in my stomach and rising all the way up to my tongue, is something I can actually taste: salt and copper. I feel my pulse in my eyes and hear it, too, like a bass drum in my head.

"Do you know where morphine comes from, Gwendolyn?" Dr. Simon asks.

I rack my brain; maybe a right answer will please her. "Poppies," I say. "Morphine comes from poppies."

"That's right," she says. " And how about aspirin, where does that come from?"

Again, I work my memory but this time come up with nothing. I shake my head.

"From a process that turned coal tar into fabric dye. Imagine that— aspirin from coal tar and dye." She sighs, marveling at science and its wonders. "But we're beyond that now. That psychiatrist I mentioned, the East German, Stanislaw Richter—he did it, Gwendolyn, actually cracked the code. But me, I took it to the next level."

The whisper comes out hoarse and feeble. "Congratulations."

"What we've discovered—oh, Gwendolyn, it's wonderful. Can you guess what it is?"

I look up at her. "No."

Her eyes widen and appear wet, as if she's about to cry. She pinches her lips between her teeth and shakes her head, still not able to believe it. "We found—what love is made from."

I blink, twice, three times, her words making no sense. I pull tight at the restraints.

"That's right, Gwendolyn. The chemistry of it. Of love." She walks slowly to a steel counter at the back of the room and picks up a leather case. "Know what the key ingredient of love is, Gwendolyn?"

"I—don't."

"Come on," she says. "*Guess.*"

A raspy sound comes from my throat. "Kittens," I manage. "Rainbows."

She turns her head to me, lips pursed like an elementary school teacher's to a wiseass. "Turns out, it's venom." Blue rubber gloves snap over her hands. "Venom of the bullet ant. A special neurotoxic peptide unique to a single species in Brazil. Took forever to isolate. Weird, huh?"

My stomach clenches and I strain at the leather cuffs. "I can give you whatever you need. Information. Money. Whatever. I'll tell you..."

The needle of a syringe pokes through the red cover on a little vial. She pulls back the plunger. "Most ferocious stuff in the world. Had to recalibrate the whole way we measured pain. Unbearable, it's said. But, Gwendolyn"—a flick to the needle with her finger—"turns out, it *is* bearable."

A bead of sweat tickles its way from the top of my wrist, over my palm, to the bottom of my hand. I look and see it's blood from where I've pulled and twisted at the leather cuffs around my wrists until they've reopened my skin. "What do you want?" The words are raw, coming from someplace far deeper than my throat. "Please. Whatever it is."

"That's the trouble. What I want, so hard to put into words," she says, approaching calmly, like the doctor she is, gentle and wise in her movements. "Far easier to show you."

My teeth clench and my body bucks against the restraints. I lunge at her with a bark.

But there's no fear in her—the restraints have made fear unnecessary—and, curiously, there's no malice, either. Just pale lips feigning a clinician's smile.

The needle puckers the skin over a blue vein on the inside of my elbow, then slides through.

Her thumb depresses the plunger slowly, and the drug creeps like warm water through my arm to my heart and to my head. She tells me to shush, then caresses my bicep. The warmth of her fingers shines through the rubber.

The pain, the toxic nausea—I clench my face in anticipation of the first wave from this unbearable-bearable venom. But it doesn't come.

Instead, delirium and pleasure. It does not wait. Does not build to something better. It just takes hold, all at once.

A cartoon sun. A child's yellow marker, soaking through the paper. Hypersaturated. The salt-and-copper taste of the terror is replaced by sugar and cherries.

It is not the sensation of flying; it's stillness, of the world coming to me. I hear a gasp, then a laugh—mine from my O-shaped mouth. I close my eyes. See springtime.

She's there, next to me. I can feel her breath roll over my ear to the skin of my neck and cheek. *Like?* she asks. I don't answer. I hear the white film on her lips crackle as it pulls apart. She's smiling.

She's smiling because I've made her happy.

Sometimes she's there, next to me. Sometimes no one is. Sometimes someone else is. A handsome, unshaven man, fit and lovely, curly hair, in scrubs the color of a perfect day's sky. He asks me questions and I answer and he takes notes on a clipboard. Are they even words, the sounds coming out of my mouth? He leans over, to check the leather cuffs on my wrists, and I strain at the strap over my chest to smell him.

There's music playing—a Tibetan singing bowl the size of the Earth—a single-note tremolo containing all notes. It's the sound the planets make. *Musica universalis.* The harmony of the spheres.

Do you know what sunshine feels like on your bare shoulders and your ass and your tummy and the soles of your feet all at the same time? I do. I know what it's like and wish I had the words to say.

Three thousand people who love me kiss me with three thousand mouths and stroke my flesh with six thousand hands.

My blood is champagne.

These are not metaphors.

This Dr. Simon—she is a caring doctor indeed. Such a gift she's given me. And how cruel I was to her. How awfully I had misread her intentions. She loves me. The handsome man is writing more notes, so concerned is he with my welfare. Checking my heart rate, my blood pressure—notice the concern on his face? That's compassion, right there. Squinting gorgeously as he makes careful numbers. He loves me, too. I know it.

And maybe there's sleep, but who knows the way these things work, with Dr. Simon's magical elixir love potion, made of peptides from the bullet ant, native of Brazil. Time passes, not enough of it, and it all ends just like that. It doesn't scale down gradually, ebb away the way wisdom-teeth-Percocet does. It's like a drop from a high place, very sudden. A drop from a high place that ends on pavement. Every muscle pulses with the exhaustion of effort, and my wrists and ankles sting with fresh bite marks. When my eyes flutter open, I'm alone in the room. The countertop where Dr. Simon had laid her leather case is bare. The sensors hooked to my chest and temples are gone. As is the machine that flashed out my vitals in green and, later, red lights.

My mouth opens to call out to someone, but my throat is on fire and a thick paste coats my tongue. I want water, but even though the words form, they won't come out as anything but a hoarse whisper. Where's the concern? Where's the love? Above me, the lights seem brighter than before, brighter and whiter. They shine through my eyelids when I close them. A wave of nausea crawls from my stomach up into my throat and I gag. I try to crane my neck and wipe the bile on my skin onto my hospital gown, but I can't, and the bile just hangs on my chin and grows cold.

The beating of my heart is too fast. I feel it thumping against my ribs, sending out shock waves that travel to my fingers and toes and make my temples pulse. My cells ache. Each one. As if they're reaching for something and can't quite grasp it. My cells *want*. The shivering starts a few minutes later. Another wave of nausea comes.

. . .

There is indifference on Dr. Simon's face as she wipes the slime from my chin with a paper towel rough as tree bark. Blue-gloved hands tilt my head, turn it right, turn it left, as her eyes squint at me. A penlight appears and she tells me to look right at it. I try but have to look away after a second. She tells me to try again.

When Dr. Simon is finished with her exam, she takes her chair and opens her laptop on her knees.

"Nausea," Dr. Simon says, not looking up. "Zero to five?"

I blink at her. She repeats the question.

"Five," I say.

"Restlessness in limbs?"

"Five," I say.

"Difficulty concentrating?"

"Five," I say. "What is this?"

"Anxiety index, modified for pharmacology studies." She types something, peers at the screen. "How about blurry vision? Ringing in the ears?"

"What did you give me?"

"I call it Theta Compound, but it's not quite ready yet. There's still more work you and I need to do." Dr. Simon puts her laptop away, then stands and walks over to me. From here I can see every pore on her face, and the line below her chin where her makeup ends. "What is the therapeutic purpose of morphine, what's its point?"

"To get high."

"No. That's a side effect. The therapeutic purpose of morphine is to relieve pain." She rests her hand on my arm. "How was it, my Theta Compound? Just subjectively, I mean."

I nod, swallow. "Good."

"Come on," she says, mouth breaking into a smile. "It was better than good. Better than amazing."

I look away.

"Like love, right? Because it is love. Love and saline. But again, that's

272

just a side effect." She places a finger on my chin, turns my head to her. "A philosophical question, Gwendolyn: What is love? On a basic level?"

I don't answer.

"Love is want, Gwendolyn. You want what you love. And what you love, you're *loyal* to. That, *that*, is the therapeutic purpose of Theta Compound. The political purpose."

I close my eyes in order not to see her. But the light comes through anyway, stinging the raw nerves of my retinas. I'll just do what she asks. I'll just comply. "What do you want from me?"

"What we want—what I want—is for you to want us. For you to love us."

"Us?"

Dr. Simon places her hands on her knees, presses down, breathes slowly, like she's meditating. "You're a citizen," she says after a while. "The state, your government, it needs you. A body can't live without, say, the pancreas. And you don't see a pancreas walking around without a body, do you?"

I blink at her. "I'm—I'm the pancreas."

"You are," she says. "You are the pancreas."

My face stretches, and despite everything, I laugh. Dryly. Coughing out my laugh until I taste blood. I laugh at her metaphor, and her pancreas. I laugh at her suit, at her good leather briefcase from the mall, at her rubber laptop inside it. When I stop, when I make myself stop, there are tears cooling on my cheeks.

It gets worse, the wanting. By the time she leaves, my veins hurt like they'd been stretched and my brain itches so badly that if I could get my hands out of the restraints I'd pull my hair out to squelch it. Waves of fever and chill roll over me, and sometimes my head is freezing while my feet sweat, and sometimes it's the opposite. The fluorescent lights are deafening.

The door opens at some point, and the man with curly hair who wears scrubs the color of a perfect day's sky comes in. The concern I'd seen on his face is something more now. Worry. His eyes are narrow and jaw is set as he takes my temperature and checks the restraints. He puts on blue gloves and produces a tube of some kind of balm, then smears it on the abrasions on my wrists and ankles. His touch is warm and gentle and hurts so bad I wince.

"How's the nausea?" he asks.

The voice, I recognize it from somewhere, but it's too much trouble to try to place it. I shake my head and say, "Bad."

He pats the pockets of his scrubs, then takes out a single tiny pill. "Zofran. I'll put it under your tongue," he says. "Don't swallow it, just let it dissolve."

But as soon as the pill touches the saliva in my mouth, I'm dry heaving over the side of the bed. The man pulls a crescent-shaped steel dish from below and catches the strings of saliva, then wipes my mouth with a cloth.

"You need an IV," he says.

He leaves and comes back wheeling a pole already carrying a flaccid bag of saline.

"What's your name?" I manage to ask.

He looks at me from the side as he wipes my arm with a brown fluid that looks like oil. "I've missed our games lately," he says quietly.

Max. His name is Max. Now I recognize the shape of his hands even through the gloves, the stubby fingers that slaughtered me in chess. And his face, the corner of it I saw through the slot in the door, I recognize that, too. "Are you a doctor, Max? What's wrong with me?" I say.

"Nurse. Army medic before this," he says, readying the needle. "Squeeze your hand into a fist. You'll feel a poke."

It's agony, the needle, but over in a second and already taped down by the time I open my eyes.

"*Krankenschwester,*" I say.

"What?"

"Nurse. In German." I watch as he sticks a syringe into a plastic port on the line leading to my arm. "It means 'sicksister.'"

"Sicksister. I like that."

"What are you giving me?"

"We'll try the Zofran intravenously," Max says, sticking a syringe into a plastic port on the line leading to my arm. "Nausea should be gone soon. But don't tell her I gave you anything more than saline."

"Why not?"

"Nausea is part of the withdrawal," he says. "That's—what this whole thing is about."

I study his gloved hands and try to remember what Dr. Simon had said. "Love is just a side effect."

Max's Adam's apple shifts up, then down, as he swallows. "I'm sorry about all this," he says, voice low. "Really. You don't deserve it."

"So cut the straps," I say. "Let's go."

He closes his eyes, peels off the gloves. "I'll try to make you as comfortable as possible," he says.

I'm mostly better by the next day, the IV having done what Max promised, relieving the nausea. Or maybe it was just time that did that, the drug, Dr. Simon's magic love potion, her Theta Compound, having been sweated out through my pores. When Dr. Simon arrives, she checks the needle in my arm.

"Aside from needing some hydration, you handled it well," she says. "That crash when it's over, though. A real bitch, isn't it?"

I don't answer.

"Come on, Gwendolyn. I want your opinion. Wasn't it awful?"

"What do you want from me?"

A shrug, casual, like the question hadn't occurred to her. "We just want you"—and now a smile, real, not even pretending—"to *feel* the love. To *understand* it. In here." She taps her chest where her heart is.

She takes a prefilled syringe from her pocket and attaches it to the port in the IV line, just as Max had done with the antinausea medication.

No ceremony or buildup this time. She inserts the needle into the plastic junction in the IV line. The rush hits me stronger than it did the day before, like she's upped my dose, pushing it as high as she dares to go.

I'm bending backward, backward through the mattress, through the floor, my body bent in a C, my spine impossibly flexible, as I tumble through lavender light that licks my skin.

Twenty-Nine

Four or five times this happens, a quick visit, another injection, another glide through the universe on lavender light, kissing all I meet with loving-kindness, and getting loving-kindness back in return. Each dose becomes heavier and the trips longer and better. Each crash becomes harder and more violent. The injections of Zofran, delivered in secret by Max, seem to do less and less. So he changes the sheets and my scrubs soaked in sweat and bile and piss and tells me with grave concern and frustration bordering on naked fury that I should give her what she wants, give her what she wants and end this. But Max knows nothing about love.

Each time she steps into the room and readies a fresh dose, my eyes gleam with a kind of love I'd never known.

Turns out, I'd gotten the emotion all wrong. Admiration? Respect? Lust? The embodiment of all that's good in the whole wide world? Bullshit. Those are poets' definitions. Children's definitions. Dr. Simon was right: Love is want. And what we want, we're loyal to.

All this she gives unconditionally. Other than a few simple questions from her anxiety index after each dose, there is no other interrogation from Dr. Simon. She gives me her love unconditionally.

So that's why, after that fourth or fifth trip, I suspect nothing as she detaches my IV and orders Rossi and LaBelle to haul me out of bed. Surely, Dr. Simon has benevolent reasons in mind, loving me as she does.

Rossi's strong arms hoist me by the right armpit, while LaBelle's hoist me by the left. They walk slowly, accommodating my slow shuffle like the good sports they are, guiding me out of the room and down the hallway to another room, this one very near the end where the tunnel is unpainted and the doors are battered steel shot through with bolts.

This cell they help me into is utterly bare and the floor is slicked with water a few degrees above freezing that glows brown under what little light there is. As Rossi and LaBelle let me go, I stagger forward, regaining my balance just in time to hear the door slam behind me. My arms beat on the door and I call out, but no one comes. No one comes, because that's the point. Even a mind in my dull state can recognize that much.

The pain, the terrible afterward, was just starting when they lifted me from the bed. I was a few minutes out of my high and still catching my breath. But the stretched veins and itchy mind are coming back now with fierce earnestness. Fever and nausea, too. I stumble to the far wall, wet like the floor, very nearly greasy, and press my body to it. It helps a little, cooling the noxious waves of heat shuddering through me. Then the wall moves, sliding this way, then that, but not really. It's just the vertigo, the up-down-left-right gyroscope in my head still spinning wildly. I lose my balance and slide to the floor, the icy water slicing through the pink scrubs.

I need a reference point, something for my mind to hold on to. My eyes bounce around the room for anything to pull me through the agony that's just starting and will get worse until such time as it becomes unbearable. The walls and ceiling and floor are all identical in size, forming a perfect cube, broken only by a yellow lightbulb trapped in its cage like a sad, dim canary. Only the lightbulb. And no camera.

Not just alone, but unseen. Uncared for. Outside God's love. Outside the state's embrace, as Dr. Simon had said. So here, Gwendolyn: Let me show you exactly how alone.

I retch, stinging yellow slime coming up from my empty gut and forming a solid cord of bile between my throat and the fetid water on the floor. As I pull away, the cord snaps and bounces back into my mouth, tasting of iron and whatever else is down there. A wave of fever turns cold, and my whole body shakes violently, vibrating as if I'm being driven along a shitty, rutted road at a hundred miles an hour.

My arms are curled around my knees and I'm shuddering with cold when the door opens very suddenly, a deafening screech of metal being ripped in two and crying out in pain. Two figures enter and take me by the arms, trying to get me upright, but my legs are too shaky for my own weight. I manage only to raise my head and see a silhouette standing in the entrance.

Dr. Simon gives a nod to the guards. They release my arms and I buckle, my knees striking the concrete. I catch myself with a hand then raise it to my chest, where my heart hammers away, as if trying to get out. I leave behind a shit-brown palm print.

She takes a step forward, then crouches so her face is even with mine. There's soft pity in her eyes, and sadness—this hurts her, too—and her lips are slightly parted, bare and dry, like we're about to kiss.

"Nausea," she says evenly. "Zero to five?"

My mouth flutters open and I struggle to say something, but as my breath touches her, she recoils.

"Restlessness in limbs?"

"I can't even stand," I manage.

"So, five. And concentration?"

"I'm dying."

She places her hands on either side of my head and tilts it up. "You are not, Gwendolyn. You are not dying. Not yet."

"Help me," I whisper.

Dr. Simon withdraws a hand from my face and digs for something in her pants pocket. When she pulls it out again, there's a small capped syringe resting on her palm. "This what you want?"

I look down, away from her. And nod once.

She tilts my head up again with a finger under my chin. "The love you give is the love you get."

"What?"

"The love you give. Is equal to the love you get," she says.

"Tell me how."

An easy shrug. "Think of something." Then she stands, crosses her arms, and paces through the filthy water. Her shoes will hate her for this.

A shudder comes through me, not fever or chill or nausea, but a sob, dry and soundless. How tiny my body is. How weak I am. Give him up. Give him up, and feel God's love. Pathetic, but so what? It was always going to come to this. Tomorrow or a week from now or in a month. I would still be here, my body frail and desperate, and the water would still be cold, and the math would never change: your happiness for his life.

"He has a doomsday device," I whisper.

Sudden footsteps to my side, then she's crouching again. "Good, Gwendolyn. Good."

"His—testimony. He tells everything," I say softly. "An account on a cloud service. The links, ready to send out. In the drafts folder."

"Send out to whom?"

I look up at her; her face is so tender. "Media. CNN. *New York Times*. Everyone."

She snaps her fingers, and I hear one of the guards opening a notepad and clicking a pen.

"Username and password, Gwendolyn."

I rattle them off slowly, deliberately, making sure she gets the spelling, the special characters, the nonsense phrases of the password just right. She double-checks, then shows me the actual paper.

"That's it," I say.

She hands me the syringe, and a moment later, they're gone again and the door is shut.

It won't be enough, though. They'll realize that account is just one of the many I'd set up. In the morning, they'll be back for the others. I'll string them along as best I can for as long as I can, until there's nothing left. As to what I do after my information runs dry, I have no idea. But that's a problem for then.

I bite the cap off the needle, pull the filthy sleeve of the scrubs up, and stab myself in the shoulder.

Max checks my pulse and lets out an audible breath when he finds there is one. With the back of a gloveless hand he feels for a fever, then touches my cheek.

"Try to sit up," he says quietly.

I do try but can't, so he does it for me, circling an arm beneath my shoulders and heaving me into a seated position as if he were posing some enormous dead-eyed doll. There's a blanket around my shoulders a moment later, and another one under my ass, folded thick enough so that it doesn't get saturated.

"Thanks," I whisper.

He squeezes both my hands in his, then massages my forearms, heat through friction. I'm wet and cold and he's dry and warm and the effect is both painful and marvelous. In a moment, I'm coughing, and I feel blood coming back to my face. His hands move to my shoulders and squeeze hard, then he's slapping my cheeks, alternating left, right, left, right, until I actually smile and try feebly to push his arm away.

"Dr. Simon says no more IV, even saline," Max whispers. "But I've got a patch I can put behind your ear. Or the Zofran pills again. We can try."

I manage to raise a finger at the mention of the Zofran, so he shakes a pill out of a bottle and tells me to open. I don't vomit this time, and in less than a minute, it's dissolved under my tongue.

The shivering is starting to come back and I pull the blanket around me more tightly, barely able to hold on to it. Max checks his watch, then tells me to lean forward. Before I understand what's happening, he's sliding his body behind mine, pressing his chest to my back, and wrapping his arms around my torso. I can feel his breath on my neck. "You need to warm up," he says. "Hypothermia."

I nod and continue to shiver, but each tremor of my body now is being absorbed by his, bouncing into warm flesh. "Are, are, y-you"—the stuttering is too much to control—"go-going to g-get in . . ."

"In trouble?" Max says. "Yes. If you tell them."

"Ma-Max . . ."

"Yes?"

"Mm-Am I"—I swallow, trying to force the stutter away—"going t-to die?"

No answer from Max.

I swallow again. "Max . . ."

"Shh," he says, arms tightening. "Relax. If you can."

"Max," I say again. "Get me out."

When I wake, the blankets, and Max, are gone. My right side is paralyzed, or at least that's how it feels, because I'm lying on that side and the water and floor are so very cold. I think about turning over, but that's all I do, think about it. Because I would just get other parts of me wet, and I don't have the energy anyway.

It's the sound of the door opening that wakes me, that terrible scream of pain the steel makes. The guards come in, then Dr. Simon.

"Your father's—testimony, whatever that was—is pretty innocuous, I'm afraid," she says, no hint of gloating in her voice. "The public, nothing surprises them anymore. A day of outrage, maybe. Then it's chum for the conspiracy bloggers. Sorry."

I blink at her.

"You should know also, we found the duplicates. NSA did a global search using the—I don't know what they call it—file hash, checksum, whatever. All the copies are gone now." She crouches beside me, wipes the hair out of my eyes and tucks it behind my ear. "You're so strong, Gwendolyn. Doing the right thing like that. Couldn't have been easy."

All the copies, gone, just like that. The idea that the NSA is so potent it could scrub the Internet and find all of them comes as a shock, or would if I gave a shit any longer. Because now it's time for the child hero, example to all, to receive her hero's reward. Slowly and with effort, I prop myself up.

"He's out there somewhere, your father," Dr. Simon says. "How long since you last checked in with him? He's probably wondering if you're okay."

At the mention of him my mind snaps back, just enough to form a clear, or clearish, thought. No, my father's not wondering. He's desperate. Panicked. Fearing the worst, because really, what else could it mean, my going dark like this? I picture him in my mind, someplace hot, because that's where people always run to in the movies. His shirt is sticking to his back as he sits in a grungy Internet café, drumming his fingers, waiting for the TOR to connect, and praying today's the day I come back. The buzz in his mind is louder than the buzz of motor scooters out in the street.

"You use an e-mail address to contact him."

"Yes," I whisper.

"It wasn't a question, Gwendolyn. We know about it. It's how we tracked you down, actually."

"It was encrypted."

"Yes. And it probably slowed the NSA down by a few minutes. Anyway, Gwendolyn"—the concern on her face, it's so real—"your father may know it's compromised, which is why he doesn't answer you. But we're sure he's at least monitoring it." Dr. Simon pulls a notepad and pen from her pocket. "Go ahead," she says. "Write down what you want to tell him, to let him know you're okay."

My hands tremble as I take them from her. The idea of thinking something cogent, and then setting it to paper, seems impossibly hard. But I have to warn him. Somewhere I'll have to work in the duress signal, *All's going fine, so don't worry,* which is to be written or said exactly that way, innocuous and banal.

Which is what Dr. Simon wants.

To tell him I've been captured. That I'm in danger. That I'm going to die.

I know him, and so does she: He'll reappear in an instant—a phone call to make a hasty deal, his freedom for mine, then a cab to the nearest consulate. And that will be that. Neither of us will be seen again. How had Max put it? A helicopter ride over the ocean.

I hesitate, the pen pressing into the paper, a circle of ink expanding outward like a wound bleeding blue.

My body shakes, but I manage to rise to my feet and stand uneasily. I print the word *DAD* in sloppy caps, then *IM OK DO NOT*—but then my hand freezes, refusing to go any further.

The male guard, LaBelle, takes a step closer.

And then, from somewhere, it comes, a burst of power, what you get when you hold a match to fury. I dive toward him, spiking the pen into his right shoulder.

Then my body jerks into the air, carried on pulses of light and sublime, rhythmic pain. I land on the floor, conscious of every muscle convulsing in time to a racing metronome at my side.

I inhale spit, taste blood, cough, and feel pee flow warm and steady down my legs.

Dr. Simon stands, a stun gun loose in her hand.

LaBelle approaches, hand pressed to his bleeding shoulder, jaw set. He's going to drive a boot into my side, but Dr. Simon raises a hand and he steps away.

She crouches beside me, presses two fingers to my neck to take my pulse. "That was *very* naughty, Gwendolyn," she says. "So off to bed you go without your supper."

. . .

My heart rate, frantic, is too fast for my breathing, which is too slow and shallow to keep up. I don't even feel the cold anymore.

Withdrawal is the point of Theta Compound. The love is just a side effect. Still, I would do anything to have it back, Dr. Simon. Come now, tell me what to do and I'll do it. Tell you anything. Even pull the trigger myself. How many iterations of your love potion had come before, and how many lab rats just like me had it cost? However many it was, it's worth it, though. Here in your lab, your lair—underground and off the grid—you can do whatever you like. No oversight. No consequences. Just you and your noble work, curing citizens like me of what ails us. You're the god here, Dr. S. So show me your forgiveness.

He's holding me, again, Max. As he did the last time, with his chest to my back, and a blanket around us both to keep the heat in. He's given me another Zofran, and it's finally kicking in. "Do you want some broth?" he says.

I swallow, try to think whether I do or not, then can't remember the question. "Can you get it for me?"

"The broth? I brought some. In a thermos."

"Another syringe," I hiss.

He squeezes his arms tighter. "It's killing you."

"I know."

Max wraps his arms around me tightly. "You've been twenty-four hours without it. So stay strong. Fight."

He unscrews a thermos and pours broth into a plastic mug, the steam rising luxuriously. The warmth of the cup in my hands makes me tremble with gratitude. I take a sip. It's the same chicken broth they served me before, too salty and tasting of metal. But it works.

"Easy," he says. "Take it easy."

A pang of nausea, but just a pang, easily suppressed. I take another sip. "Why are you doing this?"

"Doing what?"

"Being human." I turn my head a little so I can see his face. "Your patients, they must love you."

"You're the only one." He works the blanket in front of us to close a gap. "The last one."

I shudder, wondering again how many there have been. Is the timing right to push him further? But it's a stupid question: There's no time left.

"I have a million Swiss francs," I say. A lie, but so what. "We can split it."

Another long silence. I see his jaw tighten as if he's chewing the words. He shifts his weight to the side and I touch his hand.

"I don't care about money," he says.

"Everybody cares about money. Can you do it?"

Max breathes in and out, fast and nervous. I feel it, hot and nice against my neck. Then his mouth is next to my ear. "I gotta go."

"Max. Stay."

"Sorry—"

She wakes me by whispering "Morning, sunshine," six inches from my ear. But my eyes don't open, so she checks my pulse and I hear her tell the guards to sit me up.

They prop me against the wall.

"Sleep well?" she says, readying a stethoscope. She listens to my heart, takes my temperature and blood pressure. Jots them down in a little notebook.

"Can you hear me, Gwendolyn?"

My lips flutter out of sync with the words. "I-I n-need . . ."

Arched eyebrows. "Yes?"

"Blanket."

"You want a blanket?"

I nod.

"Tell me the message you want to send to your father," she says softly. "Then you choose: blanket or Theta."

My mouth opens again, but no sound comes out.

"You want to tell me the message, Gwendolyn?"

I shake my head.

She motions for the guards to leave, then turns before she steps through the door. "Last chance," she says.

I stay where I am, staring blank-eyed at the sad yellow canary in its cage.

The door closes behind her.

I picture a syringe of Theta in my head. A syringe of amber glass, or amber plastic that looks like glass. And an impossibly slender needle at the end. Hard to imagine that such a universe of wonders could pass through something so narrow.

I'm not shivering anymore. I don't feel the cold.

Get here soon, Max.

I'd shown Dr. Simon my best bitchy self, the proud petulant child who braves whatever punishment might come. But she'd responded coolly and in kind with her own bitchy best, *you chose this, not me.* Now, the consequences of my behavior. Of my disloyalty. Of my unlove.

Tick tock, Max.

I strain to hear the world beyond the cell, anything at all. But the steel and stone give up nothing.

He lost his nerve, poor Max. His dedication to a righteous mission, faltering in the transition from my world back to his.

I won't be here when you come back, Max.

Thirty

The first thing I'm aware of is the sensation of vomiting. This is what wakes me. When my eyes open, I'm upright, kind of. Max has his arm around me, and my arm is around him, but he's holding my entire weight, the only thing that's keeping me from falling over. My bare feet are red from cold and are pointed inward.

Max hisses at me to be quiet and hold on. There's a pool of what I'd spit up on the floor, but it's not the floor of my cell. It's diamond plate steel, scraped up and dirty. Above me, an engine is whirring and I feel motion.

We're in an elevator.

My eyes sweep around, trying to make sense of my surroundings. Max's jaw is set, but his eyes are all worry. He holds a small Glock pistol in his right hand. It's the preferred toy among CIA types, but given the unease with which Max holds it, the preference probably doesn't extend to CIA nurses. The elevator itself is enormous and designed for cargo far bigger than two humans. The engine above alternates between a purr and a whine as it hauls us upward.

"Wh-where—"

"I'm getting you out," he whispers. "Can you stand on your own?"

In principle, or right now? I want to ask. But I nod that I can, and so Max slowly lets go. I wobble side to side for a moment, catch myself on the elevator wall, then find my balance, an accomplishment that in that moment feels absurdly big.

"When the door opens, we'll be in a garage, on the surface," Max says. "I'll go first, then you. Six or seven meters ahead, you'll see a red sedan. Get on the floor of the backseat. Understand?"

I squeeze his shoulder. "Thank you."

"Save it for when it's over," he says. "I don't want to jinx it."

How prepared is he? How good is his plan? I want to take his gun myself, and while we're at it, the keys to the car, too. But just as this thought manages to come together in my mind, nausea sweeps through me once more and I buckle at the waist. I can barely stand, which means whatever comes next is up to him. I'm just a wobbling, puking piece of luggage along for the ride. Why is he doing this? Why does he give a shit about me? The million francs? Or could it be that a human on this earth is motivated by goodness alone?

A groan of metal colliding with metal, then a jolt. I fall against Max's shoulder as the elevator shudders to a stop. As the doors slide open, Max lifts the pistol and releases its safety.

The smells of motor oil mixed with mildew drift in. Over Max's shoulder I see the red sedan, a small Volkswagen, maybe two decades old with rust along the fenders. Behind it is parked an unmarked white delivery van. Max steps into the room, waving his pistol slowly back and forth, then hisses, "Go!"

I stumble forward, barely keeping upright, and land hard against the sedan. The latch for the back door suddenly seems impossibly complicated and my mind struggles with how to open it, as if it were a calculus problem.

Behind me, an explosion, the report from Max's gun echoing off the vaulted ceiling. My eyes snap in the direction Max fired and see the guard LaBelle standing at the back of the garage ten meters away.

His own pistol is raised and tracking Max's movements. Max fires again, and this time LaBelle staggers backward into a stack of cardboard boxes before sliding to the ground.

Then I'm on the floor of the backseat pulling a plaid wool blanket over my body. Max starts the engine, and the tires chirp on the floor as we burst forward.

The road is unpaved and I bounce in an uneven rhythm as we speed through darkness. Max's window is open, and I can smell pine and mountain air. I can taste it as I inhale deep, grateful breaths, the air itself sweet and dense. With effort, I lift myself up so I can see out the windshield.

A forest at night, with a narrow dirt road cut through it, illuminated by overlapping yellow cones from the headlights. Moths scatter madly as we race along. I reach forward to squeeze Max's shoulder.

"It's not over yet," he says.

Shining through the chills and waves of nausea, my chest pounds with love for this man, a kind of love that has nothing to do with romance or Theta. Love as admiration, of the desire that the whole world could be filled with people just as good and kind and brave as he is. "Where are we headed?" I ask.

"You tell me," Max says. "Toward Dresden if we're going east. Nuremberg if we're headed west."

"West. Go west."

We round a corner at speed, the back end of the car kicking out before straightening again. "West to where?" he asks.

"I don't know yet. Just drive."

Then, ahead of us, a chain-link fence topped with barbed wire, and a closed gate. Even in the yellow of the headlights, I can tell it's new and sturdy. Max slows to a stop, takes a pair of bolt cutters from the passenger seat, and exits the car, leaving the engine running.

I watch him, his uncertain steps, his fumbling with the chain as he searches for a weak spot—*they're all the same, handsome; any one will do.* He's a brave fool, risking his life, and almost certainly losing it, to save mine. But maybe that's not exactly right. Maybe I'm just a variable in this equation, and my life is swappable for any other. Maybe he's doing this for the sake of some principle, some idea of justice, larger than me, but invisible and abstract. So, yes, a brave fool, with the accent on the second part.

He's back in the car again, spinning the tires as he guns first gear, and revving the motor all the way up before throwing it into second. We burst past the gate and continue down the dirt track, the trees blurring by faster and faster. I can see his clenched-teeth grin in the rearview mirror. I can even smell the adrenaline on him like sweat. One million francs that I don't really have well spent.

Stillness and the sound of birds, then the sensation of cold air on my face, nearly freezing my nostrils as I breathe in. My eyes flicker open and I see an old-fashioned alarm clock, hands stuck at 1:24, and beyond it a wood-paneled wall.

My body is encased in something warm and soft and wonderful. I can tell from the feel alone that it's a fat eiderdown, heavy and weightless all at once. I roll onto my back and feel the mattress beneath give way and suck me in like an act of supreme welcome.

But it's not so easy to sit up in. My elbows tilt and falter as I try to raise myself, every muscle fighting back, telling me to keep still. The pain from even this simple movement shoots from my head like steel bands bent the wrong way, through my abdomen, radiating up and down my legs and arms. It's literally incredible, defying belief, like the summary of every workout I'd ever had, every fall off the beam in gymnastics, every torn muscle, every bruise, has come back for some sick reunion in my body. Then the room spins and I tumble back down into the mattress, where I'm stuck in infinite softness. I fight back the nausea but feel pressure going the other way, too.

I stay just where I fell, hoping it'll go away if I don't move. The light in the bedroom is soft and gray, and it comes in through windows of warped, old glass fenced in between diagonal mullions. It floats gently over a sturdy and uncomfortable-looking wooden chair, painted with swirls of blue and white, and an intricately carved chest of drawers with a white ceramic washing bowl on top.

It's a cottage. Missing only the cheerful singing of seven dwarves.

The idea of cheerful singing, and cartoon dwarves, and cottages as such makes me ill. My veins thrum like guitar strings, and then the compulsion to purge through vomit and shit roars back.

I try again, forcing myself up to a seated position, then swing my legs over the side of the bed. I taste the puke, spicy bile, in my throat, but I hold it in as I climb to my feet. Somehow I'm dressed in thick sweat-pants and a too-large sweatshirt—Max's maybe—but the air outside the embrace of the eiderdown is frigid nonetheless. I scramble toward the room's only door, praying the bathroom is nearby, then see that the uncomfortable, intricately painted chair is a kind of toilet, with a hole in the center of the seat and a porcelain pot beneath. I pull the sweat-pants down just in time and snatch the bowl from the chest of draw-ers. Everything comes out both ends at once, the smells wretched and commingling.

My body shudders in the cold, and each shudder sends more con-vulsions of pain coursing through my muscles and bones. Even through the pain, I imagine a syringe of Theta floating in front of me like Mac-beth's dagger. I imagine grabbing it, shooting it into my arm. I imag-ine the tsunami of love that would come seconds later, sweeping away the cold and nausea and diarrhea.

The itching in my brain descends like cascading water to my face, my neck, my collarbone, my chest and arms. I scratch at my skin through the thick fabric of the sweatshirt, and when that isn't enough, I take the sweatshirt off and scratch harder. The cold air is sharp and wonderful, but still, the itch won't relent. My nails dig harder until my skin turns red.

Breathe in, I tell myself, *one-two-three-four*. Hold it, *one-two-three-four*. Exhale, *one-two-three-four-five-six-seven-eight*. I repeat the ritual again and again until my body stills and the itch fades into something manageable. I study my hands and feet and see that Max cleaned them, along with the rest of me, too, wiping away the filth from so many days in the cell. Even the abrasions from the restraints are better, and slightly greasy to the touch from the ointment he must have applied. I puke one last time, then thank the gods Max left a roll of toilet paper for me.

I rise and shuffle to the far corner of the room and press my ear to the rough pine door. A clock is ticking in the room beyond, but otherwise, there's only silence. Slowly, I turn the latch and pull the door open, revealing the rest of the cottage, complete with stone walls and plank floors and thick timber beams running in parallel lines along the ceiling. There's a fireplace with embers still smoldering, and an old couch with a bedsheet and blanket, rumpled and slept in.

My feet pad across the floor, the boards creaky and smooth with age. There's a battered teakettle on a black potbelly stove that's still hot to the touch, and a wooden counter where two empty cans of baked beans and a heel of bread sit neglected. I walk to the fireplace, throw a few more sticks in, and stir it up with an iron poker until they catch. As the warmth seeps through the thick cotton of Max's gym clothes, I take down a framed photo from the mantel. It's an ancient black-and-white family portrait, three generations of men in lederhosen and women in long wool dresses assembled formally on a grand staircase.

Behind me, a door opens and a wave of cold air rushes in. I snap around, wincing at the pain of the movement and nearly dropping the photo.

Max stands in the entrance, barely managing a large box overflowing with groceries. He jumps at the sight of me.

"Jesus," he says. "What are you doing out of bed?"

"Where are we?" I say, and put the photograph back on the mantel.

"A hunting lodge. An old man in town rented it to me."

"A hunting lodge where, Max?"

"The Alps. Two hours outside Zurich," he says. "I drove west. I just figured."

The obvious direction, and precisely where Dr. Simon would be looking. I curse myself for being so stupid. "We need to get out of here. At least I do."

"Get out of here?" he says. "Gwen, look at yourself. You're sick. I had to get you someplace where I could put an IV in." Max sets the box on the counter and begins unpacking. A box of rice. A loaf of bread. "Another few hours, and you wouldn't have made it."

I feel a sore spot and fresh bandage beneath the sweatshirt sleeve where he'd stuck me with the IV needle.

"It was killing you. The withdrawal," he says, almost angry now as he takes out apples, potatoes, meat in butcher paper. "That's why I got you out of there when I did."

I lower myself to the couch and pull my legs up against my chest. "You—you gave me a bath."

"I'm a nurse. It's part of the job."

"No, I mean, thank you. For that. And rescuing me." I swallow hard, my arms starting to shake again. "How long have we been here?"

"Three days," he says. "I gave you some saline, nutrients. A Naloxone variant. Something to help you sleep through the worst of it."

I nod toward the bedroom door. "I had a—I'm sorry, I was sick. It isn't pretty."

"I'll take care of it," he says. "Now get back to bed."

Dusk outside, and getting colder in the cottage with every minute. My body shudders, even under the eiderdown. The stretched veins, the itchy mind, the nausea and fearsome pain, they are what it feels like to want and not have. What it feels like to be disloyal.

But stillness and want taste awful together. Both feed off each other, becoming noxious, like bleach and ammonia, so I climb out of bed and lower myself to the floor. I'm sure I could see my breath in the cold if there was any light at all. The planks beneath my toes and hands are smoothed by age, and I press down on them with everything I have, trying to lift myself into a push-up. I make it only halfway before falling, then try again. Ten is my goal; I'll make it there or die trying.

It takes forever, and it's brutal, but in the end, I make it all the way to twenty. I swap bad hurt for good, itching for cold, and anxiety for exhaustion. When I climb back into the bed and close my eyes, though, a fresh needle is waiting for me in my imagination.

I sleep for a time, or something like sleep. When I come back, the smell of soup cooking on the stove in the other room torments me with hunger, a new kind of want. It must be a good sign, wanting something I can actually have without it killing me. It smells of simmering carrots and potatoes and something strange and savory, a vegetable or spice I'm not familiar with.

The door swings open, Max pushing it with his foot. He elbows on a light switch, and in his hands he grips the edges of a chipped bowl.

"Fennel soup," he says, setting the bowl on the table next to me. "My grandma used to make it. 'Sick soup,' she called it. Here, let me help you."

He arranges the eiderdown and pillows just so, then holds the bowl under my chin, raising a spoonful to my lips. There's no metallic taste from a can, no salt covering up synthetic chicken flavoring generated in a lab. Just vegetable tang and what I assume is the fennel, bits of all of it floating in the broth. Max catches a tickling stream of it down my chin with a spoon, then brings back more.

"A folk remedy," he says. "The fennel, it's supposed to help with the nausea. Sometimes the old ways are best."

Every slurp brings fresh energy into me, the warmth in my stomach pushing steam through my veins and into my head. I hold up my hand when I've had enough, and Max brings me a glass of water. It's from a well and stinks of sulfur, like from those hot springs said to heal arthritis or eczema with a few sips. I hold my nose and drink, knowing the medicine is good for me.

"You're through it, the worst part, anyway," Max says. "Congratulations."

The fennel soup sits uneasily in my stomach, but ultimately there's no nausea. "Sick soup?" I ask.

He pushes himself up on the bed. "I made it from memory, so maybe I got it wrong."

A soup made from memory, Nana's secret ingredient. "Not bad," I say.

"I figure we can go in a day or two. If you're feeling well." Max wipes my mouth with a dishcloth. "You have hard copies, right? The originals of your dad's testimony."

I look at him. Sometime in the last few days he'd shaved and now his skin is bare and pink, like a kid's. The sharp features inherited from wherever his grandmother came from have blended together into a distinctly American prettiness. How is someone like this going to live on the run? I lift a hand and touch his cheek. "We do that, and they'll kill you. You know that, right?"

He just shrugs, like it's the least important thing in the world. "It doesn't get better, this world, if people like us are afraid to do what's right," he says.

"That simple."

"That simple," he says. "You and I, we have a clear shot. All we have to do is take it."

Four days without Theta, going on five. The Naxo-something he'd given me, and the food, are working. And so is time, which dries up the urge like sunlight evaporates water. I want it, badly, but not as badly as I did a few hours ago, or a few minutes ago. The desire is unbolted from the ground now, and if my mind puts enough muscle behind it, I can shove it a few centimeters out of the way, just enough for other thoughts to get through.

Despite the cold and the sheer effort it takes, I climb from the bed and begin the push-ups once more. Ten, then twenty.

Fucking Max. Of all the patients he'd had, what is it he saw in me? The chance to use a murderer to become a saint? His words haunt me. *People like us*, he'd said. People with integrity like his. Good people. That stretch in my veins again.

Thirty.

So is it betraying my father, releasing the information? Or is it the only thing that can save him? The logic of it is twisty, full of backtracks and detours into contradiction. By the time he's killed or captured, whatever good can come from the doomsday device will be of no use to him. But it turns out this isn't a contradiction at all, because my dad never meant it as an insurance policy for his life, but for mine. And if it's mine, can't I do with it what I want?

Forty.

Handled right, it could be the one thing that saves us both. Besides, look what Dr. Simon and the others did to me, what they put me through. So it's fitting I be the one to deliver what's coming next to them. Max's principles and my lusty revenge, they snap together nicely, make a pretty couple. She's right, Dr. Simon. To want is to love, and what we love, we're loyal to.

Fifty.

The endorphins and adrenaline do what they're supposed to. Lift the spirits. Fill one with helium confidence. I go into the next room quickly, before I change my mind.

Max is crouched beside the potbelly stove, shoving sticks into the fire, his face flickering orange. He looks up as I enter, eyebrows raised. "I was going to make some tea."

"It's in a safe-deposit box," I say. "At a bank. In Zurich. Feldman Capital Services."

"Feldman Capital Services," Max repeats. As he starts to rise, he grabs hold of the stove's hatch, then jerks his hand away, waving it frantically.

I approach and take his hand. Pink-gray blisters are already forming along his palm and fingers. "Let me get you some water," I say.

"I'll be fine. And the well is all the way down the hill." He pulls his hand away from me, wraps it in a dishcloth. "Your father's doomsday device, you mean. You're sure you want to."

"You were right. About people like us," I say. "How the world is, when we don't act."

"Tomorrow," he says. "We'll drive to the bank. I'll find someplace we can scan it."

The pain from the burn is still evident in his face.

"Come on," I say. "Let me get some water. For your hand."

Before he can say anything, I'm lifting a pail from the counter and heading toward the door. I slide into his hiking boots and shut the door on his protest. The air is frigid and delicious, tasting of rain and pine sap and wet soil. For a moment, I linger on the small porch, hand on the railing, and just feel the air soak through my sweatshirt and pants. A puff of steam comes out of my mouth, evaporating into the sky. Crickets scratch all around me, and wind stirs the branches.

It's a long staircase to the forest floor, and I navigate it slowly, the boards slick beneath my borrowed boots, untied and too big. Max is coming down the steps behind me in stocking feet, telling me to come back. The ground at the bottom of the staircase is muddy with half-disintegrated leaves. I start down the path, then feel Max's hand on my shoulder.

"Stop," he says. "Gwendolyn, please. It isn't safe, not at night."

Before I can say anything, he's already steering me back up the staircase. Always the nurse, lovely Max. Head full of caring. He'll be a good dad someday, if he lives.

I raise my hands in mock surrender when we reach the top and step out of his boots. He takes the pail from me and gives me a scolding smile. "Inside," he says. "Get yourself warmed up."

Then he's gone, taking the stairs two at a time and disappearing down the path.

I wander to the bedroom and the chest of drawers and porcelain bowl of water for washing, overtaken suddenly with the desire to be clean. For him, maybe. Or because of tomorrow's trip to the city. It's the first time I've allowed myself a look in the mirror above the porcelain washbowl since we arrived here. The reflection of my face is warped and distorted, narrow forehead and heavy chin, the better to show a constellation of pimples running from the corner of my mouth to the edge of my jaw, bright red against gray, lifeless skin. I wince when I touch them, then move my fingertips up to my nest of hair and start picking through the snarls. Leaning in close to the mirror, I part my hair to the scalp. Jesus, is that gray? No, couldn't be. Not at nineteen. I squint: Not gray. White.

They say that happens sometimes. To a convict, the night before his date with the guillotine. Or to a murderer, in the days following the murder. Age never factors into it, just the weight of the trauma and sin. I splash some water on my face, try to rub some life back into my skin, and lean in close to my reflection to inspect my progress. Then, between the cracks in the mirror's surface, something moves.

Just a little. Like an insect shuffling its feet.

I pull back from the mirror and stare at it. Just paranoia, I tell myself. Exhaustion. Bits of Theta still on the loose. Still, I lean in close again, squinting into the crack.

The edge of a black circle, twisting first to the right, then the left.

I close my eyes, sure that when I open them again, I'll discover I'd imagined it. But let's be honest, Gwendolyn, you haven't been able to tell the difference between real and imaginary for quite some time.

My fingers wrap around the edge of the porcelain bowl. Then I'm lifting it, feeling the water slosh over me, turning my gray sweats to black. Then I'm hurling it forward, watching as the porcelain splinters the glass of the mirror into a spiderweb, then passes through it, into the space behind, a cavity in the wall twenty or thirty centimeters deep. The bowl catches the edge of a video camera mounted to a gimbal and twists it to the side, the lens whirring in and out, in and out, trying to regain focus.

My feet slide on the wet floor as I scramble for the outer room. I snatch up a frying pan from the counter and swing at the light fixture. The bulb makes a pop and explodes sparks and shards of white glass over me. But down comes a black plastic cylinder the size of a tube of lipstick dangling on a wire, its glass eye seeming to wink at me even in the newly arrived darkness. I launch toward the grandfather clock and see another lens in the center of the face, where the two hands are anchored. With all my weight, I drive my shoulder into the body of the clock, waiting impatiently as it lingers as if on tiptoe for a second before toppling to the ground with an enormous crack of splitting wood and the cartoon *boing* of springs going off.

He'll be back any second, Max my savior. I throw open the drawers in the kitchen, grab a battered knife with a serrated edge, and bolt for the door. My bare feet slip on the wet planks of the steps, and I tumble down the last half of the staircase, landing on my side in the mud at the bottom. But I'm on my feet within a second, dashing down the path, barely aware of the branches and stones cutting the skin of my soles.

I'm fueled by fury, and my muscles are suddenly as powerful as they've ever been. Even my vision is sharper, as I make out shapes in the darkness, differentiating shades of gray as if they were as starkly separated as red and yellow. It's as if running in terror and fury is my natural state, the way a cat is most a cat when stalking prey. I sprint along the path, deeper into the forest, and see Max up ahead. He's rushing toward me, discarding the pail in his hand and lowering himself into a tackle.

Then comes a series of baritone pops and the humming of electricity as floodlights erupt from high up in the trees, four of them, no, six, filling the world with white clarity. I glance up, and one of the lights shifts so that it's shining directly into my eyes. My arm goes up to block the glare, but a hand grabs me by the wrist. I lash out with my other, the blade of the knife streaking through the air and landing in something soft. The hand lets go and a figure staggers backward, face all blown-out white and the blood welling from his stomach blown-out red. It's not Max. It's LaBelle, the guard from the lab whom Max had shot—or appeared to shoot—as we'd fled. LaBelle's mouth is open, a dark featureless hole sucking at the air. He sways back and forth for a moment, as if idly dancing to a song, then he pitches forward, collapsing into my arms.

Two shadows move in from either side, and I whirl around with LaBelle still clinging to me. A metal baton whistles through the air and catches LaBelle in the back of his head. Blood flecks my face like drops of rain. I drop LaBelle to the ground as I thrust the knife toward the center of the silhouetted figure. It recoils and swings the baton again. But I dodge it and step to the side just as the second figure reaches for me. A stun gun sparkles viciously in the darkness, giving me a point of reference. I aim my free hand for the space six inches behind it and grab hold of the second figure's forearm. I jerk it forward, pulling Max into the light.

I get my arm around Max's neck and hold the knife close to his bulging artery as I maneuver him between me and the first figure. I recognize the silhouette now as Rossi's, and she circles me slowly, trying to get me positioned so the light is directly in my face.

"Please," Max rasps. "Gwen, come on, I was trying to . . ."

I make a show of repositioning the blade over Max's carotid, knowing Rossi knows just as well as I do how quickly he'll bleed out.

"Gwendolyn?" An inquiring voice from behind me, a few meters away. "Gwendolyn, can you hear me?"

Dr. Simon. Polite as ever with her shrink's permanent calm.

"There's nothing you can do, Gwendolyn. Know where you are?"

What had Max said? Just outside Switzerland. Two hours outside Zurich.

Her footsteps crunch through the leaves as they come toward me cautiously. "You're eighty meters from the door to the lab. That's it. You never even left the grounds."

My mouth beside Max's ear: "It is true? What she says?"

I loosen my arm around his neck just enough for him to answer. "Yes," he gasps.

I steal a glance in Dr. Simon's direction. She's in a quilted coat and high boots, just the right outfit for a hike in the woods. In her hand is a small pistol, the muzzle pointed at me and the implication clear: My usefulness is over. "We appreciate your help, though," she says. "Really, we do."

My eyes dart back to Rossi as she takes another step to the side. I can feel Max tense up as he tracks her with his eyes. Then two other figures step into the light, both with raised assault rifles.

Black tactical gear covers their bodies and they move with perfect precision—operators whose careers are spent in the field hunting far deadlier prey than me. They'll drop me the moment I cut Max's throat. Maybe even before, taking him down, too.

Max's hands flash upward and seize my wrists, snapping the knife away and yanking my forearm from his throat. Rossi is on me a second later, tackling me to the ground.

A struggle of silhouettes, shadows that kick and drive fists and elbows into my body.

Thirty-One

No need for an ambulance or car back to the lab. The two operators hand off their assault rifles to Max and simply carry me the few dozen meters to the garage door of the facility, already open like the mouth of a waiting python. Strong, these men; I can feel their muscles even through their many-pocketed tactical clothing blistered with equipment. I should be flattered that two of America's best were put on the case of little Gwendolyn Bloom.

They carry me horizontally, one of them with an arm looped around my chest just under the armpits, squeezing hard, and the other holding me by the legs. The pressure on my chest is asphyxiating me, making my vision tunnel out as if I'm seeing my surroundings through a white tube. With everything I have, I fight back, bucking against them, screaming, trying to sink my fingers into someone's flesh. But with a dwindling supply of oxygen, everything I have isn't much.

We're in the elevator, going down. We're in the corridor, going straight. There is no purposeful brutality in the way the operators carry me. It's what they've been trained to do, all function, no cruelty intended.

Then I land on the floor and gasp, inhaling to the point of bursting.

My vision returns quickly, and I see we're in the hospital room, bright lights above, the air heavy with disinfectant that stings my eyes. Apparently, the two operators dropped me by mistake, because they're looming over me again, reaching for me to hoist me back into the air.

My hands flash forward, grab the nearest of the two by the front of his many-pocketed shirt, and yank him toward me. My teeth spike into the soft flesh of his cheek and suddenly I'm deaf from the sound of his scream. His body wrenches in a seizure and I shove him away in time to fire a bare foot into the stomach of the second operator. It's a weak stab on my part, improvised and sloppy, but he was throwing all his weight into the effort of grabbing me, so it hits him hard, exploding his breath from his mouth as his body wraps around my leg. I redirect his momentum to the side, where he crashes into a stainless steel medical cart and sends instruments flying.

These are, I'm sure, the only freebies I'll get. They'd underestimated sickly, barefooted me, maybe even felt something like sympathy as they'd trundled me back into the lab. But that's all over now. The face of the first operator is a mask of blood, but he's on his feet as soon as I am, lunging toward me, driving an expert jab toward my chin. I sidestep it, knock his arm out of the way, drive a knee hard into his groin. As he buckles, I catch his chin in the palm of my hand and snap his head back, pitching his body into the wall behind him.

Steel forceps and scalpels and round-tipped probes scratch on the concrete floor beneath the second operator's boots. He's using the hospital bed to pull himself up while his free hand draws a pistol from an ankle holster. The training from Orphan Camp, pounded into me as deeply as the instinct to breathe, doesn't flinch or hesitate. I cross the room in two long strides, snatching up a scalpel from the floor as I go. My hand seizes the pistol and twists it away before the operator even finishes raising it. The blade of the scalpel slashes cleanly across his throat and he buckles to his knees.

I take up the pistol and wheel around, catching the first operator unholstering his own. I tell him to drop it. He hesitates. I shoot him just beneath the right eye. In the confines of the room, the gunshot's echo is like the hollow clang of an enormous church bell.

My bare feet slide through the blood on the floor as I approach the door and exit, pistol first. Max is standing against the wall five meters down the corridor, pistol raised uncertainly, his breathing fast and nervous.

With my sights on his chest, and his sights on mine, we both freeze. Rossi and Dr. Simon and who knows how many others are still somewhere inside. But the two dead operators in the room were supposed to be enough to handle me, so it's clear Max's presence here, by himself, wasn't planned.

The corridor is dim, the lights maybe at one-quarter power, leaving the hallway with deep shadows in places the light doesn't reach at all. A semicompetent marksman could hit me without my even being aware of their presence. Thus, I need insurance, or at least a shield.

"Was it from the beginning, Max? The first chess game?" I shuffle to the right, then edge a few centimeters closer. "Or did they flip you later?"

His eyebrows furrow. "Does it matter?"

"Not really," I say, taking another step. "Broke my heart a little, though. For the record."

"Yeah. Mine too," he says. "Now put down the gun."

I take another step.

"Put down the gun, Gwen."

Two strides, three, and the distance between us is closed. I catch his gun hand as my shoulder slams him back into the wall. His breath comes out in a baritone grunt. My fingers dig deep into his hair and gather a tight grip as I kick his pistol away.

"Where is she?" I hiss, with the muzzle of my pistol pressed to his cheek.

In the ringing silence of the corridor I feel my body shaking with exhaustion. The nausea at the thought of LaBelle and the two operators swells like a seawater wave in my belly. Yet I know Dr. Simon is watching on the camera feed, so I hide it as best I can behind a stoic expression and straight back.

I push Max forward by the shoulder, the muzzle of my pistol pressed into his back between his shoulder blades. "Who else is here?" I whisper.

"Dr. Simon. Rossi. One other guy, tactical specialist."

"Who else? Tell me or I'll kill you."

"That's it," he answers. "And you're going to kill me anyway."

He says this so flatly I almost want to lift his spirits, tell him he's wrong, but he'd never believe it, and it would just make me a liar. "Why'd you do this, Max?"

"For America, Gwen. Cheap gas and pumpkin spice lattes and pants with elastic waistbands." He turns his head and actually grins at me. Then he starts singing, loudly and terribly. From the gut. "*Oh-oh say can you see . . .*"

"Shut up, Max."

"*By the dawn's early light . . .*"

I squeeze his shoulder and dig the muzzle of the gun deeper. "Shut the fuck up."

But the volume of his voice only increases. If it weren't for the sarcasm gleaming from every off-key syllable, he'd sound like an embarrassingly drunk uncle at the start of a baseball game. "*What so proudly we hail . . .*"

And that's why I neither see nor hear the blow coming. The baton strikes me in the kidney, just below my ribs, and explodes in a searing white light through my torso. My knees buckle, then the baton catches me around the neck and pulls hard. I claw at my throat to get my fingers around the metal bar while I swing the pistol over my head, trying to point it at my attacker without blowing my own head off.

From the shadows ahead of us, Dr. Simon steps forward, along with another operator in tactical clothes. There's a professional sort of panic on her face, the fret of a manager very much displeased with her team's

306

performance today. She's shouting something at the operator as he raises a pistol, the end of which mirrors every thrash of my body as it tracks me.

The blackout is creeping closer, I can feel it. The baton is crushing my windpipe, and the blow to my side seems to have shattered some glass jar inside me filled with poison that is now seeping into my organs. The gun drops from my hand and bounces on the floor. But I'm not so far gone that I can't see Dr. Simon and the operator. She's shouting again, pointing at me, and even without hearing it I know what's coming out of her mouth. As for what happens next, I recognize it from ten thousand drills: the operator's body tensing a certain way, his eyes narrowing a certain way. Just a fraction of a second before—

With everything I have, I jerk down on the baton and arch forward, lifting my attacker's body enough to wheel around. I feel the impact of bullets slamming into flesh travel through his body and into mine. There's a pop behind my ear, and a spray of something wet and hot as candle wax blasts across my cheek. I push backward a few steps, the impacts still coming even as my attacker's body tumbles to the ground. Then the baton is in my hand, arcing through the air. If I'm judging the distance and speed right, it should land—yes, just there, on the side of the operator's head. It snaps sideways, and Dr. Simon screams. I swing the baton again, catching the operator's head from the other side and sending him into the wall, where he bounces and rolls to the floor.

Dr. Simon and Max are scrambling for the pistols the operator and I had dropped. My foot catches Dr. Simon under the chin just as she's about to grab one, and I take it up instead. Max is already raising the other, but I land the baton hard on his wrist and send him sprawling. I pick up the second pistol, too.

I scan up and down the corridor looking for others, but it's empty, or seems to be. Only now do I recognize my attacker with the baton, the blood forming a widening pool beneath Rossi's back where the operator had shot her.

Peering between her shaking fingers, Dr. Simon's eyes are wide with terror. Delight rolls through me, seeing her like this, powerful as a shot of fresh Theta, and glaring brighter than even the pain in my side. I point one pistol at Max, the other at Dr. Simon.

Max isn't even trying anymore. There's no straining at the duct tape fastening him to the chair. He doesn't even ask for water. Dr. Simon, on the other hand, now clear of the initial shock, is very much in her zone. Despite being bound at wrists and ankles and chest, somehow she still manages prim smiles, and even tosses her blandly pretty hair now and then as she makes a point. This is, for her, a subject worth study, perhaps even a paper. *Duct Tape and Its Impact on Therapeutic Modalities.*

I keep an eye on the monitors, looking for other operators or other Rossis and LaBelles, but there's no one. The only sign of humanity is the bodies—two each in a hospital room and the corridor—and they remain where I left them, impossibly still.

"Quite something, what you did out there," Dr. Simon says, a tone of real admiration, as if I'd just scored the winning basket at the buzzer.

"Should've hired more guys." I open a metal cabinet and drag my finger over a row of external hard drives arranged like books.

"There it is, the famous Gwendolyn Bloom arrogance," she says. "Just performative, of course. But hey, fake it till you make it, right?"

I slide one of the hard drives out. It's a slim thing, the upward-facing edge covered in dust. Written on a piece of masking tape stuck to the front is a name, ABERNATHY, JEROME. I slide out another, that one marked RANDALL, OCTAVIA. There's at least four dozen drives here, four dozen names. I look to Dr. Simon, tap the shelf with the muzzle of my pistol.

"Copies of your predecessors' therapy sessions," she says. "You should give thanks to them, maybe make a little shrine. The version of Theta Compound they got wasn't so refined as yours."

The words she'd first used to describe Theta play back through my head. *Bullet ant venom: had to recalibrate the whole way we measured pain.* I'm about to ask her what became of the other victims, but there's a smug tightness to her mouth that gives me the answer.

At the row of tables I see an open laptop with my own hard drive attached, BLOOM, GWENDOLYN. I sit down in the chair before it and mouse over to the drive. Folder after folder, sorted by date, each loaded with video files. I click one open, see a split frame of one of my early nights here. On the left side, me strapped to a bed, the VR headset buckled on, thrashing midseizure at the restraints. On the right, the images from the headset, throats being cut, bodies melting to dust.

I open another file: me in a chair, slumped shoulders, knees together, a pile of tissues in my lap as I sob.

And another: Me on the toilet in the cottage, body convulsing with chill.

"You said these are copies?" I say.

"What?"

"The hard drives. You said they're copies." I swivel in the chair and face her, studying her face for any sign of guilt, or really, anything human. "Where are the originals? Washington?"

"Oh, no. Washington wants no part of this," she says. "Experimental protocols. Human testing. Strictly black book. Off the grid. All they care about is results, results, results—*never* process. God forbid they give a damn about the actual work." She coughs, as if offended by the idea, then gives a little sniffle. "Do me a favor, Gwendolyn?"

"A favor?"

"Yes, a favor. A *kindness*," she says. "After you kill me, *show* them. *Show* the world. We found what love is made from. And you helped."

The gun twitches in my hand as if it were alive, like one of her bullet ants, pissed and desperate for a target.

She nods toward a laptop at the far end of the table, the nexus of a nest of cables and external drives. "The big one there, standing upright," she says. "Six terabytes. From the first patient all the way to you."

I move the chair and wake the computer, then open the drive. There they are, just as she said: Abernathy, Jerome. Randall, Octavia. Bloom, Gwendolyn. My hand trembles as I scroll down past dozens and dozens of others. Americans. Latinos. Chinese. Russians. Arabs. Mostly they're men, but there's thirteen or fourteen women, too. A mad scientist's collection of specimens, swapping glass jars and formaldehyde for ones and zeros.

"I suggest you send a copy to the best psychiatry journals," she says. "You can Google them. But to the press, too. I'm not under any illusions here, Gwendolyn. Political psychiatry is radical work. Radical."

"Don't worry," I say quietly, closing the laptop and detaching the drive. "I'll make sure everyone knows all about it."

"Look, I'm not expecting a Nobel Prize. They'll call me a monster. Everyone will."

"Because you are," I say.

The duct tape bunches up as she shrugs. "For now," she says quietly. "But in a hundred years . . ."

There's a rush of blood to my head as I rise to my feet, and I have to grab hold of the back of the chair to stay upright. I raise the gun, aiming it carefully at Dr. Simon's head, at the small spot just between her eyes. Then I lower it to my side.

"Go on, Gwendolyn," she says. "We've done enough work together."

"Have you—have you ever tried it?" I say.

She gives a single shake of her head.

"Would you like to?"

Her cheeks expand into a smile, and her eyes suddenly glisten. "Oh, Gwendolyn," she says.

I look around the room, find her little black case on a shelf, and open it. A row of new syringes, still in plastic envelopes, and small bottles marked THETA 6.2.

She watches as I unwrap a syringe and fill it halfway, then I look up and she nods for me to continue. I keep drawing more until the syringe is full.

"My arm," she says. "If you don't mind."

But her arms are bound to her sides with duct tape, so I unbutton her blouse, tug the collar open until I see her shoulder. "Here okay?"

"Oh, that'll be just fine," she says.

Her eyes track the needle as I lower it to the fleshy part just beneath her shoulder bone. The impossibly narrow line puckers her skin, then breaks through. I push the plunger gently and see her body relax, as if collapsing in on itself, the last moments of her life the very best.

I drop the empty syringe to the floor, take Dr. Simon's hand, and give it a squeeze.

Everyone deserves to die happy.

I wait until her breathing stops five minutes later. Then I take up the black leather case and turn to Max. His eyes are still wide with horror. "How about you?" I say. "Want some?"

He shudders, a motion I interpret as no.

"What do you think," I say, picking up one of the vials. "Should we take it with us?"

"Us?"

The first word he's spoken since I tied him to the chair. It comes out raspy and small.

"I don't even know where we are. So, yes, you're coming with me." I dig around through a drawer until I find a pair of scissors. "Do we bring the Theta, yes or no?"

He clears his throat and swallows. "It could be—useful. For research. Given the right people."

I cut the duct tape, starting at his wrists and working up to his left shoulder. Then I place the scissors in his hand so he can do the rest.

"Might be," I say, picking up my pistol again. "Or maybe there are no more right people left."

He struggles to free himself with the scissors—his left wrist swollen and black where I'd struck him with the baton—while I study the vial of Theta in my hand, watching the light refract through it. Then I glance toward the body of Dr. Simon and feel jealousy. My veins stretch inside my arms, and my brain starts to itch.

I drop the vial to the floor, dump the others there, too. Do it quick, I tell myself, before you change your mind. With the butt of my pistol, I smash each one, and grind them into the wet concrete.

Thirty-Two

The little red Volkswagen speeds west along the highway through fairy-tale forests and industrial towns, passing trucks loaded with enormous pieces of mining equipment that strain at the cables holding them onto flatbed trailers like captured giants trying to get free. The air is gray with smoke you can actually taste on the tongue, dirt and sulfur and diesel.

I find it all marvelous.

My eyes sting, from the smoke and exhaustion, but also from the brightness of even this dull light. *Erzgebirge* is where the lab was. Ore Mountains. Where communist East Germany went for iron for steel and uranium for nuclear missiles. We'll head west for a time—Max at the wheel, me in the backseat, pistol on my lap—skirting along the border between Germany and the Czech Republic, then turn southwest through Bavaria. We'll be in Zurich by late afternoon.

I dig through the bag of food we'd gathered from the lab, tear the plastic off another perfectly circular cookie. I've been at it for an hour, devouring whatever I can, circular cookies, square sheets of ham, rectangles of chemistry-set orange juice. My blood tingles with sugar and salt and fat.

"How's the wrist?" I call out to Max, bits of cookie falling from my mouth.

"Okay," he says, eyes not leaving the road.

"Still hurt?"

"Like hell. Thanks for asking."

He had moved like a robot as we left the lab, terrified and doing everything I said without complaint or hesitation. Why, yes, he knew where the food was kept. Why, yes, he knew where Dr. Simon kept her things. He dug a gym bag out from a closet, stuffed with her workout clothes. I cleaned myself up as best I could and changed into her yoga pants and pink neoprene athletic jacket and purple-white sneakers a size too small. In her purse, I found three passports, all with her photo but none with the name Dr. Simon. Each identity had two credit cards and a few other supporting documents—library cards, gym memberships, dog-eared electric bills.

There's no way I can pass for her, not even with the new white in my hair, and it's too dangerous to use the credit cards. But I packed it all up in her gym bag anyway, along with the hard drive and her laptop, and keep it by my side in the backseat.

The shush of the tires on the highway stretching like a black satin ribbon through the smoky forest is making it hard to keep my eyes open. Five more hours, I tell myself. Six tops. We'll get to the bank in Zurich just before it closes; then I'll pay Max off and we'll part ways. At least that's what I told him.

"Eighth of a tank," Max announces.

I slide forward in the seat, look over his shoulder. "Next town," I say.

We pull off after another few kilometers. A large way station, a section for trucks, one for cars, and a restaurant in between. I climb out of the car with Max and never leave his side. In the restaurant, I buy some junk food, a German newspaper, a phone, and spare SIM cards, paying for it all with Dr. Simon's cash.

As we leave, my eyes go to the date on the newspaper.

Four months. I've been away four months.

The paper rattles in my hand and I wind it into a tight roll. I could kill him with it. They showed us how at Orphan Camp.

"You took four months of my life," I say quietly.

But the drive has done much to ease his terror, and he looks at me dispassionately. "Better than taking all the months," he says. "And anyway, it wasn't me. I had no choice."

"No choice," I repeat. "Really."

"Once you're in—there's no leaving. Ever." Max unlocks the back door, motions for me to get in.

"Helicopter ride over the ocean," I say. "Yeah, you already said."

"That's right."

"Just a victim then, huh, Max?" I say. "Poor you."

We ride for another hour without speaking, the anger like steam in the small confines of the VW. Finally, I roll down the window a little for some air. He tells me to roll it up. I tell him to fuck off. Then we're silent again.

Somewhere past Nuremberg, I take a try at the newspaper, but right now I'm so exhausted that my mind skitters and slips over words that are too long and sentences with the verbs all piled up at the end.

"You read German?" Max asks cheerily, as if trying to start fresh.

"I try. Do you?"

"Never could get the hang of it."

"Why bother, right?" I say. "You're American."

He ignores the jibe. "For what it's worth, you didn't miss much. I mean, you picked a good four months to be, you know, off the grid."

I open a bottle of Coke from the gas station and drink.

"A few celebrities died, old ones, no one big. Some bill in Congress, Republicans were pissed. Or Democrats, I forget."

I set the newspaper aside and look out the window. The roads are like something from the future, sleek and dark with rain that must have just passed. Buildings that look like they're made of ice cubes are stacked tidily just beyond the Autobahn barrier. No speed limit here, and the low, aerodynamic cars that pass us with a hiss rather than a roar remind us our old Volkswagen simply won't do.

"What's it like?" Max asks. "Being on the run?"

I turn my eyes back and see him glancing at me in the rearview mirror. "Tiring," I say.

"But you get used to it, though, right? After a while."

"No."

But I can tell he wants more, so I sigh and lean forward. "It's not the running," I say. "It's the—watching. Over your shoulder. You never see them coming. That's what my dad said."

"Is that true?"

"You tell me. I'm not the one who's CIA."

"Former," he says, drumming his fingers on the wheel. "Same as everyone there. We were all contractors."

"Still. You've seen it. A steamroller that never runs out of steam." I play with the Coke bottle, watch the brown high-fructose diabetes-juice slosh around, wish I hadn't gotten rid of all the Theta. "You'll need a new passport, first thing. For you, Australian would be good. Learn the accent."

"Gwendolyn . . ."

"Grow your hair out. Get a job on some beach. I hear Belize is nice for that. . . ."

"Except, Gwendolyn, that's not how this ends for me, is it?" His eyes on mine again in the rearview mirror. "I appreciate it, though. Beach bum in Belize. Nice touch."

Idly, I flick the safety on the pistol back and forth.

An hour outside Zurich, the highway comes to a standstill. I seethe with impatience in the backseat, carving ridges in the upholstery with my thumbnail until I actually break through the fabric. A police car, then a second one, races down the shoulder and disappears as the road curves behind a mountain.

Max turns on the radio, twists the dial—a commercial in German for an appliance sale, this week only; a news program in French, the interior minister will surely have to resign this time!—until he finds some chipper, bleating American pop music. A woman's voice I recognize but whose name I forget, singing about wanting a second chance. Backup rap vocal by a male: *No such thing as second chances,* he says.

Eventually, we make it around the curve, and an overturned tractor trailer comes into view. A spray of logs from its flatbed is tossed carelessly along the highway like a spilled box of toothpicks. Police are directing traffic to an off-ramp.

Max glances at the clock. "We're not going to make it to the bank before five."

I close my eyes, feel the impatience swell.

"So what do we do?" Max says.

I put a SIM card in the phone I'd bought and look for lodging. "Take a left at the exit. There's a little motel ten kilometers away. Cheap."

But we're not the only ones with that idea. When we arrive, only a single bed is available, and even this we have to argue for. Our lack of passports is a problem, and so is our insistence on paying cash. *Sehr unregelmässig,* mutters the clerk over and over as we fill out our registration, *sehr unregelmässig.* Very irregular. Max quietly suggests we offer her a bribe, but judging from the tightness of the clerk's hair bun, this would only get us kicked out. So in the end, I speak to her in pleading French, pretending to be a clueless foreigner.

The room is shabby and worn but clean. A bed for one abuts the wall and we have to climb over an armchair with blue-turning-threadbare-beige upholstery to reach the tiny bathroom. It's a weirdly intimate stage set for a captor-captive relationship, but neither of us has a choice. He showers first, door open at my insistence. I shower next, putting my pistol on a shelf with the shampoo, and making him sit on the toilet until I'm done.

"You take the bed," he says when we're dry and dressed. "I'll take the floor."

But I tell him no, order him to move the armchair against the door, then settle into its collapsed comfort for the evening. We turn on the TV, watch an engineer from Leipzig win a vacation to Disneyland on a game show. When it's over, we watch an American reality series about desperate housewives plotting against one another that culminates in a blond throwing a glass of chardonnay in the face of a brunette in a strangely empty restaurant. *Such a waste of alcohol*, I think.

"There it is," Max says from the bed, head propped up on a pillow. "What I'm going to die for."

I'm so tired, I can't detangle the sentence in my mind. "For—what?"

"This," he says, gesturing at the TV. "Them. America. This show."

Not even a hint of blame in his voice, though. Like it's an inevitable conclusion in his mind. He's going to die, and it's me who's going to kill him. I open my mouth to respond, but really, what can I say.

"Mind if I turn the channel?"

"Sure," I say.

He scrolls through a weather report, a soccer match, a symphony, back to the soccer match, forward to the symphony. It's the music they use in a lot of movies, always at the climax, a big full-throated orchestral drama complete with an entire chorus chanting in the background like a magical incantation.

"*Carmina Burana*," Max says.

"Never heard of her," I say.

"It's the name of the piece. *Carmina Burana*," Max says. "My nana took me to see it. Detroit symphony. Blew my mind. I was, I don't know, seven maybe. Started piano lessons the next week."

In the blue light of the TV, his face is happy and sad at once. "Sick soup," I say.

"Sick soup?"

"Nana's recipe," I say. "Or was that bullshit, too?"

He clicks off the TV, rolls over on his side, head balanced on his hand. "I had leukemia, when I was a kid. Fennel soup was what kept me from puking. After the chemo."

318

"I don't care, Max."

He shrugs. "And I don't care that you don't care." He flops onto his back, stares at the ceiling. "I told Dr. Simon you weren't going to make it. She said that it didn't matter, that you were just a data point. I said if we get the intel, we'll get more funding. She said, okay, try it your way."

"My hero," I say. "I'm sure Nana would be proud."

Max closes his eyes, breathes in deep. "The cottage, the care, all that. I wasn't just in it from the beginning, Gwendolyn. It was my idea."

"Sorry it didn't work."

"Sure it did," he says. "You're alive."

He falls asleep sometime after midnight, snoring softly. I stay awake by reading a tourist brochure and translating it in my head into Spanish and Arabic and Russian. It works for a time, but my eyes keep going back to Max. It'll have to be tonight. I'll get to the safe-deposit box and be out of the country on Lila Kereti's passport before they even find his body.

The gun is too loud and obviously out of the question. A megadose of Theta would be best, but I'd use it myself if I had any. So the pillow then. Quiet and quick. Or at least quickish.

Leukemia. Chemo. Nana's sick soup. Fucking liar. But even if it's true, what a cheap ploy. Hold on, Max, let's try again, this time with violins while you gaze through a rain-spattered window. I slide the tourist brochure onto the seat next to me and move to the bed, sitting down on the mattress carefully so as not to wake him.

But there's only one pillow, and it's under his head.

So I'll have to cover his mouth, jerk the pillow away, and do it. My hand moves slowly, trembling just a little, and hovers over his face.

I touch his cheek instead.

The clock reads 1:50. No rush, I tell myself. Let him have another ten minutes.

I lean over, rest my head on the mattress next to his arm, and watch the clock turn to 1:51.

Terrance in a suit, looking sharp as hell, reclining in the plush red banquette just so. "You remember my mother," he says to me. The woman next to him reaches across the table and shakes my hand softly. Gorgeous umber skin, and with that same warm glow Terrance has, as if there were a lamp inside her. Her hair is clipped short, and she looks great in a cream-colored dress that's probably real silk. I make out her age to be about twenty.

"I thought you died in a sailing accident," I say.

Mrs. Mutai pours me a glass of water from a carafe. "You look thirsty."

"I'm just tired," I say.

I look down at the necktie and blue blazer with brass buttons the maître d' had loaned me and feel ashamed I'd shown up in filthy pink hospital scrubs. "There are no prices on anything," I say.

"Everything is free here," says Terrance. "I already ordered oysters for the table."

"Very rude, Terrance," says Mrs. Mutai. "What if Gwendolyn keeps kosher, then what?"

"Gwendolyn doesn't believe in God, Mom," Terrance says. "She used to be Hindu, then kept getting reincarnated as something she didn't like."

"You don't believe in God, Gwendolyn?" Mrs. Mutai says. "So what happens to us when we die?"

I struggle for an answer and am grateful to be interrupted by a band starting up on a stage in the center of the room, a full orchestra, and a chorus, too. *Carmina Burana*, loud, almost deafening.

"This was Hitler's favorite piece of music," a woman's voice says.

I look up and now there's someone new on Terrance's other side. Hair in a bob, colored red with cheap drugstore dye, and pale skin like a translucent sheath pulled over something darker. She's barely out of her teens and wears a green sequined gown with an army name tape sewn over her left breast that says SAFIR.

"Like you even know what Hitler's favorite piece of music was." I'm angry for some reason. Here I liked the music so much, and now this newcomer ruined it.

"Eat your oysters or no dessert," she says. "I mean it, Gwen."

I pick an oyster out of the water glass that Mrs. Mutai poured for me, bend it open. The inside is filled with gray gel, and I gag at the smell.

I look up at her defiantly. "It's against God's will to eat shellfish, Mom."

She looks at Mrs. Mutai. "Children, they think they know everything." Then she turns to me and smiles with kindness. "So save them for your dad. He'll be here any minute."

I stand up, something pulling at me to leave, compelling me to do it right now. Weaving my way through crowded tables of men in suits and women in gowns, I nearly knock over the maître d', who comes complete with haughty mustache and red carnation in his lapel.

I strip off the blazer and necktie, then start counting off bills from a brick of 1,000-franc notes that never gets any thinner. "Here," I say, shoving the bills at him. "Just don't let him have any oysters."

"Everything is free here, Ms. Bloom," the maître d' says, voice offended. Then he points over my shoulder. "Alas, little goat, you missed the boat."

I look. My dad's at the table in my spot, laughing with my mom and Mrs. Mutai and Terrance, adding an empty oyster shell to the pile growing in front of him.

I jump upright and feel Max's hand over my mouth. My elbow fires back, lands hard in his stomach, and he lets out a pained yelp. My feet crash across the floor, catching on the handle of the gym bag and sending me to the ground. I'm up again in less than a second and leveling the pistol at Max's chest.

"Jesus, Gwen," he hisses. "Jesus, don't shoot."

"You were trying to suffocate me," I hiss.

"You were screaming, Gwen. A nightmare. Jesus, I was trying to help you."

The light in the room is dim blue, and the clock says 5:33. I lower the trembling gun, sink into the armchair.

He climbs out of the bed, kneels down on the rug in front of me, touches my arm. "Are you all right?"

"Fine," I whisper. "Wash up. We're going."

He nods, gets up, heads to the bathroom. Too late for the pillow. So maybe a pit stop on the way to Zurich. A quiet side road, a ditch. Or not.

By some miracle, we find a punishingly tight parking space for the VW between a Bentley and Lamborghini only a block away from Feldman Capital Services. We walk to the front doors in rain just heavy enough to remind us, next time, to bring an umbrella. Behind the brass doors shined as bright as gold, a trim clerk in a gray suit and starched collar gives us a curt nod. *You're welcome to come in*, the nod says. *Sneakers and pink neoprene jacket are fine. Really. Just don't steal the pens.*

But evidently this happens sometimes with clients who use the biometric safe-deposit boxes. A young woman greets us with an actual smile once we're buzzed into the anteroom of the vaults on the floor below. We're shown to a comfortable leather couch, and coffee is served to Max and me with ceremonial manners.

The young attendant asks me to look in the retinal scanner, then shows me to a booth and sets down my steel box on the counter. *Thumbprint like so*, she says, indicating a reader along the front. *Take all the time you need.* I follow her with my eyes as she exits and shuts the door behind her. I'm certain she's seen her share of moguls on the run and fugitive ex-dictators going into the booth dressed like bums and coming out in a suit, clutching a shiny Gucci overnight bag fat with cash. How disappointed she'd be at my own meager kit.

I raise the lid slowly, stare down at the stack of children's notebooks, a plastic bag of identical SD cards, a passport, a packet of

1,000-franc notes. My lips tremble and broaden into a relieved smile; it's all here.

I shove the passport and an SD card into my jacket beside the pistol, slide a second card into my shoe for the sake of redundancy, then thumb through the money—300,000 francs—and put it in the gym bag.

Max is, of course, gone when I return to the lobby. But the clerk is there, waiting for me behind a podium, typing on a computer.

"My friend," I say. "Did he . . . ?"

"Left a moment ago."

I nod. "Thank you."

But there's a surprise waiting for me on the steps of Feldman Capital Services: Max, leaning against the railing, one hand in his pants pocket, the other holding a bottle of beer. He looks up as I come toward him, just slightly curious, but not too much.

"You're still here," I say.

"Needed a drink. Figured, why not?" He clears his throat, studies his shoes. "Can you even drink on the street here?"

It's Switzerland, so either emphatically no or emphatically yes. "No idea."

"Well then, I'll live dangerously," he says. "How'd it go, in the bank?"

"*Alles ist in Ordnung*," I say.

"One thing they do well here, it's *Ordnung*." He raises his bottle in a mock toast and takes a long drink. "So how do we work this?"

"Work this?"

"I expected you to do it last night, when I was sleeping. Then this morning." He looks around, wipes his nose with his sleeve. "Now what? You can't just shoot me in the street."

My eyes narrow. *Can't I?* I slide my hand into my jacket pocket, brushing against the gun. "I just, you know. Changed my mind."

"Well," he says, taking another drink. "That's nice."

My hand comes back out, holding a fat packet of francs folded in half. "Here. Your cut. One hundred thousand."

Max looks at my hand. "So, not a million."

"I lied about that."

He shrugs. "Yeah. I figured."

"Take it," I say. "You'll need it."

"Oh, that's right. Australian passport. Grow my hair out." Max takes the money indifferently, puts it in his pocket. "Feel like getting breakfast somewhere?"

I shake my head.

"All right, then," he says, pushing himself off the railing. "Take care of yourself."

"You too," I call out after him. "Have a nice life."

He raises a hand in a casual wave as he walks away. "All five minutes of it," he calls back.

Part Four

MARIKE

Thirty-Three

A mistake. Obviously. Or maybe not. But it leaves my stomach ebullient to see him disappear, alive. My breath soars; my heart beats evenly and without guilt. A part of me—most of me—is furious and calling the rest of me a sentimental idiot. But I just couldn't do it. Not another one. Not today. Not tomorrow, either. I walk for a while, two hundred grand in my pocket, along with a clean passport and a gym bag full of justice. As for the gun, it'll go in the river. Not now. But soon.

I stroll for a time, crossing and recrossing the river on different bridges, nearly getting hit by a streetcar and laughing about it, buying a pretzel from a street vendor and thinking it's the most delicious thing I've ever tasted. By lunch, I find myself in the Old Town, strolling like a tourist past shops for millionaires that line the streets. Then I remember my suit, the one I'd paid for months ago. Can I find the shop again?

Of course, Lorber's Haberdashery is right where I'd left it. Marcel, the man who'd helped me, recognizes me instantly. "We were afraid you'd... Well, in any case, welcome back."

"Thank you," I say. "Good to be back."

I try it on, the midnight-colored suit that isn't blue or black but both and neither.

Marcel smiles. "One feels—sublime. Does one not?"

I turn in front of the mirror, tugging at the jacket button, cinching the waist. It's sleek and close-cut, shimmering just a touch as it follows the curves of my shoulders and back. "Yes," I say. "One does."

"A little loose. We can take it in, of course," Marcel says.

"Don't bother," I say. "Room to grow."

Marcel helps me find a blouse and stockings and shoes, and I leave wearing all of it.

From an old woman on the street, I buy a 10-franc umbrella for twenty and whistle as I cross the river yet again.

I head into the less bougie quarter east of the Old Town, to the little antiquities shop where Miriam Sonnenfeld sells novelty collectibles that look remarkably like the real thing.

She greets me with unambiguous distaste, even curling her lip. "Are you on drugs? You look like an addict who stole a suit."

With my gaunt, sallow face and ratty hair, I don't blame her. "Just had—some trouble come up."

She appraises me, tapping the pungent red nails against a wrinkled chin. "The raid at the Obelisk Grande, was that you?"

"Yes."

"So that identity I created—what was her name, Kereti?"

"Still alive, for the moment. But I need another. The best you have."

Miriam gestures with her head to the back room. I follow her down the stairs, careful of the third, broken one, and into her studio. She moves a stack of papers from the middle of her desk so she can see me across it. "The best I have," she repeats. "Best at what? Crossing borders? Want to be a Yale graduate?"

"I need—something permanent," I say. "I don't care where I'm born or where I went to school. I just want to be normal. Get a job. Rent an apartment."

"So what's wrong with Lila Kereti?"

"She has a history. I want to be new. Clean."

"So see a priest," Miriam says.

"What I need is paper," I say. "Can you help me or not?"

She looks off at something in the distance, the artist lost in thought. "Birth certificate. School transcripts."

"If possible," I say.

"Expensive, all this," she says, leaning forward.

"I know."

"No. You don't." She holds up a battered old Swiss passport. "When everything was, as you said, paper, it was a question of skill. Now, it's biometric chips and databases. Skill is just the beginning."

I swallow. "How much?"

"Full identity—as you said, *clean*—fifty thousand."

She's screwing me. Or maybe not. I close my eyes, then nod. "I'll pay in full now, and contact you where to send it."

"Work like this, it's a giant pain in the ass," Miriam says. "But you have my word, when it's done, you won't need to come to me ever again."

She won't give me a time estimate and says only that it will be done when it's done. I leave her shop an hour later, after more questions are answered, after she takes my fingerprints and photo. Between Miriam and Max, I've spent half of my money, and it isn't even night yet.

But my day isn't done, not by a long shot.

I'm outside Naz Sadik's office a half hour later and take up position across the street. At 4:45, I get a coffee and come back. At 5:00, the door to her building opens and Naz steps out.

Bright pink hijab today. Goes nicely with her sky-blue umbrella and sky-blue trench coat. Even in the rain, Naz shines among the Zurich crowd in their drab grays, which makes her all the easier to follow. She climbs aboard a streetcar, using the middle door; I climb aboard in the back. I peer through the canyons between shoulders and catch slices of her checking her phone, unwrapping a piece of gum, checking her phone again, smiling this time, as if reading good news.

Eight or nine commuters get off at her stop, so I blend in with them, hanging back as I follow. I see her pull out her keys, and I close the distance. I'm nearly beside her as she slides a key into a door lock.

"Naz," I say quietly, neither a whisper nor a hiss.

She jumps a little anyway, flicks her head around. When she sees me, she inhales sharply, touches her chest. "Lila Kereti," she says. "My God—how did you . . ."

"I followed you from your office."

"Ah. Well. Of course." She fumbles with her keys, wondering whether to go inside or keep the trouble confined to the front stoop. "Look, what happened. With the money. I told you, I had no control over it."

"I know. That's not why I'm here." I look around, making sure the street is empty. "I need your help."

"If you call my secretary, I'm sure we . . ."

"The last thing you need is me showing up at your office," I say, reaching a hand into my jacket pocket. "It has to be now. Tonight." I pull out the small pistol, holding it by the muzzle, and push it toward her butt first.

She looks at it. "What's this?"

"Your insurance policy. That I won't hurt you."

Naz takes the pistol, unlocks the door.

Dim yellow light rolls sleepily over a pair of butter-colored love seats and a curved maple table loaded neatly with a Sotheby's art auction catalog, a copy of *Vogue*, and a vase of white lilies. They look expensive and fresh, like everything in Naz's living room. I run my finger along the spines on her bookshelf. Arabic and Turkish titles, German, French, and English, too. On a lighted pedestal sits a silver teapot in a glass display cube, like at a museum. I study the teapot—nice enough, weirdly squared off—but whatever makes it so valuable is beyond my comprehension.

"You're a fan of Dresser's work," Naz says, a statement rather than a question, as she enters from the kitchen carrying a tray.

"The teapot?" I say.

"Christopher Dresser. Looks modern, but he was designing these in Victorian England. Whole new aesthetic paradigm." She sets the tray down on the table beside the *Vogue* and Sotheby's catalog. A plate of artfully arranged crackers and cheese. A glass of water for me. Scotch for her. "That one there. A prototype. Never went into production. You sure you don't want something—harder?"

I shake my head and sit down on the love seat. "I didn't think a teapot could be, I don't know. Important."

"It isn't. It's a teapot." Naz collapses in the love seat across from me, folds her legs under her. "Works the same as any other. For what that cost me, I could have put a kid through college."

The unpretty idea hangs in the air for a moment, like the aftershock of an obscenity polite people should never say aloud. Then I sip my water, let out a little laugh.

"Fucked-up world," she says, raising her glass as if toasting it. "But you know all about that, right, Lila? Or are you using something else?"

"That's why I'm here," I say. "I was . . . being held. Four months."

"I heard," Naz says. "When you didn't show up again, I feared the worst."

"It's over now. I think. For a little while." I make a sandwich for myself with two crackers and a piece of cheese. "Terrance. Have you seen him?"

"Damn." Naz sighs, takes a sip of scotch. "Just when I thought we were going to pass the Bechdel test."

I look at her.

"Bechdel test. In a movie, or book, whatever. When two female characters have a conversation that's not about a man. You'd be surprised how rare that is."

I close my eyes impatiently. "Do you know where he is or not?"

331

"Budapest. He came by, day after the raid. I made a connection for him, a new passport."

"Budapest," I repeat.

"That's all I know. What name he's using or whether that's where he really went, who can say?" Naz sets down her drink and leans forward, hands folded. "Lila, may I give you some advice?"

I nod.

"Running. It's hard enough on your own. But with two . . ." She cuts herself off, takes another drink. "Love. Attachments. These are privileges you don't have."

"Look, I get it. And thank you." I run my hand over the leather on the armrest, look around the room, Naz's home, comfortable, clean, very much hers. Everything permanent. "I'm here because I need—a plan. Also, a place to stay for a night or two, to get things sorted."

"You can stay here," she says. "Hourly rates apply, of course."

I almost smile as if she's making a joke, but she isn't. "I have a hundred and fifty thousand francs. That's it. That's all that's left."

Naz leans back in the love seat, pushes her hair over her ear, and smiles.

"What?" I say.

"My favorite, this part. Broke client." She gets up from her seat. "Let me show you something."

She disappears into another room and, a moment later, comes back with a file folder. She rests it on her knees and starts paging through it. "The paperwork you gave me. The companies. Webb-Rosenthal. España Shipping. Fomax Optical. You remember?"

"Of course."

"And the bank accounts."

"Which are empty. Thanks to you."

Naz eyes me in a way that means *don't push it*. "Then there's this," she says.

A packet of papers slides across the table. I pick it up. It's a lease from someplace called Ports Francs et Entrêpots de Genève SA, signed by none other than Lila Kereti. I remember it now, glancing over it in my room 33 at the Pension Alexandra. It was Lila's signature that drew my attention, but I hadn't given it more thought than that.

I look up at Naz. "A lease—but for what?"

"For a strong room, it's called. At the Geneva free port. Used to be for grain, cotton, anything that was in transit. The merchant could keep it there, tax-free, no questions asked, until they shipped it to its final destination."

"I don't need grain, Naz," I say. "Or cotton."

"Used to be for that. Then the rich, the same ones who pay a fortune for teapots, figured out you could keep other things there. Artwork. Wine. Anything worth money. Dollars and yen go up and down, but a Picasso is always a Picasso."

"So what's in it?"

"I have no idea," Naz says. "But whatever it is, it belongs to you."

The warehouse for the rich is a beige rectangle of prefab concrete next to the railroad tracks just south of downtown Geneva. There's a McDonald's a block away, and a pizzeria, and buildings that look like warehouses. But this is a deception, Naz tell me. Inside these buildings that look like warehouses are art galleries, insurance agents, lawyers—the professionals who set up shop like street hawkers wherever the rich are found. Money in this part of Geneva isn't merely quiet; it's hidden.

We'd left Naz's house at exactly six o'clock this morning, driving her Mercedes south for three hours in dense but fast-moving traffic. I did my best to minimize my expectations, but I tapped my fingers on the armrest ceaselessly and my stomach cramped the whole way. We pull into the parking lot just as the clock on the dashboard turned from 8:59 to 9:00.

Thérèse, forty or close to it, with brown hair worn in a stylish mop and a gray peaked-lapel suit, steps into the lobby from a back office the moment we enter from the front, as if our arrival had been timed to the second. She greets us in English.

"This is, ah, your first time here?" asks Thérèse.

"Yes. The lease was—arranged," I say.

"Then welcome. Would you care for coffee or tea . . ."

"Just show us to the room, please," says Naz.

As Thérèse examines Lila Kereti's identification in the back office, Naz grips my forearm. "A reminder. It may be empty. Be ready for disappointment," she says, looking at me over the rims of her Audrey Hepburn sunglasses.

Thérèse reappears, a comically large key in her hand, and motions for us to follow. We ride a gleaming steel cube of an elevator to the fourth floor, then walk past polished concrete walls and heavy steel doors, three sets of heels clicking and echoing as we go.

"I'll be exactly here," Thérèse says as she unlocks the last door on the end. "If you need anything, just call."

With professional tact, Thérèse turns her back as we step inside and turn on the lights.

Thirty-Four

A single wooden crate, ESPAÑA SHIPPING stenciled on the side. I run my fingers over the rough wood and look at Naz.

"And me without my tool belt," Naz says.

But the problem is soon remedied. Thérèse knocks politely at the door less than a minute after being dispatched and hands me a crowbar and hard rubber mallet. I decline Naz's offer to help and am rewarded with a grateful smile. She alights to the hallway to wait with Thérèse while I go to work, pounding the crowbar beneath the lid and pushing on it with all my weight until the nails squeak free.

Clothing, carefully folded, makes up the first layer. Blue jeans, a puffy ski parka, a pretty scarf. Then bedsheets, good ones, and a red satin duvet cover, king-sized. It's all very intimate, and no different, really, than any storage locker anywhere. Just like that, I'm back in New York, in Queens, in the storage locker my dad had rented there. I'd broken into it, looking for clues after he went missing, only to find my old life inside.

A toy racetrack, an enormous stuffed elephant, gray and well-loved, Disney DVDs, and a bundle of children's clothes—sweaters and corduroy pants thin at the knees and beat-up, tiny sneakers. Then, photo albums.

I urge myself, just as I did in Queens, to set the albums aside, leave the memories unvisited, but of course I don't. Inside, pictures of a little boy, three or four. At a park. At a swimming pool. On the seat of a rowboat. And in each one, the same woman is with him. Dark hair, brown eyes, dressed indifferently in jeans and sweatshirt. If I were seven or eight or ten years older, she could be me. The most striking thing about her is her evident love for the boy. Her son. I'm looking at Lila Kereti and her son.

I remind myself that this is not merely a storage locker. Not in the sense mine was. It's a climate-controlled strong room in a vault for the rich, complete with a multilingual attendant quick to fetch you coffee or a crowbar. So I set my sentimentality aside with the photos and dig deeper.

A worn-out Oriental rug bundled around something. I spread it out on the floor—the rug old, worn, and to my eyes, meaningless—and find inside two objects. The first, a warrior's mask, bronze and ancient, and the second, a figurine ten or twelve inches high, a goddess carved in marble and holding a bowl.

I place them along the wall of the strong room and fish out the next items, a trio of cardboard cylinders, each a meter long. They feel empty, nearly weightless, but when I pry the cap off the first, I find a roll of old and fragile paper. I unfurl it carefully and see a charcoal drawing of a man's anguished face, just the shadows, though, no high-lights, not even an outline for the rest—a face rendered entirely by the unseen parts. In the second tube, another drawing, this one of a do-mestic scene: a well-off family in sixteenth-century dress at a table, Papa laughing at something his daughter is saying, Mama setting a loaf of bread on the table, smiling slyly. In the third tube is a small collection of more modern drawings: Cubist fish swimming in a Cubist sea. A nude woman with a tiny head and rectangle arms.

In the crate beneath the cylinders, I find a set of flat cardboard sleeves. I run my finger through the seam of the first one and peel it open. Inside, the top of a gold frame, and when I pull it free, I see a still life, a bowl of fruit and a dead pheasant, rendered as sharp-edged pixelated blocks of color. In the second sleeve, something older and more traditional, a woman in a Victorian dress, turning her head away from whoever's making her portrait, but eyes looking back, daring the artist to continue. And in the third, a riot of color exploding from beneath a protective sheet of glass. Greens and yellows and blues and oranges distinct and separate, then melding together into an abstracted seascape. Along the right edge, Chinese characters, large, then small.

I recognize none of the art, none of the few signatures written on the bottom. Each piece is different, and there's no unity to the works until I step back and take in the entirety of the collection all at once. When there are faces, they are never ordinary, never merely satisfied or glum, but faces bursting with love or sadness or joy, the outer limits of what a human can feel. When there is color, it is blinding, forceful, insisting it be seen and heard. Someone, maybe Lila, brought these together under the same roof because she loved them.

When I'm done, I find myself standing, fingers trembling as they touch my lips. I've never seen such beauty before, and certainly never collected together in the same place. I find myself thinking it's like a family reunion of all the good things that ever existed in this world.

Then I find myself wondering how much it's all worth.

I sit with my back against the gold filigreed headboard, bare feet on a duvet cover made of pink satin. Beyond the translucent curtains, Geneva glimmers the way Zurich glimmers, modestly, lights like carefully stacked gold coins, but not too many, lest the city be seen as too showy. Naz has shed her suit jacket and paces in front of the bed in just her skirt and sleeveless blouse, somehow the exact same pink as the duvet cover. She nods as she says, *ja, ja, ferstehe* into her phone; *I understand, Agatha, of course, morning is fine.*

She clicks off, pinches her face in happiness, and jumps in place excitedly. "Full report by morning, Agatha says, but it looks good. Really good."

I try to smile.

"Honestly, a once-in-a-lifetime thing, what happened today," Naz says. "And here you are, looking like I do when I my scotch is gone. Speaking of . . ." Naz points to the minibar.

"Sure," I say. My eyes follow her as she almost skips across the room, radiating an undiluted happiness, lawyers' happiness: *You got yours, I got mine, what else matters?*

"It's just—last time I was in a hotel like this . . ."

"Last time was last time," she says. "This time is this time. The important thing is, we move quickly."

"Naz, listen . . ."

"I started the paperwork already. A new company in the Canary Islands." She empties a tiny bottle of brown liquor into her glass. "Don't worry. I have a new e-mail and the best encryption money can buy."

I cross the room, take her glass from her, and set it down on a table. "This, what we're doing. It isn't right."

"You're a rich woman," Naz says. "You can do whatever you want."

"Lila Kereti is a rich woman."

"According to your passport, you are Lila Kereti."

"Legally."

"Is there any other way that matters?" She snatches back her glass and eyes me as she sips. "God bless her, wherever she is, but Lila Kereti 1.0 is gone. Now here's Lila 2.0. Younger, faster, smarter."

She finishes the rest, sets down her glass, and gives me a tender smile.

"Get some sleep," she says. "I'll be in my room, setting up Lila's empire."

She's gone a moment later, and I hear her whistling, actually whistling, in the hallway. I fasten the chain on the door, draw a bath, and lie at the bottom of the tub as it fills. Warm, plush, rich people's water creeps up a millimeter at a time, encasing my ears and making the world go dumb.

Lila, where have you gone? Where's your son? Dead, the both of you, or just one of you?

The water covers my nose, makes the world go airless.

Why haven't you come for your treasures, Lila? No need for worldly things where you are? A Buddhist monastery. A convent. Under the dirt.

I open my mouth, let the bubbles rise to the surface and pop.

Agatha Lupo wears silver cowboy boots and a yellow cape and a pink skirt that's almost a ballerina's tutu, permanently floating as if she'd been spinning and the skirt just stuck there. Asian, from her appearance, and the same age as Naz, she strides around the strong room at the Freeport as if it were a dance floor, then hands down her verdict: "You have, Ms. Kereti, excellent taste."

"Thank you."

"The rug alone," Agatha says. "*The rug alone.*" She slips on a pair of white cotton gloves and examines the rug's fringe. "Persian. Kerman province. Let's say, hm, circa 1700. One never sees a sickle motif with vine scroll and palmette anymore. Not in this condition."

I shake my head, no, one certainly doesn't.

"Conservatively," she says. "Conservatively, at a good auction, the rug will fetch twenty. Twenty-five on a good day. How does that sound?"

"Good," I say, nearly laughing at the absurdity of a rug going for so much. "I mean, great. Twenty thousand sounds great."

A look between Agatha and Naz that contains a whole wordless conversation.

Naz places a hand on my forearm, leans in close to my ear. "Twenty million," she whispers.

I turn my head, blink at her, *twenty million what?* "I don't understand."

Now it's Agatha's turn. She pulls a stack of papers from a briefcase leaning against the wall and motions for me to come over. It's a long list: item numbers, estimated values, final sales price. "Textile and rug auctions from the last seven years," Agatha says. "Look at these numbers, and none of these are as good as yours. Most buyers are anonymous, but we know they're almost certainly from Gulf countries, usually royalty."

"Twenty million," I say. "Dollars?"

"Conservatively," Agatha says.

The air seems to shimmer, and suddenly I'm leaning against the wall, grateful for cold concrete. I close my eyes and am back in the cell at Dr. Simon's lab. My veins stretch.

"Get her a wastebasket," I hear Dr. Simon shout. "Goddammit, hurry."

Rossi and LaBelle are holding me by the arms, Dr. Simon is patting my face.

"Take some water," Dr. Simon says. "Here, some water."

My eyes flutter open to see Naz crouching before me, a bottle of water held out like an offering. Agatha sits next to me on the floor, holding one arm, while the attendant, Thérèse, is holding the other. Naz pours a little water in my mouth and I swallow.

"I'm sorry," I say.

"Don't be sorry," Naz says. "You're in shock. It happens."

"No," I say. "I mean, I'm sorry, I don't believe you. This is bullshit. Twenty million for a rug. That's not real."

"Bullshit in your world." Agatha smiles gently. "But not in mine."

The mask is Etruscan bronze, the goddess is Cycladic marble. The seascape is a late-period Zhang Daqian, and the still life an early and underappreciated Braque. As for the painting of the woman in Victorian dress turning away, eyes looking back at the artist, it's unsigned, but Agatha has theories.

The drawings include a study by Modigliani and a rare Ferdinand Bol, a student of Rembrandt. As for the charcoal of the anguished face, Agatha presses her fingers together and tells me in a voice like a solemn prayer that it's by Raffaello Sanzio, and has been missing since 1916. Who's that? I ask. Mostly he's known just as Raphael, she says.

Although the best prices are to be had at a public auction, Naz and I, to Agatha's disappointment, rule it out. All transactions are to be done discreetly and—Naz is adamant on this point—here in the Geneva Freeport, where no government need be informed and no taxes paid. This, I learn, is the very point of the Freeport: a secret world hidden inside a nondescript building next to the railroad tracks where the rich can conduct their business beyond the eyes of any authority.

Once Naz has my company set up—LK Marketing Services—and Agatha has phoned her buyers, I sit through three days of meetings in the Freeport's own viewing room. A platinum blond, eighty years young, strokes a tiny dog with jeweled fingers as she squints at piece after piece, then whispers a price to her gallery boy when the Braque is presented. A Russian man with a shaved head and a shiny suit buttoned over a ballooning chest growls into a mobile phone as his stick-figure girlfriend says yes, the Modigliani will be perfect for the Chamonix ski lodge. A chinless aristocrat from London wearing a brass-buttoned blazer and an actual ascot—the first I've seen in real life—harrumphs and wheezes as he runs a yellow fingernail over the marble goddess and grins with yellow teeth.

The Ferdinand Bol drawing goes to a Chinese businesswoman, the rug to a Qatari prince, who at the last second glances at the Etruscan warrior mask and announces he'll take that, too. There seems to be a rule that no one speak to me directly. Instead, prices are conveyed first to a member of the buyer's entourage, then to Agatha, then to Naz, who presents me with a number written in pencil, underlined if Agatha thinks it's acceptable.

The sense of unreality, of total disbelief that all this is not only possible, but legal, never leaves me. The things, which are not mine, are turned into money, which is mine. From time to time I excuse myself, go to a stall in the bathroom, and cry. The dreams and memories and chimeric combinations of both that had tormented me in Dr. Simon's lab seem more real than what's happening now.

Frau Schürr, a woman of sixty in leather pants and oversized sweater, eyes the charcoal drawing of the anguished face by Raphael, her head cocked, weight on the heel of a boot. Her husband sits impatiently on a steel-and-leather chair, reminding her every two minutes of his lunch appointment.

The other man Frau Schürr has brought with her, a child of thirty with a head of wispy blond hair who wears jeans and pink eyeglasses, mirrors her pose.

"I don't want to live with sadness on my wall," Frau Schürr says in German.

"It's a Raphael," pink eyeglasses says. "So hot right now. You can resell the damn thing in a year for thirty percent more."

Agatha takes a step closer, shows the man a catalog.

"See," he says. "It's not about sadness, my love. It's about your return."

Frau Schürr consults with him for a moment, and a number is passed along to me. It's underlined three times, and Naz is giving me a look. I shake my head.

Naz leans in close. "You're an idiot to pass on this," she whispers.

I rise from my seat, brush my hands over my pants as if wiping dust off my thighs. "The Raphael is no longer for sale," I say flatly.

Frau Schürr, pink eyeglasses, and even her husband look at me.

"I'm keeping it," I say. *"Danke für deine Zeit."*

Naz follows me out of the room and when she catches up, I see she's wrestling with how to play this, firm or compassionate. She goes with the latter.

"What's wrong? That was an excellent offer. Better than excellent."

I stop in the hallway, wait for someone to pass. "I want it put back in the strong room. Wrapped up, just like it was."

Naz blinks at me, mouth open. "We have other buyers interested . . ."

"Just like it was," I repeat. "You work for me, remember that."

Naz is pissed but is doing her best not to show it. A forced sense of celebration as she insists on ordering champagne. But Agatha demurs, then reminds me with a steely smile it's perfectly understandable to have seller's remorse. "If you ever, *ever*, want to liquidate the Raphael, just give me a call," she says, kissing me on each cheek before bouncing away.

"*Liquidate* the Raphael," Naz says, signaling the waiter. "It's her business, so we can't really blame her, but *liquidate*. It's just crass."

Playing the ally now, but that's all right. It's what I'm paying her for.

"Everything will be cleared in a day, maybe two. I've set up a separate account, all cash, here in Switzerland. Which reminds me, it came in this morning." She pulls a manila envelope from her briefcase and slides it across the table. "My secretary drove it down here himself. Your—delivery."

My new identity. I don't even know my new name yet, but the envelope is pleasingly thick with a passport and paperwork. I slide it onto the seat beside me.

"The lease on the Freeport strong room was, what, twenty years?" I say.

"Paid in advance," Naz says. "You left a lot of money back there."

"The Raphael stays where it is. That's the way I want it."

The waiter arrives with the bottle of champagne. As he fusses through the business of opening it and filling our glasses, I watch the other people in the restaurant, couples and families, business partners, all of them prosperous-looking, swallowing foie gras and Wagyu beef so casually I wonder if they even taste it.

"I'm not—indifferent," says Naz when the waiter is gone. "I want you to know that."

I look at her.

"To her. Lila. Or anyone." She takes another sip of champagne. "My father came here when I was two. Worked as a cabdriver and was lucky to get that. 'Be a cork,' he told me."

"A cork?"

She picks up the cork from the champagne bottle. "You take this to the bottom of the ocean and let go, what happens?"

"It—goes up," I say. "To the top."

She drops it back onto the tablecloth. "The Raphael. Why do we say it belonged to Lila Kereti? Because it was there wrapped up in her things? If she earned it, then how? If it was a gift, then who gave it to her?"

I shrug. "It doesn't matter."

"My point exactly. So why can't it belong to you, the real Lila Kereti, the *legal* Lila Kereti?" she says.

A solo toast, her glass to mine, which I leave on the table, untouched.

"You're on the top now, darling," Naz says. "Where corks belong."

Thirty-Five

From the window over her IKEA couch, Marike Saar can see the river and, beyond, the hills of the Buda side. She takes coffee on the couch in the mornings, and in the evenings, tea. On the mantel of the fireplace, filled with candles, is a photo of Nick and Imre, the kind boys from whom Marike has leased the apartment while Imre works a three-month film-editing gig in Berlin. On the IKEA coffee table is a book of Nick's poems, *Budapest by Night*, published by a small local press.

Marike ventures out twice daily into her neighborhood on the Pesht side, pronounced just that way, Pesht, the way the locals pronounce it. In the mornings, she does her shopping at a grocery on the pedestrian street a block away. When Henri is standing outside his salon smoking, she stops for a chat, inquires about his two corgis, Trinidad and Tobago. Her first week in Budapest, Henri had colored her hair to get rid of the premature gray (*Tragique*, he'd said) and scissored the stringy mess on her head into a chin-length bob, no bangs.

At night, Marike visits one of three cafés for dinner and seeks out a bar with live music, usually jazz, which is easy to find here. In between the twice-daily outings, she reads, takes many naps, and studies

Hungarian with a university student who comes by the apartment to tutor her. It is a quiet existence that does not change much from day to day. The routine of it is her joy.

Marike finds it easy not to think about her father too much. The anonymous package to the local bureau desk of the *New York Times* or *Guardian* is always a project for next week. Nothing would be the same after that, and as noted, Marike's joy is in her routine.

She stops by a café on an evening during her third week in Budapest and finds Henri and his boyfriend, Jan, at a table in the corner. They motion for Marike to join them, and she does. Marike is tired of the paprikash, which is fantastic, but since she eats it every time she's here, she lets them suggest something unpronounceable and off the menu. It might be veal, which Marike is against, in principle, but which she eats and enjoys just the same.

On the TV over the bar is a news program in German. After the weather (unusually sunny), and the fútbol scores (Dusseldorf lost), a story comes on about which the newscaster seems to care very little, but there's a minute of airtime to kill, so here it is: A methane gas explosion in the Ore Mountains incinerated an abandoned subterranean laboratory once operated by the East German government. No injuries, says the newscaster, and because of its remote location and links to a dark chapter in the country's history, the government has decided to seal it up with concrete, and let it burn beneath the ground.

Jan asks Marike if she's bringing a date to Trinidad's birthday party Saturday, but she doesn't answer at first. He has to ask a second time before she says no, she's coming alone. Her face is like that of a person in shock, Henri notes as he reaches for the check, but good shock, happy shock. Like she's just won the lottery. Marike takes the check from Henri's hand and pays the bill. On the way out, she gives them hugs and kisses, tells them she'll see them Saturday.

Like Judita before her, I can't help seeing Marike as an outsider might, standing at some distance, as if she's not me. But I'm glad she is. I like the way she dresses and styles her hair. I like the cafés she goes to and the food she orders. And I like what Marike is not. She is not angry or devious and unkind. Marike is a cork. Bobbing from day to day, always on life's surface.

That night after the dinner with Henri and his boyfriend, I walk across the bridge to the Buda side just as the clementine-orange sun is setting behind the hills. There's a gallery I'd heard about that has live music on Thursdays and Fridays. It takes me a long time to find it, what with the streets a rat's nest over there. I even ask directions in my crude Hungarian and am proud of myself that I understand the answer.

A half hour into the first set, I arrive at a shabby warehouse. A girl guarding a cooler just inside the front door sells me a bottle of mineral water. In the corner, a wild-haired trio plays bass, drums, and grunting baritone sax. The crowd is around my age, college students in T-shirts and jeans, and they sprawl out on the floor, drinking beer from bottles and passing joints between them. I find a place near the back, sit cross-legged on the dirty concrete, and close my eyes.

The trio is a bleating, glorious mess, with a melodic line I have to hunt for amid dissonant harmonies and a rhythm the percussionist hammers out on everything from a gong to a plastic bucket. But no, I discover after five minutes, not a mess. Exacting perfection, just in a way the rest of the world can't hear unless they listen for it. Perfection for its own sake, well hidden within chaos that isn't chaos at all.

Math music. That's what I used to call it. Like a calculus problem you can hear with your ears and feel in your chest. I open my eyes again and drag my gaze over the others in the audience. They nod along with the music, staring into the middle distance as if thinking. My eyes move to the art on the walls, paintings and photographs, childish, shitty, disciplined, wonderful.

When the set ends, I wander along the edge of the gallery, stopping at a black-and-white photograph of a woman's shoulders and back as she lies on a bed. One arm is pulled up under her head, disappearing beneath tangled dark hair. The light follows the contours of muscles and folds of skin on her back, undulations of highlight and shadow and all the gradations in between. She's beautiful, but maybe she doesn't know it, only the photographer does. A mole, a scar from a burn—she's a little ashamed of these things, but here they are, gorgeous to whoever took the picture.

I suppose it's possible someone else in the world has a mole just there, with a scar from a curling iron she got when she was thirteen right above it. Still, it surprises me how long it takes to recognize myself. And when I do, I'm still not entirely sure. I look at the little notecard pinned to the wall beside the frame. *Sleeping Woman*. Albumen print. Carlo Frei.

The next set is starting, but I make my way to the girl at the entrance. I point to the photo.

"Who is Carlo Frei?" I say.

She raises her eyebrows.

"Ki Carlo Frei?"

She holds up a finger for me to wait, then comes back with a beat-up brochure for a photographic printing shop. At first, I wonder if she understood, then she taps it with a fingernail painted black. "Carlo Frei," she says.

At the train station in Geneva, I'd said *Budapest*, when the clerk said *Where to?* I'd never been, after all, and remember someone telling me once it was one of the world's perfect cities. *Hard not to fall in love there,* is how she put it, I think.

Thus my presence in front of Foto Jó, a shabby little storefront in the Jewish Quarter, around the corner from the big synagogue. Hasidic guys in yarmulkes and beards and side locks, the fringe from their prayer shawls peeking from beneath white shirts, argue in front of the yeshiva next door to the shop. They pay me no attention, used to all the hipsters who've moved into the neighborhood lately.

Wrong to surprise Terrance at work. I'm a ghost to him, and maybe an unwelcome one. It takes special concentration to remind myself he didn't betray me, that the voice I heard in the Ore Mountains lab wasn't his. It's the way you're angry at a friend who did something cruel in a dream—I know, in my head, he's innocent; but my heart and gut haven't caught up yet.

So I linger out front, watch the shadows shift as day becomes evening. At five o'clock a woman comes out—pretty face, pierced nose, hair clipped short on the sides of her head, long and dyed electric-blue on top. She lights a cigarette, checks her phone, then the door opens again and Terrance comes out. He's grown his hair out a little, and he wears glasses with big plastic frames. He puts his hands in the pockets of tight jeans and the two of them start walking together toward a wide boulevard just a few blocks away. I follow at a distance, overhearing snatches of conversation every so often. He's trying to communicate something in Hungarian, but it's rough and self-conscious, like mine is, and the woman keeps laughing and switching over to English.

A Hasidic boy in his teens, red-cheeked with a patchy beard, shouts hello to Terrance, and Terrance shouts hello back. The two continue on, walking very close to each other, then they stop before a store window and discuss something they see. Terrance makes a point, and she makes a counterpoint, touching his arm as she does so. Boy, she laughs a lot. What he's saying can't be that funny, my friend, so knock it off.

It's crowded on the busy boulevard, and I have to get closer so I don't lose them. At a subway entrance the two stop again. She stands up on the toes of her red Doc Marten boots and gives him a kiss on the cheek. He squeezes her arm, smiles, and follows her with his eyes as she gallops away down the subway stairs.

So what, I tell myself. So what if he is. So what if they are. He has a right to whatever happiness he can find. Terrance heads down a side street, stops at a street vendor, and buys some kind of breaded sausage that smells delicious.

Must be nearing the end now. This is a cheap residential block, filled with people just like him in cool glasses and tight jeans. Just the right place for a printmaker to live. But Terrance keeps walking, edging closer to the Danube. I stay a half-block behind, always keeping at least a few people between us. Then, up ahead, a crowded streetcar stop on a line that heads over the bridge to the Buda side. Terrance quickens his pace to a jog, then a run. I keep up. A streetcar pulls in, disgorges passengers, swallows more. He's nearing the stop, twenty meters away, fifteen—

The doors close, a bell sounds, and the streetcar jerks forward. Terrance slows, puts his hands on his hips, follows the tram with his gaze. Resigned to a long walk, he heads toward the bridge, and I follow.

The hills of the other side of the river are silhouetted in the gathering darkness. Behind them, the sun burns gloriously, rays visible through the smog like spotlights searching for someone. The wind is picking up, and in the shadows of the Buda hills, cold arrives. I zip my leather jacket, huddle down, and see Terrance do the same ten paces ahead.

I had no plan and have none now. Follow him. See where he goes. Read his mind if I'm able. That was the extent of it, but now here we are, the both of us. The Buda castle, grand and golden, springs to life, its evening lights coming on and turning it into a sun of its own. A tourist couple stops; the woman pulls out a phone to take a picture. I hurry past them, not caring that I'm ruining their shot.

I call after him, his new name, Carlo Frei, Carlo the Free. But we're headed into the wind and he doesn't hear. I pick up my pace, feel the lace from my right boot lash against my left shin, feel my father glowering from wherever he is, reminding me just how dangerous an untied shoe can be. But my father's not here, and Terrance is, so my jog turns into a sprint, and I call his new name again, *Carlo!*

He turns with near panic, then realizes it's just a solo someone. An acquaintance from a gallery maybe. Or a customer from Foto Jó. Terrance blinks at me. Confusion only. No fear.

I nearly trip as I come to a stop, then I laugh. As for when he sees that it's me, when the moment of recognition actually arrives, I can't say because my vision is blurry. There are no words, just gasps as our chests pull together and rock back and forth there on the bridge between Buda and Pesht.

Part Five

EPILOGUE

Thirty-Six

It all worked out, didn't it? The ending I wanted, or close to it. Even if there's too much history between Gwendolyn Bloom and Terrance Mutai IV for things to ever really be okay, there isn't any history at all between Marike Saar and Carlo Frei. They can start fresh. New lives in a new city. And as for the woman with the blue hair, it turns out, she's nothing to him. A coworker with a crush. How tidy.

But here's the thing about endings. They only happen one way, and it isn't this way. To end a story at a particular point is to tell a lie. Because lives continue until they don't, and there's no such thing as a fresh start.

I learn that immediately. Right there on the bridge. Terrance invites me back to his apartment, but really, what else could he do? When we get there, he boils water for tea on a hot plate on the floor. I take a glass from him—one of the two glasses he owns—and sit cross-legged on the couch, which is also a mattress, which is also on the floor. It's good, though, whatever's in Terrance's tea. Mint, licorice, the label is in Hungarian, so neither of us can really tell.

He apologizes once again for how small and dingy his place is. Once again I tell him it's fine, nice actually, bohemian and cozy. He sits on the mattress next to me and drinks from his glass.

"It's done now," I say softly. "I think done. Anyway, it's done as far as I'm concerned. Over, I mean. All that."

The words just bubble out, and I hope he understands them. I want him to touch me, just a shoulder, or an arm, but he doesn't. Hasn't since the bridge.

"What—what did they do to you?" he says. "I mean, if you want to tell me."

"They kept me, four months, I guess." My voice is flat, barely audible. "In a—cave thing. A CIA black site. Underground. A research facility is what they called it."

He looks at me from the corners of his eyes. "Jesus."

"There was this . . . psychological thing. Sounds. Images. Torture. At first. Then, drugs. Well, *a* drug. Then . . ." My voice trails off. The tension radiates from him like a fever, his desire for none of this to be happening. I stand, but in the tiny space, feel like I'm looming, so I sit again, this time on the floor across from him. "Doesn't matter. Like I said. It's done now."

He breathes in deep, lets it go. "You can talk about it. I don't mind."

"Maybe later."

"What are you going by these days?"

"Marike Saar," I say. "I like it."

"What is it, Dutch or something—Finnish?"

"Estonian."

"Do you speak Estonian?"

I poke him playfully. "Alas, no. Marike grew up in Paris."

"Good bit," he says. "A little convenient, though."

"A little," I say. "And you—Carlo Frei."

He nods. "Weird name. Means 'free' in German apparently."

"*Frei*," I say. "Like *Stadtluft macht frei*."

"What?"

"Nothing. Something I saw on TV. 'City air makes you free.'" I touch his forearm, just two fingers' worth, and am glad when he doesn't pull away.

"You found your thing, didn't you? Working with, what's his name, Jó."

"Miksa Jó," he says. "He started me with cyanotypes, other kinds of contact prints. Worked up to albumen."

"Cool."

"Platinum prints. I'll learn those in, I don't know, a year or two. They're pretty hard."

I pinch my lips between my teeth. There's genuine happiness seeping out in his words. "That's how I found you, you know. You had a print at a gallery. Of me. I was so flattered."

He looks down, lets out a laugh that ripples the surface of his tea. "It's like—fate."

Something in the way he says this, that fate isn't always for the best. Or maybe that's just me, reading into it. I look up at the wall behind us. It's an orderly grid of pinned-up black-and-white prints.

"These yours?"

He nods. "Yeah. Practice."

Street scenes. A portrait of a Hasidic guy holding hands with his daughter. An old lady being helped onto a streetcar by a conductor. A woman, pretty face, pierced nose, long hair on top, sides clipped short. "Very good," I say. "I mean it. You're—these are exceptional."

He follows my gaze. "Marta. You'd get along well. She's a coworker."

"I'm sure I would."

"Really into jazz. Like you."

"And like you," I say.

His eyes are on mine—I feel them—but I can't bring mine to his. Instead, I cheat, focus on the skin just beneath. "I don't know what we're supposed to do," I say.

"Me neither."

"You're happy here."

"I am," he says.

I'm happy for his happiness, every bit of my soul meaning it, and feel bad that all I can do is nod and force a smile. "Anyway," I say. "I have a—well, there's lots of things. We should talk. I mean, some other time."

He pats the mattress next to him. "Come here," he says.

Sometime after three in the morning, I get up to pee, trotting in bare feet down the hallway to the shared toilet, leaving the door to his apartment propped open with a shoe so it doesn't lock behind me. My eyes are red and hurting, and so are his, but this is from lack of sleep. At no point did either of us cry. At first, I was glad for that, but as the hours wore on, it made me angry. Maybe we'd simply run out of our lifetime supply. Or maybe something inside both of us had broken and crying just wasn't a thing we could do anymore.

The toilet seat is cold, and someone left a pair of underwear bunched up in the corner. I'd whispered into Terrance's ear a fifteen-second version of the Geneva Freeport story, leaving out the part about how much I'd gotten, but telling him it was enough to be comfortable. His response was a shrug, a quiet *That's great, really.* It wasn't sarcastic the way he said it, or bitter, just a thing someone says when good fortune falls upon someone they don't know very well.

I pull my phone from my pocket, check the time. By now I'd expected to be—I don't know—back in love. Or at least naked and next to him. But maybe that part of us has broken, too. I wipe, pull up my jeans, and rinse my hands and face with cold, brassy water from the tap. *Let's be rich together, Terrance,* I say to the reflection in the mirror. *Or just together.*

When I slide back under the blanket, his eyes catch the light. They're serious and tired but not at all sleepy. He drapes an arm over me, runs a finger idly along the fabric covering my collarbone.

"Terrance, if you—need anything. Money. You can have whatever you want. You should consider it yours, too."

He breathes in and out calmly for a moment. "I'm set. You should keep it."

I close my eyes, fighting back irrational anger. Fucking rich kid, even if he's not anymore.

"What do you mean, you're 'set'? How can you be 'set'?" I say.

He shrugs. "I'm—good. I'm happy. Like this."

"Bullshit. You always had money. I didn't."

"Okay," he whispers.

"It's not like—look, you don't understand."

"Okay," he says again.

I slow my breath, try to just feel him there. What makes him 'set'? The woman, Marta. Or maybe his job. That's all he's after, all he wants.

I reach up, squeeze his forearm. "Sorry," I whisper. "I'm just—I don't know."

"It's all right." He presses his mouth to my temple, not sensual or sexy, but just to do it. "So," he whispers into my hair. "How long are you in Budapest?"

By morning there's nothing left to say, neither about the four months behind us, nor whatever time—a week or five minutes—is ahead of us. At dawn, we decide to eat something, and so we head out into his neighborhood. At a corner table in a café that has just opened for the morning, we eat fresh bread and drink coffee and wait for the pastries to be done. The waiter is a dick, upset at our intrusion into what I guess must usually be a quiet hour.

"Your dad," Terrance says as the waiter retreats into the kitchen. "How is he? Have you—have you heard from him?"

I shake my head.

"No? So what are you going to do?"

I don't look up from the bread I'm buttering. "He has to wait."

"For what?"

"Until I get tired of—grocery shopping. And taking care of a houseplant."

A confused smile flickers on his face. "I don't understand."

"Know what my biggest worry is? Know what keeps me up at night?

Hungarian verb conjugations." I focus on the movement of the knife across the bread. "Selfish bitch. You can say it."

"Gwen, it's *your* life. Your *life*." He reaches across the table, squeezes my hands. "It belongs to you. You don't owe it to him. Do you think he wants you to die for his sake?"

I look away.

"He'd rather you be here, rather you be happy. So stop feeling guilty."

An old man comes through the front door, tweed coat, hat, newspaper under his arm. He calls out a familiar *good morning* to the waiter, who calls a familiar *good morning* back. There's a jokey line from the old man as he takes his seat—his usual seat, I imagine—and the waiter laughs. Outside, the sun is coming up and little wisps of steam rise from the streets.

"You like it here? In Budapest?" I ask.

"I stay careful," he says. "There are nationalist militias in the streets now. Jobbiks. They beat up immigrants, blacks. Jews sometimes."

"Then why stay?"

"I'm a New Yorker. I can take care of myself."

"That's not what I mean." I turn my coffee cup in its saucer, the ceramic so hot it burns my fingertips. "Are you happy here?"

He bites his lower lip as he thinks. "I get up in the morning. I make art. I learn things. I see friends. We talk and drink."

A routine that plods forward, more or less the same day to day, week to week. "So, yes, you're happy," I say.

"I don't know a better definition." He sighs, and it turns into a laugh. "We could have done all this—coffee, breakfast—in Buenos Aires, you know. Skipped that whole middle part."

"Guess so."

When we finish, I try to pay, but Terrance won't let me. As the two of us are standing on the sidewalk in front of the café, he tightens the collar of his jacket. "Going to be warmer today," he says.

"Yeah, maybe."

"We should do this again."

"Maybe dinner," I say. "Next week."

"Or—there's a gallery show tonight," he repeats. "You should come."

I nod. "Okay.

"I'll text you the address."

"Okay."

Making plans for later. That's how one does it, I guess. How one sets the foundation for where one will be tonight, and thus tomorrow, and thus a pattern and a normal life. I walk to a main street where I can catch a tram to the Pesht side. But the day is, as he predicted, warmer than yesterday, so I decide to walk instead.

I'll meet him at the gallery show. Maybe meet this Marta, too. On the bridge, I have to shield my eyes with my hand because the sun is so bright today. It reflects off the river, making its choppy blueness as bright as the sky. Maybe I'll surprise him by inviting Marta out with us afterward. But probably not.

The bridge between Buda and Pesht is longer than it appears, but I don't regret my decision to walk. Plenty to think about. We'll slip away from the show, find a little place where there's music, order two of the cheapest things on the menu.

But look at me, lost in imagination. As if someone in my position could afford to lower her tactical awareness for even the length of a stroll. Turns out, I'm not alone on the bridge. Despite the early hour and morning chill, there's a figure thirty or forty paces behind me. A tall man with good posture in an overcoat, gray hair clipped short, giving him the bearing of a military man out of uniform. Even from this distance, I'd recognize Brent anywhere.

Thirty-Seven

The pedestrian part of the bridge ends at an overpass that serves as both an informal skate park and homeless camp. I linger there, waiting for the figure to catch up. When he does, he simply keeps going past me, and I fall into step beside him. Not even old acquaintances, the two of us, just two pedestrians headed the same direction at the same time.

Makeshift shelters of plastic tarp and wooden crates are coming to life around us. It's mostly Europeans, but a few Arab and North African refugees who've managed to avoid the cops and fascist patrols. Breakfast is being made and water for tea boiled over cans of gelled fuel burning blue.

"Well, congratulations," Brent says. "I mean that. Really."

"For what?"

"You not only survive, kid. You come out golden."

Anger, misdirected or not, crawls out. "Who put the CIA onto me? Was it your team?"

"We're the ones who warned you," he whispers. "At the hotel. The phone call."

I thrust my hands into my pockets. "No offense, but I don't want to see you again. I'm done, okay? Completely. I've paid enough."

"Sure. No problem." But he concedes this too easily, which is why I'm not surprised when the next part slips out of his mouth: "Although . . ."

"*What?*" I hiss.

"We have information you might be interested in. About your father."

I close my eyes. "Is he alive?"

"We hear you spent some time in the Ore Mountains, at a lab there. Were you responsible for what happened to that psychiatrist, Dr. Simon?"

"What about my father, Brent?"

"I'm using Paul now. And answer the question."

We near the end of the camp, and both of us start up a stairway to the street level. "Well, *Paul.* Dr. Simon is the one responsible for what happened to Dr. Simon."

"Maybe you can pass the message on, then, to whoever killed her. The world is forever grateful."

"Goddammit. Tell me about my father."

He stops when we reach the top of the stairs and looks around, surveying the empty sidewalk. "We want to know about the program Dr. Simon was running. What she did. Who else was there."

"I took a hard drive when I left. I was going to release it to the press."

"Mind if we take a look first?"

"My father. Tell me, and I'll give it to you."

He inhales and leans back against the railing, pretending to mull the idea over. "You been to the Dohány Street Synagogue yet? Really something. You feel this connection, you know?"

"Do we have a deal?"

"Sabbath services. Tonight. You should check it out."

He pushes off just as a tram slows to a stop, then disappears inside it.

. . .

A Budapest cop in uniform and two security men in leather jackets and black yarmulkes preside over the steel gate before the synagogue. I hang out in the little park outside the entrance, watching the tourists consulting guidebooks and taking duckface-peace-sign selfies beside the Holocaust memorial. Only when services are about to start do I approach.

The security guys—lean and very thorough—usher me through the metal detector and search my backpack. The duplicate I'd made of the hard drive gets extra scrutiny, and why not? Six terabytes of human suffering. But I tell them it's for work, and after consultation, they let me in with it. A sparse crowd for tonight's service, men in the center section, women and children off on either side. I take a seat midway toward the front, two rows away from anyone else.

The place isn't particularly ancient by European standards, but it's weighted down with the compressed history of the twentieth century, all of it bad. This had been the center of the Jewish ghetto during World War II, and then the Soviets came, used it as a stable. But the synagogue had been restored, cyan and gold frescoes brought back to life, the minarets out front cleaned and gilded.

The congregation is a mix of locals and visitors, with the Orthodox seeming to prefer the front, where they greet one another, *Gut Shabbos*, and chat amiably until the service starts. A woman in a good Burberry trench sidles into the pew next to me, and I know before even looking up that it's Mazal. She is the only woman with brown skin in the synagogue, and people turn and look. A few children even point before having their hands slapped down by their mothers. Mazal shows no reaction.

I can't remember the last time I've been to services—the wedding of one of my father's friends, maybe, or someone's bar mitzvah. Mazal and I follow the lead of the congregation, standing when they stand, sitting when they sit.

"Do you have it?" Mazal whispers.

I push the backpack toward her. She lifts the flap and takes a peek inside.

"Your turn," I whisper back. "My father, what's happening?"

"Relax. He's safe, or that's what we think."

"Where?"

"In Qatar. With the Al-Saqqaf family. A guest of the sheikh."

That name, it's familiar. I squeeze my eyes shut and work my memory. "I—know him," I whisper. "I was there once. At his house. Eid."

Breaking the Eid fast, the sheikh straddling the lamb, running a knife across its throat.

The congregation suddenly stands, and Mazal and I follow suit.

"A guest? You're sure?" I say quietly.

"When we got him out of Uruguay, we took him by plane to Recife, Brazil, hooked him up with new papers. Last we saw, he was getting off a plane in Doha and was met by a car registered to Al-Saqqaf. It appeared—consensual."

I wait until a prayer starts, the congregation calling out in unison, before speaking.

"Do you have intelligence on the sheikh?"

"A whole filing cabinet. He's old-school, hates politics, hates the Islamic radicals more. He's safe there, your father."

I close my eyes, feel the desert sun on my face. "I need to get in touch with him," I whisper.

"That's up to you," Mazal whispers back. "As you can imagine, the Al-Saqqafs don't answer phone calls from Mossad. Maybe your new friend can help."

"New friend?"

"Dragoslava Zoric. The sheikh and her father did business together, once upon a time." Mazal hefts the backpack into her lap. "You were right, by the way."

"About what?"

"About the Zorics closing up shop. We confirmed it. Resources can now be directed elsewhere."

"You're not hunting them anymore?"

"As I said, resources have been directed elsewhere. We no longer

365

consider them an active threat." She rises, slips the backpack over her shoulder.

"Don't leave," I hiss. "We're not finished."

Mazal gives my forearm a squeeze. "Once again, the state of Israel thanks you for your efforts."

She's gone a moment later, slipping down the aisle and out the back. I look down at her seat and see she left something behind.

It's a book of matches: *El Gran Castillo, Sarajevo,* says the cover.

I stay through the end of services, sitting and standing along with everyone else, drinking the sweet white wine that was handed out in paper cups—the first intoxicant I've had since my last dose of Theta— hoping it'll help me feel it, hoping I'll feel the rabbi's words in a language I don't understand bring me the same peace they seem to bring everyone else here.

When it's over, the worshippers file out, and a woman who'd sat near the front pauses in the aisle beside me. She's herding her two children toward the door, but she stops for some reason and waits for me to look at her.

"*Beszélsz magyarul?*" she says.

"*Csak egy kicsit,*" I say apologetically.

She switches to slow English. "You are visitor here or are you alive in Budapest?" I sort out her words—are you alive in Budapest. "Yes." I nod. "I live in Budapest."

"Not so many young people, but we are trying," she says. "We have classes. In evenings of Wednesdays. If you are interested about this."

She tells her kids to stop fighting as she digs through an enormous handbag and pulls out a brochure. "Sometimes in the world, we lose— sorry, my English—our selfs, our spirits, you know? Who we are on the innards. This world is very—difficult. Am I saying what makes sense?"

"Yes, I understand perfectly." I take the brochure, tuck it into my jacket. "I'll think about it. Thank you."

In a moment, I'm one of only three or four others left in the temple, others who need the extra time with God. For reasons I can't explain, I kneel and fold my hands. This is how you're supposed to do it, I think, how one prays.

No names, no images of who this message is going out to—nothing in a beard, no human-shaped anything. That would make it too easy to not believe. So just hope, then, that there's something there to catch it. I can't sort through the thoughts well enough to put them into words, so I just let the mess roll out of me, bits of data, stillborn ideas, half images, prethoughts. Loyalty. Father. Running. Tired. Happiness. This.

I wipe my eyes on my sleeve, reach to my backpack for a tissue, but remember Mazal took it. Blood rushes to my head as I stand, so I have to sit until the dizziness passes. Had something heard me? Had the message found an ear? No reply. No blinking light. No indication I'd done anything more than ejaculate madness from my mind out into the world.

On the way out, I check my phone. An address from Terrance, followed by, *C U at 22:00.*

I sigh, standing at the entrance to the Metro, looking at his message, and seeing instead, *R U alive in Budapest?*

The gallery is out by the university, adjacent to a park, where there are stalls and food carts serving beer and delicious things I can't pronounce yet. Budapest's young set. Its smart set. Its knows-about-art set. I somehow make it through the crowd into the gallery, sliding sideways between knots of people who know one another. I find myself at the wall, next to a black-and-white photo taped to cardboard matting. Title, Platinum Print Number 8. Artist, Marta Nagy. The subject, Terrance, nude, reading in a chair. There's nothing sexual about the photo, just matter-of-fact. He is, though, dazzling in his nakedness, the position of the lamp over his right shoulder draping light over half his face, over his collarbone, catching the end of his penis where it rests against his left thigh, and the light continuing all the way down to the ridges of his left foot, which is pointed, finishing the diagonal started by the lamp. This is how I remember him in our best moments together. And it's obviously how Marta remembers him, too.

I spot Terrance near the back, arms raised with four beer bottles as he pushes through the crowd toward a woman with blue hair smoking a cigarette. Just as I'm about to turn away, he sees me and grins, motions for me to come over.

When I get there, Marta is holding court, explaining in English how tricky platinum is to work with. Terrance is nodding along in agreement. That platinum, such a pain in the ass. I fold my arms over my chest and look down, wishing I hadn't come. Then Terrance is saying, "Everyone, everyone, this is my friend Marike."

It takes my mind a second to realize he means me, then I look up and give a forced smile.

Marta smiles. "Carlo told me all about you."

"I heard about you, too," I say.

"Did you see the photo I made of him?"

"Yes. It's great. Beautiful work."

She rolls her eyes. "*He's* beautiful. My work is okay, not great. But thank you. That was sweet."

"Is it for sale?" I ask.

Terrance flashes me a look.

"For sale?" she says. "Well, I suppose everything is, no?"

Terrance clasps a hand on my shoulder. "Marta, excuse us. I have to talk to Marike about something."

He takes my hand and leads me outside. Cigarette and weed smoke is thick here and we escape to a corner of the park.

"Hey," he says. "Hey, are you all right?"

I pinch my eyes closed and nod. "Just—out of place."

He takes my shoulders in his hands and squeezes gently. "I didn't know she was showing that one."

I pull away from him. "It's fine. I've seen you naked before."

"That's not what I mean." He sighs, lets his arms collapse to his side. "She's cool. I like her. We slept together. But we're friends now, that's it."

"Yeah. Cool. None of my business."

He takes my hand and leads me to the sidewalk. We walk slowly between the park fence and the cars lining the curb. It's deserted, thankfully. I remember his warning about the Jobbik militias.

"I got news today," I say suddenly. "About my dad. He's alive. Doing fine, apparently."

"What? That's great!"

I don't reply for a long time. He touches my chin, turns my face toward his.

"I mean, you wanted that," he says. "You wanted to find him."

"Yeah. I did."

We reach the corner where the street joins with a long boulevard that stretches into the distance. I start walking, and Terrance stays at my side.

I take his arm, slide my hand into his. "This feels like, I don't know, a vacation," I say quietly.

"What does?"

"All this. Normal life. How long does it last, do you think?"

He laces his fingers between mine. "As long as you want. If you choose it."

I feel my lips trembling as I try to smile. "They won't stop, you know. Ever. Looking for us, I mean."

He steps back, pulling our hands apart. "And I don't care. I don't. This is where I want to be. And you need to decide."

I look at him but don't answer.

Terrance gestures to the crowd behind us. "Look, I'm going back to the gallery, to see my friends, have a drink. You coming with? Because you're welcome to. I want you to."

I turn and look down the boulevard. It stretches into the distance, to a vanishing point a long way from here. "I think—I think I'm just tired," I say.

He nods, closes his eyes. "Call me tomorrow, then," he says. "Or whenever."

I swallow hard. "Tell Marta I like her work. Really."

Thirty-Eight

There was a war here, decades ago or yesterday, hard to tell. A gleaming office building of a modest, suburban size sits on one side of the street. Across from it, another building, a ring of rubble surrounding the foundation, baring the building's interior, the apartments inside naked for all to see. Faded wallpaper—yellow plaid in one home, pink flowers in another—and pieces of furniture left as they were when the building was cleaved in two by artillery shells. A kitchen table beside an open refrigerator. A wrought-iron bed, tattered sheets still fluttering in the breeze.

Sarajevo Landscape #1. That's what Terrance would call it. He would tell the driver to pull over and be out of the car a second later with his camera. He would squint at the scene, framing it just the right way, the way only he can. He would lift the camera to his eye, one or two disciplined frames, that's it. He would shift positions, squint again, take two more shots. He would do all of this if he were here.

I left the morning after the gallery show, sliding an envelope with the key to the apartment under the store to Henri's salon with a note asking him to water Nick and Imre's plant. As for Terrance, I'll catch up with him when I come back. If I come back. But I decided on the train to Belgrade—eight hours on a Communist-era local, the only kind they run to Belgrade—that going back is unlikely.

In Belgrade I learned there was no train direct to Sarajevo, what with the recent genocide having soured relations between the two capitals. I could get there through Zagreb, a twenty-hour detour, or hire a driver and car and be there in three. Outside the station I met Midho, who makes a living shuttling passengers between Belgrade and his hometown of Sarajevo in a well-cared-for VW hatchback he calls his Ferrari. I paid in cash, a hundred Swiss francs, and introduced myself as Sveta, a throwaway pseudonym.

Midho flicks a finger toward the ruins of the building. "Sorry for the mess," he says. "Maid's day off."

I give him an uneasy smile, and he laughs in that way people who've seen too much tragedy laugh—the world is hell, no sense dwelling on it.

Virtually every building older than I am bears scars, star-shaped wounds from shells, crudely patched over, seams of bullet holes from machine guns, too small to bother with.

Then we turn a corner and an enormous mosque looms before us, white marble and gold. A muezzin has just started the call to prayer, and figures are streaming into the structure, men in simple white pants and long shirts that come almost to their knees, and women in hijab and full burkas.

"Saudis," Midho says, pointing to the mosque. "We need factories and schools, they give us that. Before the war, Muslims like me, my wife, we never wear stuff like that." He shakes his head at the idea. "Only Zoric family makes work here now. Furniture factory, you know. And hospital, good hospital."

"You like them, the Zoric family?"

"Viktor Zoric, he is killed since a few years." Midho fumbles for another cigarette.

"He was Serbian, no?"

"A Serb, but Bosnian Serb, *our* Serb. Criminal, they say about him, but *pfft.*"

He taps a finger to his temple. "His daughter, very smart. All that money, she could live anywhere. But she stays in this shithole. Loyal, like her father."

"There's a place I heard about. El Gran Castillo. Do you know it?"

"East, a little. Viktor's hotel. Big gangster parties every night before he died. Now, nothing." Midho exhales a jet of smoke. "His daughter owns, I think."

"Can you take me there?"

El Gran Castillo. The Grand Castle. An inexplicable Spanish name for an Austro-Hungarian hotel owned by a Serb in Bosnia. It sits away from the city by several kilometers in what Midho told me was, a century ago, a neighborhood for the old Austro-Hungarian authorities. When the Serbs retreated after the war, they took everything they could carry from it and burned down most of what they couldn't.

He drops me off outside the empty parking lot. Not many visitors to the hotel since Viktor's death, Midho explains. But the area around it is a popular tourist destination among visiting Arabs from the Gulf, families used to endless stretches of sand seeking out the green and lush.

What comes next will be a tricky play for me. When I'd approached Lovrenc and Dragoslava the first time, it had been as an adversary. Now I'm coming in search of their help. So I'll wait to be noticed, make myself seen, no stealth. I walk down a muddy road next to the hotel, beneath an archway of unkempt trees, just surveilling the area. Every once in a while, an old mansion slips in and out of sight behind the foliage, the serious, down-to-business architecture losing the battle against weeds and rain and winter. Midho had been right about the looting. Windows aren't broken and doors aren't hanging ajar; the windows and doors are simply gone, leaving black rectangles garlanded with vines.

Up ahead, I spot movement and hear children playing. They grow quieter as I draw nearer. It's a Romani camp, a collection of sheds made with scavenged wood and metal, a few women hanging out on make-shift stoops in bright green and orange and pink dresses. The children approach me with curiosity but keep their distance as they size up the newcomer.

The road turns right just at their encampment and continues to a shelled-out brick building with debris extending for twenty meters in every direction. When I come before it, a wave of desperation hits me suddenly, and I stagger back a step. The frames of children's beds are strewn around, impossibly bent and mangled. The things of childhood—brightly colored chairs and low tables, teddy bears and plastic toys—are spread across the courtyard, barely recognizable beneath the char of the initial explosions and two decades in the open.

The desperation is accompanied by silence, and I realize the Gypsy kids have vanished. Scared of ghosts, I assume. Then I see the real reason a moment later: a sign in four languages on a post: DANGER: MINES. I stare down, searching the ground around me, scanning the charred body of someone's stuffed bear, the head of someone's beloved doll, the hulk of a melted plastic car. I've stumbled into someone else's war, bumped into someone else's tragedy.

I turn back, keeping to what there is of a little footpath, until I reach the road where the Gypsy kids are still gathered. They part as I approach, keeping away from the stranger who walked through the forbidden place, the place they've been told never, ever to enter. One of the mothers rises from the stoop and rushes toward me, hissing something, making some gesture with a contorted hand that looks very specific, very meaningful. A curse, I'm sure, and from her expression, not one meant to protect me.

Judging from the vacant parking lot of El Gran Castillo, the place is obviously closed for business. It's only when I draw closer and catch sight of the dining patio, every place immaculately set with china and silverware, every ashtray and crystal goblet spotless, that I realize it's just enormously unpopular.

I enter the restaurant, where a waiter in bow tie and vest is standing at attention. He'd seen me, I suppose, and scrambled up from his chair and tucked away his newspaper. Or maybe not. Maybe that's the way he always stands, on the off chance a customer might come in.

The place is empty, not in the sense of having few customers, but in the sense of having literally zero customers, except for me.

"Would mademoiselle desire for herself a table for dining?" he asks in proudly enunciated English.

I nod that mademoiselle would. Absurdly, he checks a reservation book, dragging a finger over an empty page, before plucking a menu from a rack and showing me to a table for six with an excellent view of the parking lot.

"Just a coffee," I say.

He bows formally and disappears into a room I assume is the kitchen.

The place doesn't stir the entire time he's gone. Not a single figure enters the restaurant, and no one comes into the parking lot. The waiter returns twenty minutes later with a silver tray, a tiny china espresso cup, and an elaborate silver service consisting of a coffeepot, a pitcher of cream, a tray of cookies, a dish of jam, a glass of water, a bowl of various kinds of sugar, and a pair of silver tongs.

"Excuse me," I say. "Where are the other customers?"

"Weekday afternoons," he says, shrugging amiably.

I stir a cube of sugar into the coffee, the bitter Balkan kind, thick like river mud. "Has Dragoslava been in today?"

His eyes actually flutter and he wrings his hands. "Dragoslava? Ah, no. No. Enjoy your coffee, mademoiselle."

It turns out I was wrong about how empty the place is. A moment after he heads into the kitchen, he appears again in the doorway, a man in a suit beside him who looks me over, gives the waiter whispered instructions.

They leave me alone for a half hour longer, then the waiter appears with the check. "Will there be anything else, mademoiselle?"

"Oh, I'm just waiting for a friend," I say.

"A friend?"

"Dragoslava Zoric. I believe I mentioned her."

He sets the check down and heads off into the kitchen.

A moment later, he's back, carrying a mustard-yellow telephone, the cord trailing behind him. The man in the suit waits in the doorway, hands folded in front of him. "A call for you," the waiter says, setting the phone on the table.

I pick up the receiver, press it to my ear.

"*What the fuck are you doing?*"

Dragoslava. Unmistakably.

"I was in the neighborhood," I say. "Thought I'd stop by."

"Stand up," she says. "Look out the window."

I do, and I see a black Mercedes sedan pull into the parking lot and crawl to a stop.

"A car just pulled in," I say.

I hear her breathe angrily. "Pay for your coffee, and get in."

That there is no blindfold or bag over my head is cause for alarm. It means one of two things: The first is that secrecy is unnecessary because we're headed somewhere public. The second, and more likely, is that secrecy is unnecessary because I'm about to be shot.

The driver and the guard are new to me. They're well-dressed versions of the bodyguards I'd met on the *Erebus*, thick men in suits and ties, and their demeanor is professional and efficient. There's a quick frisk and search through my backpack, then the driver reminds me to put on my seat belt.

I ask where we're headed, but I am told only "To Dragoslava." The car speeds through the city, and I find relief in the idea of meeting her in some crowded, public area. Then the Mercedes turns onto a winding road that leads into the surrounding hills, and my relief turns to unease.

"Are we almost there?" I ask.

The guard in the passenger seat turns his head. "Near the end now."

The car slows as a block of ruins comes into sight, shattered buildings that used to be three or four stories tall, blown open, exposing interior walls and doorways, a bulletin board, a sink dangling on a pipe. It's not an office or apartment building—my mind scrambles to decode the subtle signals of its identity, not wanting it to be true. The furniture is institutional, and the walls at one time had been a certain kind of white, hospital white. I catch a scorched mural of cartoon rabbits and chipmunks playing in a meadow under a rainbow and watchful yellow sun. A cartoon doctor in a white coat. A cartoon nurse leaning over the bed of a cartoon child.

"What is this place?" I say to the men in the front seat, first in English, then in Russian, the words coming out in a panicked gasp.

"Dragoslava," answers the driver.

The sedan passes between two of the shattered buildings, creeping along pavement that is surprisingly new and smooth until it emerges on the other side. The road climbs to the top of a hill, where a new hospital sits, gleaming glass and clean white brick, people moving busily past the windows or lingering on the sidewalk. A man pulls a bald child in a wagon. A teen in a wheelchair smokes a cigarette. A mother and father walk patiently beside a daughter on crutches. The sedan pulls beneath the carport, and a woman walks purposefully from the lobby to the curb. A blouse and skirt, stockings and pumps, the scar covering the side of her face visible only when the wind rustles her dark hair.

She opens the back door before the guard in the passenger seat has a chance to, smiling radiantly at me, an old friend. Only her eyes tell the truth, stabbing into me as I climb out and she pulls me into an embrace.

"*How dare you*," Dragoslava hisses, so close my ear is wet from her breath.

I try to smile, but it comes out twitchy and unsure of itself. Dragoslava turns to the guard and driver, says something in Bosnian, and leads me away down the sidewalk with an arm over my shoulder.

"I came for your help," I say quietly.

"Shut up," she says.

Only when we've cleared the hospital and the last of the patients on the sidewalk does she turn to me. The smile she hadn't meant in the first place is gone.

"Turn around," she says.

I do as she orders.

"What do you see?"

"A hospital," I say.

"Describe it," she says.

I swallow. "Large. New."

"Do better."

I close my eyes, try to imagine the words she wants to hear. "Useful. Important."

She shoves my shoulders hard. I stagger and turn back to her.

"Life," she says. "Hope. Goodness."

I nod as if I'm understanding what she's getting at. "Yes," I say. "Yes, all those things."

"Expensive," Dragoslava continues. "Also, fragile. We opened seven months ago. And now a fugitive wanted by the CIA shows up in Sarajevo, asking for me."

"I'm sorry," I say. "I thought . . ."

"The world is full of people who need help," she says. "Not just Gwendolyn Bloom."

We walk for a while in silence along the edge of the hospital property, cracked soil, patches of weeds. No matter which direction we travel, the ruins seem somehow always ahead of us, never out of sight.

"It worked out for you," she says eventually. "Switzerland. You got what you wanted."

I wonder how much to disclose. "Yes," I say. "There was—something left."

"A lot?"

"Yes."

Her pace slows for a moment, and I can tell she's debating whether to ask for a figure, an amount, some gauge of her generosity.

"You killed Bohdan Kladivo before he could kill me. So I paid my debt to you, and I have no intention of going back on my word," she says. "But there was a condition, remember? That you never come near me again."

"If there were any other way..."

"You're not rich enough to solve your own problems now?"

"It's not that kind of problem," I say. "It's about my father. He's with Sheikh Al-Saqqaf. In Qatar. He's a guest."

"Need a ride to the airport?"

"I need to get in touch. You did business with him."

"My father did business with him," Dragoslava says. "I haven't seen the sheikh in years. Why can't you find out who his attorney is? Call his business office?"

"How many months of voice mails, messages left with secretaries?" I stop, wait for her to face me. "A phone call, an introduction. That's all I'm asking."

"The English phrase is 'vouch.' You need me to vouch for you."

"Yes. I need you to vouch for me," I say. "Just like I did for you. With the Israelis."

She squints at me. "The message I asked you to pass on."

"They found me in Zurich, and I told them you were out of the arms-trafficking business. They found me again in Budapest and said they confirmed it." I take a step closer to her. "You're off their list. 'No longer an active threat' is how they put it."

"And you believed them?" she says.

"They have no reason to lie," I say. "That should be good for at least a phone call."

"Then why should I believe *you*? We don't even know each other." She tilts her head toward a grove of green just off the hospital property, a section of lush forest. "See those trees?"

I nod.

"Look what's around them," she says.

Worn roads, flattened yards around decaying houses, the edge of a city abutting its opposite, unspoiled nature.

"You saw that boy out in front of the hospital, in a wheelchair?" she says.

The teenager off to the side, smoking a cigarette. "Yes," I say.

"He was trying to take a picture of a bird, wandered into a forest like that one. Now he'll never walk again. He ignored the first rule every child here learns: Trust only what's old and worn out. Because in anything green and pretty, the devil left land mines there."

The breeze picks up, the trees in the grove of land mines sway with it. I fold my arms over my chest.

Hawkers of polyester silk scarves and local trinkets made in China crowd the pedestrian arcades. Toy guns that look like the real thing beside dolls in Bosnian dress. Souvenir ashtrays from the '84 Olympics, when shelled hospitals and ditches filled with bodies were still a few years off.

The street empties into a cobblestone square bordered with café tables. A boy of four or five slips his hand from his mother's and races forward, scrambling a flock of pigeons airborne. They swirl like a cyclone around a bride and groom grinning for photos before a fountain, he staring at the camera with wide, nervous eyes, she gripping the strings to a bouquet of a dozen balloons. An orange one breaks free, and for a moment the entire square stops mid-step, mid-conversation, mid–coffee sip, to follow its progress into a cold gray sky.

Are we meant to feel bad for the bride or happy for the balloon? For a few seconds, this is the single shared thought. Then the transition back to more important things happens just as quickly, chatter swelling, paces resuming. Only I and the child who scattered the pigeons are still watching the shrinking dot of orange, zagging across three dimensions that look like two. He's imagining a grand voyage, a trip across a sea, a desert, a jungle, camels and tigers looking up with curiosity at the lucky adventurer.

What marvelous things are possible when we're free.

I wander deeper into the neighborhood beside the square and find a hotel where a 100-franc note and a lie about a lost passport allow me to register under the name Svetlana Petrov. Visible from my balcony, just across the Miljacka River, is the white marble mosque Midho had pointed out to me on the drive into the city. I lean on the balcony railing, watching the traffic crawl three stories below me, and dial Naz's office.

She answers at once, a cheery hello for her favorite client.

"I need you to look something up for me," I say. "The English name is the General Children's Hospital of Sarajevo."

I hear the keyboard click beneath Naz's fingers.

"Yes. Here it is," she says.

"Is there a charity associated with it? An organization, maybe?"

Another pause, more clicking. "Yes. Run by—the Lovrenc and Dragoslava Zoric Foundation."

"And it's—legitimate?"

"Appears to be."

From the mosque across the street, the muezzin starts up, the call to afternoon prayer sliding outward from the minarets across the city.

"I want to make a donation," I say. "Use whatever account you think is best."

"How much?"

"Ten million," I say.

A long pause, silence of a certain kind. "Lila . . ."

"Do it, Naz. Today. Right now."

"It's very . . . generous of you."

"Naz?"

"Yes?"

"Are there any—has anyone left a message?"

A sad breath. "A message," she says. "I'm sorry, no."

Pedestrians on the street below stream across the bridge toward the mosque. Long robes. Burkas. Jeans. Bare, blond heads. I wade through another few moments of polite small talk with Naz, small talk for which she'll no doubt bill me, until we both hang up.

Ten million. How easily the sum had been said, like ten million grains of salt. It was the other sum mentioned—no messages, zero messages—that hurt. I push back from the balcony railing, shut the doors, draw the curtains.

Marike Saar's apartment had a balcony like this balcony, had curtains like these curtains. How quickly they'd been exchanged, that room for this one. Budapest for Sarajevo. Carlo Frei for no one. I sink into the bed in the darkened room, close my eyes, imagine alternate had-I-stayed me beside alternate had-I-stayed him. Marike and Carlo, maybe having coffee in Marike's apartment. Marike and Carlo, maybe kneeling on the floor, Carlo's photos spread out on Marike's IKEA coffee table. I'd *mm* and *hm* as I finally got how the artist's eye sees, and by the end, Marike would perceive the world just as Carlo does, all the little dramas and walk-on characters that make life so interesting and beautiful.

But I didn't stay. And now Carlo is alone in his alternate free-jazz-Budapest reality where there's a melody underlying the chaos if you look for it. A logic underlying the chaos, and therefore justice, and therefore safety. Good people leading good lives; why should anything go wrong? I purge the Marike-Carlo fantasy from my mind with a long wince, then flop onto the mattress, press a pillow over my head. The sheets smell faintly of chemical detergent and cigarette smoke. Marike's smelled like lavender.

The night passes like a time-lapse movie, black sky turning blue, traffic lights ticking off the seconds, the marble mosque dialing up its radiance. All this I observe from a chair I pulled onto the balcony when I realized sleep wouldn't come. It's only at the sound of the hotel phone (*get out get out get out get out*) that I move, stumbling on numb legs into the room. I clutch the receiver to my ear. "Yes?"

It's a visitor, the clerk on the other end says. Someone waiting for me in the lobby. The clerk knows more but doesn't say more.

I brush my teeth, wash my face, comb my hair, and find Dragoslava waiting for me on a couch next to the front desk. The clerks, the bell-men, are rigid with respect. She rises when I appear at the bottom of the stairs, and we walk out the front door together.

"How did you find me?" I say.

"I know everyone in Sarajevo," she says. "It wasn't hard. You should be more careful with your aliases. Svetlana Petrov. Might as well have registered under Jane Smith."

We cross the street and start down the sidewalk beside the river.

"Did you receive it, the money?" I say.

"You thought you could bribe me?"

"It's for the hospital," I say. "Unconditional. Whether you help me or not."

"Ten million," she says. "We needed a burn center, now we'll have one. What should we call it?"

"Anonymous Donor Wing," I say.

"Not the Lila Kereti Wing?"

I look at her, but Dragoslava shows nothing.

"It was the name on the accounts," I say. "Was she—was she a real person?"

"One of my father's girlfriends. His favorite. They had a son to-gether." Dragoslava stops at the low stone wall running beside the river. "At least someone can make use of what she left behind. Since she can't."

I'm about to ask for more, but something stops me, an instinct that this is unwelcome territory.

Dragoslava gestures to the other side. The buildings there range from the very old and traditional to the very new and defiantly mod-ern. "Serbs were over there, all the way to the shore. We were trapped here." She turns, points to an intersection. "The snipers on their side would aim for civilians on ours. When you came to a place where the street was open, you ran like hell. Children first, before the snipers could react. Then the parents."

Dragoslava folds her arms in front of her, the memory so old and scarred over she doesn't flinch at it anymore. "I went first, then my mother. The bullet caught her in the stomach. They did that sometimes, the snipers, avoided the kill shot. So it lasted longer. So they could watch."

I stay silent for a moment, images of my own mother flashing across my vision, all of which stop before her final moments, which I had been lucky enough not to see.

"And—what did you do?" I ask after a time.

She looks at me from the corners of her eyes and shrugs. "I watched it, too. A few men, they dashed out to try to carry her out of the intersection, but the sniper got excited, started shooting everything in sight. So someone threw out the end of a chain. She was too weak to hold on."

I extend my hand tentatively, squeeze her forearm. She tries to smile.

"Three hours," Dragoslava says. "That's how long it took her to die."

I can only nod, look back at her with wet eyes.

Dragoslava lets out a sigh, then shakes her head. "What you said yesterday. About the Israelis."

"It was true. You've been cleared. That's what they told me."

She pushes away from the wall, straightens her shoulders. Meeting over. "I'll call the sheikh this afternoon," she says. "In the meantime, you're staying with me."

Thirty-Nine

Bullet holes stitched across the exterior walls remain unpatched, and jagged sections torn from the roof are covered with plastic tarps that rustle and snap in the wind. A woman in a maid's uniform who introduces herself as Blanka greets me at the front door and shows me past construction scaffolds and pods of workers, up a grand staircase with its railing missing.

There's a hole on the floor of the second story to match one in the roof, and Blanka glides effortlessly around it, calling a warning as she goes to be careful, especially if I've been drinking. My room is in the back and overlooks a yard with a stable and guesthouse and long shed that I assume is a kind of dormitory for the Zoric family army that I see patrolling the grounds with assault rifles and regal German shepherds. Dinner, Blanka says, will be served in the dining room at seven. I thank her and, when she disappears down the hallway, close the door.

Once—a decade ago or a hundred years ago—the walls had been painted yellow. Now plaster flakes like dandruff onto scuffed wooden floors. My bed, however, is a wrought-iron masterpiece of comfort with white linens and a fat eiderdown folded down the center of the mattress.

The groan of drills, the rapping of hammers, the whine of electric saws, all sound far away now, a floor below and all the way across the expanse of the mansion. The floorboards creak with every step, and I notice a rectangle of paint on the wall that appears nearly fresh, as if a dresser had stood there for a long time. Who had been here before Dragoslava had taken it over, and what had happened to them?

I don't believe in ghosts but will make a one-time-only exception for this place. Bloody feuds going back to Alexander the Great. Burnt churches. Burnt mosques. Burnt synagogues. All the ghosts of the last century wander a road that leads back to Sarajevo. I lean on the window-sill, the curtains to either side of me dancing listlessly in the breeze, and stare at the lush, gorgeous green minefields beyond.

Dragoslava is working late, so it's dinner for one in a dimly lit dining room. Patties of meat in a thin, spicy tomato sauce, along with a salad of cucumbers and tomato and onion peeled into narrow ribbons of white and pink.

"*Hvala vam*," I say slowly as Blanka sets the plate in front of me. Thank you. My first words in Bosnian, carefully memorized.

Blanka restrains a chuckle and smiles. "*Nema na čemu*," she says, enunciating each syllable for my benefit.

"You're welcome," says a woman's voice behind me.

I turn to see Dragoslava silhouetted in the dining room entrance, a dark, tired shape drooping at the shoulders, leaning against the doorway for support.

"I know," I say.

"No, I'm saying you're welcome." Dragoslava peels off her pumps with her toes and pads into the room, stopping at a battered sideboard and pulling the cork out of a half-empty bottle of wine. "For letting you get this far. Against my better judgment. You want some?"

"I'm fine with water, thank you."

She sits in a chair opposite me and takes a long sip. "Lovrenc is skiing," she says.

I blink at her. "Skiing?"

"You know, mountains, snow, uncomfortable boots."

"I know what it is."

Dragoslava twirls the wineglass, looks inside idly at the whirlpool. "Aspen, maybe. Or wherever there's snow this time of year. It's what he does. It's all he does."

"Sounds—nice."

Dragoslava closes her eyes, inhales slowly, the exhaustion coming off her in waves that are almost visible. "A woman came in today. Her nine-year-old daughter needs medicine that costs three thousand euros a month. State won't pay for it. Says she's terminal."

"So you paid for it," I say. Not a question but the obvious answer.

"You did," Dragoslava says quietly. Her eyes open, and they're suddenly sharp and alert. "Do good things, Gwendolyn. With your money. Don't waste it on bar tabs in Aspen. People died for what you have."

I nod that I understand, that I'll do as she says.

"I reached him, by the way," she says. "The sheikh."

My silverware clatters against the plate. "And?"

The corners of her mouth creep upward, a reluctant smile. "You can talk to him tonight. After dinner."

"Talk to the sheikh?"

"Talk to your father."

I stand on Dragoslava's patio with her enormous satellite phone pressed to my ear as the call goes through. My father's voice answers in English, a tentative "Hello?"

"Dad."

I actually hear the smile crackle across his face. "Hi, kiddo."

Silence for a long moment, or as silent as an encrypted line connecting two phones to a satellite can be. Whirs and chirps and harmonic tones drift in and out like electronic clouds passing through the signal. I think of Terrance, or the voice I thought was his. My body stiffens.

"Kiddo? Can you hear me?" the voice on the other side says.

"My guppies," I say. "When I was nine, remember?"

A crackling pause, then, "Yes."

"What were their names?"

"Monkey and—was it Lollipop?"

I close my eyes. "That was two of them. What about the third?"

Another pause. "Stinkface," he says.

I tighten my grip around the phone. "There was no third guppy," I say flatly.

"Wait—yes there was, kiddo. Lollipop died first, remember? I got you Stinkface to replace her. Then I used the wrong cleaner on their bowl, and, you know."

I laugh silently, remembering now. Monkey, Lollipop, Stinkface—that tragic trio who had no idea what they'd mean to me a decade later. I manage to choke out, "Dad!"

He laughs genuinely, a sound I recognize, and just as good as dead guppies for confirming it's him.

He switches to Spanish and, even then, speaks quietly and indirectly. "I'm getting fat, kiddo. You won't recognize me."

I reply the same way. "They're feeding you, Dad?"

"Muslim hospitality, you know how it is. The sheikh and I, you were here once, remember? Eid? The lamb?"

"Yes. I remember. So—you're a guest. Not a . . ."

"No. I mean, yes. I'm a guest."

"We had a duress code, do you remember it?"

"Sure. I remember her very well. I haven't thought about her in ages, though." Another long silence, the whir and hum of distance over the line. His voice tightens around the words as he speaks. "When you left, that was—the hardest thing."

I squeeze my eyes shut, pressing back tears. "Yeah," I say. "Yeah, I know. For me too. They held me, Dad. For four months. Did you know that? Four months."

His breath shakes, and I'm certain he's picturing it, the details foggy but the important parts clear enough. "Baby," he says. "My baby, I'm sorry."

"But I won, Dad. I won. You remember the thing we talked about, just before I left?" I have to restrain myself from saying too much.

"Yes?"

"I got the—the person whose papers you left for me. At the inn. You know?"

"Yes. The papers—they were supposed to be an insurance policy."

"Well, it worked, Dad. It worked. Lots of—we'll be eating doughnuts forever. As many as we want."

"Doughnuts are what makes the world go round, right?" He chuckles sadly. "I'm proud of you, kiddo. I want you to know that."

My eyes feel like they're shriveling, and I bite my lower lip. "I tried to tell you. You didn't answer."

"The e-mail was compromised. I couldn't get in touch. It might be how . . ."

"How they found me," I say. "I know, Dad."

"But I got away, Gwen. Our friend, with the American haircut, you know? He got me out. Then I came here."

"The man you're with, he's a good guy?"

"The best." I can tell from his voice that he means it.

"I think I—I think I'd like to come there. See you."

Another pause. "Yeah. I think I'd like that, too."

"Very soon."

"Okay." He lets out a sigh. "I love you, sweetheart."

"I love you too, Dad."

"See you soon?"

"See you soon."

Even after the connection is dead, I keep the phone pressed to my ear. He did it. He actually did it. He lived.

It's only when Dragoslava sets her wineglass on a stone table behind me that I become conscious of her presence. I turn and catch her face half-illuminated by the light coming from inside the house, a single brow raised inquisitively.

"Well?"

The words come out in a hushed tremble. "He's fine," I say. "He's fine."

It's the unscarred side of Dragoslava's face that's visible, and a soft crescent of cheek rises up in satisfaction. "So what's your plan?"

"I'll go to the airport tomorrow. Maybe be in Doha by nightfall, if I can catch a connection."

"Or I can take you," she says.

"Take me?"

An embarrassed chuckle. "My father left us a plane. Tacky thing. Looks like a flying strip club. I can't bring myself to sell it."

"You're sure?"

"For ten million, it's the least I can do." She touches my shoulder, her fingers lingering there. "Get some rest. We'll leave in the morning."

More ghosts, the night air stirring them up. I can hear the German shepherds growling at them as they whisper through the perfect trees in the minefield. What had Midho said when we arrived from Belgrade? That Dragoslava stayed here out of loyalty. But it's not to the ghosts; it's to the living. To the legless teen and the terminal nine-year-old. To their parents. To a city struggling to stay breathing.

In my life, I've only ever trusted a few people. If I thought about it, I'm pretty sure I could count them on one hand. But, foolishly, Dragoslava is among them. I can't point to a list of reasons, but I can point to the totality of her and the absurdity that of all the people in the world I could entrust my life to, it's the daughter of a gangster who only months ago had been asked to kill me.

Snuggled beneath the eiderdown in the room, I close my eyes and listen to the howling of the wind through loose slats in the wall and gaps between windowpanes. He wouldn't have understood, Terrance. He wouldn't have accepted the logic of the absurd. That's what it comes down to, I think. Being okay with the idea that none of this makes sense and will never make sense. He scrabbled together a life for himself, the name Carlo Frei and a job that would allow him to make beautiful things.

So long as he never looks up from his work, the illusion can persist. But see how quickly it had been snatched away from us in Zurich.

Tomorrow, I'll head to Qatar. And the day after that—there's only a blank page, something absurd yet to be discovered.

The jet is unmarked except for the tail number, and the interior smells of old cigarette smoke and cologne. Everything that's not fake wood paneling and black leather is plated in gold, with the initials *VZ* engraved liberally throughout.

Dragoslava settles into the seat across from mine, cracked taupe leather, sweat-stained on the armrests, and pushes a duffel bag toward me. I haul it into my lap and open it. Bricks of cash wrapped in plastic and new iPhones still in their boxes.

"A gift for the sheikh," she says. "It's a million dollars—the nice round number matters—and phones for his grandchildren. He has fourteen. Remember that."

"I'll pay you back," I say, embarrassed suddenly I hadn't thought of it myself.

"Of course you will," Dragoslava says as the plane starts to taxi. "Nice suit, by the way."

I look down, brush a piece of lint from my right arm. "I got it in Zurich," I say.

She leans forward, rubs the fabric, watches as it turns from blue to black. I ask her about her own suit, and just like that we're discussing clothes like two old girlfriends. It's the first conversation of its kind I think I've ever had.

As the wheels lift off the runway, I'm pressed back in my seat and feel the rush of giddy nausea creeping from my stomach into my veins. Only a few hours left now. The duffel bag slides across the floor and I brace it with my feet. How kind Dragoslava had been to loan it to me, how kind she's being. I find myself studying her, the contours of her scars, the way her jaw is set, and her eyes, always focused, always perceptive, drilling through the plane's window to the world outside. She understands its dangers. The cowardice and awfulness of the people who inhabit it. Yet the orphan girl turned gangster's daughter who has every reason to hate chose something else instead.

"She looked like you a little," Dragoslava says over the roar of the engines.

I blink at her. "Who?"

"Lila."

I think of the photo albums, her with her boy. "I saw his picture. Her son," I say. "Your half brother."

"So what?"

"So nothing," I say. "Just mentioning it."

"Never met him." She closes her eyes, leans her head against the seat.

"I left something for Lila, in case she comes back. So she's provided for."

"Lila's not coming back."

"Her son, then. I didn't want—to leave them with nothing."

Dragoslava lets out a little snort. "Why? You didn't even know her."

"When I opened her things . . ." My voice trails off as I work out how to say it. "It was so personal. Somehow, I thought—I don't know. I wanted it to suddenly make sense."

"Find a connection, you mean. Between you and her." She opens her eyes suddenly and leans forward, elbows on knees. "What did you think you'd find, the missing half of a gold locket?"

"It's stupid. Obviously." I look out the window, the green Bosnian hills shrinking below us, being replaced by skeins of white-gray clouds. "My mother was here, you know. In Bosnia, with the peacekeeping force."

She looks at me, eyes firm. "We're not half sisters, if that's what you're wondering."

"Of course not."

"I mean, we might be," she says. "My father fucked a lot of women."

The muscles in my shoulders tense. "I was just—looking for a link. For it to come full circle. Find out the pieces fit together."

"Family, you mean," Dragoslava says.

"I guess."

"That link, what you're talking about—family, tribe, nationality— that's what gives us minefields in forests." She closes her eyes and leans back again. "It's what my father built his business on."

"I know."

"So stop looking for it to make sense. Stop telling yourself you're some special princess who's just getting what's rightfully hers." She grimaces at whatever she's picturing in her head. "You didn't win because of shared DNA. You won because you're smart and lucky. Let that be enough."

The engines of the plane whine as we climb higher into the clouds, the earth below us gone.

Forty

The plane touches down in heat that shimmers off the tarmac, bounces a few times, then rolls to a stop. The airport buildings—two small Quonset huts and a single-story building of bare concrete blocks—are spartan and almost deserted. A snaking line of three vehicles, two white Toyota Land Cruisers and a black Mercedes limousine, appears, then pulls up beside the jet.

For a visitor of Dragoslava's importance, Sheikh Al-Saqqaf will apparently take no chances. There are four men apiece in the Toyotas, locals in flowing robes carrying Kalashnikov assault rifles as casually as students carry backpacks. A handsome attendant in a suit waits for us at the bottom of the stairs, smiles a welcome, and ushers Dragoslava and me into the backseat of the Mercedes.

"There's a sandstorm coming, apparently," Dragoslava tells me. "Should end in a few hours. We'll be wheels up after dinner with the sheikh."

Beyond the private airport, there is only desert bisected by a black ribbon of pavement pulled taut across the surface of the earth. There are no other vehicles on the road, so the drivers speed up, racing toward whatever lies ahead. Whether it's out of some sense of urgency or this is the way they always drive here, I have no idea.

"The Al-Saqqaf family, they're kind people, and always good friends to the Zoric family," she says, shifting her eyes to the driver so that I understand.

"I'm very grateful to the Al-Saqqafs," I say, following along. "They are powerful and respected."

Dragoslava gives me the smallest of smiles in return. It's not lost on me that however important Dragoslava is, we are both at the mercy of our hosts.

I check the time, swallow nervously—less than an hour. I'll see him in less than an hour. I don't have a plan worked out and don't even want to picture it too clearly in my head. Just a schematic of the conversation we'll have. Naz. The money. How I'm not going to run anymore. Marike Saar will live her life, and he's welcome to be a part of it. But as for her living where she wishes, as she wishes, that part is nonnegotiable.

We drive for fifteen minutes more, deeper into the desert, the road ahead disappearing and reappearing as waves of sand move across it. Every so often, the driver's radio comes to life with a quick comment in a hyperlocal dialect of Arabic I can't understand.

Another burst of something on the radio and the two SUVs behind us drop their speed. Our driver picks up the handset and says a few words back. The Mercedes slows to a stop in the middle of the road, while one of the Toyotas pulls around and stops just ahead of us.

"Find out why we've stopped," Dragoslava says.

I lean forward and ask the driver, doing my best to stay polite and appear unworried. The driver just shrugs and tells me in Arabic, "We were told to wait here."

I translate into English, then catch sight of something up ahead. A kilometer or so down the road, the spectral figure of a vehicle appears, shimmering in and out of sight like a mirage. Then I see it's not a single vehicle, but several, a convoy like ours.

Men are climbing out of the SUVs now, shouting at one another, taking up positions on the road, assault rifles not raised, not quite, but ready.

"We'll be safer outside," I say quietly to Dragoslava.

The two of us exit the car, leaving only the driver inside. The sudden heat is crushing, and the wind has picked up, blasting sand-filled air that scorches my lungs with each breath. The security men are tense and uncertain, squinting at the approaching vehicles as their leader orders them to spread out.

The lead vehicle is a Land Cruiser like ours, and it's followed by a Mercedes limo like ours. The security men start laughing and relax their guns as the convoy pulls to a stop directly in front of us. The back door of the Mercedes opens and an ample-bellied man in sunglasses and black-turning-gray beard in resplendent green-and-white robes climbs out. The guards all fall silent and step out of his path.

I recognize him now. The same man who'd straddled the lamb, gave it a reassuring rub between the ears.

The sheikh calls out a happy greeting to Dragoslava and embraces her, patting her back jovially. I reach into the car, take the duffel bags of gifts.

"*Salam*," the sheikh says, taking my hands in his, a wide smile beneath the mustache. "*Ahlan wa sahlan fiki fi dari.*"

"Peace be upon you. It is an honor to be welcomed onto your land." I speak in very formal Arabic, head slightly bowed, then hold the duffel bag forward. "These are gifts for you, honored sheikh, and your blessed grandchildren."

He peeks into the bag, at the iPhones and watches and the bundle of 1 million euros, then gives me a rough pat on the shoulder. "You've grown," he says in Oxford-degree English. "You visited me before, do you remember? We broke the Eid fast together."

"I remember," I say. "Thank you for having my father as your guest. You have no idea what this means to us."

"An honorable man is always welcome here." He smiles warmly at me. "Your father, he was pacing so nervously. I thought, why not meet you on the road. You can ride together if you wish. You must have much to talk about."

"He's here?" I say. "My father's here?"

The sheikh turns, gestures to the limo. The rear door opens again.

The beard and hair are trim and neat, tight up against a healthy, grinning face, red from the sun. My father has filled out, too, just as he'd said, putting back on some of the weight, making his white shirt and khaki pants look almost the right size.

My legs are trembling and can't seem to move, but that's all right, because he's walking toward me—walking, not running—the gait exactly as I remembered him when he was confident and strong. He spreads his arms wide, then circles them around me, pulling me into his chest.

Back in Montevideo, I thought it would be the last time I heard his heart beating, but I was wrong. Here it is, even, steady. I look up and see his eyes are wet with tears. "Sweetheart," he says. "Last time we do this, okay?"

He rocks me back and forth, arms so tight he's almost crushing me. Dragoslava turns away to give us our privacy, but the sheikh and his men look on, their faces alternating between polite warmth and boredom.

Above my dad's words and the men's banter and the blowing of the wind and the sedate growl of the vehicles' engines, I hear something else. A hum that starts as a tinny buzz and grows into what sounds like a sustained chord on an organ. The sheikh looks to the sky, and his men do, too, their eyes searching back and forth for the sound's origin.

Then, a second sound to accompany the first. It lasts just a second or two. Ripping fabric that starts low but climbs the register until it's a screeching whistle. The security men start scrambling for the open desert, while the sheikh turns his eyes to me and my father, disappointment heavy on his face. The Mercedes he arrived in disappears in white-orange flame, then the Mercedes I arrived in does the same.

My father is crumpling around me, his body wrapping mine as he pushes me to the ground beneath him. There's a third explosion, and a fourth, and a fifth, all of which I feel rather than hear. I feel them through my father's body and through the ground as it lifts beneath us.

I pull myself from my father's arms slowly and climb out from under him. He is half of himself now. His face, his chest, are intact, but the reverse side has been peeled away, exposing burnt flesh and organs and bone and brain matter. I sit cross-legged on the ground, holding his head in my lap, looking at his perfect, sleeping face while my hands try their best to gently smooth and mold the back of his head to the shape it should be.

I turn and call for help, but the rest are dead, too. Sheikh Al-Saqqaf's security men are littered about the road, some having made it as far as the edge of the desert, some lying where they stood. As for the sheikh himself, he has disappeared, replaced by a blackened shape in the resplendent green-and-white robes, the duffel bag of gifts beside him, my symbol of gratitude and trust.

Sound is starting to come back, but now it's just the wind and the crackle of burning vehicles and flesh. The banter of the guards is gone, and so is that odd buzzing, that strange drone.

My hands flutter to my face, understanding now, understanding what's happened. When my fingers touch my skin, I feel wetness and a peculiar, oily texture. I look at my fingertips and see blood, but also bits of flesh, bits of myself, where shrapnel tore into me. It's that way on the back of my left arm and shoulder, too, and on my right calf. Funny, there's no pain.

One vehicle is intact. A Land Cruiser that had accompanied us from the airfield. One vehicle intact, and one person. Dragoslava is pulling herself along the ground toward it, a dark streak on the pavement trailing along behind her from her useless legs. Panic wells up from my gut, then rage.

I stumble after her, calling her name, but she ignores me. My hands grip the back of her blouse and I flip her over. Her hands flutter to my chest and her mouth opens and closes without a sound. She's bleeding from her abdomen, a field of red and pink, light and dark, every shade, pulsing in the air swirling with sand.

Her hands circle my head tenderly, and she pulls me close. "You did this," she says.

I crane my head, surveying the carnage around us, the wreckage and burnt shells of at least a dozen lives, looking for an enemy who isn't here. I can picture them, chuckling in an air-conditioned conference room, picture them in rolled-up shirtsleeves, biting their lips, watching a screen, grunting as the first missile found its target.

Dragoslava cries out in agony as I lift her by the armpits and drag her with shuffling steps toward the Toyota. I arrange her on the floor of the backseat as best I can, fish through the body of the nearest corpse for the keys, then climb behind the wheel.

The tires crunch over debris as I turn the truck around and head back the way we came. I keep one hand on the steering wheel, and the other on Dragoslava, calling out to her, telling her she'll be all right, telling her I'm sorry.

Dark, rolling demon clouds of sand are starting to swirl over the road, and their arrival is accompanied by the first onset of pain in my face and shoulder and calf. The hurt is exquisite and strange, burning matched with gouged flesh, terrible in ways I'd never imagined. I drive blindly, unable to see anything but sand and motion, glimpses of pavement coming only every few seconds, and then disappearing just as quickly.

For a very long time, I crawl the vehicle forward, moved by faith that the road is straight and the airfield lies ahead, moved by the slowing metronome pulsing on Dragoslava's neck beneath my fingertips. The journey ends when the front bumper of the Land Cruiser crashes into a light pole, slamming me forward into the steering wheel. Ghost figures materialize through the sand, ghost helpers who pull Dragoslava and me from the vehicle. The pilot and copilot carry her aboard the plane as I stumble up the stairs after them.

An hour into the flight, Dragoslava dies.

I lie beside her body the whole way to Sarajevo.

Prologue

Mein Ruh ist hin.

Mein Herz ist schwer.

The third time the woman sings it, Marike raises her hand to her eyes. Dark mascara on the fingertips of her cream-colored gloves now, which may or may not come out. A stupid purchase anyway—who wears gloves anymore, even to the opera?—but they'd been so pretty and did such a good job of covering the scar tissue on her left forearm.

Beautiful Johnny touches her thigh through the black beadwork dress. A loving gesture, an inquiring gesture. Johnny's boyfriend is right next to him, after all. Marike catches Johnny's eye, mouths the words, *I'm fine.*

He hands her a handkerchief, pulling it from the breast pocket of his tuxedo jacket. Linen and white as snow, which means she'll ruin that, too. Marike wonders how much it cost, because it's possible she'll see a bill for it. But probably not. Janal Purohit isn't that kind of attorney.

Let's celebrate, beautiful Johnny had said. Mohammed and I, we have an extra ticket. Jessica Chen, tell me you've heard of her. No? Darling. *Darling.*

Marike Saar is not into opera, does not know this impresario from Beijing, and does not like crowds. And it's not even a real opera, just songs by Schubert and Rachmaninoff. Thus Marike can't even lose herself in the plot.

But celebrate she must. It would be rude not to. Provisional Singaporean citizenship had been granted, and all it had cost her was a 60,000-dollar application fee, whatever Johnny was billing her, and a $20 million investment in a company run by the nephew of Singapore's foreign minister. She should have her provisional passport in a week or two.

An intermission, thank God. Ranks of tuxedos and evening gowns file out of the theater and into the lobby. Marike dashes ahead as quickly as she dares in these shoes to be one of the first at the bar. Two glasses of red wine, one of which she downs and disposes of on her way back to Johnny and Mohammed. They've run into someone they know, an associate at Johnny's practice, and Marike hangs back until Mohammed motions for her to come over.

"So sad," the associate says. "Broke my heart."

"Mein Ruh," Mohammad says. "Mein Herz—wish I knew German."

"Marike does," says Johnny.

They all turn to look at her, but the associate quickly averts his eyes. Despite her efforts to grow her hair out long enough to cover her left cheek, it still doesn't hide the lava bed of scar tissue—bright pink, bright white—which is there for all to see.

Marike clears her throat, looks down into her wine. "My—my rest, you know, like inner peace, is gone, or ran away," she says. "And the second part means 'my heart is heavy.'"

"Ah," says the associate as he forces a laugh. "Well, *that's* uplifting."

Marike smiles politely, which creases and folds the scar tissue in a way that hurts her. She is suddenly conscious of the crowd around her, the deafening chatter, the closeness of their bodies. She glances around at a thousand unscarred faces, feels her veins stretch as if being pulled taut like violin strings, feels her stomach ball up, squirting fear and want into her heart.

Lights dim and come back brightly, twice, three times. Intermission over. She pushes through a knot of people toward the restroom, approaches the sink, and does not look into the mirror. Instead, she scoops water into her mouth, opens her clutch, and finds the bottle of pills they'd prescribed after her second or third surgery and which she's faithfully renewed with a pliant doctor every month since. Marike scoops more water into her mouth and swallows them down.

The restroom is empty now, or almost. Behind her comes a flush, and the clack of a door bolt being opened. The woman who comes out of the stall wears a burgundy cocktail dress that looks good against her brown skin. Her hair is cut short these days, or shorter than Marike remembers it, but she recognizes the fine features, the woman's slender nose.

Wordlessly, the woman washes her hands at the sink beside Marike, dries them with a towel, and walks away.

Marike picks up the folded square of paper the woman left behind, tucks it into her clutch.

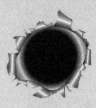

Thank you for reading this FEIWEL AND FRIENDS book.

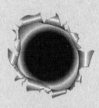

The friends who made

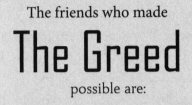

The Greed

possible are:

JEAN FEIWEL, Publisher

LIZ SZABLA, Associate Publisher

RICH DEAS, Senior Creative Director

HOLLY WEST, Editor

ANNA ROBERTO, Editor

CHRISTINE BARCELLONA, Editor

KAT BRZOZOWSKI, Editor

ALEXEI ESIKOFF, Senior Managing Editor

KIM WAYMER, Senior Production Manager

ANNA POON, Assistant Editor

EMILY SETTLE, Administrative Assistant

EILEEN GILSHIAN, Production Designer

MELINDA ACKELL, Copy Chief

Follow us on Facebook or visit us online at mackids.com.

OUR BOOKS ARE FRIENDS FOR LIFE.